HEART

of

HOPE and FEAR

BOOK THREE OF *THE ORDER OF THE CRYSTAL DAGGERS*

◊   ◊   ◊   ◊

C. S. Johnson

Psalm 111:10, NIV

The fear of the Lord is the beginning of wisdom;
all who follow his precepts have good understanding.

To him belongs eternal praise.

This book is dedicated with much love to Sam, as always. I always wonder what you'll think if you read it, and then I am terrified that you actually will.

Second, this is for my own little prince and princess. You will not always be so little, but there will always be a crown in the kingdom of my heart just for you. I may write legends, but I gave birth to them, too.

Third, this is for Terri, who did everything short of holding me at gunpoint to make sure this book was finished, and Cathy, who dragged me through my points of depression and uncertainty as I made my way through the book. Without Cathy pulling me through and Terri pushing from behind, I wouldn't have made it, and I wouldn't have made it as well as I did.

Fourth, this is for Faith. In a world of princesses, you reign as queen, and I am honored to call you my friend.

Fifth, I live in a world of half-imagination and half-reality, but it is all wonder thanks to my family, friends, and fans. I owe so much to each person who has touched my life, and I am grateful for the chance to be a part of each of yours, even if it is only through the magic of a book—and the magic you sense, as such it is, is only a small pittance of the love and joy that lies beneath.

And finally, this book is also dedicated especially to my favorite friends and fans who made sure that I finished this book. The road has been very long and as cumbersome as tiresome, and I am eternally grateful for those who have given me their company and goodwill.

My (Almost) Famous Readers:

Bryn S.
Cathy H.
Jennifer S.
Laura P.
Krissy F.
Rebecca B.
Priscila P.
Malissa P.
Rebecca L.
Beth C.
Darla A.
Donna S.
David S.
David W.
Daniel S.
Terri R.
Tina M.
Christian S.
Jacob A.
Natalia K.
Jerilyn B.
Marty H.
Crystal M.
Ani S.
Marty H.
Jeremy R.
Mary S.
G. E.
Kara G.
Stephen D.
Jan K.

1

◊

"Eleanora."

Against the darkness of the lingering night, I heard my grandmother calling for me from the other side of my bedroom door.

It could've just as easily been the other side of the world, and I still would've heard her, I thought groggily.

Even though I had not known her long, I knew there was no ignoring Lady Penelope Ollerton-Wellesley—especially when she demanded my attention.

The shadows of her toes began to tap impatiently from the other side of the door. It was too easy to believe St. Peter would simply open the pearly gates at her command, rather than calling her into heaven himself.

"Eleanora, I know you're awake. This is no time to languish."

I frowned at her sharp tone. *Assuming she makes it into heaven.*

Frustrated, I shifted my weight onto my elbows and eased myself up from the softness of my mattress.

"What is it?" I flinched at the stark sound of my voice as it cut through the early morning air. I did not want to wake yet, but between Lady POW and the wintry chill, I knew there was little hope of finding sleep again.

"You have training this morning. And you are late." Lady Penelope's sour tone hardened, as if she sensed my resistance.

I stifled a groan. She only ever seemed pleased when I was miserable, and in the month since our meeting with Empress

Maria Anna, the former ruler of the Austria-Hungarian Empire, pleasing her was more than impossible.

"I will be there in a few moments," I promised.

"See that you are. Also, I need you to tend to Lumiere. He's been drinking the absinthe again."

At the mention of the infuriating, incorrigible Frenchman who was currently our prisoner, I clenched my fists into the folds of my blankets. Lumiere had been drinking in excess since his arrival, and it was a miracle the rest of us hadn't followed suit. He regularly insisted that if he was stuck here, he'd make sure we were fully aware of it every cursed moment of our lives.

So far, I was the only one who had any success when it came to shaming him. Even Tulia could not stop him, and she'd never had any trouble getting anyone to heed her orders, even as a mute. Yet Lumiere only laughed at Tulia's silent chiding, calling her his favorite old crone and insisting her ugliness kept the devil at bay. Seeing Tulia so uncharacteristically helpless disturbed me far more than I wanted to admit.

Perhaps it was because Lumiere was more than a legitimate threat. Quite proudly, he'd admitted to orchestrating the attack on Tulia's house before the Advent Ball and organizing several other murders around Prague. He never repented of those transgressions, either; instead, he insisted everything he did was supposedly under the direction of his father, and he even assured me I would thank him if I knew the whole truth. But when I would ask what he meant, he only devolved into a fit of laughter.

Lady Penelope reprimanded me for paying any attention to him at all, and this made me even more upset.

How could I be anything but horrified at Lumiere's delighted confessions?

Tulia was severely burned because of his orders. Outside my family, others were dead, and the future of the kingdom was more uncertain than ever.

And after all that, why should I have to be the one bringing him to heel, as if he was a wild dog?

"I need you to hurry." Lady Penelope let out a long sigh, forcing me back to the moment at hand.

I unclenched my fists, letting the feeling come back into my fingertips. Lady Penelope could have sent anyone else to fetch me—Xiana, Amir, or Tulia, or one of her maidservants; if she had come for me, there was a good chance she hadn't been able to sleep herself.

As much as I suffered because of it, I could understand her restlessness. So much had happened after the *Salacia* had blown up in the harbor.

"All right," I replied carefully.

"Fine. Do not disappoint me, Eleanor."

I winced as she called me by my mother's name. Before I could correct her, Lady Penelope's shadow whirled around and disappeared down the hall. As she turned down the corner, I could hear her skirts fluttering angrily.

"Thank you, Lord." I let out a quiet sigh of relief before slumping back onto my bed.

An arm reached out from the shadows beside me and curled me into a tight embrace. I smiled as the scent of lavender and mint flickered around me, hinting of musk and carrying the warmth of flesh.

"Why is she bothering us this early in the morning?" Ferdy's voice was muffled by his pillow.

"It's Lumiere. He needs to be subdued, apparently."

THE ORDER OF THE CRYSTAL DAGGERS

"I would've happily taken care of him for you, if I'd been allowed."

I grimaced at his dark tone, recalling how often in the last few weeks Ferdy had fought with Lumiere. "Lady POW told you to stay away from him if all you were going to do was argue."

"I'm happy to do more than argue." He shifted closer to me. "Besides, I don't take orders from your grandmother."

"Then think of it as a request from me." I patted his arm gently. "I don't like seeing you get hurt. Besides, Lumiere enjoys getting you into trouble. He doesn't deserve such happiness."

"What of my happiness?"

I leaned into him. "You must find it elsewhere for now."

"It's no wonder why I love you." Ferdy chuckled before his lips touched my shoulder. My skin tingled with the whisper of heightened awareness.

"You know I need to train this morning." My heart beat in warning and anticipation. "Our position with Lady Penelope is tenuous enough. For now, I'd rather you not risk her wrath."

"I wouldn't dare," Ferdy playfully assured me as he pressed another kiss on my neck.

"Ferdy." My voice was full of warning, but he was eager to ignore me.

"Come now, you already trained plenty last night." Ferdy drew me even closer to him. "Lady Penelope should appreciate enthusiastic *training* such as ours."

Even in the dark, I blushed. "Ferdy."

"Ah, *chérie*, you know I love hearing you say my name. Such a ploy is sure to make me spill all my secrets." His voice was still slightly slurred with sleep, but I knew he was stirring awake as his lips found mine.

His mouth was irresistibly warm. I twined my arms around his neck, moaning softly in momentary surrender. My lips were still swollen with his kisses from the night before, but the more I had of him, the more I wanted.

Ferdy, for his part, seemed to be in complete agreement. His one arm kept me pinned next to him, while his other held my head closer to his.

I giggled, reluctantly pulling away from him as the stubble of his beard tickled my neck. "Come, now. You know Lady Penelope is the leader of the Order, and I have to listen to her."

"You're my bride, and I'm your master now." As if to prove it, he rolled over and tugged me underneath him. The heat between the two of us crackled like lightning through the room, made more clear and certain as it met February's bristling chill.

"You might be the master, but she's still the spymaster." It was so hard to remain resolved. I let him kiss me a few more times before I slid out from under him.

"Now you're just torturing me."

"*Absolument.*" I freed myself from his grasp and rolled off the bed to grab my chemise. As I dressed for training with Harshad and Xiana, I could see Ferdy's cheeky smile in the dim morning light.

I climbed into a pair of breeches; I usually trained in my stealth habit, but with the colder weather of setting in, I opted for warmer clothes.

"You get such joy out of wounding me like this, Ella." Ferdy sat up and crossed his arms over his chest, watching me. He was clearly enjoying himself, even if he insisted on making everything harder. "Weren't you the one, just a few weeks ago, who tried to convince me that parting was such sweet sorrow, and then promptly fell into inconsolable despair after leaving me?"

Recalling the incident he was referring to, I almost smacked him.

"There is quite a difference in believing you're dead and knowing you're just a few corridors away," I retorted. Despite the flare of my temper, I was glad for his goading. There was no doubt Ferdy was infuriating at times, but that was all the more reason to make him suffer—and it would help me keep my promise to Lady Penelope. "Besides, you know this is important. I'm certain Lady POW would've shot Lumiere herself by now if he wasn't our best lead on Lord Maximillian, and we need to find him if we're going to save Karl."

Ferdy groaned. "If there's one thing that will kill the mood, it's mentioning my wayward brother." He climbed out of bed, wrapping a sheet around himself. "But then, I suppose I have things to attend to, as well."

"What do you have to do?" I asked, genuinely curious. Ferdy was not a member of the League of Ungentlemanly Warfare, nor was he a member of the Order of the Crystal Daggers, as I was. He chose to remain at my side, even standing against his mother and Lady Penelope to do so, but he had no official orders.

"Oh, nothing much," he assured me, his tone too casual for comfort. "But if you must know, I've decided to use my time on a few special projects."

I frowned, suddenly suspicious. "What does that mean?"

"Just that if Clavan and Jarl don't see me at the Cabal every once in a while, they'll be concerned."

My cheeks filled with heat, recalling my more recent, embarrassing moments there. "Especially after I thought you were dead?"

"Especially now that I'm married," Ferdy said with a gentle chuckle.

I could almost smile back at him.

"Don't tell me Jarl is listening to your advice," I warned, thinking of our friends down at the publican house. "I won't let Faye suffer because of your antics."

"Never," Ferdy promised, once more making me suspicious with his quick appeasement. "Remember, Jarl happens to know his fiancée is not a spy or an assassin. Since that's the first rule for finding a bride, I'm willing to gamble he'll be fine in the end."

"We're *not* assassins," I murmured, knowing my objection was useless. Ferdy and I would likely never see things the same way; he observed the Order from the outside, while I was a member on the inside.

That was not all he was observing, either, I noticed, watching as his eyes followed the shadowy outline of my form as I dressed.

I pretended to ignore him, letting the next few moments pass in tense, mutual silence.

"You shouldn't worry about Karl." Ferdy finally spoke again, surprising me as he returned to our initial argument.

"Why not?" I asked, genuinely flustered. "The former empress told us Lord Maximillian's guest house had been abandoned, Karl hasn't contacted her, and even Harshad's informants haven't found a lead on their whereabouts. Aren't you worried?"

"Karl is resourceful, and if he's capable of threatening Lady Penelope, he's more than capable of taking care of himself," Ferdy pointed out. "Even if he's been kidnapped."

"If that's really what you think, then it's no wonder why I'm worried. You don't really care about him at all, do you?"

Ferdy scowled. "Of course I care, but he's stuck in a situation of his own doing. This is how justice works. Should I have endless amounts of compassion when it's better that he's gotten his comeuppance?"

"He's still your brother."

"Yes, but my brother is not your brother."

I stepped back, stricken at his words. Of all the recent shadows that had been cast over my father's manor, it was the distance I felt between myself and my older brother that haunted me the most.

"Ella." Ferdy softened at my sudden silence. "Karl's not Ben, and you shouldn't compare them in this case. Your brother is upset with me, but he hasn't tried to dislodge the kingdom from the empire or framed anyone for murder."

"I know," I murmured, still despondent even if Ferdy was right. Ben would always be a weakness of mine, and in more ways than one; it was hard for me to imagine hating my own brother. "But we're not sure what Lord Maximillian will do with Karl."

"What does it matter? It's unlikely he'll kill him. The worse that can happen is Karl will be held prisoner until his Tripartite Council convenes. And despite what Lumiere says, we all know excessive boredom isn't the same as death or torture."

"Ferdy! That's still not good enough," I objected. "Besides, what of your mother? She wants him back, and it's already been weeks. I don't want her to be even more upset with us."

"And so what if she is?" Ferdy shrugged. "There's nothing she can do, now that we're married. Even she's not able to nullify our vows."

I said nothing at his remark; instead, I began to pull my hair back.

While I was still irritated at Ferdy's flippancy regarding Karl's fate and his mother's distress, I was torn between my greatest joy and deepest pain.

It was still a miracle to me that in the past few weeks, Ferdy's cheeky grin and irreverent comments had become as necessary to me as his searing hot kisses and sincere moments of kindness. After everything we had been through, even though I did not deserve him, I could not stop myself from embracing him, especially when he made it clear he was determined to marry me.

And I truly was so happy we were married. I'd found a kind of freedom in our love, one that I had never even imagined possible. It gave me security in the midst of adventure, and it was a place of arrival, as much as the milestone on the way to a greater destination.

Even if coming home from the castle as his bride had soured the already-salted wounds between me and my brother.

My fingers slipped; my hair tie fell to the floor as I stood there, remembering the look of angry shock on Ben's face when I told him the news.

"Let me help," Ferdy offered.

"I don't need your help," I snapped, my voice surprisingly harsh. "I just need to do what I am supposed to do and then everything will be fine."

The tense silence returned briefly, before Ferdy let out a sigh. "Do you know, Ella, that despite everything, I can't feel the smallest measure of remorse for the trouble we're in?"

I scowled, keeping my face hidden from his. "What Karl did isn't your fault."

"Well, that's certainly true, and you know I'd never take on the burden of guilt when it's not mine. But I'm here, just as you are." His voice was just shy of cheerful, but still deeply sincere. "Once we find Karl and appease my mother, I'll do whatever I can to make this up to you."

"It's not me you'll have to make amends with," I murmured, thinking of Lady POW's soured expression and recalling Ben's ire. Ferdy was not the only one who was wondering how to find a way to get his brother back, even if he was considerably less eager to do so.

"Anyway, Karl will be all right, Ella." Ferdy sat down on the bed again. "Lord Maximillian needs him to secure the Bohemian throne, so he'll be fine. And Karl deserves to be frightened for at least a few weeks."

"But—"

"But nothing," Ferdy insisted. "He kidnapped your grandmother to force you to marry him."

"Yes, but your mother—"

"No mother wants to see her child suffer, but no mother wants to believe he might deserve it, either." Ferdy frowned, and all trace of cheerfulness disappeared. In the morning shadows, he suddenly seemed so much older. "Karl's the reason Lumi hired assassins and attacked my friends."

"Oh, Ferdy." I sat down and draped my arm around his shoulder, pushing aside my anger as I sought to comfort him.

After the ballroom walls of Prague Castle had fallen, back when I first doubted Ferdy, I woke to find I was trapped in his room, and I was equally trapped in my doubt. I had left, torn between the love of my heart and the logic of my mind. That pain was only resolved when he earned my trust and I embraced my love for him.

But while we had a new life together, we still had the past to face. Now was not the time to distance myself from my greatest ally.

"I'm sorry." At my apology, crushing agony shot through me, and I tightened my grip on him. "I didn't mean to sound so upset. I'm just worried."

Ferdy drew my hand into his and kissed it, before holding it over his heart. In the dim lighting, I could see all of his usual mockery and irreverence was gone from his eyes.

"I'm sorry, too. I know how much you strive to honor and serve those you love, *chérie*, and I would do anything to keep you safe," Ferdy said.

"I feel the same for you," I whispered back.

"I know. But you don't have to fear my mother's disappointment—or your own mother's, either."

At the mention of my mother, my heart stilled, overwhelmed with a sudden mix of shame and despair.

"The promise she made to my mother was kept, remember?" Ferdy smiled at me. "You saved my life at the Advent Ball."

"Thank you." I pressed into him gratefully, as my heart began to beat regularly again. His assurance, even if it was misplaced, was more comforting than I could say.

"I love you, Ella." Ferdy pulled me into his arms. "That love has saved me more than once."

THE ORDER OF THE CRYSTAL DAGGERS

"It would have to; I can't bear to lose you." I trembled, recalling just how close I had come to that fate in recent weeks.

An overwhelming flood of love washed through me. The instinctive drive to comfort and protect was at once so primal and yet supernatural; I longed to offer him every ounce of goodness inside of me, all with the hope of pushing back against the pain he carried.

Before I knew it, we were falling back onto the bed behind us.

The second before passion consumed me, I sighed. "Lady POW is not going to like it if I'm late."

"Please don't leave me," Ferdy whispered, his voice desperate and his hands already seeking the warmth of my skin. "I'll write the apology letter for you myself."

"I suppose that's fair." My response was slightly muffled as his mouth covered mine.

THE ORDER OF THE CRYSTAL DAGGERS

2

◊

It was roughly an hour later when I finally headed for the west parlor. I was late for my training, but I had difficulty caring. My body was still tingling from my husband's touch, and I was amazed all over again that such marital joy was not only sanctioned by God, but encouraged.

A pair of servants rushed past me, careful not to call attention to themselves. I slowed my steps a little, thinking of how things had changed so drastically in such a short amount of time.

After the Advent Ball, Lumiere had captured my family's household, and then stationed them aboard the *Salacia*. They had served as working hostages during the holidays and the new year celebration. Now that they were back at the manor, they avoided me and the others under Lady Penelope. Even my friends, Betsy and Mavis, seemed unsure of whether or not to approach me.

At first, their distance felt strange, but after my hasty wedding, it was easier to accept; it was even a relief not to have to explain certain things.

And Ferdy was far from the only thing I did not want to explain; there were others I did not even want to think about.

Such as my mother's promise to Empress Maria Anna.

My steps slowed, thinking how Ferdy mentioned her promise.

From what I knew, *Máma* had come back to her childhood home of Bohemia in 1847 as unrest threatened King Ferdinand and Empress Maria Anna. She vowed to protect them and their family. Not long after that, my father saved the king when he was attacked by an unknown assailant.

My mother's promise to protect Ferdy's family was one I could wholeheartedly embrace—even if I was a little unnerved by it, as well.

That was one of the main reasons I stayed in the Order, despite my mother's wishes for a better life for me and Ben, and despite my own uncertainties.

And because Lady POW hasn't dismissed me for all my failures—yet.

Perhaps that was why *Máma's* promise bothered me so.

Such a promise was no easy undertaking, and thanks to Karl's disappearance, I'd already failed to keep it.

I slowed to a stop and leaned against the wall in the middle of the empty hallway. I put my head in my hands as I relived the most intense hours of our adventure—the ones I spent in Prague Castle, speaking with Ferdy's mother.

"Ella."

Ferdy said my name quietly as he squeezed my hand, attempting to comfort me. But neither his encouragement, nor Lady Penelope's calm demeanor or Amir's presence, could give me any peace as we stood there, waiting.

We had just been escorted into a private throne room, similar to the one I'd seen the day of the Advent Ball. We were there to prove Lady POW was innocent of killing Ferdy—a relatively easy task, as he was standing next to me— but then we had to explain Karl's abduction and Lord Maximillian's treachery. Thanks to Harshad's contacts, we knew that they had been last seen heading east from the

Vltava, but no other sign of either man had been confirmed in the hours since; we had nothing hopeful to offer the former rulers.

Finally, seemingly endless moments later, Empress Maria Anna came into the room and made her way to the throne. She was younger than Lady Penelope, but she seemed so much older, even since the Advent Ball. Her downcast eyes carried the weight of grief, and all her jewelry and ornate trimmings only seemed to add to her weariness.

She waved to the guards as she entered, a telltale sign that King Ferdinand, Ferdy's father, would not be joining us. Briefly, I wondered if he was feeling well. The former emperor had a history of physical ailments, and the events of the past few days were no doubt strenuous for him.

I tightened my grip on Ferdy, but with my other hand, I held onto the hilt of my mother's dagger, the one I carried as a member of the Order. It was hidden away between the layers of my skirts, and I was never more aware of it than when I needed to remind myself to be brave.

Máma told before me that my life could change in a moment, if I was brave enough to let it. As I stood there, I could only think of how life could change in the worst sort of ways.

Lady Penelope cleared her throat and scowled at me and Ferdy, before nodding toward our joined hands.

Quickly, I looked to Amir for guidance. He'd seen Lady Penelope in trouble before, and after all we had been through together, I could trust him to tell me if Lady Penelope was overreacting or not.

So I was surprised when he nodded curtly. I gave Amir a questioning look in return, and only when he indicated he would explain later did I acquiesce.

THE ORDER OF THE CRYSTAL DAGGERS

Ferdy frowned at me as I let him go, but before he could argue, Empress Maria Anna gasped.

"Ferdinand," she cried, realizing it was her son who stood before her.

Given Ferdy was dressed in one of Ben's older shirts and his right arm was bound up in bandages, I doubted I would've recognized him myself, especially if I was used to seeing him in his princely apparel.

"Mother." Ferdy stepped forward and opened his arms as he hurried up to her.

The former empress collapsed into him. Ferdy flinched as she brushed against his wound, yet he said nothing as her arms wrapped around him in a very ardent and tender manner. She spoke softly with him, and while I was not able to hear her words, a moment later Ferdy gestured toward me.

I felt the heat rise in my cheeks as Empress Maria Anna glowered at me. She signaled to the guards again, and they marched us forward. Ferdy took his place beside his mother as she gave us a chilly welcome.

"As you can see, Your Imperial Highness, I clearly did not murder your son," Lady Penelope said.

Empress Maria Anna's frown deepened, no doubt impugned by Lady Penelope's manners. But then, Lady POW had been imprisoned at Karl's insistence, and my grandmother had her own dignity to defend—even if she defended it poorly.

"You have my sincerest apologies, Lady Penelope," Empress Maria Anna said ruefully. "My oldest son has a rather large imagination at times, and it seems his rigorous education has only worked against me in this instance."

"That's certainly putting it mildly," Ferdy retorted, and his mother gave him a sharp, silencing glare.

"I must agree with your younger heir," Lady Penelope replied, taking another step forward. She unsheathed her dagger and held it before her as both part of her identity and her fealty. "Prince Karl's fevered imaginings of taking back the Bohemian throne have led to disaster several times in recent weeks, and it is time to put a stop to it."

She nodded toward Amir, who stepped up next to the queen and knelt as he held out a bundle of letters. I could not read the different scrawlings from where I stood, but I had a feeling the letter Lumiere had demanded of Lord Maximillian was among them.

As much as I did not trust Lumiere, there was no denying he made securing proof of treason much easier on us.

"It seems Prince Karl has been involved in several disruptive activities in the last several months," Lady Penelope said. "He is leading a political coup with the hope of overturning the emperor's authority and freeing Bohemia from the empire."

"That is not possible." Empress Maria Anna's brown eyes flooded with tears.

"I'm afraid it is," Lady Penelope said, her voice lacking any sympathy at all. "The Emperor is holding the Tripartite Council to discuss Bohemia's place in the empire, thanks to Karl's push for Bohemia's sovereignty."

The former empress shook her head in disbelief. "There is no isolating our country as we might have in the past. Karl knows this."

"Does he believe it, though? He is quite ambitious," I said.

"I am relieved to hear that you have made such a thorough study of my sons of late, Lady Eleanora." Ferdy's mother narrowed her eyes at me. "I must confess, given our last conversation, I was surprised to hear of your engagement to Karl through the papers."

THE ORDER OF THE CRYSTAL DAGGERS

My face burned with stinging heat. "I regret to inform you, Your Highness, that Karl made the arrangements with the papers. I did not agree to an engagement."

"Well, that's not entirely true," Ferdy interjected. "Ella has agreed to marry me."

His mother gasped. "What?"

Everyone turned to look at me, while I could only gape at Ferdy.

This is not the best time to discuss this.

I wanted to shout my silent words, but I wasn't capable of speaking at all.

"I love her, and she loves me," Ferdy said, ignoring my stunned look.

My heart began to race inside my chest. Each second of silence was more unbearable than the last. It was scandalous that Ferdy would love me at all, but the way in which he presented his claim on my heart was more than inappropriate—especially given that in the eyes of Society, Karl was the one who was rightfully engaged to me.

Ferdy cleared his throat. "We would like to speak with the archbishop while we are here."

"Today?" The former empress stared at him, still clearly stricken.

"Yes." Ferdy stepped down from beside the throne to stand beside me. He took my hand and brought it to his lips.

"Ferdinand … " Empress Maria Anna looked from Ferdy to me, and then back at her son. She seemed aghast, and I did not know what would calm her fears, if such a thing could be done at all. My own stomach was turning and twisting into tight knots.

"I have fallen deeply under her spell, Mother, and I would hate to fall even further into scandal and temptation," Ferdy continued, his eyes sparkling with mischief and amusement. "It would be such a stain on our family's virtuous history."

The former empress flushed as she turned back to me, and I was still too shocked to assure her Ferdy and I were not engaged in an affair.

But even if I did say anything, I worried Ferdy would only speak more about our stolen moments together, vaguely enough that everyone would assume the worst.

Some measure of relief came as Amir gave me a small smirk; it seemed he approved of Ferdy, and I was glad for that.

But as for Lady Penelope …

In that moment, I did not know what she was thinking, nor did I want to. I deliberately kept my face turned away from hers as Ferdy continued.

"It was only a few days ago that my life was endangered as I made my way back to Silesia," Ferdy said, so smoothly I did not even call him out on his lie. "Life is so fragile, Mother, and I have been waiting for Ella for so long."

He looked back up at his mother, resolved and proud but still pleading for her approval.

Ferdy had told me before that I was the more determined one between us, but as his fingers curled into mine, in a manner so seductive, yet so innocent, I wondered if he'd been lying.

Empress Maria Anna shook her head. "But your duty to the kingdom—"

"There is no better way to serve the kingdom, and show it my love, than by marrying Ella." Ferdy held steady as she looked down her nose at us, clearly skeptical.

Once more, I began to feel uncertain. I knew we would face some adversity if Ferdy and I remained together, but I never considered what he would have to give up for me.

I did not want to be the reason his family disowned him.

"What of your brother and his claim on her hand?" Empress Maria Anna asked.

"Karl is not here to object," Ferdy pointed out. "And considering his own villainous behavior of late, I know he would take Ella as his bride if he were in my position."

I tightened my grip on Ferdy's hand, sickened by the thought of Karl's manipulative behavior.

It would also be much easier for me to refuse.

Lady Penelope stepped forward. "If I may speak, Your Imperial Highness. I would prefer Eleanora to stay under my custody." She looked over at Ferdy with a slanted gaze. "The Order requires her service, and I would not want to interrupt any newlywed bliss, Prince Ferdinand."

Ferdy gave her a calculated, saccharine smile. "I assure you, Madame, you would only add to my joy. After all, I know how fond Ella is of you and the rest of your cohorts. And as for the Order, what better way to explain Karl and Ella's sudden disappearance from Society than an actual wedding?"

"What of your father's approval?" Lady Penelope argued. "Perhaps the question is better left to him."

"Excellent idea," Ferdy agreed. "As it happens, I have already secured his approval. I told him of my intent to marry Ella the night of the Advent Ball."

"That was before you knew about me and the Order," I whispered.

"Nothing has changed my feelings for you, Ella. Not even that." Ferdy looked back at his mother. "And just think,

Mother. Soon, you could even be a grandmother—possibly even by the end of the year."

Empress Maria Anna's face went white, while Lady Penelope's sharp gaze traveled down my midsection, as if her squinting would allow her to see if there was indeed a baby already growing inside my womb. It dawned on me belatedly that the dress I was wearing, with its plain, simple fabric and unfashionable cut, was exactly the sort of dress I would wear if I was trying to hide a pregnancy.

The former empress' voice croaked with disbelief. "I suppose if it's too late … to … to prevent you from manifesting your affections, and your father has already given his blessing, I am unable to stop you."

"Are you saying you would, if you could?" I asked.

"I want only what is best for my sons." Her eyes frosted over. "This will hurt my Karl, even if it makes my Ferdinand happy. How can a mother willingly choose between her children?"

I swallowed hard, unable to think of a suitable answer.

That did not stop Ferdy, of course.

"That's simple. You can let them choose for themselves." Ferdy gave her a cheeky grin, but I frowned.

"Ferdy," I hissed.

"Oh, Ferdinand." Empress Maria Anna sighed. "At least I can take comfort that he has chosen you as his bride, Lady Eleanora. I trust your mother's promise to my family will remain intact?"

"My mother's promise? What promise?"

Empress Maria Anna frowned at me, more irritated at my ignorance. "She promised me when I was carrying Karl that her family would always protect mine."

"She did?" I blinked in surprise. There had been no hint of guile or deceit in the Empress' words as she spoke. I looked to Lady Penelope, whose expression was full of withering disdain.

The Order must not have sanctioned her promise, I realized.

"I'm surprised you've never heard the story," Empress Maria Anna said. "Before my husband abdicated, I found her promise somewhat naive, but then your father saved my husband from an assassin, and Lady Eleanor's promise proved useful."

Lady Penelope groaned. I did not have to glance behind me to know she was growing more agitated by the minute.

Still, hearing of my mother's promise of protection from the former empress made me feel proud, as though God in all his wisdom had woven these precious moments together, just for me. I took it as a sign that I was walking in the right footsteps afforded to my fate.

Empress Maria Anna cleared her throat. "If I give you my blessing, I want your oath that you will uphold her vow."

"You have it," I promised, smiling over at Ferdy. I already wanted to protect him.

He reached over and took both of my hands, a devoted look in his silver eyes.

"You will protect my family," Empress Maria Anna insisted. "And that would include Karl."

Ferdy squeezed his fingers around mine. "She already knows that," he said, failing to notice I had indeed forgotten about Karl in those few moments.

But I quickly nodded in agreement. If I worked with the Order to save Karl, keep Ferdy safe, and secure the kingdom, not only would I earn the Empress' approval, I would also honor my mother.

It was everything I could ever hope for, and everything I wanted.

"Yes, I will protect Karl, too," I vowed. "We will find him and return him to you."

"Then you can see he is adequately punished," Ferdy added, as his mother scowled at him again.

"Come here, Ferdinand," she said, beckoning him forward.

Ferdy let his hand linger around mine as long as possible before letting me go. The moment he began talking with his mother, Lady POW scooted over to speak with me.

"This is unacceptable, Eleanora," she hissed. "I didn't come here to discuss marriage."

"You didn't object to the thought of Ferdy wanting to marry me while we were on the *Salacia*," I reminded her.

"I'll humor ideas to get where we need to go, but this is ridiculous." She shook her head. "Should I remind you that you specifically told me you did not want to end up married before?"

"I did not want to be married as a bargaining chip." I did not want to argue with her, but I would fight for Ferdy. "And, well … I really do love him."

"There is no room for love in the life of a spy."

Off to the side, I saw Amir flinch. His pain strengthened my conviction.

"I will make room for it, then," I insisted, annoyed by Lady Penelope's stringency.

Why did Lady POW even have such rigid, unbending rules? There was nothing in her own life that seemed worth the price of giving up Ferdy. She had Harshad's contentious friendship, but she never allowed herself to love him more than the mission would let her; she'd supposedly trusted Amir, but at the first sign he had stepped out of line, she condemned him; and even now I knew my own mother had deserted the Order quickly enough after being freed from Lady Penelope's oversight.

"Eleanora." Lady Penelope's eyes were a chilly blue as we stared down at each other. "Are you to end up like your mother? Giving up the security of nations and the lives of others, all for your own selfish happiness?"

I gulped. It was almost as if she knew I was thinking of *Máma* in that moment.

"This would be her revenge against me, wouldn't it?" Lady POW's lips curled into a snarl. She glared over at Amir, who quickly looked away. "Perhaps you have gotten too close with your mother's former lover?"

"Amir is a good man, and he loved my mother very much."

"I'm not a fool, Eleanora. Even though she's been gone nearly fifteen years, I can see Amir still loves her," Lady Penelope murmured quietly. "But that is another reason why you should reconsider the younger prince's offer. There is no room for love in the life of a spy, because the instant you have it, you suddenly fear losing it. Can you imagine the pain you would feel if the younger prince were to die—especially if it was your fault?"

A thousand moments of terror hit me all at once; my heart leaped into my throat and I struggled to breathe, recalling how I'd felt when I thought Ferdy had been killed.

I couldn't lose him.

But I couldn't let him go, either.

Hadn't that exact truth been proven to me in the last several hours?

At my silence, Lady Penelope's frown deepened. "We can't be allowed the luxury of love; we can't be compromised by loss. So much depends on us. If you marry him, you will only put him—and others—in more danger."

I stood there, silently fuming, barely able to breathe. Lady POW was right, but she was also wrong—even if I couldn't exactly explain why.

Before I could say or do anything else, Ferdy kissed his mother's cheek, hurried back over to me, and grabbed my hand.

"Mother told me Archbishop Filak is in the *Hradčany*, over at *Katedrála svatého Víta*, St. Vitus," he said. "Come with me, Ella."

After only a second of hesitation, I nodded.

Barely ignoring Lady Penelope's red-faced fury, I bowed again to the Empress, who waved us off with a disappointed look on her face.

It was only when we were alone that I voiced my uncertainty.

"Are you sure about this, Ferdy?" I asked as he led me down through the myriad of palace hallways. "Your mother is not happy."

And neither is Lady Penelope.

"Mother's always been worried about me. And Karl, too." He paused for a moment. "It makes sense she would object to this, even if it would ensure my happiness. Karl and I weren't supposed to be born, you see."

There was nothing more antithetical to my world than that statement; Ferdy was supposed to be here, just as I was.

THE ORDER OF THE CRYSTAL DAGGERS

Of course, given my mother's history, it might have been that we were so well suited to each other precisely because neither of us would have existed had things happened differently.

"Because of your father's illnesses?" I asked, tentative but still curious.

"I shouldn't say anything, but you might as well know. My parents had an arranged marriage, like most royals. While they're friends now, my mother was very lonely early on in their marriage. She grew quite desperate for a child to love. But my father couldn't give her one. So she looked for a physician willing to help them conceive outside the accepted practice," Ferdy explained. "The physician she eventually found was a protégé of John Hunter and one of King George III's best surgeons."

"I can see why you're not supposed to say anything," I murmured, thinking of the man who had championed artificial insemination in animal husbandry. "The church doesn't look kindly on unnatural birthing methods."

"If they could look on them at all." Ferdy started laughing as I groaned. "Come on, Ella. Those of us born into this world don't get to choose our families, or how we are conceived. I certainly didn't choose to be born a prince. But if there is any chance in this life for me to choose my princess, then I choose you."

I knew at that moment I had no choice but to follow him through the chapel doors.

Ferdy let me wait in the chapel's foyer as he set off to speak with the chaplains.

The next several moments passed as I remained still, letting the enormity and gravity of the situation wrap itself around me. The majestic sanctuary was a source of both suffocation and comfort, and I was only truly relieved when Amir quietly appeared at my side.

He stood with the practiced ease of a soldier, his feet positioned straight and his arms held behind him. There was a tiredness anchored in his deep brown irises. The previous night he had likely gotten only a little sleep, if any at all, thanks to the work he had done in taking care of Ben and the others.

I did not know what to say, if there was anything I could say at all, and I was glad when Amir spoke first.

"Your beloved is right to do this."

"Do you really think so?" I asked.

"Yes." Amir's answer was quick and sure, forthright in its insistence, but still gentle in its delivery. "If you truly love him, and you love him too much to let him go, then don't step back from him now."

"I'm worried he will regret this," I admitted softly; I did not want even the angels in the vespers to hear me. "He is really too good for me, Amir."

"There is always a risk when it comes to commitment. But if you falter now, Lady Penelope will not allow you to reconsider." Amir placed his hands on my shoulders. "The former empress is not eager for the union, either. If your beloved had not already received the blessing of the king, you would not be able to marry him tonight."

"I don't know about that. It seems Ferdy's mother is worried I'm carrying her grandchild."

"Lady Penelope would not see that as an issue." Amir shook his head. "Xiana told me a long time ago that there are herbs women can take to rid themselves of an unwanted babe; in fact, it's the Order's silver thallis that is used in one such mixture."

Lady Penelope's words, seemingly from a lifetime ago, echoed in my memory.

"The Order is sworn to serve the truth and protect the innocent. That includes our children. I would hate to have you live up to our family's reputation in this matter."

My eyes went wide. "My mother didn't do that, did she?"

Amir looked shocked at my question, and I immediately regretted saying anything.

"I'm sorry." I quickly stammered out my apologies, terrified I might have hurt him. "I'm sorry. I didn't mean to say that. I am so sorry, Amir … Amir?"

He stepped away from me and hid his face, much as he had when Lumiere had brought up Nassara during their scuffle.

I was terrified I'd hurt him, and then I was suddenly even more horrified I had stumbled upon the truth.

In the background, I could hear Ferdy, talking with a man who could only be Archbishop Filak, but my world was slipping away as Amir's silence dragged on.

"Eleanora." Amir's expression was grim as he finally spoke. "I apologize for my comments. I only wanted to let you know that if you want to marry your beloved, this is the only chance you will get."

I noticed he refrained from mentioning my mother, and I was more relieved than I felt comfortable admitting. I clung to his lead and focused on the question of my marriage.

"What about the Order?" I hesitated to ask, knowing Amir had painful memories of his own. "I wanted to be free before. Lady Penelope pointed out that this is the opposite of what I wanted. I can't help but feel she is right."

"Wanting to be free is not a sin in itself," Amir told me softly. "Only when that is everything and held to the highest priority is it so. We are loyal to the truth, Eleanora, but the truth is complicated, and freedom can be painful."

I couldn't stop myself from wondering if he was talking about my mother when he said that.

Still, I gave him a half-smile. "I suppose you'll tell me that good things are often painful, won't you?"

His eyes twinkled, and it was enough to give me hope. "Yes. But there is pleasure, too. Truth must stem from love, and love gives us freedom; and freedom leads to so much more." Amir looked around us, clearly marveling at the details enshrined in the church's design. He closed his eyes, as if to let the heavenly comfort surround him and embrace him. "Part of the pain, just as its pleasure, is found in freedom's limits."

"Harshad would approve of that," I said. "Paradoxes are not the same as contradictions."

"That is how life is." Amir's mustache twitched in tired, unspoken amusement. "If we truly want to be free, we must learn to govern ourselves and recognize outside influences that work against us. It is not enough to have the power to go and the choice to do so; we must step out in faith and hold onto the goodness we fight for—even if it means, on occasion, tempering that power."

I could not find any place where I disagreed with him.

"If you want to be with your beloved, you will benefit from having the full authority of the church behind you in marriage," Amir continued. "Had your mother and I had that, Lady Penelope might not have come between us."

It was not shock but curiosity that compelled me to ask the question burning inside of me. "Why would Lady Penelope do that?"

"Your mother and I were married according to the Islamic tradition when we … fell in love," he said. There was no shame in his gaze, but there was a distinct crimson shadow to his cheeks. "A *mutah* marriage does not carry the same weight as one from the Church of England or Catholic Rome. It is one that is easily dissolved."

"But you could have—"

"Please." Amir shook his head. "After all these years, I know every alternative path I could have taken. It is one thing to look back on it, and another thing to live through it. When Lady Penelope confronted us, and then Naděžda lost our Nassara, and then everything else … I did not want to fight any longer."

"And that was when you stepped back from the Order?"

He nodded. "After … after the last time I saw her, Naděžda agreed to stay with the Order. For a few years, I went back to Constantinople and joined the military, still passing information to Harshad. The Ottomans hesitated to trust me, as a convert to Christianity, but they appreciated my skill as a doctor. I did not hear from Naděžda ever again. Lady Penelope informed me of her marriage to your father, citing her letters, and blamed me for Naděžda's decision to leave. I did my best to push aside her memory for good, but after I learned of Naděžda's passing, I returned to the Order."

"I'm sorry," I whispered, comforting him now. He'd carried so many secrets, and this was one burden we could share.

"Harshad was the one who told me," Amir said. "He was always Naděžda's champion. I went to investigate his claims. She died traveling across the North Sea. There is a small memorial at Rotterdam for the crew. It was constructed after Maas merchants discovered pieces of the wreck."

I clasped his hand in silent comfort.

"I carved her name in the gravestone there." Amir pulled back from me as he looked away, lost in his own memories. "You and Ben are not alone in seeing the Order as a way to connect with her."

Ben?

After all this time, it was strange to think of Ben missing *Máma* as I did, but I remembered how after she'd passed, *Táta* began neglecting him, and Lumiere had insisted rather callously that my mother initially stayed with my father only because she was pregnant with Ben.

Perhaps my father's assertation that I was proof of my mother's love was not so far off, after all.

Tears stung my eyes, and I was heartbroken for Ben. I cursed my own self-preoccupation, and my shame only grew as I watched Amir's face fill with years of lingering grief.

Neither of us seemed to notice Ferdy's irrepressible cheer and the footsteps of an aged holy man until they were directly upon us.

"It is time, Eleanora." Amir cleared his throat. "You are free to make your choice, though your choice will bind you."

"Her choice has already been made," Ferdy said, giving me a quick kiss on the cheek.

"Ferdy." My cheeks grew warm at the quiet abandon of Ferdy's affection. Even if it pleased me, it contrasted sharply with the moment of mourning Amir and I had shared, and I was left disoriented from the sudden switch.

Still, I took Ferdy's arm and walked with him toward the front of the sanctuary, where Archbishop Filak was getting ready.

"Are you worried, Ella?" Ferdy brought my hand to his lips again. "You're trembling."

"After the scene you made in front of your mother, marrying you is the only way to prevent my own assassination." I straightened my shoulders, trying to compose myself. "Did you see her face when you insinuated we were having an affair?"

"Mother will be fine. She's more upset about Karl's villainy than my perceived lack of virtue."

"You promised me you wouldn't lie anymore," I reminded him.

"I said I wouldn't lie *to you.*" Ferdy gave me a kind smirk. "But you have to admit, my mother wouldn't have believed you even if you'd denied any of our supposed liaisons."

"So, I should be thanking you for not ruining my reputation in the process of arranging a hasty wedding?" I raised my brow at the irony, but Ferdy only laughed.

"I would've bluntly insisted that I had thoroughly compromised you several times over if that meant I could've kept you."

"I'm glad it didn't come to that." I shuddered. "I think I would've been ill."

"Even better." Ferdy grinned. "It would have sold the illusion of a pregnancy, thus securing my success."

I nearly choked. "You are just awful."

"Awfully in love with you."

It was truly a work of art how Ferdy could make me wish to throttle him in one breath and then make me long for him in the next.

But he did not need to know that, I thought. I pulled back from him and crossed my arms instead, guarding the secret rush of pleasure I felt. "Enough to ruin my honor?"

"Enough to ruin it properly," he assured me. "I'll be happy to give you enough children to make even your grandmother blush."

"I know how to prevent that," I warned him, trying not to blush myself.

"Does this indeed mean that Eleanora is not pregnant?" Lady Penelope's voice seemed unusually loud within the large chapel. She had come up to us while I was distracted with Ferdy's abominable manners, and I nearly jumped at her question.

"I'm not," I insisted, forcing myself to meet her gaze without fear.

"Are you certain?" Lady Penelope studied my midsection carefully, before looking up at my face, searching for signs of deception as well as breeding. "I cannot be sure of your word in this matter, Eleanora, given your own tendencies toward secrets."

"A hereditary trait, I am sure, Madame," I bit back, trying not to let my anger override my good sense.

"Perhaps more than we would like," Lady POW agreed, and I flushed even more, thinking of my mother again.

"Excuse me," Ferdy interjected. "But I do believe it is time for us to be wed."

He'd wanted to keep me, and I would do everything I could to keep him safe. Surely, we would be able to find a way to face the danger before us.

He tugged on my hand, but I held back one last time.

"What is it?" he asked, his concern finally overriding his congeniality.

"Wait." I looked to Amir. "I need someone to give me away."

Amir nodded, giving me a sad, grateful look as I gripped his palm against my own.

I didn't know if *Táta* would approve or not, but I had a feeling my mother would. I was certain of this all the more as I watched Lady Penelope's lips wrinkle with displeasure.

Thankfully, she did not stop us. She remained quiet through the short, simple ceremony, like a demon banished just outside the bounds of holy joy.

But I forgot all about her soon enough.

Standing there, I pledged my heart and body to the man I loved, standing between him and the man my mother had loved. And as Ferdy kissed me, claiming his right to keep me, I felt the world shift around us.

It was a moment where the past, present, and future came together, baptizing me in its timelessness. It seemed that I could hear all of heaven applauding, led by my mother's cheering, as I grew into more of my true self in that moment—as I stepped into something that was both myself and greater than myself.

It was a new beginning, and all of the rest of my life was before me. I stepped back from Ferdy and saw him—truly saw him in that moment, recognizing him as my own. He looked at me the same way, as we were surrounded by an aura of contented surprise.

Ferdy reached forward as the archbishop kept praying, and drew me in for another kiss.

"Finally," he whispered against my lips. "Finally, I am yours, and you are mine."

"*Absolument*," I whispered back, unable to stop the rush of happy tears that suddenly clouded my vision.

3

◊

The gravity my wedding wielded over my thoughts was deep and seductive, much like the passion that resonated between me and my new husband. Our marriage was a shield around my heart, securing my joy in light of the future's uncertainty.

And there was plenty to be uncertain about.

I straightened my shoulders as I turned down the next corridor; if we were going to succeed in rescuing Karl, I had to take my duties to the Order seriously, no matter how mystifying and tempting Ferdy proved to be.

Despite myself, I smiled; I'd already failed at resisting him, and it was the one failure of mine I would enjoy repeating.

The clock struck a new hour just as I stepped inside the west parlor. I'd arrived late, as I'd anticipated, but still later than I'd intended. I prepared for the coming reprimand.

And it came as expected—but then, Lady POW was always more dependable than me in that respect.

"I was just wondering if I would have to come and drag you away from Ferdinand," Lady Penelope scoffed. She stood in front of the fireplace, looking like a divine judge full of sanctimonious power. The temptation to apologize was stronger than ever, and I only just managed to resist the impulse.

"There's no need, Madame," I murmured, refusing to let myself blush. "I'm here now."

"Married life has agreed with you." Her eyes darkened contemptuously. "You're much better about standing your ground, even when you're wrong."

"You are correct, even if you're displeased."

"I am displeased, and more so than you'd think. Since you neglected to rein in Lumiere as I requested, I had to take care of the matter myself."

I arched an eyebrow at her. "Never say Lumiere was too much for you to handle."

"I'm too much for anyone to handle, *chérie*."

I groaned at the sound of Lumiere's voice, unable to hide my disgust as I whirled around to face him.

He was lounging on a settee in the far corner of the room. The tired, bloodshot red of his eyes only sharpened their emerald brilliance, while his vibrant blonde hair was crimped stylishly. Much of his luxurious array of clothes and possessions had disappeared under the Vltava's waters, but he still dressed as finely as a prince—which, I supposed, given his own self-assigned title as the prince of secrets and shadows, was only appropriate.

It was then I caught sight of the iron bands around his wrists. They locked his hands together with a chain link between them, allowing only a shoulder's width of give.

"What did you say to Lady Penelope that condemned you to wear shackles?" I asked.

"Oh, these?" Lumiere chuckled. "They're mine. I wear them at my pleasure as much as for the pleasure of others."

"Unless Lady Penelope has the key, I doubt anyone is truly safe."

"We should be fine," Lady Penelope said. "He says he's willing to talk."

"He's always eager to do that." I wrinkled my nose. "Is he going to tell us anything useful?"

"Oh, *je n'ai sais quoi.*" Lumiere playfully shrugged. "But after all the excruciating *ennui* I have faced, even my father would forgive me for divulging his secrets, and he never forgives anyone."

Lady Penelope crossed her arms over her chest. "As you can see, he's still somewhat drunk, but I think he's sober enough to know when to stop playing his games."

"Ah, but I do so enjoy my games," Lumiere replied with a soft hiccup. "There is a certain amount of pleasure to be had in drawing out these violent delights."

"I assure you, Lumiere, much like your father, you give no pleasure," Lady Penelope retorted.

"There is often more pleasure in pain than pleasure itself." He stretched, putting his shackled hands behind his head. "As you will no doubt find out when the baby comes, Ella."

"What?" My face filled with heat as Lady POW immediately turned to stare at my midsection.

"There's no reason to be concerned about that," I objected vehemently, even as I hurried to calculate when my most recent monthly course began. Once I was certain Ferdy and I had been careful enough, my anger at Lumiere intensified. "Why would you say such a thing?"

"And why would I *not* say such a thing, Madame?"

I clenched my fists. "Propriety, for one."

"Propriety be damned. One does what one can, after all, *n'est-ce pas?*"

He gave me a wink, and I wrinkled my nose, quickly rejecting his charm and good humor.

"It's 'one does what one *must,*' not 'one does what one *can,*'" I snapped, infuriated by his presumptuous behavior.

"Eleanora is correct," Lady Penelope said. "Liberty is not the same as license."

"Yes, but there's also 'duty until death or defeat,' isn't there, Pepé?" Lumiere rolled his eyes and scoffed, clearly slighted by our joint rejection. "Those in power are quick to determine which rules are too sacred to be broken."

"You have enough power if you're able to break them," I started to point out, but Lady Penelope stepped between us.

"I will give you one last warning, Lumiere. If you want to experience any sort of pleasure ever again, we will see to business first, once Harshad arrives," Lady Penelope said.

I didn't know why Lady POW thought he was drunk, even if he had been drinking absinthe in excess of late. As I stared at him, I could only see how his mood was too calculating and mocking; it was more like he was pretending to be drunk, rather than actually intoxicated.

He is indeed playing his games, as he openly admitted.

"Where is Harshad?" I looked around and noticed for the first time that he was not with us.

"He is gathering his reports," Lady Penelope informed me. "He's eager to go through the available information we have. Especially given that *someone* here hasn't been as useful as we'd like."

She narrowed her eyes over at Lumiere, who only yawned dramatically.

"You always were too serious for me, Pepé. I had so hoped age would soften you, yet experience has only hardened you." Lumiere cocked an eyebrow at her. "Is there no room for nuance and fun in your life?"

Lady Penelope said nothing; her scowl only deepened.

THE ORDER OF THE CRYSTAL DAGGERS

"My father is the same, you know. If you ask me, that is largely why you never did get along with him. You are too much alike." Lumiere let out a soft chuckle. "Jakub often wondered if you harbored a *tendre* for him."

"Me? A *tendre* for Louis Valoris? Ha!" Lady Penelope let out a scraggly cough. "The very idea is beyond revolting."

While I had not yet met Lumiere's father, I easily agreed with Lady POW.

Louis Valoris was the current leader of the League of Ungentlemanly Warfare, a title that once belonged to my maternal grandfather. He had used his connections to bring Lord Maximillian and Karl together, and then assisted them with their *coup d'état*. Several lives had been lost at his direction, including Ferdy's friends, a few politicians, and my father's old physician, Dr. Artha.

When I pictured Louis inside my mind, I could only see a stark, devilish face stretched over a thin mask of flesh, his eyes glowing red with blood and fire—his monstrous visage matched only by the ugliness of his twisted soul. Anyone who could willingly unleash such chaos without concern for human life had to be grotesquely appalling.

"What foolishness." Lady Penelope shook her head at Lumiere. "Your father taught you well, I see; you certainly know how to distract the enemy."

"Perhaps you are just easily distracted, Madame." Lumiere smiled back. "But you should pay better attention, as things are only going to get worse. It's been getting worse since Constantinople."

Lady Penelope's fingers twitched, almost as if she wanted to strangle Lumiere—which she probably did, in all fairness. "We do not discuss that mission."

"Why not? It was because of Constantinople that Jakub sought reconciliation with you. He even admitted he'd been wrong about my father after the Spring Revolution," Lumiere said.

Lady Penelope scowled. "Jakub knew it was too late to reconcile with me, long before the Revolution began."

"But one would think you would enjoy such a memory. You have so few happy ones."

As much as I found him beyond abhorrent, I had to admire Lumiere's tenacity; seeing Lady Penelope's bitter expression, I knew Lumiere was gambling with his life as he kept talking. But I was also grateful for him, since then I wouldn't have to ask as many questions later.

Jakub Cerný, my mother's father, had partnered with Lady Penelope and the Order before my mother was born. Along with Louis, they had been close friends and trusted allies—until Louis turned Jakub against her, and she'd fled to London when my mother was just a child. Once there, Lady Penelope married Arthur Wellesley, the Duke of Wellington.

I paused, thinking of my own married bliss, and I felt a surprise pang of sympathy for Lady POW. It was unfortunate her marriage hadn't lasted.

"I suppose that's old history anyway, and history is boring, except where I'm involved." Lumiere laughed. "Still, everyone has regrets, *non*? And it's hardly pleasant to think of them, even if you can learn from them now, Pepé."

"You can think on your own regrets later, Lumiere," Lady Penelope warned. "If you want me to learn something so badly, why don't you tell us where Max is keeping Karl?"

"Yes," I agreed. "Tell us what you know."

"I can't tell you exactly where he is. That is my official position, and it's one I've maintained since you locked me up here like an exotic bird." Lumiere ran his hand through his hair in an impertinent, graceful manner. The elegance of the movement was disrupted by his manacles, but his grin only widened. "And for the sake of your precious propriety, I dare not even hint at my unofficial positions."

"You have contingencies," Lady Penelope pressed, ignoring his banter. "I know you do."

"I doubt Amir has said anything to you about my contingencies, Madame."

"Amir?" I blinked, more intrigued than I wanted to admit.

"Of course. Did he not tell you the story of how we met?" Lumiere clapped playfully before I could answer him. "How I envy you, as you're in for a treat. I have other plans, but I must say, given what I've done for Amir, I'm disappointed he didn't rescue me this time. I'd been so hoping to spend more time with him."

I was torn between insisting that Amir would never help him and assuring Lumiere that any past goodwill he might've accumulated was gone. But before I could speak, a new voice spoke up from the back of the room.

"Amir does not owe you anything."

I whirled around to see Xiana standing against the back wall. She wore a long tunic, and there was a small sword, carefully sheathed on her back, and her ebony hair was impeccably braided. I had not heard her arrive, but I was not surprised by that; Xiana was a longtime pupil of Harshad's, and one of the best.

As she stood there, her sunstone eyes gleamed with cold fire, sending an involuntary shudder down my spine.

"My apologies, fair lady." Lumiere's voice purred with cruel pleasure. "I hadn't realized you joined us."

"You should stay away from Amir." Xiana ignored his mocking gallantry and lowered her eyes, seeming to regret the attention she'd called to herself. In the weeks since my

41

training began, she only enjoyed speaking with Harshad and Lady POW, and Amir, if he was around. Even at Lumiere's provocation, I was surprised she had spoken at all. "It is prudent Lady Penelope is keeping him from you."

"Well, we all know how you feel about Her Ladyship's commands." Lumiere smirked. "You'd think she was at the right hand of God the way you listen to her. After all, you were always trying so hard to be just like Naděžda, *n'est-ce pas?* And you succeeded, too. Except in all the ways that actually count, of course."

Xiana's hand reached up and flexed around the hilt of her sword, but Lumiere was again right in his observations. Xiana had her *jian*, her sword, but despite her tutelage under Harshad in the past, she was not granted the same privilege as me and my mother—she did not carry a dagger of the Order.

I saw Xiana's eyes narrow at me briefly, as if she had read my thoughts, and I hurriedly looked away.

"Now that I am here, you know there is danger in acting like the clown you wish you were, Lumiere." Xiana whipped her sword out of its sheath; the firelight reflected off the double-edged blade, gleaming with deadly power. "It would be best if you simply answered the questions."

"Yes. We've had enough," I said, stepping between them. "Tell us what you know about Karl."

"Please," Lumiere scoffed. "It's not hard to see Karl was a fool."

"Was?" My eyes went wide, and I felt my heart pound in my chest. Panic strangled me, paralyzing me momentarily with despair and hopelessness. "Karl is dead?"

"Oh, calm down. I didn't mean that." Lumiere rolled his eyes. "Why would Max bother going through all that trouble to find him, and then just kill him?"

"I can think of a good reason," Lady Penelope offered. "Lord Maximillian, as a cousin to Emperor Franz Joseph, could more easily claim he deserves the Bohemian throne without Karl around."

"If that was his plan, he must be incredibly foolish—or truly a madman."

"It's been said that it takes a thief to catch a thief." I glared at him accusingly. "Perhaps it takes a madman to catch a madman."

"*Tsk, tsk*, Ella," Lumiere tutted. "All thieves are alike, because they are all unhappy in their envy. But there's no end to the diversity of madmen. Some revel in it, while others despair, and still others seek to remedy themselves by making others miserable."

"I guess we know which one you are."

"Of course. I'm not one at all." Lumiere smirked. "But I do like to pretend so. It's a great thing to be underestimated."

"You might not be a madman, Lumiere, but you know of Max's plans. Otherwise, you wouldn't have murdered so many people like Dr. Artha," Lady Penelope said as she crossed her arms. "You do not engage in murder blindly, especially when the victims are your known allies."

He shrugged. "Perhaps I am getting sloppy and indifferent in my old age."

"Perhaps. You are over forty now, and your best years are most certainly behind you," Lady Penelope retorted.

Lumiere dropped all pretense of charm as he glared at her. "You would certainly be the one to know that, Madame."

"Wait, I don't understand," I said. "Why did you kill Dr. Artha, and Father Novak, too? They were your informants." I thought back to the letter we'd found in the Church of Our

Lady of the Snows, the one the dead priest had tucked away inside his Bible.

"Killing Father Novak was easy; despite his uses, we have a bit of a painful history, but that's a story I'll spare you, Ella. Holy men can still have their faults, and I am happy to give such men the divine justice they deserve," Lumiere said, his words laced with acrimony. "But Dr. Artha was just a bit harder to kill. He and my father were longtime allies. And, of course, Tulia was quite upset with me over his death."

I closed my eyes, picturing Dr. Artha at my father's funeral as he rushed to help King Ferdinand through a seizure. Lumiere's father was not the only one who'd had a history with him, I thought. He'd been the one to declare my father dead.

Lumiere's sigh cut through my memories. "But believe me, it was an act of kindness for me to take care of him now, especially if Max and my father get their way. Dr. Artha was loyal to the Emperor, and he would not want to see the empire fall into war and chaos."

My fingers curled into fists. "Why you—"

"I see," Lady Penelope swiftly interrupted me. "So, Louis is bringing war to the Austria-Hungarian Empire, is he?"

I blinked, and then I realized more fully what Lumiere said, instead of just his callous disregard for human life. From the look on his face, he was not displeased by Lady POW's conclusion, and I was suddenly even more disgusted than before.

"War?" I repeated. "I thought Louis was the head of the League. Queen Victoria wanted peace in this part of the continent, not war."

"The Queen would not want war, but Louis wouldn't mind it." Lady Penelope sighed. "He has a history of causing chaos, and he's serious if he is murdering those he once considered loyal."

"People can only be so loyal, and war has been looming for years now. My father is only setting up the right conditions which will benefit him the most."

"Oh, Lumiere." I shook my head; I wasn't even sure why I felt disappointed in him.

"Oh, Ella, don't be foolish. It's a miracle that man is capable of mercy, not that he is able to kill," Lumiere insisted. "Remember, I could've killed Tulia before, too. But I spared her, and she knows she's lucky I did."

"You mean *you're* lucky you spared her," I muttered darkly, reaching for the dagger at my side.

"But are *you* lucky I did?" Lumiere arched his brow at me. "Perhaps you'll wish I'd killed her at some point."

"I would never!"

"We'll see." Lumiere shrugged. "My father would've killed her if he thought it more efficient to do so. He is not as forgiving as I am—and I know this well, being the one person he will never forgive—but I suppose that's another story, and one more appropriate for a confessional."

"Lumiere." Lady Penelope's voice was full of warning, and I was secretly relieved she took control of the conversation once more. "What does Louis' war have to do with Karl?"

"*C'est facile.*" Lumiere relaxed into the settee cushions, resuming his aura of merriment. "Like all the Hapsburgs, Karl suffers from impairments too great to be listed in polite company. He believes himself to be the true ruler of Bohemia, and he'll welcome war if it means he gets a crown in the end. He's a useful idiot, and he'll remain one."

THE ORDER OF THE CRYSTAL DAGGERS

My fists balled up in anger. Lumiere wasn't wrong, but still, I hated how his eyes lit up with joyful sadism as he sat there, amused at the thought of widespread destruction and death.

"I see. Karl is a front for Louis to start a war in Bohemia," Lady Penelope surmised. "What's in it for him?"

"I've already told you, Pepé. War is for the poor to suffer through and maybe even survive. But for the rich? We not only thrive, but we get richer, especially if we know how to place our bets." Lumiere smiled at me. "And I'm willing to bet Karl's death, should it be warranted, will be a grand spectacle."

"What? Why?" I asked angrily, barely able to speak. "Why would Karl have to die?"

"I didn't say he would, just that if he does, it's nothing personal. Well, perhaps a little personal. Death has to be, you know. But that's just the business of men like my father, Ella." Lumiere sneered angrily. "They get rich by promising to solve problems, and they stay in business by creating more problems to solve. We're almost fortunate for the excessive bureaucracy in our governments, or we'd be taken over by mobs every other month."

"That's terrible," I whispered.

"That's politics, *chérie*, and there is nothing good about remaining an innocent when the world will only make you pay more dearly for your ignorance."

The more Lumiere spoke, the more anger stirred inside of me. I looked over at Lady Penelope for help, but she only began pacing in front of the fire.

"Louis will profit off the chaos," she said. "The more chaos there is, the more profit he'll get. It won't even matter if Karl or Lord Maximillian rules Bohemia in the end. He will have his contingencies, too. Correct, Lumiere?"

"*Oui, oui*, Madame," Lumiere said. "*Mon père* is getting older, but he is still excited to play a new game with you, and I can see why. You know him so well."

"He would enjoy risking the future of an entire nation to prove himself against me," Lady Penelope muttered bitterly.

My fingers went numb as I gripped the hilt of my mother's dagger. Louis would willingly bring war to my country, and sacrifice Karl to get it—and all for what? Money? Chaos? Power? The thrill of facing off with my grandmother?

"We will defeat him," I declared.

"He will enjoy watching you try." Lumiere smiled. "As will I."

"Assuming you survive. Such violent delights have violent ends, as you've already noted." Lady Penelope stopped pacing. "Well then, it seems right now, the quickest way to stop Louis is to find Karl. Since Eleanora has already promised to return him to his mother, our goal has not changed."

I was enormously gratified that Lady Penelope was happier about my promise, even if it was only to stop Louis. Still, it gave me hope like nothing else to see her approve of me and my decisions.

"But our search has become more urgent," Lady Penelope continued wearily. "If we can find Karl, Louis will have a harder time starting his war."

"But what else can we do?" I asked. "We've already been looking for Karl for almost two months now. The former empress has no lead on him, and neither do any of Harshad's contacts."

"Oh, I'm sure you'll find him soon, Ella. Destiny practically demands it. Pride deserves one hell of a fall, and if anyone should get one, it's that little princeling." Lumiere cheerfully grinned, his eyes shining over with absurd delight. "I happen to like his younger brother much better, don't you?"

A protective flare lit up inside me. "Forget about Ferdy, Lumiere. I don't want you near him ever again."

"Oh, don't be such a nagging fishwife. Let him have a little fun. He and I are friends, you know."

"*Were* friends," I corrected. "After your henchmen killed his traveling party, you should consider yourself fortunate to be alive."

"As he's mentioned to me, several times," Lumiere said. "Still, we'll be fine in the end. He's someone who can handle the full truth, even if he doesn't like it."

I scowled. "What are you talking about now?"

"I'm talking about how some lives must be lost in order to save others. Ferdy would agree with me, and Tulia does, too, for that matter. After all, she certainly didn't try to stop me when I showed up at your house, and she also didn't mind taking care of your father, did she, Ella?"

"What?" I crossed my arms defiantly. "What about my father—"

"Eleanora." Lady Penelope scowled. "You're letting him distract you."

She was right, but I wanted to object regardless. What did Lumiere know about Tulia and my father?

He doesn't mean that … that Tulia actually killed Táta, *does he?*

The door suddenly opened, and Harshad appeared with a bundle of papers in his hand. He made his pleasantries and apologies before Lady Penelope began to speak with him in muttered tones, no doubt catching him up on what we'd learned from Lumiere's supposedly drunken revelations.

There was nothing I could do but glare down at Lumiere as he contentedly relaxed back into the cushions. I was about to ask him my questions when he sighed and turned to me with remorse in his large, tired eyes.

"I should apologize for teasing you, *chérie*."

I rolled my eyes. "You should, but you won't."

"You must have patience. It is not yet the right time for me to reveal anything."

"And just when is the right time, Lumiere?" I grumbled softly. "It never seems to come for you."

"You see, you have to *find* it." Lumiere pulled out his pocket watch and held it out to me. "Perhaps you'd like to take a look?"

I frowned at him, but as the fire winked off the golden watch, I was taken aback.

At second glance, I saw the elegant design, with its pierced gold carved with a *fleur-de-lis* on the cover—in a very familiar pattern.

It's the same design as the one on my father's watch.

The full force of my realization struck me again as I looked over to see Lumiere. All pretension and playfulness were gone from his face.

"You look so much like your mother," Lumiere told me softly. "But I'd rather hoped you would remember that you are your father's daughter, too. Especially since my father is eager to start another war with your family."

4

◊

"What are … why?" As I stared at Lumiere, my lips struggled to form the right question. There were so many I wanted to ask, and each one seemed more impossible to voice than the last.

"Find the right time, Ella." He plucked the watch from my hand and pocketed it before he gave me another smirk. "If you can."

I could only frown at him, unsure of anything in that moment.

Was he lying?

Was he joking?

Was he … telling the truth?

Maybe Lumiere was legitimately trying to befriend me, but I never wanted to examine that as a real possibility; the thought was as repulsive as the man himself.

I was still reeling from Lumiere's sincerity when Lady Penelope let out a loud curse.

"*Merde!*"

I turned around just in time to see her face scrunch up with displeasure. She began yelling at Harshad, speaking in an unfamiliar language, but I didn't have to know exactly what she was saying to know she was upset.

Harshad's ochre cheeks were wan and weathered, the paleness drawing out the liver spots and leathery pockmarks on his face. His condition could've been due to the weather, but I was certain the past several weeks had strained him as much as everyone else.

Perhaps even more than the others, I thought, studying the deeply furrowed, frustrated lines in his brow.

"What is the news, Harshad?" I asked, as Lady Penelope stormed back toward the mantle, furious and frustrated. "Has something happened with Karl?"

"No. But I am afraid our mission has become more complicated." Harshad walked back to the small writing desk at the back of the room and sat down. "The Prussians have captured Napoleon III just as the French government is preparing for war against the German Confederacy."

I bit down on my lip. "That doesn't sound good." I was not very well versed in international conflict, but even I knew war was never good news.

"It is not, no." He shuffled his notes as Lady Penelope let out an indignant huff.

"Of course it's not," she said. "It means Lumiere isn't lying to us. For once."

"For once," Lumiere conceded with a disingenuous giggle.

"There is more," Harshad said. "The Emperor has appointed a new Minister-President. Count Potocki has been retired earlier than he'd expected."

"Yes, yes, I've already heard from him." Lady Penelope waved her hand dismissively. "The Count believes his association with me has caused his dismissal, especially after your outrageous affair and elopement, Eleanora. He's even rescinded my invitation to his wife's ball this weekend because of all the rumors."

"It's not like you were going to go." Discreetly, I rolled my eyes, embittered by her blame and irritated at the mention of the rumors.

Ever since Karl's disappearance, and subsequently mine, whispers raged throughout Prague. There were any number of people prattling on how Karl and I were touring the ruins in Rome, attending the Opera in Paris, and strolling through Hyde Park in London. Lady Penelope had only fueled them by turning away all visitors, insisting she had taken to her bed in the throes of "irredeemable scandal."

In a very small, petty way, I imagined this was her way of punishing Ferdy for marrying me. While I doubted Ferdy was truly bothered by the rumors, it was still a callous move. When I confronted Lady Penelope about it, she only said I ought to be grateful Karl wasn't parading around with Lady Teresa Marie, before explaining to me how the rumors allowed us to work freely in the shadows. That gave us an important advantage, even if it kept us from walking out in the open.

Reluctantly, I'd decided to trust her judgment.

For now.

"If Count Potocki has been dismissed, is Karl the new Minister-President?" I asked. "The night of our so-called engagement, he announced his intent to secure the position."

Harshad shook his head. "No. The Emperor has appointed Lord Hohenwart."

I was only a little familiar with Lord Hohenwart; his wife was more memorable, with her plump figure, her voluminous gowns, and her pleasant if persistent chitter-chatter. It had been at their ball that I had been formally introduced to Prague's Society—and to Karl, too.

"That's good news," Lady Penelope said approvingly. "Hohenwart has a history of compromise. With France and Germany engaging in warfare, his appointment will help stabilize the region, even if the Emperor agreed to call for the Tripartite Council."

"With Karl missing and Count Potocki replaced, why is the Emperor still holding the council?" I asked. "There's no need to decide whether or not Bohemia should be its own kingdom now. And what about Louis?"

"The Emperor agreed to the council so he could appear to be a fair ruler, one concerned for his people. But with Hohenwart's appointment, he's shifted the players so he controls the outcome," Lady Penelope explained. "He's bought himself some time, too, no doubt in hope Karl's movement will fade out on its own."

"With Karl's disappearance, it is likely that will happen," Harshad agreed.

"Or another problem will rise to take precedence." Lady Penelope sighed. "Either way, it's political theater for the masses."

"Oh." I didn't know if I liked Franz Joseph more or less after hearing that.

"The Council is scheduled for early spring, although it's likely to be held off until September," Lady Penelope added. "Count Potocki commissioned Roman Szapira to renovate his manor before then, and he's upset that he's paying him for nothing now."

"Oh, what a shame!" Lumiere cried out, clearly enjoying himself. "A man's pride is one thing, and his job another, but his home décor? Surely that is too much to ask of him."

As Lady POW and Harshad reined in Lumiere, I could only think of Karl.

Karl will be upset Lord Hohenwart is the new Minister-President.

I clasped my hands together with grateful resolve. We would still have to save him to stop Louis, but Karl's moment to gain power had passed—and he'd failed. With the real power behind the council stripped away, Karl's own quest for power was over.

Good.

Karl spoke to our countrymen with high platitudes, but when he was with me, he callously dismissed human life and dignity. He'd been willing to kill Ferdy to secure my hand in marriage, and he was working with Lord Maximillian and Louis Valoris to gain the Bohemian throne, even if it meant war.

He wanted to be a ruler, not a leader, and any power he would've been given would have only made others more miserable.

"The news of Hohenwart's advancement will gratify Queen Victoria." Harshad folded his hands together on top of his pile of papers. "But I still have my concerns."

"Of course, and you should. After all, there is war and rumors of war, and Karl is still missing," Lumiere said. "And then, worst of all, I have been captured by Pepé, the great enemy of *mon père*, and I am now being tortured with unrelenting disdain while I only give you information."

Lady Penelope's eyes narrowed. "Is this another game for you, Lumiere?"

"Game?" Lumiere's voice was painfully insincere. "Whatever could you mean?"

"I have been wondering why you came to Prague at all. If you had stayed away and out of sight, it was always possible we wouldn't have discovered the League's rogue members and Louis's involvement."

"I do enjoy coming—and going, too," Lumiere said with a large grin.

"I see." Lady Penelope sighed. "So, you wanted this."

"Wanted what?" I asked, confused.

"He wanted us to capture him." Lady Penelope's eyes scorched into Lumiere, and he blinked at her innocently for a long moment.

And then his lips curved into a sinister smirk, before he fell into another fit of laughter.

"Well, I guess you caught me. You're right; I'm here largely of my own choosing. And I can leave whenever I want, too."

"Is that something we should worry about?" Lady Penelope arched her brow at him skeptically.

"Why would you worry? Jakub always insisted Adolf's taste in books was only rivaled by his collection of alcohol. So long as I have both, I imagine I'll be content to stay," Lumiere said. "You must admit, it was an ingenious move, to use your manor as an inn."

"And all at my own insistence," Lady Penelope grumbled.

"And your own expense, too. But don't worry, Ella." Lumiere smiled again as he turned back to me. "As long as I am entertained or drunk, it's doubtful I'll try to leave. Of course, you never know when I might feel the full weight of conviction of the Holy Ghost and run for the closest monastery."

"I should've known Louis would send you here to cause me trouble," Lady Penelope grumbled.

"I'll have you know, *I* decided to let you capture me. My father will be horrified to learn what happened. Perhaps it will hurry him along," Lumiere said. "You know, not all trouble is bad for you, Pepé. Naděžda would agree with me, as would Amir."

It seemed I only blinked, and Xiana lunged across the room, grabbed Lumiere, and hauled him up out of his seat by his belt.

Lumiere looked down with rare, authentic shock, as Xiana thrust him against the wall; less than a second later, her blade swung out in a perfect arc before pressing against his throat.

Everyone went perfectly still.

Lumiere did not even breathe. I gasped as the air rushed out of my lungs as the smallest line of blood trickled down the length of Xiana's sword.

Lumiere gave Xiana a tight-lipped smile, squashing himself against the wall behind him as much as possible. "I'll have you know I've already shaved this morning."

"Amusing … you are always so amusing, Lumiere. Why not give us another laugh?"

"Xiana," Harshad said. "That is enough."

Her eyes flickered over to Harshad, briefly, before she narrowed her gaze at Lumiere once more. "Even a little chuckle will be enough to kill you, and considering it is you, it would be an appropriate death."

Lumiere cocked an eyebrow, his drunken façade finally depleted. "It's not fair of you to tempt me like that."

"I would say it is not fair for *you* to tempt *me*," Xiana hissed.

"What can I say, *Saghira?*" Lumiere's voice growled softly, his animosity reminding me of when he'd fought with Amir on the *Salacia*. "Light shines in darkness; and the darkness comprehends it not; and all deeds done in the dark will come to light."

Her muscles tightened, as if she was about to launch another attack against him. But Lumiere shook his head, and Xiana only stared at him angrily.

He gave her a venomous smile. "Killing me would only lead to more death, and you have enough blood on your hands."

"Xiana, I said enough," Harshad repeated, this time his voice edged with rebuke.

Xiana finally released Lumiere. "Killing you would be too kind—and too quick."

"I quite understand your temptation, Xiana, and I commend you on your impressive skill and restraint, as always." Lady Penelope gave Xiana a bright smile—one I'd rarely, if ever, seen for myself. "Unfortunately, Lumiere is right; for now, we need him alive. Louis will be looking for him when he arrives. However, it would be best if Lumiere is retired back to his room. See to his care, won't you?"

"Yes, Madame." Xiana nodded curtly. Lumiere had upset her, but she was once more as emotionless, methodical, and cold as ever.

"You don't have to be so stiff." Lumiere waggled his chains along in the loudest, most obnoxious way possible as Xiana tugged him out of the room.

"Make sure you lock his door," Lady Penelope added. "And take his alcohol. No need for us to bankroll his addictions while we're stuck with him."

Lumiere glared over at Lady POW, his expression full of visceral hatred and just enough panic to make me want to giggle.

"I have my own ways of getting around you, Pepé," Lumiere warned. "I trust you would not deny me my pleasures."

"I have it on good authority that such pleasure is often found in pain," Lady POW snapped, waving him away.

Lumiere's scowl deepened with bitterness, and then he turned to me. "What can I say? Our time here is at an end. Perhaps we will find more time in the future, *chérie.*"

I turned my nose up at him. I was still angered and frustrated by his varied and strange behavior.

Strange behavior appears to be his normal behavior.

Lady Penelope shooed him away. "Drag him out by his hair if needed, Xiana."

THE ORDER OF THE CRYSTAL DAGGERS

"There is no need for that," Lumiere assured her. "It will be good to be free from your lies again, and what luck, that I even escaped with my life. Others have not been so lucky in that regard—including members of your own family, Madame."

He looked back at me one last time, with no trace of insincerity or mockery in his expression. And then his nose twitched, and he looked down at my midsection.

That's right—Nassara is dead, too.

Sadness stung inside of me at the thought of Amir's daughter, the one my mother had lost; dark uncertainty broiled as I recalled Amir's expression back in the church when I'd asked if my mother had intentionally killed her baby.

I looked back at Lady POW, who looked uncharacteristically stricken.

Before I could say anything, she hurried Xiana and Lumiere out the door and slammed it shut. The force of its impact sent a sharp breeze into the room and made Harshad's pile of papers flutter off his desk.

I waited a full moment before I put my hands on my hips and faced my grandmother. She had a right to her secrets, but I would not stand for her lies.

"What did Lumiere mean by that?" I asked.

"It means you will be training with Xiana in the afternoon instead of this morning." Lady Penelope was clearly just as upset as Xiana had been by Lumiere's commentary.

"But Lumiere—"

"Pay him no heed, Eleanora. I should've left him in his room earlier; I don't know why I thought he might be of some use today. Of course, I thought you would put in some actual work, too."

Harshad cleared his throat. "Pepé, there is no need to be so upset. I was late, too—"

"Harshad and I wish to review through our notes," Lady Penelope continued, overruling him. "There must be other ways to find Karl we haven't thought of yet. We need to find him before Louis gets here and carries out the rest of his plans."

"I can help," I offered, but she shook her head.

"No. Why don't you be a good little wife and see to your husband's needs?" she snapped. "This is serious business, and I cannot have you around right now. You are a disappointment to the Order."

"So was my mother, as I understand it."

"It is better to leave Dezda out of this," Harshad said, speaking up much more forcefully this time. "She is gone, but there is still much pain at her passing."

"I want to know what Lumiere was talking about." I knew I was overstepping myself, but if Lumiere could spend all morning doing it, why couldn't I? "Why would he bring up Nassara?"

"To distract you, if nothing else." Lady Penelope's reddened cheeks blistered into a violet crimson as she brushed off her skirts. "Enough of this. Leave, Eleanora. Need I remind you if you'd come and dealt with Lumiere earlier, he wouldn't have been here at all?"

"You're the one who brought him," I reminded her. "You said he wanted to talk."

"And so he did, and now we can see Lumiere will use what he can to sow discord among our ranks," Lady Penelope insisted. "You must remember there is nothing we can do about the past, and you cannot let it interfere with our current mission."

"Even if it will help you learn?" I asked tenuously, echoing Lumiere's earlier taunting.

"How can you learn anything when your emotions only hinder your focus?" Lady Penelope pursed her lips, clearly displeased. "You're dismissed, Eleanora."

I bit down on the inside of my cheek, forcing myself to keep silent.

Just as I stepped out of the parlor, Lady POW called back to me.

"One last thing, Eleanora: Louis Valoris is not an enemy one should underestimate. He has avoided justice in the British courts for decades now. He is cunning and ruthless, and he is always playing a deep game. As much as Lumiere says they have a tumultuous relationship, he is also Louis' most trusted associate. You can be sure that both of them already have several pieces in play—and that includes Karl."

"I know there is great risk," I said.

"But do you have any idea just how big the risk we face is? Bohemia is in the middle of the Austria-Hungarian Empire, which has treaties with nearly every major imperial force on the continent. Trade routes intersect and connect the East to the West. Civil war is possible, but with France and Germany fighting and Napoleon III's capture, it's clear Louis is setting the stage for a war larger than this world has ever seen."

Such an idea seemed too impossible to imagine, but Lady POW said it with such conviction that I could not dismiss it.

"So, Karl's fate, Bohemia's future, the threat of global war, and your mother's honor—all are at risk." She glared at me pointedly. "And all of that is easily forgotten, I assume, with a lover's kiss?"

My heart began to pound more ominously inside my chest, but I did not retreat from the confrontation. It was becoming more clear I would have to defend my husband at every turn. "I don't know why you're so upset over Ferdy. He's done nothing wrong, and he's even helped us out on more than one occasion."

"Perhaps I would be less preoccupied with him if you weren't," Lady Penelope retorted. "If you wanted him to be left alone, you shouldn't have married him."

"Well, I did marry him, and I don't regret it. And I will not let you come between us." I crossed my arms over my chest again. "Especially after the way you destroyed my mother and Amir's relationship."

"Ha." She snorted disdainfully. "Eleanor ruined it herself."

"Pepé." Harshad jumped up from his seat, his tan cheeks blanched over in horror.

"She was the one who brought it up, Harshad, and if she wants to know about Nassara so much—"

"Pepé, stop!" At the uncharacteristically angry snap of Harshad's voice, Lady POW dutifully shut her mouth.

My eyes widened as a large lump formed in my throat. I was suddenly afraid as the room went deadly silent. I didn't know if it was bravery or curiosity that kept me from running away.

"Eleanora." Harshad's voice was back to its normal volume, but I still heard a slight waver in its commanding tenor. "Please, take your leave. Xiana will meet with you for training later this afternoon."

"But what about—"

"No." Harshad straightened his shoulders and pointed to the door. "You will leave now."

Slowly, I looked back and forth between Harshad and Lady POW, and, seeing no support, I nodded.

61

As I left, the sense of discomfort I'd felt earlier came back, stronger and more vicious than ever.

Everyone has secrets.

Lady Penelope's words burned into me like never before.

Yes, everyone has secrets, I mused. My mother would have had hers, too—secrets regarding Nassara, her involvement with the Order, and her promise to Empress Maria Anna.

But at that moment, I had absolutely no desire to learn them.

THE ORDER OF THE CRYSTAL DAGGERS

5

◊

My footsteps echoed loudly across the floor as I headed for the library.

I did not want to think of the Order's mission or my mother's past, and between Lumiere's childish hunger for attention, Lady POW's disdain, Xiana's quick temper, and even Harshad's wispy sadness, it had been a long, lonely morning. My mood brightened considerably at the thought of leaving the world and falling into a new, fictional world, one far less complicated than my own.

More than ever, the library was a place of refuge—a place of books and love, family and freedom.

But just as I reached its door, it flung open, and Tulia angrily stalked out of the room.

"Tulia."

She stopped short, glaring at me, her topaz eyes full of contempt. Briefly, I wondered if she felt guilty, or even unsure like the rest of the staff. But a second later, she shook her head, brushed me aside, and resumed her determined march down the hall.

"Wait." I reached for her. "What's wrong?"

Tulia didn't answer as she slid back from me.

"Please, stop," I begged. It was clear from the scowl on her face she didn't want to talk with me, and I was suddenly afraid she hated me.

Tulia had been my mother's companion, and she was my grandfather's illegitimate half-sister. Even her alliance with Lumiere was not enough to make me doubt her; after all, I'd known her all my life and I loved her like a second mother.

"What's wrong? Tell me." I tugged at her sleeve gently. "You know I've forgiven you for working with Lumiere."

You're too kind. She signaled out a sarcastic reply as her lips twisted into a painful, amused look.

"I know you well enough to know when you regret something." I softened a little, watching her brush a stray lock of grayish white hair away from her face. Thanks to Lumiere and his hired henchman, she was covered in scrapes and small burns, adding a maimed grotesqueness to her ancient features.

Tulia pointed down each of her arms and around her face and winced in pain, before sticking out her tongue, speaking in the same language I'd known from her all my life.

You think I'm ugly, don't you?

"No."

Tulia snorted at my quick lie. *I'm not the only one who's changed. You have, too.*

"Is that why you're upset? Because I'm married now?" I asked, dreading the thought of having to defend Ferdy again. "I'm still the same person I always was, just more so."

She rolled her eyes and shook her head.

"Then what is it?" I stared at her expectantly and incredulously, starting to feel annoyed myself. Out of the two of us, I had more cause to be upset.

To answer me, Tulia jerked open the door to the library again. I peeked inside just in time to hear Cecilia's scathing voice.

"Is that you, Tulia? Did you come back with the tea, or is the Iron Dowager seeking new ways to punish me and my daughter?"

At my stepmother's screeching, I involuntarily flinched, remembering the damage she'd inflicted on both me and Ben with her wagging tongue. I quickly slammed the door shut.

"I can see why you're upset," I said, more apologetic this time.

When Lumiere "borrowed" the manor's workers to work on the *Salacia*, he'd coerced the staff into following his orders by telling them Lady Penelope would be sailing to England and dragging Cecilia to court there. Not everyone believed him, but when Lumiere instructed Tulia to keep Cecilia and my stepsister, Priscilla, locked inside the cargo hold, no one objected, either.

And then I arrived and rescued them. I'd gone directly against Tulia, who was frustrated with me for freeing them— even though if I hadn't, they would've died when the explosives went off.

"Are you there or not?" Cecilia's voice, muffled from the other side of the library door, was still as sharp and unforgiving as ever.

Tulia made a rude gesture toward the door in reply.

Despite her anger, I laughed. I stopped when she shot me another furious look.

In her own way, Tulia explained how Lady Penelope assigned her to guard my stepfamily; it was the same assignment Lumiere had given her on the ship, and she was eager to be rid of such a job.

There was nothing I could do about that. Since returning to the manor, everyone was on strict house arrest while "new plans for the future were considered," according to Lady Penelope. My stepfamily was required to remain under constant watch, and no one was allowed to go out without her direct approval—including me.

"I'm sorry you're upset," I said to Tulia. "But we need to make sure she's safe. It's unpleasant, but it's understandable."

Tulia flicked her fingers around. *An understandable punishment, you mean.*

"I'm sure it's not a punishment," I said, but as soon as I finished saying the words, I had a feeling Tulia was right. She had her own unpleasant history with Lady POW, and it would not be above my grandmother to plan something like this for the sake of efficiency.

Both Lumiere and Lady POW are good at finding ways to use people as much as punish them.

Tulia put her hands around her eyes again, making a hooded expression. Then she threw up her hands, clearly disgusted.

"Well … " I bit down on the inside of my cheek and muted a regrettable sigh. "If you'd like a break, I can take over for a bit."

Tulia's hardened expression softened, ever so slightly, before she moved her fingers in a questioning manner.

"I mean it," I told her. "It's not a trick. And I'll take care of Lady POW if she says anything."

When Tulia only seemed even more suspicious, I clasped her hands in mine. "I don't know why you think I hate you. I don't. You were the only one Ben and I could trust after Cecilia married *Táta*. And *Máma* loved you, too."

Tulia hung her head. Confused, I watched her hands as her fingers spelled out a new message.

It's better if you hate me.

"It's not like I haven't tried," I admitted softly. "I haven't forgotten how you kept us from Lady POW because of the Order, and I still don't understand why you helped Lumiere.

But I know you, and I know you did what you thought was best, even if you were wrong. So I've forgiven you."

Tulia looked heavenward, before she slumped forward, took my hand, and tried to explain things to me. She was rambling silently; all I could get was how she was saying I shouldn't forgive her so easily and that I knew nothing of the depths of her sins.

Before I could ask her to slow down, the library door opened once more.

"What could possibly be—" Cecilia poked her bird-like nose out of the room as she seethed with impatience, and then immediately fell silent. From the disgusted look on her face, I could not say if she was more enraged or surprised to see me.

"Well," Cecilia finally scoffed a moment later, before giving me the slightest of curtsies. "Your Highness. So nice of you to come and see us."

Your Highness? I glanced around, looking for Ferdy before I remembered that, as his wife, I was now a member of the royal family, too.

As much as I tried to stop myself, I blushed. "I'm not a real princess," I murmured, enormously grateful Ferdy wasn't around. He would've laughed at me, especially given how much I argued with him over his official titles in the past.

Clearing my throat, I turned to Tulia. "Go and rest. I'll see to my stepmother's care for now."

"Ha." Cecilia crossed her arms and scowled. "She couldn't at least get us the tea first, could she? Oh, never mind. After everything we've been through, she'd likely poison it."

I had to give Cecilia some credit; I wouldn't have been surprised to learn Tulia had thought about doing just that.

But when I looked back at Tulia, she was stunned, with her eyes wide and full of horror as she stared at me.

"Tulia?" I was suddenly afraid that had actually been her plan.

"Just send her away," Cecilia said as Tulia backed away from me. "Normally, I'd ask why someone with Lady Penelope's rank and privilege would even deign to keep her around, but there's no need to ask in this case. The mute has always been quite manipulative; Adolf didn't question her at all when she stayed at the cottage nearby."

I watched as Tulia's steps faltered at the mention of my father, and a sick feeling welled up inside my stomach as I remembered Lumiere's taunting, about Tulia taking care of my father, and how I might not feel lucky with Tulia still alive.

Is it possible … ?

Unfortunately, it was possible.

Táta had been poisoned with the silver thallis herb, which the Order used as their deadliest weapon. If Father Novak had been poisoned by either someone in the Order or the League, Tulia could have known who killed my father.

Or she could've done it herself.

I rubbed my forehead, my eyes burning as I willfully pushed that thought away.

Quickly, I shuffled Cecilia back into the library, regretting my kindness, as I was the one stuck watching over her now.

A single spark of comfort settled into my heart as I saw my mother's portrait hanging above the fireplace. I sat down and looked at it, remembering how *Táta* told me he'd commissioned it shortly after they were married. Her black hair was down, her straight locks dangling over a prim, white gown. Her raspberry lips were curved into a smile, and her sapphire eyes were full of mystery and kindness.

But as the time passed, and the more I studied her, the more my mother became a stranger to me. Her shoulders were too straight, her pose too practiced, her cheeks too rosy. Her face was more heart-shaped than mine, and her smile, while at first it seemed sweet, turned strangely bitter.

"Everyone has secrets, and everyone has regrets."

Amir's words, spoken to me on the night of our battle aboard the *Salacia*, took on a more haunting quality as I looked up at my mother's picture.

So much was restored of late, but so much had been destroyed, too. I had a child's memory of *Máma*; I saw her as a daughter would see her mother. But who she was, and what she wanted, seemed to shift and change the more I learned about her. I'd already lost part of her when Lady Penelope told me the truth about her and the Order of the Crystal Daggers; I did not want to lose any more of her, even if it wasn't really her.

Distractedly, I stood up and walked back to the bookshelves. I ran my hand along their spines, remembering Amir once told me my mother's handwriting filled several of their margins. Silently, I promised myself that I would look through them all and catalogue my findings one day.

"So, Your Highness, have you come to tell us what our fate will be?"

It seemed like hours had passed when Cecilia's shrilly voice called to me from nearly a world away, and I said a silent prayer for strength as I answered her.

"No. I'm only here to watch you right now." When I saw Cecilia was not impressed, I added, "I'll give Lady Penelope my report later."

The mention of my grandmother made Cecilia shudder with visible pain, and I held back a laugh.

A small movement shuffled off to the side. Priscilla was curled up by the window, with her hands folded in her lap, and a small blanket placed over her skirts. Her face was very pale, while her eyes looked tired; her hair was done up for the day, all tied back in an intricate bun, save for one long, stylish curl that fell to her collarbone. From the reflection on the glass, I could see her frown.

"Your hair looks lovely today, Prissy," I said, keeping my tone light. Priscilla was my age, but it was hard to believe I had anything in common with my stepsister; I stood before her wearing trousers, while she was dolled up like the younger version of Empress Elisabeth she yearned to be.

Priscilla had always been quick to present herself as my better, but ever since Lady Penelope's arrival, she hardly bothered to speak at all. With Alex dead, and especially having witnessed his death myself, I was not sure if we could ever be friends.

But I did hope we could get along.

"Miss Amelia did my hair this morning," Priscilla finally replied quietly. "Marguerite told her to style it the way they do in Paris."

"Paris?" I was surprised she answered me at all, but I imagined it would get quite boring if I only had Cecilia to entertain me, too.

"Yes," Priscilla said, the barest gleam of excitement lighting up her eyes. "Vienna is the music capital of the world, but Paris is where one goes for fashion. Marguerite has been showing me some of the designs from her seamstress book. She has a sister who lives in Paris who sends her new designs."

"It sounds like their whole family knows about fashion," I said.

"Yes, it is so fascinating. It's really the only part of the day I enjoy," Priscilla said, a little miffed. "I hate it when she goes off with Ben."

"Ben?"

Her eyes suddenly went wide, and she quickly clamped her mouth shut. "I forgot I wasn't supposed to say anything."

"Why not?"

Prissy stiffened. "He didn't want me to mention Marguerite was helping him. He thought you would get upset over it."

I was not sure why Ben was with Marguerite, but as I thought about it, I remembered she'd assisted Amir with Ben's leg after I'd caused his fall on the *Salacia*. Perhaps Marguerite was still tending to his injury.

"Marguerite seems nice, and she seems like a good companion. I imagine Tulia's not the best company." I was careful to keep my tone neutral as I shifted the focus away from the topic of my brother.

Slowly, Priscilla nodded. "Yes. I like Marguerite very much."

"She seems to know a lot about Paris."

"It's where her family lives. One day I'd like to go there." Priscilla hesitated. "Do you think we'll be able to, after your grandmother finds Lord Maximillian?"

"I … I don't know," I admitted.

What would happen to me and Ben, and Ferdy, too, after all the Order's business in Prague was over? Would we go back to London to await Queen Victoria's next order? Or would we stay here?

71

I thought back to the early days of Lady Penelope's arrival, thinking of the mission details she'd shared. Maybe we would even go all the way over to the West Indies.

"That's enough, Priscilla," Cecilia snapped. "You shouldn't talk to Eleanora. She'll only be happy when we're gone, and when we are, it won't be because we're going to Paris. We're more likely to be going to the poorhouse."

Priscilla stiffened and went back to staring out the window. As I tried to object, she primly jutted her chin into the air and ignored me.

Alex had been a terror all his own, but in seeing Priscilla's sad defeat, I was more sympathetic to her plight.

I turned back to Cecilia. "You know, you don't have to be so antagonistic."

"What nonsense," Cecilia muttered. "I'm being held here as a prisoner, after all. I'm under no obligation to befriend you."

"But you might want to help yourself, and your daughter, too." As I watched her scowl deepen, I was suddenly inspired. "If you know anything about where Lord Maximillian might be, perhaps we can work out a deal."

I felt clever, having thought of a way to get answers. I hoped it would please Lady POW. But Cecilia was quick to cut down my enthusiasm.

"I have already told your grandmother I have nothing to say to any of you." Cecilia stood up from her chair, keeping her posture rigid as she faced me. "I have no idea where Max is, or what he wants now."

"You knew he was after the king's heir," I pointed out. "I heard you talking about it with Alex before."

"But that doesn't matter now. He found him, didn't he? Who can say what his plans are now?" Cecilia crossed her arms over her chest. "And anyway, Alex is dead because of him."

Briefly, I saw the quiet sparkle of tears in her eyes. She let out a loud sniff, and she hurriedly straightened her skirts with a rough determination.

"I don't know why you're worried, either. You found the Bohemian prince first," Cecilia continued, poised again. "I suppose I shouldn't be surprised. You are your father's daughter, after all."

"What's that supposed to mean?" I frowned. Cecilia had never mourned for my father, only that he hadn't left her more money when he'd died.

"He was the one who found out about the former Empress' son in the first place," Cecilia explained. "Adolf was quite the researcher, and he was highly regarded even among King Ferdinand and Empress Maria Anna's circle of Bohemian Loyalists."

"Why did he tell Lord Maximillian about Karl?" I did not mean for my voice to raise, but I refused to believe *Táta* had ever helped Lord Maximillian.

"It was a mistake. Max couldn't get Adolf to admit to anything further, except that the heir was born close to the same time as Benedict. Fatherly pride did him in, in the end." Cecilia wrinkled her nose in disdain. "Or perhaps it was fatherly shame, since Adolf was complaining about Benedict falling off the barn roof. And who could blame him for that?"

As Cecilia started to complain about her various husbands and the difficulties a woman without a husband or true son faced—circumstances she faced again, with Alex dead—I ignored her.

Lord Maximillian, the Duke of Moravia, was a cousin to Ferdy's father, and he'd been in line for the throne of the Austria-Hungarian Empire before the Revolution of 1848.

From what I knew, he'd originally planned for Karl to marry his daughter; that way, he could gain control of the kingdom, if indirectly. If Karl was not embraced as the proper Bohemian king, Lord Maximillian's status as a former heir to the throne could have been used to win over more votes from the Diets and the *Reichsrat*.

Suddenly, I understood why I had been a complication for Lord Maximillian; Karl's attraction to me had been ardent enough he'd tried to renegotiate with Lord Maximillian plans. Karl thought I would win him a lot of support and goodwill, given how my father saved King Ferdinand.

I frowned.

It was strange that Karl had gone silent, and wasn't, as Lady POW had suggested, carting Teresa Marie around after learning of my deception, but I was still more concerned with my father's murder.

"Did Lord Maximillian kill my father, Cecilia?" The question left my mouth before I realized it, but I didn't regret it.

I knew *Táta* had been murdered; I did not know who did it, or why. Lord Maximillian had the motive and possible opportunity—and I wanted him to be the killer, too, if that meant Tulia was innocent.

I could already hate him for kidnapping Karl; I did not want to hate Tulia.

"What?" Cecilia nearly choked at my question. "The doctor said your father's heart gave out after a fit of apoplexy. Adolf was old, Eleanora. He worked all his life, traveled all over, and he was more than a decade older than your mother. No one killed him."

I hated Cecilia talking about my father, but her mention of my mother was even more egregious.

"Are you absolutely certain of that?" I put my hand on the hilt of my mother's dagger as I stepped closer to her.

"There's no need for such hysterics." She swallowed hard, clearly scared, but still angry. "Why would Max kill Adolf, if he still didn't know who Karl was until last year?"

We faced each other in a silent war; I watched her carefully, taking note of every twitch in her wrinkled face. As much as I hated how she'd treated me, I did not see any inkling of deceit. And her logic was sound, as much as I hated to admit it.

Slowly, I moved my hand off my dagger, and Cecilia let out an exhale in quiet, desperate relief.

And then a gunshot resounded from outside the manor.

At once, Cecilia let out a bloodcurdling scream, while Priscilla jumped out of her seat so fast, she tumbled to the floor.

"What was that?" My tongue was thick with instant fear, and it was hard to say anything as I stood there, stricken and unsure of what to do.

Another shot went off.

This time, I hurried to the window and searched for any sign of intruders or attack.

No one would think to ambush us here, would they?

A third gunshot rang out. The sound came from outside the other wing of the manor, and I knew it was time to see for myself what was going on.

"Stay here," I said, giving Cecilia and Priscilla a stern look before I headed out of the library.

"What is going on?" Cecilia cried, her cranky voice breaking with fear.

THE ORDER OF THE CRYSTAL DAGGERS

"I don't know," I said, sounding much braver than I felt at the moment. I took one last look at my mother's portrait, praying for her courage as I fully brandished my dagger. "But I'm going to find out."

THE ORDER OF THE CRYSTAL DAGGERS

6

◊

If there was anyone Karl should have wanted to kill, it was me.

There was another shot fired, and I wondered if it was possible he'd arrived to do just that. Or maybe it was Louis, searching for his vexing son?

I slowed my pace a little. Tulia told me before the Order had a lot of enemies. What if an entirely new foe had come to take care of Lady Penelope?

As I turned down another hall, I suddenly heard Ferdy and Ben both yelling.

"Oh, no!" I forgot all about everything else, as I was consumed by the determination to save my brother and husband.

I ran outside, heading toward them, as the chilly bluster slapped against me. The stunning frost was enough to leave me momentarily blindsided. My hair, already loosened by my run, danced in the wind and obscured my vision as my feet stumbled through the mushy, snow-dusted grass.

"Ben!" My voice was muffled by my windblown curls. As I drew closer, I could finally make out the words they were saying.

"That one was my shot," I heard Ferdy say.

"That one was your shot on my target," Ben argued. "You're awful at this."

I stopped short, watching the scene before me as the wind died down. My heart was pounding in my chest, and I was breathing too fast, but relief flooded through me; no one was

77

attacking us—and Ben and Ferdy were not dueling with each other, either.

The two of them were yelling at each other as they held a matching pair of dueling pistols. Beyond us, there were two squares of wood on display, each with a crudely carved target in the center.

I faltered again, seeing Ben. His stance was oddly shifted, with his right leg wrapped up in an extra layer of bandages and his foot sticking out in the cold. Nearby on the ground lay a pair of crutches.

A few days after our night on the *Salacia*, Amir told me Ben's injury was mild compared to the break he'd experienced as a child, the one he'd gotten falling off the barn roof. Amir had said he would even be able to straighten the leg a little more, though it would still pain Ben for the rest of his life.

Amir had been both kind and honest to me, but it still hurt knowing I'd caused my brother such agony, especially for a second time.

I did not think it was good for him to be outside in the middle of winter, arguing with my husband while both of them held a gun in their hands.

"Lady Ella."

I jerked around to see Lumiere's companion, Didier, standing out like a still shadow against the wintery background. Didier was a French name, and with his dark skin, it was easy to think he came from the Senegalese trading posts. But from what I'd seen of him, and from how he talked, I was more willing to believe he was actually from America. Though I had not spent much time with him, Didier seemed to be Lumiere's opposite in many instances; he was quiet, thoughtful, a little blunt, and even had a calming

THE ORDER OF THE CRYSTAL DAGGERS

presence. His black hair was short and cut close, and his eyes were a dark, bark-colored brown.

As Ferdy and Ben continued their argument, Didier bowed in greeting and gave me a slow, welcoming smile as he straightened.

"Gentlemen, please," he said, stepping between Ben and Ferdy. "We have an audience."

At the interruption, both of them looked over at me. Ferdy gave me a charming grin, while Ben only scowled.

My brother was more than content to avoid me of late; the one time I tried to check in on him in his room, he'd locked me out and ignored me for a good hour before I gave up and left.

"Great. She's come here to mother us," he said.

"I have not," I argued, trying to hide my discomfort. "But now that I'm here, what do you think you're doing?"

"Ben and I have reached an agreement," Ferdy explained. "Didier offered to teach us how to shoot, so if I ever break your heart or make him too angry, Ben can challenge me to a proper duel."

"That's terrible," I said, but I was warmed knowing Ben still cared about me enough to threaten Ferdy.

Ben scoffed. "If he doesn't accidentally kill himself first. Your husband is a terrible shot, Ella."

The warmth of the previous moment evaporated. Ben had always called me "Nora," until we came back from the *Salacia*. As I watched him now, there seemed to be very little I could do to earn his trust back.

Didier cleared his throat. "Would you like to try as well, Lady Ella?"

His voice was deep and low but still friendly as he held out his revolver to me.

"I don't know how," I admitted.

Didier nodded. "Trying is part of learning. You will likely have to learn at some point, given you are a member of the Order of the Crystal Daggers."

He was right about that. I thought of how Lady Penelope had shot her pistol while we fought on the *Salacia*.

"Go ahead," Didier said. "Take it. I can show you how to use it. I am a proficient shot, and I will make sure it's safe for you to use."

"I have no doubt of that," I murmured, still embarrassed. "But … "

My voice trailed off as I looked toward Ferdy and Ben, who were in deep discussion with each other. From the snippets of their conversation I could hear, I realized Ferdy was doing his best to befriend my brother.

I was unable to talk with Ben, but Ferdy was making sure I still had a voice in our relationship.

"They will not mind if you join us," Didier assured me. "Both your husband and brother have had quite a bit of fun getting the basics incorrect for the last several moments."

"It's not that." My voice did not sound convincing to me, and I'm sure he didn't believe me, either.

"You're not scared, are you?" Didier put the pistol back into the holster inside his coat. "But then, I suppose some are not inclined to use guns. Lumiere does not enjoy using them, either."

"Really?" I thought of how Lumiere had killed Alex on the *Salacia*. He did not seem so averse to guns.

"Of course. He doesn't like the mess they cause. Between the gunpowder and the scorch marks, there are plenty of reasons he uses them only when he has to."

I gave Didier a reluctant half-smile. "Now, *that* sounds like Lumiere."

Didier grinned. "Still, he knows I prefer them. He had these engraved especially for me shortly after we became friends."

I took another look at Didier's weapon. From the markings, I saw it was a Remington 1858 model, with gilt intricately engraved into the grip and cylinder. They were indeed beautifully made, so far as I could see.

"Perhaps I will try next time," I said. If Ferdy was trying to bond with Ben, I did not want to interrupt them. "I should go back in and see to Cecilia and my stepsister. We were worried when we heard the gunshots."

"I will make sure they stay alive," Didier promised, nodding back to Ben and Ferdy.

I was inclined to believe him; Didier was every bit as sincere and polite as Lumiere was loud and boisterous, and while I had to question his taste in friends, Didier had done nothing to alienate me. On more than one occasion, he'd even apologized for Lumiere's drunken crudeness or his unrelenting mockery.

"When you change your mind about shooting, come and join us. I will be working with both of them as we have time," Didier said, gesturing toward Ben and Ferdy.

"Thank you." I gave him a small curtsy before I headed back to the house. I glanced over my shoulder just in time to see Ferdy blow me a quick kiss, while Ben turned back to face the makeshift targets.

He shifted his weight on his crutches, and I decided I would ask Amir if Ben was able to work outside without hurting himself.

As I walked back into the house, there was a small shuffling noise to the side; I blinked in surprise as I saw Marguerite standing just beyond the window's light.

"Nora." She greeted me with kindness, but I saw her clasp her hands together nervously. "Is everything all right?"

"Everything is fine," I said. "Were you worried we were being attacked, too?"

She shook her head. "No, I was just … you don't think Ben is pushing himself too hard out there, do you?"

I stared at her. For the first time, I noticed Marguerite was close to me in age, although she was likely a little older; I also saw she was quite pretty, with her blond hair pulled back from her forehead, highlighting the intelligence and gentleness in her green eyes.

As she gazed back outside, staring at my brother, a sudden, deep concern settled inside of me.

"He's well enough," I said, suddenly eager to close that subject of discussion. "Did Lady Penelope send you to find me? I've been taking care of my stepmother in the library."

"Oh, no." She cleared her throat. "I only thought to check on Ben, that's all. I wasn't sure if he should be out there like that, no matter how much he insists he can do—"

"I'm sure Amir and Lady Penelope are well aware of his activities," I said brusquely. "Excuse me."

Marguerite nodded. "Certainly, Nora."

"Thank you." I bit down on the inside of my cheek. Nora was Ben's name for me, and as Marguerite glanced out the window again, I decided I didn't really like how she was so concerned about my brother.

That was *my* job, after all.

And it hurt; I was upset from hearing the gunshots and dealing with my brother's lingering hostility, and worrying that Ben and Ferdy were fighting over who had the better chances in a duel; I wasn't eager to discover my brother had an admirer, too.

"Actually, Marguerite, wait." I felt a little guilty as I saw her eyes light up with hope.

I didn't have the courage to ask her what her feelings were for Ben.

Just like I don't have the courage to face the other questions about Lumiere, Tulia, and my mother.

The thought pressed into me painfully, but I hurriedly pushed it aside as I faced Marguerite.

"Why don't you see to Lady Cecilia and Priscilla?" I asked. "My stepsister told me how much she enjoys your company."

If Marguerite suspected I was uncomfortable, she did not show any sign of it.

"Of course," she agreed. "I can get my sewing kit. I've been teaching her how to do some stitching."

"Thank you." Priscilla and Cecilia were a distraction that would keep her away from my brother, and I knew firsthand they were an effective one.

Realizing I was using the same reasoning Lady POW likely had when she'd sent Tulia to watch over them, I groaned and my fingers tightened into fists.

Sometimes, I really was too much like my grandmother for comfort.

Looking back, I saw Marguerite's gaze linger on Ben one last time, before she hurried away.

Wearily, I unclenched my fists.

"Please, Lord," I whispered desperately, lifting my palms upward in tired expectation. "Help me."

My voice echoed softly in the hallway, but there was no other indication my prayer had been heard. No peace enveloped me, no whisper of wings stirred my soul, no blessings filled my open hands.

My head dropped to my chest as my arms fell limply to my sides.

I was still in a fight with myself, at war with the enemy within, and there was no relief.

I was suddenly very grateful I would be working with Xiana shortly; between my thoughts and the weight in my heart, I welcomed the distraction.

THE ORDER OF THE CRYSTAL DAGGERS

7

◊

It wasn't long after my training started that I changed my mind. The melancholy weight on my heart was nothing compared to the screaming pain coursing through my body, courtesy of Xiana's instruction.

"Ground in your stance." Xiana's tone was tight and tense as she glared down at me disapprovingly.

Sweat pooled on my face, adding to its warmth as I blushed. I struggled to remain standing as I shifted my weight more into my feet.

I was more than sorry that Harshad wasn't with us, even if he would've had to witness my poor footwork. Without his supervision, Xiana did not hesitate to push me harder than usual, and since I had missed our earlier training session, it was in her right to do so. I did my best to make up for my absence, and I met her expectations most of the time, but Xiana still seemed more angry than pleased by my efforts.

Perhaps she is still upset because of Lumiere.

I couldn't blame her for that, even if I was the one who would suffer because of it.

"You are still not centered." Xiana feinted an attack to my right; I twisted around to avoid her and staggered off balance.

My fingernails scraped the sweat off the inside of my palms as I tried to show patience. "Can you show me how to fix it?"

"I have shown you." Xiana shook her head. "It is time you started seeing this as serious business. Harshad is too easy on you."

I bit down on my cheek to stop myself from replying. If anything, Harshad pushed me just as much, but he had been

85

much kinder regarding my mistakes and missteps. My complaints had no such effect on Xiana.

Instead, I took a deep breath and shifted my weight again, resolving to meet her challenge.

If Lady Penelope had intended Xiana's training to be a kind of revenge for me, she'd done well.

I gritted my teeth at the thought, but still, I put my fists up, ready for the next round.

Without hesitation, Xiana lunged forward, and once more, we began to spar.

At first, I blocked her attacks successfully. Xiana was a skilled fighter, surpassing me in technique, speed, and experience. But I was younger than she was, and while I was a little shorter, I also had a wider build; if I took careful aim and waited for the right moment, my attack could do more damage—assuming I attacked at all.

Harshad had mentioned my tendency to start on the defensive more than once, and I had to play to my strengths against Xiana if I was going to survive.

"Focus," Xiana snapped as I retreated again, still looking for an opening.

I was suddenly very grateful I'd changed into my stealth habit for our session; if I had worn my skirts, or even my trousers, it would've been a lot more difficult to keep up. In some ways, our fight reminded me of a very violent dance, one in which precise movements were mandated as much as the manners that preceded it.

Perhaps that was a weakness of mine in this regard, too; after all, I was used to following the lead and never dared to tread on another's toes—unless it was warranted.

But my goal was not to be a good follower; it was to be a competent leader—one who did what was right in the face of

THE ORDER OF THE CRYSTAL DAGGERS

evil, who would hold onto hope in the reality of despair, and who would fight for those she loved.

"Ow!" I yelped as Xiana landed a punch to my side.

"You are still not good enough." Xiana smacked my arms, forcing me back into position, and I could almost hear her silent, celebratory chiding as I whimpered in pain. "I have been instructing you for weeks now."

Swiftly, I held up my fists again. This time, her attack came just slightly slower; I managed to avoid it with a profound sense of relief.

Xiana had very little patience in dealing with me, but if I was careful, I knew I could outlast her in terms of energy. And there were other strategies I could try, too.

"Did Lumiere offend you earlier?" I asked.

"No. Lumiere is less than nothing." Despite the quick dismissal, Xiana's eyes flashed furiously, and I knew she was lying.

Everyone lies about something.

I hid a smile; Ferdy and Lady POW had made sure I'd learned that lesson. And in many ways, I did not blame Xiana for her frustration. She was usually quiet and reserved, and if Lumiere was able to irritate her in such a noticeable way, it would be something that would bother her.

I dodged another blow, but Xiana reversed and feinted. I yelped as she shoved her full weight against me; the force of her movement combined with the momentum sent me tumbling over, right into the floor.

"Ouch," I grumbled, barely catching myself. I fell hard on my hip, the one that bore the weight of my mother's dagger. I reached down to adjust it, but Xiana slapped my hand out the way.

"Get up," she ordered. "No weapons."

"I wasn't going to use it," I tried to explain, but she cut me off.

"Do not lie to me."

"I wasn't," I nearly shouted, trying to hide my growing frustration.

"If you try to use it on me, you will be sorry," Xiana warned.

"I wasn't going to; I was just trying to adjust it," I insisted, ducking my head down onto my chest.

"No." She stepped directly in front of me, her fists still balled up and ready to strike.

"Harshad would give me time to fix it." I hated how weak I sounded. It was one thing to be a noble warrior in theory; it was much more painful in practice.

A long moment of stillness passed before Xiana relaxed her stance.

"He is not here, but I will allow you to rest just this once," she conceded reluctantly.

I frowned. I had already disappointed Lady POW today; failing to meet Xiana's expectations should've been a given.

"Is Lumiere the reason Harshad is not here?" I asked, tugging the small scabbard at my side as I recalled Harshad's unusual outburst. "Or was it because of what Lady Penelope said earlier?"

I almost asked if Harshad had heard news about Karl when Xiana's eyes narrowed.

"What did Lady Penelope say?" Xiana's tone shifted immediately, and seeing her interest, I saw my chance and took it.

Quickly—but not too quickly, since I still craved a break from our battle—I explained how Lady Penelope and I had argued about my mother, and how Harshad had snapped at her.

As I spoke, I watched Xiana's stoic face carefully, looking for any small change or inflection. There was no sign of any surprise as I told her the story. When I was finished, she only nodded.

"Harshad would stop her from saying anything. He does not like to be reminded of Naděžda's great sin," Xiana said, her voice back to its usual, detached tone.

"Nassara was not my mother's sin," I snapped, standing up angrily. "No child is a mistake in God's eyes."

"In God's eyes, perhaps, but what of the world's?" Xiana's nose twitched in unspoken annoyance. "Had Nassara been born, she might've become as unhinged as Lumiere, and you might have had to kill her at some point."

Xiana's words were eerily similar to Lumiere's assertion I might one day regret he'd allowed Tulia to live, and they were no less infuriating. Tulia's actions on the *Salacia* made it clear she was not innocent, and it angered me to hear Xiana compare her with my unborn sister.

Inconvenience and innocence were different matters, and Xiana should've known better.

"Are you saying it was good my mother lost her?" I brushed a loose lock of hair out of my eyes, trying to steady myself.

"You must stay calm. Your mother is a weakness of yours," Xiana said.

"She is not a weakness." I gritted my teeth again, tempted to scream in fury, before I straightened my shoulders and composed myself. "If anything, she is a source of strength."

THE ORDER OF THE CRYSTAL DAGGERS

Xiana shook her head disdainfully. "That explains why you are so weak, then."

"I will not allow you to dishonor my mother's memory," I insisted, resuming my fighting stance.

"Eleanora, you cannot hold her up as though she was Madonna. You barely knew her, and you do not know how differently you would feel if she had lived," Xiana said. "That is the truth."

"I knew her better than you did," I objected.

"Oh, did you?" Xiana glared at me this time, furious but still unmoved. "Then you should know that Naděžda was the one who got rid of her baby."

"My mother didn't … " I swallowed the lump in my throat and tried to speak again, suddenly feeling sick and angry and full of hatred. "She didn't … "

All too clearly, I remembered the night Lady Penelope gave me *Máma's* dagger, and then Amir's words in the cathedral before my wedding. I blinked to see Xiana's glittering eyes glaring down into me, forcing me to face the earlier darkness I'd only vaguely sensed.

Máma *could've taken the silver thallis herb, enough to get rid of the baby.*

"She did," Xiana said, as if she could see into my thoughts. "I saw her drink the poison myself."

I couldn't say anything as her words, sharp as a dagger, sank into my heart and twisted violently.

I thought of my mother, combing my hair, cupping my cheek, kissing my forehead. Tucking me into bed, reading with me. Hearing her laugh. Seeing her smile.

"No." I shook my head as I found my voice again. "No, that's not true. Something else had to have happened."

Perhaps Xiana expected me to give up again, or to fall back in my fighting; I could see the spark of surprise briefly in her eyes as my fists balled up, and I launched forward in my first real offensive.

While I didn't mean to catch her off guard, it worked; Xiana only just barely slipped to the side.

"Do not be so naïve, Eleanora." Xiana grabbed my arm and twisted away, before her leg swept under mine, knocking me down again. "You have never known your mother or what kind of misery she was capable of inflicting on others."

Scrambling to my feet, I was unable to successfully retaliate at that poisonous, pernicious thought. Xiana threw out a hard, direct punch, hitting me square in the chest.

I could do nothing as my head fell back and I slammed into the hard floor. The wind rushed out of me, and I coughed at the pain.

"Get up," Xiana snapped. "We are still fighting."

Her words were muffled inside my mind as my body seemed to fight with itself.

"It's not possible," I wheezed out, struggling to move, still winded from Xiana's attack. "My mother wouldn't do that."

"She did do it." Xiana's lips thinned. "Harshad will not discuss it because she was under pressure from Lady Penelope to dispose of the baby."

"What?" My mouth barely formed the word as my hands grappled with hers. I blinked as sweat trickled down my brow, struggling to keep my vision clear; it was still clouded with memories of my mother—holding my hand, walking beside me, hugging Ben, welcoming my father home …

"That is the truth, Eleanora, and if you are smart, you will never speak of it again," Xiana said as she lashed out another

THE ORDER OF THE CRYSTAL DAGGERS

attack. "Lady Penelope was most displeased when she discovered Amir and your mother were having an affair—"

"They were married," I objected, though it affected neither her argument nor her determination.

"—and she became pregnant. Naděžda was a great beauty, and she could have had any suitor she wanted. She could have had a prince, just as you do now."

At the mention of Ferdy, I jumped up, holding my fists up to guard my face with renewed vigor. I would not let Xiana use Ferdy against me, as Lady Penelope had earlier.

"Naturally, Lady Penelope was quite upset, especially while the Order was in the middle of an important mission." Xiana's eyes narrowed into slits as we circled each other. "Lady Penelope objected to their union, and she wanted the baby gone, so Naděžda took care of it. It was an easy solution."

"Eleanor ruined it herself."

Lady Penelope's words from earlier hit me even harder this time, and tears welled up in my eyes as my mind filled up with memories.

Disbelief and shock finally gave way to fury, and I was screaming as I grabbed Xiana's collar.

I hauled her over my shoulder, and tossed her down forcefully.

Slowly but triumphantly, breathing hard, I finally managed to gain the advantage.

"I don't believe you," I told her, as she grappled wildly underneath my hold. "You're lying."

My mother had wanted children. She'd left the Order and married my father, and she not only had Ben, but she had me as well. And even before then, I knew she'd loved Amir and Nassara.

Conviction settled inside my heart like a protective cloak.

Máma would not have done anything to risk the life of her baby. It simply did not make sense, even if Xiana did see her drink the poison.

"Why would I lie?" Xiana's voice was slightly stilted as she struggled against me. "I have only told you what Lady Penelope and Harshad will not say themselves. Naděžda knew about the silver thallis herb and its capabilities, and she drank it."

Just as I started to reply, Xiana freed herself and struck out a vengeful kick.

But this time, I was ready.

I grabbed hold of her, and I forced her under my shoulder, then rolled with her and pinned her down on the floor.

"No," I said, more to myself than to her, much more determined this time. My knuckles landed hard against her jaw, and I could feel the warmth of blood.

I was shocked—but I didn't stop.

Our battle was charged with power and intent, and I was as dazzled by our mutual strength and endurance as I was befuddled by our differences.

Our deadly dance showed our distinct rivalry; it was beautiful and intense, and then it was over.

My fist was steady at her neck; Xiana's eyes widened with confused shock as I stood over her.

But my success was short-lived; she recovered in the next instant, rolling back over her shoulder and onto her feet again, reaching for my dagger. She deftly slid it out of my scabbard, and slid the blade across my armor.

THE ORDER OF THE CRYSTAL DAGGERS

I jerked back at the surprising pain. "Stop!"

I rolled to the side and clutched at my chest, feeling for any slits in the leather or any blood spilling on my skin. My lungs were on fire and my chest burned, and I was afraid, but there was no permanent damage to my person.

"As I said, you are weak." Xiana's voice was an angry hiss, even more so as she wiped the blood from her lip. "You may have had a hard life, but so did I. My parents died when I was just a child, and Harshad took me in after he lost his own family to cholera. I was raised alongside Naděžda, and I could do nothing as she endangered Amir, upset your grandmother, and betrayed the Order."

"Betrayed?" I repeated, surprised, but Xiana ignored me.

"No one even tried to stop her, either." Xiana shook her head, letting her black braid snap through the air like a whip, before she leaped toward me again, light glinting off my mother's violet-colored dagger.

"What are you doing?" I cried, watching her body tense up with deadly resolve.

Suddenly, I was terrified I'd miscalculated and greatly overestimated her integrity.

A string of half-formed words sputtered out of me as I tried to scurry away, but it was useless; she caught me, threw me onto the floor, pinned me down, and slammed the dagger down toward my heart.

I squeezed my eyes shut, scrunching up my face, angry and terrified at facing death, but determined not to scream.

And then there was a great clash, and Xiana let out the smallest gasp.

"That's enough, Xiana."

Amir's voice was harder than I'd ever heard it.

As I tentatively opened my eyes, I saw him standing above me. His own small dagger, the *Wahabite Jambiya*, was locked firmly against Xiana's attack.

"Amir." The fire I'd seen in Xiana's eyes quickly dissolved into suspicion and fear as she looked up at him.

"You were about to kill her," Amir accused, his voice full of steady vitriol.

"She has to learn how to lose, Amir," Xiana told him, her voice tight and her bloody lips sharply drawn across her face. Her cheeks were red from exertion, but there was a slight shadow of shame in her expression, one that reminded me of Cecilia in that moment.

She did not regret pushing me; she only regretted that she'd been caught.

"No." Amir's eyes were full of disappointment. "Eleanora has to learn to keep going after a loss. That's not the same thing, and you know it."

Xiana frowned, and then, in a flash of movement, she pulled back my mother's dagger, and then thrust its blade into the floor, just a hair away from my cheek.

Before I could scream, Amir was already shoving her away. Xiana began to fight back, tangling herself around his arm, but Amir shook his head.

"Xiana." Amir stood firm. "Enough."

They both stared at each other with searching gazes, reminding me of Lady POW and Harshad. They were having a silent conversation, one of hope and resentment, of admiration and admonishment.

Watching them, I kept silent; another world lay between them, and I had no notion of what they were debating with each other.

Then, reluctantly, Xiana let go and stepped away. Their eyes never left each other's; Amir looked on her with sorrow and regret, while Xiana's gaze was flat, full of forced nothingness—the gaze of a killer.

But was she really going to kill me?

I sat up, beyond befuddled. My body was numb with shock and betrayal; belatedly, I saw I was not injured beyond my pride, but my body was crying out for rest. I pulled my mother's dagger out of the floor, angered as I saw my fingers were trembling.

"You did well, Eleanora." Amir finally turned and held out his hand to me, and I took it with gratitude. "We still have plenty of time for higher levels of instruction."

"Enough, Amir. Times have changed, and so has the Order." Xiana wiped her hands off on her tunic briskly. "You cannot allow her to remain weak."

"We all have our weaknesses, regardless of how strong we are." His words were firm but soft, and I saw her give the slightest flinch at his tone. "This is not how we train."

"Then she will die."

Amir's hand constricted against mine, as if to rebuke her statement, but before either of us could say anything, Xiana shook her head.

"I was merely attending to my duties, as Madame has instructed me," she said, her voice emotionless and mechanical once more. "If you are going to prevent me from doing so, I will take my leave."

She bowed, her form as stiff and formal as ever, and turned away from both of us.

"Xiana." Amir called out to her again as she reached the door. "I would like to talk with you later. There are some things I wish to discuss."

"No, thank you. I have nothing to say to you," Xiana replied curtly. "I have been talking to you for years, Amir, wishing you would listen to me. But you have never bothered to listen, and it is too late to change anything now."

"Xiana." His expression grew forlorn. "Wishes are oddly burdensome things."

"Yes, they are, especially when such wishes go overlooked and unfulfilled," she snapped, whirling around to face him. Her eyes rippled with unspoken emotion. "After all this time, I can only return the courtesy you have shown me. Excuse me."

Then she blinked, and her expression was once more flat and impassive.

Amir and I did not say anything as she left the room.

I listened for the echo of her nearly silent footsteps as they disappeared, feeling strangely sympathetic for her. She might have won our battle, but she'd lost something more in doing so.

"How much of our conversation did you overhear?" My voice was thick as I finally broke the silence between me and Amir.

"Enough," he replied, a vacant look in his eyes.

"I'm sorry."

"It's not your fault," Amir said. "And besides, I should thank you."

"Thank me?"

"Yes." He gave me a sad, grateful look. "I am sure your mother is happy to know you will defend her honor."

"So she didn't … ?" My whisper trailed off into nothing; I still could not bear to say it.

"If she did, she certainly fooled me. Naděžda was about twenty weeks along when she went into early labor. Before that, she was always talking about being a mother."

"And leaving the Order?"

"Death or defeat is the only way to truly leave the Order." Amir's moustache twitched as he grimaced. "Or so Lady POW would say."

"That's awful," I said.

"Only if you make it awful. Any commitment is an act of both hope and fear, of courage and faith," Amir replied. "Such a pledge binds us to our choices. In the Order's case, there is room for adjustments. Remember, Lady POW allowed you and Ben to join her, and even she didn't leave the Order when she was pregnant with Naděžda."

"Why was my mother having a baby such an inconvenience, then?" I asked. "If Lady POW did it, shouldn't my mother have been able to do it, too?"

Amir shifted uncomfortably. "I suppose there were a few reasons Lady POW objected to the situation. She and your grandfather were better off financially, for one. I had just been disowned by my family a few weeks prior to Nassara's arrival. My hand was still bandaged when I held her for the first time."

"Amir." I put my hand on his, not wanting to hear any more, knowing it would only hurt him. "You don't have to say anything else if you don't want to."

But he shook his head. "For the longest time, I wondered where Lady Penelope had gotten the notion that I'd poisoned Naděžda, or if it was even true. Now I know there was at least one witness."

Both of us looked back at the empty doorway where Xiana had disappeared.

"You didn't notice anything strange when Nassara was born?" I thought of the bluish tint to my father's lips the day of his funeral. I hadn't known about the silver thallis herb at the time, nor had I known about the Order.

"No. I only saw how beautiful she was." Amir sighed. "I told myself she was too good for this world, and for me, and her death was a sign I was unfit to be a father and a husband. And perhaps I was; I wasn't much help when Nassara arrived so unexpectedly. Another doctor tended to Naděžda after her labor. He told us she would likely never conceive again."

Amir smirked as he looked over at me again. "But we know now that's not true."

I laughed a little to ease the grief that had settled in my heart. I was surprised to feel a small tear trickling down my cheek. "I'm sorry."

"Don't be," Amir replied. "As I said, you defended her honor. Naděžda will be grateful for that."

I squeezed Amir's hand, acutely aware of the scarred flesh underneath mine. "She wouldn't have done anything to hurt Nassara. We will find out the truth," I vowed.

"If we can." He was hesitant, and I could see he was only appeasing me.

"We are loyal to the truth," I reminded him.

"Yes, we are. Truth is born of love and leads us to freedom, and freedom gives us the key to beauty. In its absence, we hold on to hope, and we wait for it faithfully, with fear and trembling." Amir patted my head affectionately. "But we must realize there are limitations this side of eternity."

I was about to argue when he shook his head again.

"You will have to excuse me, Eleanora. I have an appointment with Ben. We are going to work on his Arabic today while I check his leg."

"Perhaps Ferdy will join you," I said.

"He has in the past," Amir said, surprising me. "Ben seems to enjoy having someone distract him from grammar work. It also makes our small breaks between lessons more interesting."

"Do I even want to know how they're getting along?" I grimaced, recalling how Ben and Ferdy had been arguing with each other earlier. I looked at Amir's dagger.

"I imagine you can guess." Amir patted his blade, as if to confirm guns weren't the only weapons Ben and Ferdy were bonding over. "But don't worry. I can take care of them, and Marguerite is there to help, too."

"Why is she there?" I bit my lip, unable to conceal my frustration.

"Women tame men and civilize them in miraculous ways," Amir explained. "Lady Penelope told her to see to Ben's care, but it's also nice she can help me with bandages, and stitches, if need be. She is an impressive seamstress."

"I guess I won't worry if you're there. I can trust you." I briefly thought of asking Amir about Ben and Marguerite, but I decided to save that line of inquiry for later. There were still things I wanted to say to Amir about my mother.

"Amir?" I cleared my throat, silently praying I wasn't overstepping myself. "Just so you know, I am sure my mother still loved you, even after she married my father."

I knew this to be true; in my mother's locket, a small picture of Amir had been tucked away behind my father's portrait. For the first time, I wondered if Amir had bought my mother the locket himself.

I will give it to him later.

Amir gave me his tired smile. "After all these years, my love for Naděžda has not waned, and I have not moved my heart to make room for a beauty I know will never compare to hers." He glanced back in the direction Xiana had gone, and I realized there was more to their earlier exchange than I'd thought.

"I know Xiana's not usually this hard on me," I said. "But I am glad you came to my rescue. I can't seem to win against her."

Amir nodded. "She's a tough opponent. If force doesn't work, the only way to win against her is by surprise."

"She doesn't seem to like surprises," I agreed, recalling her argument with Lumiere. "That's probably why Lumiere made her upset earlier."

"He is good at that," Amir agreed easily enough. He put his *Wahabite Jambiya* back in its scabbard. "But I am surprised she was upset at all, and to the point where others would notice. Xiana has always been very disciplined, even when we were younger."

"How long have you known her?" I asked, suddenly very curious.

"We have known each other for a very long time. She was a young orphan when Harshad took her in, and we studied under him together. Later, she worked with Naděžda and me on several missions, and of course, she taught me about the Order's use of herbs," Amir said. "We were all quite close. Naděžda and I called her *Saghira* for many years. It means 'little sister,' in Arabic."

I bit my cheek. I could understand why Xiana was so reluctant to talk with Amir, given what I knew now. "Lumiere called her that earlier," I said, remembering how Xiana had fought with him. "He doesn't seem to share her friendship."

"The French and Chinese have a contemptuous history." Amir shrugged. "But it took a while for me to see Lumi as a friend, too. I can see where she would not appreciate his style. And Lumi has always let it be known how he preferred Naděžda over her."

And he was not the only one.

My thoughts went unspoken, but Amir gave me a small nod. "She would not forgive him easily for that."

His voice was full of sadness as he spoke, and I could see he'd never fully realized that Xiana, for all her toughness, had a weakness of her own he'd missed.

Amir was a good man—I could see why Lady Penelope would want him around, and she would trust him with her life, even if she didn't trust him with her loyalty. Amir would be the kind of person to save her, even if he hated her; and my mother had loved him enough to marry him, even if their marriage did not last. And even though he'd rejected her, Xiana would know he was worthy of her affections.

"You know, there are different kinds of beauty in this world, and if you wanted to fall in love again, I don't think *Máma* would want you to deny yourself that freedom."

It was not necessary to remind Amir that my mother had given herself that freedom, too, in marrying my father.

"She would not." Amir nodded. "But I have already left her once, and I cannot seem to do it again. Others have offered me their hearts, but I'm afraid I have nothing left to give."

He was kind enough not to mention Xiana by name, and I appreciated his concern for her. Amir clearly still had a great deal of respect for her, and he would not present her as my enemy.

"But aren't you lonely?" I asked.

THE ORDER OF THE CRYSTAL DAGGERS

"Of course I am, Eleanora. But what I lack here one day will be complete. And that is what sustains me. There is also the good company I've found with Harshad and Lady POW—and yourself and your family, too." Amir paused and then laughed a little. "Even Lumiere is not so much of a burden to me as you'd think. He loved your mother, and during our time together she called him her cousin when we would meet."

"I think he sees her when he looks at me," I confessed, slightly embarrassed; Amir and I both knew Lumiere was not the only one who was guilty of that.

"It is very hard not to." His tone was apologetic, but no apology followed; I knew it was somewhat foolish to object to such a circumstance, anyway, especially when I liked being similar to my mother.

Amir held out his hand to me. "Lumi was the one who helped Naděžda and Xiana save me after my father disowned me and my cousins gave me this."

The Arabic *noon*, the one that marked him as a Christian convert and an outsider to his family, was carved into his flesh. Though it had been done decades before, every inch of its deadly cut still displayed pure pain. I shuddered, unwilling to imagine what they would have done to Amir if he hadn't escaped.

"He was docked at Constantinople that night," Amir explained. "Lumi took us to London right away, back to the Order, even though it was dangerous for him. I did not make it easy for him, either; I was suffering from blood loss and calling for Halal as we left port."

I grimaced; Amir had told me before that his older sister had been killed for helping him escape.

"I was yelling rather loudly, too. Your mother told me Lumiere used chloroform to knock me out. Later, he tried to charge me for it."

I imagined Lumiere running around his ship, preparing them to set sail, all for Amir's sake. He would've enjoyed the chaos and the thrill of risk.

"It's hard to believe Lumiere was ever good for anything," I finally murmured.

"He's a handful. But he has never failed me, even if he has always inconvenienced me." Amir put his scarred hand on his dagger's hilt.

"He said you were one of his contingencies. Is that why?"

"I don't know about any secret plans he might have," Amir said. "But I'm sure our past would be enough for him to believe I would help him if he needed it. He saved my life."

"I'll try to remember that next time Lumiere irritates me," I said. I kept my tone sincere instead of cynical; it was my turn to appease Amir.

He laughed; he seemed to know I was being kind to him. "God makes things possible, but that does not mean he makes them easy. Lumiere is on our side, even if he is reluctant to admit it, or even if we are horrified to embrace it."

"I'm quite horrified, that's for certain."

I thought of Lumiere telling me to find the right time to come and talk with him.

I was still unsure if I wanted to hear what he had to say. I didn't just want answers; I wanted the truth, and I wasn't sure Lumiere was the kind of person who would give it to me.

"He is still the one most likely to know where Karl is, even if he hasn't said anything yet. He's probably just waiting for

THE ORDER OF THE CRYSTAL DAGGERS

the right time to ensure he'll get what he wants out of the situation. That's how he usually works," Amir said, reminding me of our current mission.

I was glad for Amir's encouragement. His companionship comforted me, leaving my heart encouraged, even as we parted ways.

Just as he was about to leave the room, I called out to him again.

"What is it, Eleanora?" Amir was tired, and I knew he was busy, but it warmed me that he did not seem to mind my constant cries for attention.

Still, I could feel the sweat on my palms as I asked the most intrusive question that burdened my heart.

"I wanted to ask … if my mother did … take the poison, as Xiana said, would you still love her?"

Society did not allow for the discussion of such private matters, and even between family and friends it was hard to talk of such impropriety. I didn't want to know if my mother had purposefully poisoned Nassara, but if she did—even though it was inconceivable to me, and antithetical to all the memories I had of my mother—I wanted to know if there was still a chance that I could love her.

Amir went quiet for a long moment. I could see him thinking hard, honestly searching for an answer to give me.

At last, he spoke.

"I would still love her," he agreed. "And I would forgive her, too. But I would not be as apt to forgive myself for leaving her in a position where she believed there was no other choice. If what Xiana said was true, I could not live with such a regret."

With that, Amir excused himself, and we said nothing else. But as I watched him go, a new peace settled around me.

THE ORDER OF THE CRYSTAL DAGGERS

Even if it was unpleasant, I knew I could face the truth.

There was nothing brave or kind about feeling sorry for myself or waiting around for the right time to act. Amir deserved peace, and I wanted it for him even more than I wanted it for myself.

I rested my hand on my mother's dagger, feeling a renewed sense of urgency as I headed out of the room to go and find Lumiere. Lady Penelope had said it was more imperative than ever to find Karl, and I would no longer wait for Lumiere to find the right time.

Just as in the case with fighting and dancing, it was time to take the lead.

8

◊

"Lumiere."

I knocked hard on his door, briefly pouting as pain stung across my knuckles. After all the time I'd spent training and fighting with Xiana, my body was starting to protest at any movement at all.

"Lumiere, open up," I called again. For a brief second, I considered giving up and going to my room.

I didn't really want to deal with Lumiere. What I really wanted was a warm bath and a large supper, and then I wanted to go to bed.

But I was desperate, and curious, and left without answers—answers I suspected Lumiere could provide. Even if I couldn't trust him completely, I wanted to hear what he had to say.

After all, Lumiere knew of my mother; he'd known her before the Revolution of 1848, and he knew about my father, too. He knew about Ferdy and Karl, having met with them abroad, and he knew about the Order, and Xiana's past with Amir and Nassara.

I couldn't trust him.

But surely, if he'd loved my mother as much as everyone else did, he would give me the answers I sought.

I knocked again, this time even harder. "Lumiere, I've made the time to be here, whether it's right or not. Let me in."

There was no reply.

I pressed my ear against the door, listening for any sound at all. It was strangely quiet, and the earlier sense of regret I'd felt in deciding to talk with him suddenly increased exponentially.

"Lumiere, this is important!" I tapped my foot against the floor, waiting.

Interminably long seconds passed, and still, nothing happened. There was no answer.

Quickly but tentatively, I glanced down each side of the hallway. I checked to make sure I was in the right place, and then I looked to see no one was around as I fiddled with the lock on his door.

Lady Penelope didn't need another reason to distrust me, and I didn't need Ben to lament my poor lock-picking skills.

I bit my lip. Even if Ben did see me, I didn't think he would chide me; after all the years he'd spent building his leg braces, Ben knew he was the better mechanic between the two of us. And if he were here, he would've helped me, just as he always had.

I was the one who had trouble when it came to helping *him*—and others, too. Momentarily, my hands stilled and my eyes closed in shame; it was pure agony to remember how Alex had shot Ferdy when he'd cornered us on the *Salacia*, all because of my mistakes.

There was a small click, as the lock tumbled open.

"Oh, thank you." I opened the door, pushing my past guilt into the back of my mind. "All right, Lumiere, I'm coming in. You'd better be decent."

I was fully expecting him to assure me he was only ever decent.

But when I walked across the threshold, I was only met with cold emptiness, and my irritation turned into sincere alarm.

THE ORDER OF THE CRYSTAL DAGGERS

"Lumiere?"

The room was quiet and dark; even after I quickly drew back the curtains, the last of the day's light was barely enough to fill the room. Lumiere's effervescent personality hung in the air, and its ghostly remains lingered in the various piles of small trinkets, fine clothes, empty liquor containers.

But the man himself was stripped away.

On the bedspread, a twinkle of light sparkled like a golden flame. I already knew what it was, even before I picked it up: it was Lumiere's pocket watch, the one that he'd held up to me only hours before.

I examined it again. I could still see the similarities it held to my father's watch—the muted gold, simple design, the inlaid pierced markings. I opened it to see the elegant *fleur-de-lis* design on its clock face, encircled by a bronzed bezel. All three hands were still and silent, ominously pointing to midnight.

But for the first time, I saw the *fleur-de-lis* motif matched the princess hair combs Ferdy had given me before. It was a symbol of the Kingdom of Bohemia.

"Of course," I whispered. *Táta* had been given his watch by King Ferdinand. He'd been an ambassador, working closely with the king.

But why did Lumiere have a watch like this, too?

I looked down at the bed. There had been another item there, staring up at me, lying beside the watch.

My heart skipped a beat at the sight of my mother's journal, the one carved with the same Arabic *noon* that Amir bore on his hand.

It was a piece of her heart I never expected to find, a wish I hadn't known until I saw it.

Lumiere was the one who'd taken it, to absolutely no earth-shattering shock.

Slowly and reverently, I picked it up. Lumiere had helped *Máma* save Amir before. He would've known about the mark, and he wouldn't have had any qualms about taking the journal when he'd captured Cecilia and the others.

I leafed through the pages, momentarily awed at the neatness of my mother's handwriting. The foreign scrawl was written so smooth and straight, I could've sworn it was printed when I'd first seen it. Even the little marks and scribbles in the margins were so carefully added, it seemed to be by design rather than a doodle. My own loopy penmanship was slanted and sloppy by comparison.

There were no ripped pages, no frayed sheets, and nothing that suggested it had been waterlogged from the *Salacia.* There were a few dotted sheets with smudges, and I did not know if they were tears from my mother or someone else. I kept turning the pages, not seeing anything unusual until close to the end.

There was a small fold on the top of a page. Perhaps it was Amir's; it seemed too polite to be Lumiere's mark of progress, and its crease too sharp and fresh to be more than a few months old.

I shut the book quietly and held it against my chest. After one last fleeting glance around the room, I headed off to find Amir again.

Lumiere was missing, but my mother's journal had been found; despair and excitement both welled up inside me, and I bounced between dread and hope in a rhythm that only matched the pounding of my heart.

After awkwardly questioning a few of the staff members, I finally found Amir and Ben working in the barn. As I walked outside, the cold winter air bristled against me, but I welcomed its chilliness. My body was still sore, and walking out to the barn was like pressing my body next to a block of ice.

I paused as I reached the barn door; I could hear Ben's voice, and he sounded almost happy.

"That's what I've been wondering about ever since the night of the Advent Ball and the fire," Ben was saying. "Can you hand me that hammer, Amir? I need that one, not this one."

"Here you go," Amir answered. "What do you think? How would you go about causing such an explosion?"

"I was really worried, so I didn't think about it much at the time." Ben began to hammer at something, and it was harder for me to hear. I leaned against the door as Amir and Ben talked about the incident at Prague Castle.

"I've been trying to narrow down the list of possibilities. I thought it was nitroglycerin," Ben said. "I'd heard Mr. Nobel learned how to make it less volatile after his brother died using it, but it would be easy enough to change it back. Then the trick would be keeping it cool."

"Perhaps that was why it was in the wine cellar," Amir suggested.

"That would make sense. And it would explain Ferdy's carriage fire. As the nitroglycerin warmed, it would be more likely to detonate."

I leaned against the door, curious to hear any animosity in Ben's voice as he talked about Ferdy.

But then the door abruptly opened, and I stumbled forward.

"Ouch." I nearly dropped the journal and Lumiere's pocket watch as I struggled to keep my balance.

"Eleanora?" Amir looked over at me. He was sitting beside Ben on a workbench. From the firepit and the tools scattered around them, I could see they had been working together on a new brace for Ben and his leg.

"What are you doing here, Ella?" Ben eyed me suspiciously.

"Lumiere's gone." I came forward, desperate to cover up my insecurity and embarrassment as I handed the journal to Amir. I kept Lumiere's pocket watch in my other hand, tucked away, deciding I would worry about that on my own. "I found this in his room. I guess he had it all this time."

"I see." Amir's voice was edged with irritation as he took the journal from my hands. I was about to ask him what was wrong before he let out a sigh. "Perhaps he didn't know how much I wanted it back."

"I doubt that," Ben and I said at the same time. As we looked at each other in surprise, I wondered how much Lumiere had been bothering Ben—and what he'd been bothering him about, too.

"Thank you for this, Eleanora. I will examine it later," Amir said. "But we should find Lumiere. He was supposed to remain locked up for the rest of the day."

Dread gnawed at me from inside my stomach.

If Lumiere was missing, I wouldn't be able to ask him my questions, both about my mother's past secrets and Karl's present location.

But he might have gone to meet with his father, too—and that was even more frightening.

I shivered, but I tried to be optimistic.

"Perhaps he's with Lady POW, and they're trying their hardest to punish each other," I suggested.

Amir let out a muffled laugh, but Ben only shook his head.

THE ORDER OF THE CRYSTAL DAGGERS

"It's more likely Ferdy let him out," Ben said, carefully putting his new brace down on his worktable before reaching for his crutches.

"Ferdy wouldn't do that." My voice was harsher than I'd meant, but I was getting very tired of defending Ferdy to my family.

"So you think." Ben rolled his eyes.

"What do you mean by that?"

"I told you before, he's hardly serious about anything in particular." Ben shrugged. "It wouldn't surprise me if Ferdy thought it would be fun to let the Order's greatest asset out of his dungeon for a night."

I bit the inside of my cheek, hurt by Ben's callous tone. "I thought you were getting along with him."

"I am," Ben replied. "But he gets along with everyone until he doesn't. It's in my best interest to humor him for now, just as it's in his to befriend me. It doesn't mean we're actually friends."

I didn't like how dismissive he was, even if Ben was right about Ferdy's temperament. "You're too cynical."

"And you're too trusting."

"Ferdy is loyal to us," I insisted. "If he did let Lumiere out for any reason, it's more likely to fight with him than anything else."

Ben arched his brow at me, while my heart skipped another beat. We both knew it was too easy to believe Ferdy would do just that.

Amir cleared his throat. "Please stop arguing. You're not children anymore."

Ben and I exchanged the same guilty, knowing look. We'd hardly fought when we'd been younger, unless it was for play.

"Now," Amir said, "let's go. I believe I have some more questions for Lumiere myself."

Together we headed out of the barn and back toward the house. Ben was still using his crutches, even though his bandages had been replaced from the ones I'd seen earlier. As we walked, I peeked up at his face, happy to see that while he wore a frustrated look, it was not one of pain.

My happiness did not last.

As our search continued, there was still no sign of Lumiere. His bedroom, my father's study, and the parlor were all empty. With each empty room, my dread exponentially increased.

I couldn't help but notice that not only was Lumiere gone, but there was no sign of Ferdy, either.

"Amir, what happens if we can't find him?" There was a lump in my throat, and my lips felt very dry as I spoke. I could already guess that Lady Penelope would blame me for this, somehow—and that was just the beginning of our problems if Lumiere had indeed escaped. "What do we do?"

"We'll inform Lady POW." Amir's cool reserve steadied me, even as I saw his grip tighten around my mother's journal.

"Let's separate," Ben suggested. "I'll go check the library and see if I can talk with some of the others."

"Including Marguerite?" I asked.

Ben's jaw tightened. "Perhaps, if I see her."

I was a little gratified that, while he was annoyed at my inquiry, there was nothing in his voice that hinted at a deep, hidden affection.

"We would cover more ground more efficiently if we separate," Amir agreed. "I'll take the kitchens and the wine cellar; it wouldn't be out of character for Lumi to get himself locked in there. Ben, you should go alert the others. What about you, Eleanora?"

My fingers tightened around Lumiere's pocket watch. "I'm going to go out and look in the city. If he's already gone, surely someone would've noticed him. And depending on how long it's been since he's escaped, I might even be able to catch up to him."

"Lady POW won't like that." Ben crossed his arms. "She told you not to leave the grounds. You're supposed to be on your honeymoon with Karl, remember? The town doesn't need to know it's all a lie."

"She's already disappointed in me," I said with a shrug. "This shouldn't surprise her; in fact, given what she's told me about trusting people before, she's probably expecting me to disobey her."

"She still won't be happy when she finds out," Ben argued.

"She's never happy anyway."

"Eleanora." Amir glanced up at the windows. "It's nearly nightfall. If you are intent on leaving, you should go now."

"You're not just going to let her out of the house, are you?" Ben asked, his expression incredulous. "What about our orders? And we're not done searching here yet."

"We can take care of the grounds here while Eleanora searches the city," Amir told him. "Lumiere might have left, and she will have better luck in getting him to come back if that's the case."

"But she shouldn't go out alone. I'll go with her."

"No," I said, trying to be tactful. "Amir just said you can help him here. I'll draw less attention if I'm by myself."

He glanced down at his leg. "Well, that's true enough, isn't it?"

"You know that's not what I meant." I felt the blood drain from my face, as though I'd hurt him all over again.

"Come." Amir put his hand on Ben's shoulder. "We're wasting time. Eleanora will do her part, while we do ours."

There was a small pause, but Ben finally nodded, resigned. "Just promise me you'll be careful, Ella."

"Of course I will," I promised, giving him a brave smile. His concern was touching, even if he wasn't calling me Nora anymore.

"And don't forget to look for Ferdy, too."

My smile disappeared; I could feel my nostrils flare in anger and my fingers curled into fists. I didn't know if Ben was teasing me more out of contempt or concern, but I hated to even give him the benefit of the doubt.

As they headed off and moved out of sight, I steadied myself.

It was time to go.

I pushed away my anger, and embraced my chance for freedom once more.

9

◊

Moonlight was shining at its fullest by the time I reached the Vltava's riverbank. The small waves and the soft lull of wispy winds carried the unspoken promise of adventure, while the starlight hummed a melody all its own.

I had spent years peeking out from my windows, watching the city skyline, wondering at the majestic walls of Prague Castle and the buildings my ancestors built and sculpted hundreds of years before. The tall, sprouting trees of the city softened its edges. Now I knew more of the sadness of its streets and the strife it carried in its quarters; I knew of the places poisoned by sin and tainted beyond mortal repair. In that way, it reminded me of Moses' burning bush: the fire's bright destruction, coexisting with nature's subtle power, in an ongoing battle both constrained and encouraged by heavenly forces.

I was still mesmerized by the majestic sight as I crossed the Stone Bridge and the Prague astronomical clock began to ring. The tolling of the bells added a new depth to the darkness, while the resplendent towers of St. Vitus Cathedral, where Ferdy and I had been wed only weeks ago, called for reckoning and judgment.

I shuddered, suddenly grateful I'd thought to wear my cloak. It was too thin to keep all the winter chill away, but it had been a gift from my friend Faye. It was a reminder to me that I was not alone, and that I did not have to be afraid.

But it was not enough to be unafraid, I thought, aspiring to be brave as I reached for my mother's dagger.

That was when a voice spoke to me from the shadows.

"It is no coincidence you are captivated, Madame."

"Excuse me?" I was surprised to see an older man standing just off to the side behind me.

"This city is full of beauty," the man explained. "And it is no coincidence that you are captivated by it."

The older man was carrying a small box and a pile of papers, and his one hand was smudged with ink and charcoal from his sketching. From his plain, orderly cloak, I guessed him to be one of Prague's many resident artists.

The assessment fit; with his neatly combed, white hair, receding in some areas, he reminded me a little of Harshad. His boots were black and clean, and the only touch of color I saw on him was a patch on his sleeve, one that bore the signet of the University.

"This is one of the most magnificent places in all of Prague." The man gestured toward the top of St. Vitus, and then to the Old Town Tower on the Stone Bridge. "On nights like this, the moon sets behind the top of the main tower. It shines down on this whole bridge, illuminating it with heaven's light and calling dead souls to their eternal rest."

"Oh, yes. It is really beautiful," I agreed, noticing the man was alone, just as I was. He seemed harmless enough, if a little lonely, and eager to speak with another soul.

He pulled out one of his drawings and held it out to me. Inspecting it, I saw a sketch of the cathedral and the bridge, and I was taken aback at its lines of confident simplicity.

"Petr Parléř built both this bridge and the cathedral," the older man continued. "He took great care in his calculations. Do you know why that number is on the tower there?"

He pointed to the east end of the bridge, where the number "135797531" was carved in the stone.

"It's when they started building it," I said, surprised I remembered *Táta* had told me about it once before as we crossed the bridge to go into the city.

"Yes. The number is a palindrome, the same backward or forward. It was meant to be a blessing," the man said. "So you see? Nothing this captivating happens randomly. It is all by design and care, and any artist who wishes to capture even a hint of its beauty must be attentive, precise, and decisive, without regret or remorse."

"Your picture is lovely." I examined the drawing again. Even from where I was, even in the poor lighting, it truly was brilliant; the lines were straight and its shadows aligned perfectly to the scene before us. "You are a talented artist. This is perfect."

"Well, not quite perfect," he said with an amused half-smile. "As beautiful as it is, there are still imperfections, and they must not be ignored or overlooked."

"But it looks just like the city," I insisted, looking back at the church and the bridge and the moon, unable to see any deviation.

"The city itself has its defects. See the water line? And this slope along the wall here?" He pointed down to every flaw on his paper before looking back out to the city. "This city was designed for beauty, but it was not built on a sufficiently firm foundation. You can see the erosion of time and circumstance the more you study it … Such defects ultimately cause rot and undermine the glory of a master's design."

"Perhaps the imperfections serve to make things more beautiful," I said, looking back over at St. Vitus and the bridge and the river. I was unable to stop my smile, remembering Ferdy and our wedding. Prague was part of my history as much as I was part of its memory.

Perhaps the defects of my soul and my city were reminders of our struggles and triumphs over the years, and perhaps we should be grateful for any beauty at all in a fallen world such as ours.

"Oh, gracious, no." The man shook his head with a small laugh. "One must never indulge such thoughts. Complacency only leads to irreverence and destruction. If the foundation is not properly built, no matter how beautiful it is, it will not endure."

"Perhaps." I did not agree with him, even if I was unable to articulate why. "But I fear that means even a talented artist like yourself will be forced to remain a student forever."

"Yes. Still, such a position has its advantages." His light-colored eyes twinkled at me playfully. "We have an appreciation for history few can rival. Even if we are not the best conversationalists, perhaps?"

His smile was wrinkled and teasing, and we shared a small, sweet laugh. Then the older man folded up his sketch, and I winced at the creases in his beautiful work.

"Wait," I said. "If you're only going to dispose of it, I'd be happy to take it."

Without hesitation, he handed it to me. "It would be my pleasure, Madame."

I smoothed the drawing out, before rolling it up into a scroll. I thanked him for it, and then I quickly curtsied and excused myself.

"My apologies for keeping you," he said. "Where are you headed?"

As I held the picture, I decided it wouldn't hurt to tell him the truth. "I am going to the Cabal, a publican house near the *Josefkà*. They have meetings where they discuss all sorts of topics, including history and art and politics. Perhaps as a University student, you would enjoy it, too."

"I know of the place," the man said. "It's been several years since I've visited, but I see I will have to go back. For now, I must return to the University."

He held up his box of tools, as if to explain.

"Farewell, Madame," he said, giving me a formal bow. "You are just as captivating and beautiful as this city."

"Thank you." I was gratified by his kindness. He seemed like a lonely man, and I was glad he had his art to keep him company.

As we parted ways, I tried tucking his drawing into my cloak. When it wouldn't fit there, I put it into the pocket inside my tunic, underneath my corset. It was a little itchy so close to my skin, but it was safe.

I resumed my quest. Soon, the light emitting from the Cabal's windows was cozy and welcoming, as was its chatter and laughter; I even listened for Lumiere's voice, expecting to hear him making a fool of himself or someone else.

My hope quickly withered away once I was inside. There were plenty of patrons around. Clavan was pouring wine and drinks, and Helen, his wife, was talking with the customers as she wiped down the bar.

But Lumiere was not among them.

Jarl called to me from the far corner of the room, and my disappointment faded.

"It's good to see you, Ella." He showed me the stack of papers in his hand. "I'm glad the crowd will be a friendly one. I'm supposed to lead one of the talks tonight."

"What will you be discussing?" I asked.

"The ethics of politics." Jarl tapped his pipe between his teeth. "So you know I'm prepared."

"Yes," said Faye as she came up behind me, balancing three cups in her hands. "You'd never guess he's been fretting over his papers for days now."

It was then I saw the papers in Jarl's hands and noticed they were all blank. "You've been working on that for weeks?"

"Yes," Jarl replied proudly as he held them up proudly. "Perhaps it will make a good book one day, don't you think?"

Faye giggled. "I'm sure it'll be a bestseller."

"It should be, if you're the one who's proofing the final manuscript for the publisher," Jarl replied. He took a sip from his cup and grimaced. "I wanted whisky, not tea."

Faye only laughed as she handed me a cup, too, and she gestured for me to join them.

I gave in and sat down, letting Jarl and Faye share the latest news and gossip around the city. Thankfully, they avoided rumors about me and Karl; Ferdy had told them about my fake scandal, but I didn't want them to worry about the Order, or what it demanded.

Every so often I would look for Lumiere, hoping he would make his appearance. I began to wish for Ferdy to arrive, too, as Faye started talking of their wedding plans.

"It's just a few weeks away now, and Dad is inviting the whole town. I'm sure this place will be packed," she said. "Did Ferdy tell you? I invited you both to come and celebrate with us, if you are able to."

"I am excited for you and your wedding. We should be able to attend," I said, although I didn't actually know if that was true. Still, I did want to go.

"Good. I'm happy you'll be there." Faye gave Jarl a loving look. "I know you must be busy, especially since your own wedding happened so quickly."

"Yes, it did." I blushed, but I hid behind my teacup as I took another gulp.

Marriage was a serious business in Society, and that was as true in Prague as it was in London and Paris and other places. Some unions were arranged by parents since the birth of their children, and others were left to the deciding factors of titles and money. Few married for love, as Ferdy and I had, and even fewer did so in such a quick manner.

Of course, I suspected I was alone in marrying a hidden prince in haste because of Bohemia's secret *coup d'état*. The people who enjoyed clutching their pearls and crying "Scandal!" would be perpetually appalled if they knew how scandalous my marriage actually was.

I almost laughed at the thought, but then Eliezer arrived, and I could hear him starting to argue with some of the other patrons.

"I'm going to remind him that he promised to let me talk tonight," Jarl said, excusing himself. Faye and I took our empty teacups to the bar, and while she talked with her mom, I looked over at Clavan.

He was as patient and welcoming as ever. "Lady Ella, welcome. It's good to see you're here to join us," he said, smiling at me.

"Thank you." I had come to find Lumiere, and even though he wasn't there, I was truly happy I was. "It's a good crowd tonight."

"An early judgment, perhaps." Clavan gave me a playful wink. "Eliezer's about to inform Jarl he's going to discuss Count Potocki's dismissal from his position as the Minister-President and the future of the Diets."

"I have heard there is unrest abroad, too," I said, thinking of Harshad's news of war and the rumors of war across Europe.

"War in France has been coming for a long time," Clavan said. "Many of their institutions have broken down, and that which has not the will to survive, won't. Jarl's Uncle Rhys arrived from Berlin recently, and he says there's plenty of rot in the German Confederacy, too."

"What of the Austria-Hungarian Empire?" I asked, genuinely curious as I pulled out Lumiere's watch.

"Well, no one knows the future," Clavan said. "But if I were to speculate, I would say only trouble is certain. The American Civil War has ended, and it will take time for healing. But ever since America's creation, Europeans have such a mutual disdain and envy for it, I can't help but feel they will try to follow them."

"You believe a civil war is in our future?" My hand tightened around the pocket watch in my hand.

"There has always been war, Ella. Ever since the fall of man, we have known conflict, and we either must fight to overcome it, or it will overcome us." Clavan leaned forward on his elbows. "That is why freedom is only truly found in the present. You cannot be trapped in the past, nor cast too far away into the perceived future—for one is a memory, and the other a dream. But the question of what will happen, for certain, in specific terms, remains hidden until the time of revelation."

"You could just say you don't know," I replied, making him laugh.

"Oh, but where is the fun in that?" Clavan smiled. "You know this is true of your own life. You seek out freedom, but not freedom from struggle; rather, freedom is only found through struggle."

"That all sounds so complicated," I said, suddenly feeling weary.

"Still, there should be plenty of fun to balance out the struggle freedom requires. And speaking of which, where is your rascal of a rogue tonight?" Clavan looked around.

"I came alone. I wanted to ask you about this," I said as I presented him with Lumiere's watch.

Clavan's eyes, hidden behind his small, golden spectacles, gleamed in recognition and he reached out his palm. Without a word, I handed it over to him, studying him as he examined it.

"This is the pocket watch of a Bohemian Loyalist," he said.

"Bohemian Loyalist?" I repeated the words carefully, recalling Cecilia had mentioned it only this morning.

"Yes," Clavan said. "Before he abdicated the throne, King Ferdinand V was attacked at the beginning of the Spring Revolutions of 1848. While he survived the encounter, it was said to be a significant failure of his own guards and officials, many of whom he'd erroneously trusted for years."

"My father was one," I murmured.

"And more importantly, your father remained one," Clavan continued. Since he didn't ask me any questions about *Táta*, I assumed he'd already known. "This watch was made in the early 1840s, as part of a small collection. They were a special gift for those the king considered trustworthy. They were also given plaques, which are on display at the University's *Karolinum*. After the attack, King Ferdinand sentenced the traitors to death. Their watches were collected and destroyed. Only a handful remain."

He held the watch out to me. "So you have quite a gift here."

"Is there anything else you can tell me about it?" I asked. As much as I was enormously grateful to hear of my father's honor, nothing Clavan told me gave me insight into Lumiere's thinking or his possible whereabouts.

"Nothing particularly useful, although this one seems to be broken. With the wind-up mechanism locked, it's not good for telling time. If you'd like to have it fixed, I can see about getting it done for you." He gestured toward the crowd in the Cabal, which had steadily grown. "I know a few people."

Despite my disappointment, I laughed and eagerly handed him the pocket watch again. "Thank you. Please send me a message when it's ready, and I'll come over with the payment."

"Consider it a belated wedding present for you and Ferdy," Clavan said. "It's a pleasure to help you with your questions. And as it happens, despite some of the difficulties I've had in living in Prague, it's my home, and I feel a debt toward loyal men like your father who helped it get here. Even if it's still working out some of its issues," he added, as Eliezer began challenging Jarl's arguments and Faye looked on the scene, clearly a little distressed.

"Mr. Clavan," I said carefully, "have you heard anything about Karl Marcelin of late?"

"You mean, anything official, especially regarding how you don't want it known you've refused his hand in marriage, all for the heart of a street urchin?" Clavan gave me a conspiring look. "No, he's still keeping out of the public eye. But since you're here tonight, perhaps he'll soon feel compelled to leave his castle and rejoin Society, too."

"Castle?" I asked.

Clavan frowned. "Didn't Ferdy tell you? I sent him a message two weeks ago that he was right. Karl Marcelin has taken up residence at *Vyšehrad*. He's trying to keep his

THE ORDER OF THE CRYSTAL DAGGERS

presence quiet, but there are always a few guards eager to brag about such things after a few drinks."

My heart felt hollow as I struggled to speak. "I see. So Karl is at *Vyšehrad.*"

Prague Castle was the primary residence for royalty in Bohemia, but other castles were scattered throughout the kingdom that were available to them. *Vyšehrad* was one, and it was not just a castle, either, I remembered. It was also a military fort—making it an ideal location where Lord Maximillian could wait for Louis' arrival.

Ferdy lied to me. He lied to me!

Ferdy had known about Karl all this time—and he'd kept it from me.

Anger stirred deep inside of me as I sat there, dumbfounded and deceived.

"If you will excuse me," I said, cutting Clavan off mid-sentence. Briefly, I folded Clavan's hands tightly in mine, trying to silently convey just how grateful I was to him for his help and kindness. "I have to go home. Thank you so much for your help."

And then I left, letting the crowds and their commentary blur into background noise. I couldn't even look up from the ground as I walked out the door.

Tears stung my eyes, but I refused to cry. Another trance of sorts now mesmerized me—but this time, I was not overwhelmed by beauty and mystery, but rather heartbreak and agony.

"Ella."

I stopped in my tracks as the spell was broken, and there was Ferdy, standing there, outside the Cabal. I blinked, wondering if my despair had somehow summoned him.

THE ORDER OF THE CRYSTAL DAGGERS

Ferdy's hand reached for mine, and he wore one of his charming smiles on his face. It could've been the same as any one of our other encounters in the city.

If only he hadn't lied to me.

His fingertips had just grazed my arm when I flinched and stepped back.

He looked confused. "Ella?"

I shook my head and turned away. I began to walk quickly, heading back toward the manor, torn between my desire to fight him and escape him.

"Where are you going?" Ferdy followed me. His voice was full of concern—and maybe, just maybe, a small measure of guilt. "What's wrong?"

"What's wrong?" I whirled around, no longer uncertain. I was ready to fight now. "What's wrong? You found out where Karl was and you didn't tell me."

Ferdy's smile disappeared, and then he sighed. "I was hoping you wouldn't find out."

If I'd harbored any hope that he would tell me I was mistaken, that I was rushing to judgment, or that there was some kind of misunderstanding, it died in that moment.

"I can't believe you did this," I hissed. "You promised me you wouldn't lie to me again."

"And I didn't," Ferdy said. "I just didn't tell you the truth."

"That's the same thing!"

"Secrets and lies are not the same thing." He reached for me again, but I slapped his hand back.

"Don't touch me," I yelled, turning away from him and heading down the street. "I can't even look at you. After all

THE ORDER OF THE CRYSTAL DAGGERS

the pains I've endured for your sake, how can you betray me like this?"

"Betray you?" Ferdy finally dropped any pretense of cordiality. He caught up to me and forced me to face him. "Are you mad? I'll admit I knew where Karl was, but I'm not about to apologize for keeping you safe!"

"Keeping me safe? By lying to me?" I tried to move out of his way, but Ferdy stayed firmly in front of me. "You didn't like it when others did that to you."

"It's not the same thing."

"Of course it is." I put my hands on my hips. "How long have you imagined me a fool?"

"There's nothing to imagine," Ferdy grumbled. "You didn't know about Karl until today, and he's just fine. He's stuck at *Vyšehrad*, watched over by Lord Maximillian, and nothing has happened. Nothing. He's being punished, effectively, and I say he's earned it."

"What about the Order?"

"I'm not your lapdog, nor the Order's," Ferdy snapped.

"You're my *family*."

"And you're mine," he argued back. "It's my job to keep you safe, Ella."

"And it's my job to return Karl to his mother," I countered.

"Why? She can't stop him." Ferdy's scowl deepened with impatience. "That's the reason we're in this situation in the first place. If you free him, he's not going to give up trying to regain Bohemia for himself. At least now, he's unable to make things worse."

I shook my head. "I can't believe you don't see how wrong all of this is."

"And I can't believe you're so upset." Ferdy's eyes sparkled with fierce lightning. "Karl murdered my friends, Ella. He's working with insurrectionists to disrupt the kingdom. He hired someone to kill me, his own brother. And who knows what he would do to you if he ever got his hands on you? He's not a prodigal son who needs to go home, Ella. He's a willing agent of evil who needs to be brought to justice."

"At the cost of my mother's honor?" I studied his face carefully. "And the word of the Order?"

"Yes," Ferdy insisted angrily. "Karl can't hurt you now."

"Yes, you're doing that well enough on your own."

"How am I wrong?" Ferdy asked. "Tell me. He's fine, you're safe, and the Order is on alert, watching for Louis Valoris and his grand appearance. We couldn't ask for better circumstances."

Pressure built up behind my forehead painfully, and I finally turned my back to him and walked away.

"I was going to tell you eventually," Ferdy said, softening his tone only a little as he spoke. "I was just waiting for enough time to pass to ensure his failure."

It was more than a chore to speak as I stopped in my tracks. "And when was that supposed to be?"

"After the Tripartite Council. Once Cousin Franz rejects reforms, Karl won't be able to do anything else. His dignity will never be salvaged, his ambition will be neutered, and then we can take him back to Mother." Ferdy put his hands on my shoulders. "Don't you see? All we have to do is wait, Ella, and everything will be fine. Trust me."

His hands reached up and caressed my cheeks, and he touched his forehead against mine. Staggering intimacy flushed through me, but instead of reassuring me of his love, it only strengthened my revulsion.

"No." Briefly, I saw the surprised look on his face and felt even angrier.

He'd been expecting me to soften against him, to minimize his sins and rationalize his trespasses against me; he might've even believed I would assure him that he was right, all for the sake of wanting a kiss and his declaration of love.

"Stay away from me." I pushed myself away from him again.

"Ella—"

"No! You lied to me, after you promised you wouldn't lie to me ever again. Don't you remember that?"

I met his gaze now, and I thought back to the morning I'd woken up after the Advent Ball, when Ferdy and I had finally seen each other for who we were: a spy, and a prince, with a world of differences and dishonesty between us. We had known, back then, that the only way we could be together was through love and trust—and he'd just broken my trust.

Ferdy looked away in shame. "I had good reason to lie to you this time."

"That's not good enough." I shook my head. "How can I trust you?"

When he had no answer, I finally turned and hurried away from him. This time, he didn't try to stop me.

Desperately confused and angry and sad and upset, I made my way down the alleyway and turned onto a new street. I barely paid attention to where I was going until I realized I was making a large circle around the *Josefkà*. Anger and humiliation burned even further into me.

Quickly, I righted myself and headed back towards home.

It wasn't until I crossed the Stone Bridge that I stopped and looked around.

This was where I'd been standing earlier, I realized. It was the place where I'd seen the older man sketching the city, and I'd been caught up in the magic of the night.

Could it have been only an hour ago that my life seemed so much brighter?

An hour ago, I was a happily married woman, and a determined spy, on a quest to find a roguish runaway. True, I wanted to find him more for past, personal reasons than anything that had to do with the Order's mission, but I'd had a clear objective.

And now I was not only alone, but I'd failed to find Lumiere, and I was fighting with Ferdy.

I walked over to one side and put my elbows on the stone barrier that lined the bridge. My body ached more than ever as I watched the water below. It was too far down and dark for me to see my reflection, and I was relieved; I did not want my mother's ghost to stare back at me, not when I was consumed by another failure.

And then it struck me—Lady Penelope had been right.

Oh, my goodness, Lady POW was right.

She'd said Ferdy was a complication, and he would betray my trust at some point. I could almost see her gloating now, and my knees buckled; I was more horrified than ever. Was I going to face another round of disappointment if it was indeed Ferdy who let Lumiere go free?

I looked back at the city; moonlight now seemed to highlight its flaws, and I couldn't help but wonder if the foundation between me and Ferdy was just as scarred and eroding with hidden decay.

"Ella!"

Ferdy called for me, as a rush of silent wind flew behind me.

I was going to tell him to go away again when I saw Ferdy was calling me from downriver, from off to the side where the city was—but the steps were behind me.

I spun around just in time to see a figure, dressed all in black.

A shadowed fist lashed out, hitting me directly in my heart, all before I could prepare to fight.

The air rushed out of my lungs, and my lingering pain reawakened in full force. I slammed backward and then slumped against the stone partition, unable to even scream as I choked.

My enemy attacked again, this time pushing me hard and sending me flying backward over the edge.

I was still fighting for breath as I fell, headfirst, down into the stinging cold river.

THE ORDER OF THE CRYSTAL DAGGERS

10

◊

I hit the waves of the Vltava with a devastating splash. Immediately, the weight of my cloak drew me further down into the river's unforgiving embrace. Pain bounded through me, baptizing me in panic. I floundered, looking for the surface, unable to determine up from down, all while I couldn't breathe, and there was nothing but darkness around.

My body was trapped, tangled up in the folds of my cloak; my skin was tingling with weakness and numbness. As seconds passed and death drew closer, I swore I could almost feel my mother there in the water beside me.

This was how she'd died.

I shivered, too cold and afraid to move otherwise.

"Ella."

I heard Ferdy calling out to me from far off, just the same as he had the night of the Advent Ball. His voice was only a muffled whisper against the tides, but it was enough. My eyes squinted open under the waves, and I saw a sliver of moonlight push through the clouded water. It seemed so far away.

My ears popped, and new pain split across my temples, while I was still trembling and already nearly frozen.

But I began to fight.

I reached down for my mother's dagger. The blade sliced through my cloak as I made slow, staggered cuts through the drenched fabric. I mourned the loss of Faye's gift while I sliced at my skirts, wishing I hadn't given in to wearing them. They no longer offered me any extra warmth as they dragged me further down into the water.

THE ORDER OF THE CRYSTAL DAGGERS

Once I had my weapon secure, I swam furiously for the surface, even as my consciousness began slipping away.

Just as my vision blurred over, a pair of hands caught me and hauled me upward.

The air struck me hard and fast as we breached the surface. Water sputtered out my mouth.

"Ella. Oh, thank God you're all right."

Ferdy was beside me in the water, his voice frantic with worry as he held onto me with one arm while he swam with the other. I tried to tell him I could swim, but I was coughing uncontrollably.

"We're over here," he called toward the shore, waving his arm. The movement, combined with my weight, sent him under the surface again, but he bubbled up just as I blinked the last of the water out of my eyes.

My stomach lurched as the city lights blended together in my vision, and I struggled to reorient myself.

Gradually, we made it to the riverbank. Ferdy was still talking, though if it was to me or someone else, I couldn't say. Between my constant coughing and water-logged ears, I couldn't hear him properly.

A new pair of hands took hold of me and lay me down on the hard, frozen ground.

My lungs were on fire, my body was imbued with frost; my coughing slowed as I lay there.

"We've got her," an unfamiliar man said to my right. He turned back toward the bridge. "She's breathing!"

I was able to hear a small murmur of approval from out in the distance; apparently there were some onlookers by the bridge who'd watched my dramatic rescue, and my cheeks flushed with cold embarrassment.

"Can you help me get her home?" Ferdy's voice was shaking as much as my body was, now that we were out of the water.

"I'll talk to Eliezer," Jarl offered. "He's got a carriage we might be able to use."

"Of course he does," the first voice said. "But let's see if he'll let you use it."

"Uncle, please don't underestimate Elie's capabilities for charity," Jarl admonished, and I saw the man was Jarl's Uncle Rhys. I'd only briefly seen him before; he was a bigger man, with a burly stature and a gruff face. His voice held hints of the many nights he'd spent smoking his cheroots and drinking hard liquor.

"It's not his charity I would question, but his inclination to humor you," Rhys explained. "After tonight's debate, I'm not even sure you'll be allowed back in the Cabal."

"Clavan won't let him refuse," Jarl said.

"I'll pay him if needed," Ferdy offered.

"That sounds like a better deal," Rhys said.

While Jarl laughed and the two talked with each other in their familiar ways, Ferdy pulled off his shirt and thrust it over my head.

"Sorry it's cold," Ferdy whispered to me. "But I don't have anything else to cover you."

I felt myself nod limply, before I coughed again and shivered even more. My fingers were frozen as I reached for my mother's dagger again. Once I found it was still there, secured to my side, I relaxed and allowed myself to rest.

Another jacket was tucked around me. I coughed again, flooded by the smell of pipe tobacco—Jarl's coat, I realized.

The dizziness returned, amplified by the cold. Ferdy called out my name again, but I didn't answer him this time.

Instead, my thoughts turned to my mother—to her death, to how lonely I felt without her. And then the last of my reality disappeared, and my consciousness fell away.

◊   ◊   ◊   ◊

In the world between dreams and memories, everything felt real, just as real as it had been when I was a child.

I was a child again, sitting with *Máma* in her bedroom, as she carefully brushed my hair. There was a mirror in front of me, and my five-year-old self blinked back at me with large, innocent eyes.

"Grandmother would simply adore your curls, Eleanora," *Máma* said.

Through the mirror's reflection, I drank in the sight of my mother, seeing her own ebony locks elegantly brushed back for the day. Her locket, the one hidden in my room along with my father's pocket watch, was tucked just underneath the lacy edge of her bodice. Her eyes were just like mine, but for the first time, I saw the hidden depth of their secrets and shadows.

She was everything I remembered, and everything I'd forgotten.

The door to her bedroom opened. I blinked, surprised to see *Táta* come into the room.

"Dolf." *Máma's* lips turned up into a genuine smile and lit up her eyes. "Were you looking for me?"

"Only all of my life." My father stood straight and tall; his coal-black hair was as ruffled and messy as the rest of him, but his eyes were cheerful and his step was energetic as he kissed *Máma*'s hand.

He picked me up and held me close to his heart. I cried happily for my *Táta*, though my voice seemed much more hollow; my older self still knew how he would neglect Ben, plunge himself into his work, and marry again after losing my mother. But my small body stayed there, curled against him, listening as he told *Máma* he'd been called to represent the king—Ferdy's father—on another trip to Constantinople.

"Oh, Dolf," *Máma* murmured, clearly dismayed by the news. "Must you go?"

"I'm sorry, my love," he replied. "But it's my duty. And I'll get to practice more of my Arabic."

"Duty to family should come before duty to the kingdom."

"Duty to family is only possible through duty to the kingdom." My father sighed. "I am the king's ambassador. I warned you when we were married this would happen."

"And I warned you I would still complain."

"Eleanor." My father sounded heartbroken, and I remembered how he never liked to see her sad. I glanced over to see my mother's nose twitch, and then a second later, she masked her face with a large smile.

"I am only teasing," she said, her tone both apologetic and dishonest. "You are a good man, Dolf. The world doesn't deserve you, and I hate to have to share you. Especially as often as I do. It is very lonely at times."

I could still see her as my head leaned on *Táta*'s shoulder. Ben had been right about her melancholy. As much as she loved my father, and her family, I could see now there were secrets in her past that isolated and imprisoned her.

THE ORDER OF THE CRYSTAL DAGGERS

"Your cousin is still here," *Táta* replied. "Unless he's decided to end his stay early?"

My mother chuckled at his hopeful tone. "Lumiere always stays until he is escorted out. I'm sure my father will take care of him soon."

"Take care of Lumiere? You don't happen to mean Jakub will murder him for me, do you?" My father let out a jovial laugh.

I understood he was making a joke, and on any other given day, I could offer him my sincere sympathies and perverse pleasure. But this time, I could only frown at his remark; I didn't know why. I only knew the words struck me much more harshly and more familiar than I would've liked.

"No, but you needn't worry about seeing him out." *Máma's* fingers curled around her locket again. "You can stay as pure and as kind as you've always been, my dear husband. Let others sully their hands with such unpleasantries."

"First Jakub gives me permission to marry you, and now he will handle Lumiere? He spoils me with his graciousness."

"He was always very grateful for how you saved me that day in Constantinople," *Máma* said softly. "And how you've been so good to me every day since we reunited."

"It is a joy and privilege I seek to honor every day that I am home." He touched her locket delicately. "I will bring you home an even more extravagant necklace."

"You know I prefer books, Dolf." *Máma* smiled sadly. "Besides, you gave me this when we were engaged, and I would be devastated at its loss."

She took me from his arms, and then *Táta* leaned in and kissed her on the forehead.

"You think me pure and kind, but I am nowhere near as perfect as you, Madame wife," he said as he left the room.

139

Once my father was gone, my mother put me down again. I watched as she put her hand over her locket and fumbled with it anxiously. Her eyes clouded over with a vision I couldn't see as she let out a small, forlorn whisper and clasped her hands together in a quick, fervent prayer.

I reached for her. "*Máma.*"

"Eleanora." She bit down on her lower lip and then tucked her locket back beside her heart in a dutiful manner.

As she positioned me in front of the mirror, I blinked to see my face in the mirror had changed. I was no longer a child, but a grown woman.

But *Máma* did not change. She only patted my curls down again and sifted my curls through her fingers. "What is it?"

"What should I do?" I asked.

"Why, Eleanora, what we must do what we must." She let out a sad sigh, but she was resolved, steady, and firm. "We must be kind, and we must be brave."

I looked at her expectantly. "And then what?"

"We must have faith we made the right choices."

"And if we didn't?"

Máma looked away from me as her confidence faded and weariness shadowed her eyes; she toyed with the locket around her neck again. "Everyone has regrets, darling."

"That doesn't help." I frowned. "This is too hard."

Máma laughed softly and gathered me into her arms. "Well, don't lose hope. After all, my dear Eleanora, my lovely one, your life can change at any moment; you need only be brave enough to let it."

I was hoping for a better answer.

THE ORDER OF THE CRYSTAL DAGGERS

Ferdy had willfully kept vital information from me regarding the Order's mission, to punish Karl while also protecting me. For as little as he thought of the Order in general, he was certainly willing to act in a way that Lady POW would applaud, if only he were on her side.

I would've loved to talk with *Máma* about anything and everything, but especially about Ferdy. How I loved him, how I couldn't trust him, and how I couldn't live without him— quite literally, thanks to our current circumstance.

Of course, she'd had her own secrets, and she might've felt more sympathetic toward Ferdy than I would've liked.

My vision swam out of focus as *Máma* leaned her head down on mine. "There's still reason to hold on," she whispered.

Tearfully, I clung to her, even as I fell back into dreamlessness.

As I slept, the darkness felt long but familiar, and the more I slept, the more I began to fear waking.

It was only when I heard Ben yelling angrily that reality forcefully dragged me back to the present moment.

"What did you do to my sister?"

I stirred; I was in my room, in my bed, with multiple layers of bedsheets on top of me. I had my nightdress on, though it was loose and the ribbons were all tied incorrectly. My hair was unbound and free, and full of sweat, all while my body ached with pain and frost and my forehead was continuously burning.

"I didn't do this," I heard Ferdy reply, and I knew both of them were in my room along with me. "She was standing on the bridge, and there was a man who came by all dressed in black and pushed her into the river."

"And where were you? Out drinking with Lumiere?"

"What? No." Ferdy scoffed. "You know, if you want to be mad at someone, you should be mad at yourself. I would've never noticed her at all that day if it hadn't been for you."

"What are you talking about?" Ben asked, still fuming as he demanded answers.

Yes, I wondered, still half-asleep and feverishly dreaming. What was he talking about?

"The first time I saw Ella in Prague," Ferdy snapped, moving back quickly as Ben advanced on him. "That day, the two of you were waiting around outside Wickward's, debating over which books of yours to sell. You were loud enough that it wasn't hard for me to listen. She wanted to keep one of them, and you said no, and then you went inside to pawn that one with the rest. The book had a red leather binding."

He could have been describing several of our trips into the city to sell *Táta*'s books. But I had a feeling I knew which trip he was talking about.

"You were spying on us?" Ben's voice was getting louder, and so far, neither of them had noticed I was waking up.

"No," Ferdy said. "I was dressed as a street urchin. I was only a few weeks into my charade back then. I'd managed to steal an apple from one of the vendors in Market Square when I heard you arguing and headed over. Being poor can be boring at times, so I went over to see what was going on. And there was Ella, making a fuss, with all her soft, pretty tears, begging you to let her keep the book. But you didn't."

"No, I didn't," Ben said. "Cecilia wanted money and would've beat her again if we didn't get it. As it was, we nearly didn't get enough."

My eyes were closed, but I still felt the world start to spin all around me as I recalled that day, nearly two years before.

That was the day Ben and I had to sell *Táta*'s copy of *Morte d'Arthur*, one of our favorites. I'd been devastated at the loss; it was akin to losing our father all over again, but Ben remained firm.

"I knew you were unhappy with the price Wickward gave you for it," Ferdy said. "I could see it on your face when you walked out. And Ella saw it, too. But she ran up to you and hugged you, and when I saw her smile up at you, I ... "

"I recognized you."

I could hear the words, even if he didn't say them aloud. The memory of Ferdy's tenderness on the night he first kissed me hit me hard and left me breathless.

Ferdy wasn't going to say that to Ben; there was no need to explain how he'd remembered me from my father's funeral.

Instead, he cleared his throat. "Well, that was when I started spying on you more, I guess."

After he returned from dealing with Wickward, Ben promised that one day he would get the book back for me, and when Liberté was finally established, it would be in our freedom to decide to sell it or not. I hadn't known Cecilia had threatened to have me beaten again; Ben never said anything about it. But that made it even more appropriate how I'd hugged him and told him he was a good man, and he was the kind of person who did what was right even though it was difficult—and even if I was the one making it difficult.

"I didn't have any money on me at the time," Ferdy continued. "So I wasn't able to buy your book before it was resold. But I did look for better book dealers and collectors. That's how I found Clavan, and when I finally did get to meet Ella last year, everything came together in a way I'd always dreamed, but still never expected."

"I wasn't with her that time." Ben's voice was full of grim defeat.

Ferdy chuckled. "As I said, just as I'd dreamed."

When Ferdy stopped laughing rather abruptly a second later, I didn't have to look to know Ben had glared at him threateningly.

"But you do see, don't you?" Ferdy whispered, his voice much more hoarse and weighed down with worry. "I love her, too. And I can't lose her, either."

There was a long pause between them, or perhaps I imagined it; my forehead was full of drilling pain, and I couldn't keep track of the time.

It could've been hours later when Ben finally replied.

"You should just be grateful you're still alive," Ben grumbled. "Especially now that she's come home like this."

"I didn't do this to her." Ferdy's voice was much more unsure this time. "I wasn't with her when it happened. I was nearby and when I saw her fall, I was able to get some friends of mine to help me save her."

I heard Ben let out a long, unhappy sigh. "She's all the family I have left, Ferdy."

"I know you're not happy with me," Ferdy said. "And I'm sorry if you feel like you've been cast aside or forgotten. But I promise you're not losing your sister. We are brothers now. And I'd like to be friends, one day, too."

I had to remind Ferdy he was part of my family earlier, and I suddenly wondered if he'd changed his mind about keeping Karl's location a secret. Hope fluttered through me.

"One day, perhaps," Ben retorted. "But not today. Prince or not, you're still not worthy of her."

"On that point, *mon frère,* we are in full agreement."

"This isn't a joke," Ben snapped. "You need to take this seriously. And if anything happens to her, you and I will face each other with pistols at dawn."

"If anything happens to her, I'll let you shoot me." Ferdy shuffled his feet. "I was supposed to keep her safe. The instant I found out she'd left for the city, I hurried after her. I might not have pushed her off the bridge, but it's still my fault she was almost … she was almost … "

Ferdy's voice trailed off, and in the several moments of silence that followed, I knew he was thinking of Philip, and his other friends Lumiere's henchman had killed. He seemed unable to make out the words properly, and my heart caught in my throat. Ferdy was always so irreverent; he enjoyed a good laugh, and he eagerly brushed aside the gravity of a situation with a quip. But this time he was too hurt and traumatized to even speak the truth, let alone make fun of it.

I wondered how I'd failed to see just how afraid Ferdy was. He'd been angry over Karl's actions, and while our wedding might have offered him some distraction, it was clear when he'd found out I'd gone out earlier, he'd been terrified.

There was a small knock at the door, and it opened. I half-opened one eye and saw it was Marguerite. She peeked in and looked at Ben, but he quickly shook his head. She nodded and then quietly left.

Ferdy laughed softly. "She's been standing outside for a while now. I wondered how long she was going to wait for you."

"Shut up," Ben growled.

"Just an observation," Ferdy replied, amusement still in his voice. "I happen to know how she prefers waiting with you."

I recalled the time I'd gone to Ben's room to talk with him, and he'd locked me out and told me to go away. I'd stayed there an hour waiting, but he still hadn't budged.

Was Marguerite in there with him?

As if he could sense my curious displeasure, Ben shifted toward the door.

"I'm tired of dealing with you," he told Ferdy. "Keep watch over Ella. I'm going to go talk with Amir and see about Lumiere, or if there's any other news yet."

I held my breath, waiting for Ferdy to tell Ben that Karl was at *Vyšehrad* with Lord Maximillian. He didn't even have to say when he'd learned about them, I just wanted him to say something.

But Ferdy said nothing.

As Ben hobbled out of the room, I felt my heart sicken even further as my earlier hope died.

I wanted to scream, to sob, to cry out, but I didn't move. I couldn't speak; there were too many things to say, and I wanted to say them all at once. Ferdy didn't want to help me get Karl back, and he didn't want to help me honor my mother's promise.

Suddenly, I felt trapped.

Ben was barely out of the room before Ferdy gently slid down onto the bed next to me.

Weakly, I turned away, but he only pulled me up into the crook of his shoulder and wrapped his arms around me protectively.

THE ORDER OF THE CRYSTAL DAGGERS

"I love you." He pressed a kiss on my shoulder. While his touch radiated with love, I could also sense his hesitancy. "I'm sorry about before."

"I know." I managed to croak out a reply, and I cringed, hearing how unintelligible it sounded.

"I did promise you I would do whatever possible to make this up to you," he reminded me, but I said nothing back.

Was there anything I could say to this man—this man whom I loved but couldn't trust, this man who loved me but didn't understand me?

After several long moments, Ferdy shifted away. Perhaps he seemed to realize my heart had hardened toward him, or that as much as I was grateful he'd saved me, we had once more come to an impasse.

In truth, I wasn't sure I would be able to say anything else anyway. I was already feeling sick and disoriented again, and as I lay there, I suddenly and desperately hoped I wasn't pregnant.

"Get some rest," Ferdy whispered beside me. "I'll be back to check on you soon."

He kissed me softly on my forehead, and before I could object or say anything else, he was gone.

And then I was alone.

11

◊

It was hard to say how long it was before I slipped into sleep, or when I began to emerge from it. But when I did wake up again, I was certain I was not alone.

When I blinked my eyes open, I was not surprised to see Amir was keeping watch beside my bed. He was sitting in a chair, peacefully dozing; one hand was on his cheek, and the other was tucked inside my mother's journal on his lap. There was a small light beside me, with the wick flickering brightly against the darkness of night.

"Amir." My voice came out as a hoarse croak, and I cleared my throat to try again. "Amir."

Guilt trickled through me as he jolted awake. I had no notion of how long I'd been asleep, and it was still dark outside. But there was enough light in my room I could see the traces of silver winking at Amir's temples and the ragged shadows under his eyes. He seemed much more frail of late, weary and restless at the same time.

Still, he smiled as he saw I was awake, and his countenance cheered me considerably.

"Eleanora." He shifted in his seat, clearly uncomfortable. "Pardon me. I did not mean to fall asleep. How are you feeling?"

"Cold," I admitted weakly. "Did we find Lumiere?"

Amir's smile disappeared as he rose out of the chair, walked to my wardrobe, and pulled out another blanket. As he tucked it around me, he shook his head. "No, we did not."

"Was it Ferdy who let him go free?" My voice remained weak, but this time it was not because of the chill in the air.

"No," Amir said. "Didier is still here, and he's insistent that Lumiere told him only that he was going outside to smoke."

I closed my eyes and fell back against my pillow. "So I failed again."

"No." Amir took my hand. "Lady Penelope actually blames Xiana this time. She was supposed to ensure his door was securely locked while she trained you."

"I'm surprised. I didn't think Lady POW ever got angry with her." I bit my lip, not wanting to overstep myself. I also didn't want to admit I'd struggled with the lock on Lumiere's door myself, so I knew Xiana wasn't as guilty as Lady Penelope thought her to be. "You didn't tell Lady POW about what happened at my training session, did you?"

Amir shook his head again. It seemed Ferdy wasn't the only one keeping information to himself, although in this case, I could excuse Amir's decision more easily. I imagined he wanted Xiana to save face in front of the others, and he likely didn't want to discuss her unrequited affections, either.

"She did stop by earlier to apologize, to the both of us. She even brought some tea, but she took it away when I told her that you were asleep."

"I'm glad," I said. And I was glad.

Glad she apologized to Amir and me, and glad I didn't have to talk to her about it.

At last, I squeezed his hand and then let him go. "How long have I been indisposed?"

"Not long. It's nearly sunrise, although it may snow yet." Amir reached over and felt my forehead. "Your fever has improved."

Just then, my stomach rumbled loudly.

"That's also a good sign." Amir let out a quiet laugh while I politely excused myself. "The others will be happy to see you awake. Plenty have come to check in on you since your return."

"I'll wager Lady POW didn't," I murmured darkly. "She would've seen what happened to me as divine justice for going against her orders."

"Providence is full of divine mercy, too," Amir reminded me. "And as it happens, Lady Penelope did come to see you. She didn't even try to wake you up, either."

"Where's Ferdy?" I asked, trying to keep evidence of my lingering hurt out of my voice.

"He was in his old room, last I saw him." Amir gave me a thoughtful look. "He thinks he's to blame for your fall into the river."

"Unless he was the one who pushed me, he wasn't," I said with a small, disdainful snort. "But I know he feels terrible about what happened."

"Any husband would be alarmed for the fate of his wife."

"No, it's different than that." I shook my head. "He knows where Karl is. And he's known for the last fortnight."

There was a long pause between us before Amir simply nodded. "I see. Tell me what happened."

It wasn't hard to talk with Amir. His presence was a remedy in itself. He sat next to me, calmly listening as I explained what happened at the Cabal, and then at the bridge. Sometimes he asked questions, and I did my best to answer them. I told him about Clavan's information about Lumiere's watch and the Bohemian Loyalists, about Faye and Jarl's approaching wedding, what Ferdy had told me about Karl, and I described what I could of my attacker.

When I was done, I looked at him expectantly.

THE ORDER OF THE CRYSTAL DAGGERS

Amir put his hand on his chin thoughtfully. "It's good you left Lumiere's watch with Clavan. Otherwise you might've lost it."

"Oh, yes. I guess so." I shrugged. "But what about Ferdy?"

"What about him?" Amir shifted in his chair again, looking uncomfortable.

"He knew where Karl was and didn't tell me. And he hid the information from the Order, too."

"Do you suspect he's working with the League against Lady Penelope, or others?"

"No, of course not." I sighed. "But … he didn't tell me."

I knew I was being silly the moment I said it, but I couldn't stop myself from feeling so blindsided and betrayed.

"What were his reasons for keeping it a secret?" Amir asked.

"He said it was to keep me safe," I grumbled. "And that it would be better for Karl to be stuck at *Vyšehrad* until the Tripartite Council was over. He was quite content to keep the Order from interfering."

"Does your beloved have a reason to distrust the Order?"

"No. I mean, he thinks we're assassins," I said. "But he said he would help me as I worked with the Order. And even the Empress said *Máma* had promised to keep her family safe, remember?"

"I do not believe your mother promised that for the Order. If it was after her arrival in Prague, and her marriage to your father, she might have been promising that on her own behalf—or more on behalf of your father's oath, if he truly was a Bohemian Loyalist. It would mark a turn in her allegiance, and in her life." Amir pulled out her journal to show me the little he had left. "I am making progress in my reading."

I nodded in approval. "Thank you."

"And as for what to do about your beloved, the only suggestion I can give you would be that you speak with him. You see this as a breach of trust between you, and that should be mended first," Amir said. "It helps that he is right about Karl being unable to do much otherwise."

"Hey!"

"I can agree with his reasoning at that point, even if his actions have hurt you," Amir said. "Karl's ambitions have been interrupted, but most believe it is because of marriage. If the truth were to come out, his reputation would be tainted with truly irredeemable scandal. Your beloved makes a good case for keeping him under guard, even if it's the enemy that's watching him. Karl is likely upset with both of you, and there's no telling what he would do to you if he could get a hold of you."

"I didn't want you to take Ferdy's side," I groaned. "I don't care if he thinks he's protecting me. If our positions had been reversed, I wouldn't have done this to him."

"It is uncharitable to condemn others for their worst failings while we judge ourselves by our best intentions."

"Well, what about Louis?" I asked, quickly changing my approach. "Lady POW said we need to keep Karl away from him."

"Louis is playing a deep game with the monarchy and other surrounding nations," Amir agreed. "But Ferdy wouldn't have known that before yesterday, same as you. In fact, I'm not certain he even knows about it now."

I swallowed a groan; Amir was right, of course. Ferdy wouldn't have known about Louis or his plans, but he'd still known what it meant to me for us to return Karl to his mother—and that was why I'd been so upset with him.

"All right, I don't want to talk about this anymore," I said.

Amir gave me a sad smile. "Are you sorry you asked for my opinion now? Perhaps next time you will save yourself the disappointment."

"I was hoping for a better answer." I rolled my eyes, before ruefully smiling back at him. "But it seems even now, you and *Máma* are of the same mind."

"What do you mean?"

"I had a dream about her." I looked down at my hands as I clasped them together in my lap. "It felt like a memory of sorts, but I was living it again. She was talking with my father, and he had to go on a trip, and … "

My voice trailed off, and as much as I was mortified of giving credence to a dream, I couldn't stop myself from believing it had been real.

"Eleanora." Amir moved his chair in closer to me. "Tell me something. If you had to choose between Ferdinand and the Order, which would you choose?"

"What does that have to do with my dream?" I asked, slightly irritated.

I had already been disappointed with his answers once; did he really need to upset me again?

"Be patient with me," Amir said. "Tell me your choice."

I crossed my arms, feeling a little flustered. Ferdy had deceived me, even if he hadn't technically lied, and I was angry at him for being hypocritical and high-handed. But as for the Order, it might be better for them if I stepped back. Hadn't I failed them numerous times already?

"I would choose Ferdy," I said. "But I'd at least like to finish this mission first. For *Máma*'s sake."

"I thought as much," Amir said. "This is about Naděžda more than anything else, isn't it?"

"Why wouldn't it be?" I scoffed. "That was the promise of the Order to begin with—that I would learn the truth about her."

"Eleanora, as much as I love Naděžda, I would not want you to be her," Amir told me quietly. "I beg you, do not carry her mission as your own mantle. She would not want you to."

"Because she left the Order?" I snapped back, angry Amir had seen through my façade.

"No." Amir put his hand on my shoulder gently. "Because she loved you. She would not want to burden you with her failures, real or imagined or otherwise. I have no doubt her spirit will carry you throughout your own mission, but you must not confuse it with hers."

"If she loved me so much, then why did she leave me?"

Amir gave me a pained smile as I realized what I'd said. He shook his head before I could apologize. "She has never left us, Eleanora. We still remember her; we still love her. And we will carry her in here, until we meet again." He placed his hand over his heart. "You have her spirit, but you have your own life to live. And I am here, as are the others, to help you as you do so. She loved you—as do I, and as your brother and husband do."

"What about Lady POW?" I asked, brushing the tears back into my eyes.

"I have learned not to speak for her." Amir gave me a rueful smile.

"Probably for the best."

THE ORDER OF THE CRYSTAL DAGGERS

"She has to learn, too. She has to learn to see who you are beyond Naděžda's shadow." Amir's hand tightened on my shoulder. "Don't hold back on who you are, Eleanora. You are your mother's daughter—and your father's too, if Lumiere is to be believed."

"What do you mean by that?" I asked.

"I knew of Adolf Svoboda," Amir said. "He was enchanted by your mother, as any man with seeing eyes and a beating heart would be."

"You don't have to be so kind," I whispered. "He had his faults, too."

As if Amir and I had the same thought, we both glanced off to the side, in the direction of Ben's room.

"That is true," Amir continued slowly. "And some part of that, I wonder if it wasn't my fault."

"Did *Táta* know about you?" I asked.

"I cannot say for certain. But I wouldn't be surprised." Amir gestured toward *Máma*'s journal, and my mouth went dry as I thought back to my dream. *Táta* had been learning Arabic. If he'd been able to decipher her code, he would've been able to read it.

While it had been a dream, I was still certain it held some truth.

Amir sighed. "Naděžda was … captivating, illuminating, invigorating. Her humor was infectious. But there was a darkness inside her, too. And as bright and lovely as she was, there were times when I saw it slip through. I imagine after a time, your father likely figured out she wasn't quite the person he had fallen in love with. People change, sometimes even while you get to know them, but you also find they reveal themselves more; they change, even as they stay the same."

THE ORDER OF THE CRYSTAL DAGGERS

"I'll wager Harshad taught you that."

"You're already changing yourself by adopting more of Ferdy's gambling predilections," Amir pointed out. "So you know it's true. Although if anything, Harshad is the exception that proves the rule."

I let out a sigh. "Ben told me he remembers *Máma* was melancholic."

All the light and humor in Amir's eyes flickered away. "Undoubtedly, she was, after everything that happened … "

His voice drifted off, and then he cleared his throat.

"But as I was saying, regarding your father … From what I know, he was very loyal to Bohemia. He worked with Jakub Cerný, your grandfather, to protect Prague from Louis Valoris and his previous attempts to weaken the Empire. Back in 1845, in Constantinople, Louis ordered his men to steal a shipment of weapons. They were to go to revolutionary leaders in different countries, including Bohemia."

"Lady Penelope doesn't like to talk about Constantinople," I murmured, thinking of her anger over the topic.

"She has a lot of reasons for hating that particular mission." Amir's tone was easy and light, but I could see his expression was full of longing. "Lumiere being one of them, of course. It was then we met, and I saved his life."

"You saved his life?" I asked.

"Yes." Amir smiled as I made a face. "In return, he helped us find the missing weapons. It was easy, since he was the one in charge of stealing them. In the end, Lumiere got away, of course, but that is when we first became friends."

"I can see why Lady POW doesn't like Lumiere, but why would she have a problem discussing that? It doesn't sound that bad."

"There are other reasons." Amir looked away from me again. "After we left port, we found out I'd saved Lumiere from a group of Bohemian Loyalists your grandfather had sent to find the same weapons."

"This is really complicated," I murmured.

"International politics always are," Amir replied. "The League is British, even if it has members from other nations, but the Order is now largely working under Queen Victoria, too."

"Why have two groups working like that?" I asked. "Don't they do the same thing?"

"They gain power and money by rather sundry and ill-advised means. In some ways, it is ingenious to have two sides fighting each other, while their master watches and pulls the strings from the shadows."

I grimaced at the thought. Ferdy had always seen the Order as a group of assassins, and perhaps I should not have brushed the accusations aside so quickly.

But I'm not an assassin, and Ferdy knows that.

Amir cleared his throat and continued. "Jakub eventually figured out there was a split in the League, and Louis was working to undermine the ruling elite all over Europe. Louis had cast Lady Penelope as the villain before, and Jakub finally reached out to her to make peace. She rejected his offer and refused to forgive him."

"That sounds like her. She would hold a grudge."

"As much as she tries to hide it, your grandmother is a very loyal woman, even stubbornly so at times," Amir said. "The worst thing such a person can experience is being wrongfully accused of harmful intent or selfish ambition."

"Like the time she accused you of poisoning *Máma*?"

Amir only nodded, and I felt ashamed again. I was about to apologize for overstepping myself when I remembered *Máma*'s locket.

"Amir? Would you open that for me?" I pointed to the drawer that held my father's watch, my mother's locket, and the set of royal hair combs Ferdy had given to me.

Amir opened it and picked up the pocket watch. "I thought you gave this to Clavan?"

"No. The one he has is Lumiere's; that one is my father's," I said. "Can you hand me the locket?"

Amir handed it to me graciously, and then I opened it for him. Inside there was the small miniature of him, and I smiled as I gave it to him. "My mother wore this in her dream," I said. "And I remember it from the past, too. It was hers."

"Thank you, Eleanora." Amir swallowed hard as he gazed down at it. He turned it around carefully in his hand, looking at the date and the small picture *Máma* had drawn on the back.

I didn't tell him it was tucked behind the pictures of *Táta* and me and Ben, but the picture was the smallest thing I could give him.

Or so I thought.

"Eleanora, may I see your dagger, please?" Amir barely looked up at me as he held out his other hand.

"Sure." I looked around, puzzled, before I saw my mother's dagger on the night table. I reached for it and handed it to Amir without hesitation.

Only to object when he twisted the hilt and dislodged it from the blade.

"What are you doing? Stop!" I protested, although it was too late.

I was about to yell at him, but then Amir carefully tugged on a folded sheet of parchment, and I realized why he'd broken my weapon.

I leaned forward. "What is that?"

"Naděžda's last letter to me," he whispered as he took it and unfolded it carefully.

There were lines of English faded with age and blurry with water damage, but I could still read some of it from where I sat. I watched as Amir's face lit up with remorse and regret and wonder, and I knew the exact instant he was finished reading it.

He pushed it toward me. "Here. You can read it."

"Are you certain?" I held the thin, moist paper with trembling hands. By the time Amir nodded, I was already halfway through reading it.

My mother's voice echoed along inside my mind as I tried not to cry at seeing her true self come out.

Dearest Mr. Qureshi, devoted doctor, sweet Othello, and my darling mongrel,

After all these years, and despite our history, I still smile as I write these words and think of you. Of course, I think of you quite often. Every day, in fact. While it has been nearly two years since I have seen you, I only need to close my eyes to find solace in your memory.

After everything that has happened, I fear I have done more than a disservice to you with my silence and my secrecy. I am determined in part to correct that with this letter, as cowardly and unkind as it may seem if it ever does find its way to you.

You have no doubt heard what has happened to me by now. Uncle has always been good about seeing to your care, whether you knew it or not. It seems he suspected all along you and I would find a way to be together, even if we were not destined to stay together, and I know his love for you is the same as a father's for his son.

I found a good man to marry—one you would even recognize. It seems Sir Dolf the Bohemian is good at keeping his word, even though it has been several years since we last saw him in Constantinople. I met him on the way to Prague, and we have since then become engaged and wed. He is a good friend of my father's, and it has been nice seeing him again without the colorful lens provided by my mother. Admittedly, I am a little disappointed to find that rather than a half-demon, my father is fully human, and thus more sympathetic in his failings. He and I have reconciled since my arrival, and he is delighted to have met my son as well.

Yes, I am a mother now—or at least, I have a son.

And this is perhaps my greatest failing to you. Once more, I have believed that I deserved to suffer without you, that I deserved to suffer my life alone after the loss of our beloved Nassara.

It seems that God in his grace did not deem that to be my fate, but in my foolishness—of which you know well —I truly believed it was justice to let you go. But now, even as I see my son grow, as my belly rounds with another child, and as much as I love them, I cannot help but think of you.

In some ways, I wish I could forget you; longing for you poisons what I have now, and I do promise Dolf is a very loving husband. He suspects I do not love him as much as he loves me, but he loves me nonetheless. I want to be a good wife to him and a good mother to my children more than anything.

But I keep remembering you, and above all else, I fear losing you.

There are unspeakable wishes in every human heart, and you know mine as no one else will, just as we both know life is not so kind to our hearts' wishes.

For now, I am letting the Order go, as my father desires, and of which my husband remains ignorant. But I know, even as I tuck my heart away and fulfill my duty to my family, of which there is no greater joy in my life, I am not letting you go. As surely as I secure this letter inside my dagger's hilt, you will remain with me all of my days, and I will never stop looking for you.

Even if death should separate us, your face will be the last one I see as I die and the first one I see in heaven. Until then, my heart remains faithfully yours, and I will ever be

Your Nadĕžda

As I looked up from the parchment, Amir gave me my mother's dagger back, its hilt fully restored and secured in place. There was a new glumness in his eyes as he held out his hand, silently asking for the letter back. I gave it to him at once, letting my eyes linger on my mother's ever-prim penmanship until he refolded it and tucked it into his jacket.

"Are you all right?" I bit my lip, worried I'd made him unhappy, when I'd only meant to do the opposite.

"Yes."

He was lying, and he was tired, but he still put effort into making it seem like his assertion was the truth; perhaps he was even hoping it was, or hoping that it would be.

"Then go rest." I made no attempt to hide a yawn. "I need to sleep, too. Especially if I need to be well enough to go looking for Lumiere again soon."

Amir nodded. As he reached my bedroom door, he paused. "Have you decided what to do about your beloved?"

I shrugged.

"Would you prefer I keep our conversation tonight between us while you decide?"

From the way he looked at me, I could tell he seemed to know the answer to that question, and I was more than grateful for it. Amir was willing to let me take the lead on an issue that directly impacted our mission. Ferdy thought I was a fool when it came to being a member of the Order, and perhaps he was right; but Amir believed that even if I was a fool, I should have the chance to learn from my mistakes.

"Yes, please don't say anything. I'm not sure what to do right now," I said. "But I'm sure I'll make up my mind soon."

"Of course you will." Amir bowed his head as he excused himself.

Once he was gone, I leaned back against my pillows and curled into my sheets, wrestling inwardly with myself, bound to complete agony as I was divided over what to do—about Ferdy, about my mother, about my mission.

For a long time, I lay there, wide awake, lonely and angry and frustrated, thinking and not thinking at the same time. Part of me kept waiting for Ferdy to return, and when he didn't, I only grew more frustrated.

And then all at once, I fell asleep.

THE ORDER OF THE CRYSTAL DAGGERS

12

◊

The next time I woke, there were no more dreams left. There was only the harsh reality of the present day, where all the complications of the past collided with the uncertainties of the future.

My fever was gone, or enough so that I was able to get out of bed and dress myself, even if my movements were clumsy and stiff. There was a small ringing in my ears as I worked through the motions methodically and patiently.

Everything took twice as long to complete, but as soon as I was ready, I had a plan—and this time, I decided I would talk with Lady Penelope.

I took a deep breath as I left my room. I was ready, even if I didn't feel prepared.

As I passed by Ferdy's door, I paused to listen for any sound or movement. I was still angry with him, but I hoped he was recovering, too. When I didn't hear anything, I squeezed my eyes shut and pushed myself away from his room, further resolved to find my grandmother and do my best to forget about him for a little while.

Amir had given me his counsel, and I sincerely took it to heart. But my heart was broken, both by Ferdy's overprotective callousness and a sorely renewed sense of abandonment by my mother. I loved them, and like all mortal love, the abundance in its certainty was only rivaled by the emptiness in its brokenness. It was too painful for me to fully contemplate, and in the meantime, there were other things I needed to do.

Such as find Karl and return him to his mother.

If I did that, I would fulfill my mother's promise and uphold her honor, and if I wanted, I could quit the Order and go in peace.

We would stop Karl, we would stop Louis, and I would stop being a failure.

Sunlight and silence followed my steps as I walked through the halls of my home. I couldn't tell if it was a blessing, allowing me to go over my plan in peace, or if it was an ominous omen, one that allowed dread and fear to grow inside of me. I was even willing to bet it was both, a test to see if I could cling to the good and eschew the bad.

I almost smiled; Amir was right about Ferdy's gambling habits growing on me.

But I didn't have to be a gambler to know Lady Penelope would be in an unpleasant mood when I found her in the west parlor.

What I wasn't counting on was that she was not alone.

"—cannot believe you would be so irresponsible," Lady Penelope was saying harshly. "This is too important, Xiana. Louis Valoris has come once again to ruin everything, and we were so close to gaining the upper hand. We had Lumiere in our grasp, for goodness' sake."

I inched closer to the door, slowing down and eventually stopping so I could listen.

"He did say he could leave when he wanted," Xiana objected. "I did just as you asked. You know I have always worked so hard to make you happy."

"I don't need you to make me happy; I need to be able to trust you," Lady Penelope snapped.

For all I winced at her tone, I agreed with her logic.

"Is there reason you believe I might have made this error on purpose?" Xiana asked.

There was a lingering moment of silence, and I could almost see Lady Penelope shocked that Xiana would question her reasoning.

"Harshad and I have no reason to doubt you."

That was all she said, and I wondered if Lady Penelope knew what happened at my training session.

Amir had told me he hadn't talked about it with Lady POW, but maybe he'd mentioned it to Harshad.

Neither of the women said anything else, until Xiana brusquely apologized and excused herself.

As quickly and quietly as I could, I scrambled back down the hall and pretended I was just coming around the corner. Xiana saw me as she left the west parlor. She scowled at me as I waved to her in greeting, and then she turned and headed off in the other direction.

I headed back to the parlor door. When I peeked inside, Lady Penelope was alone, and she was her usual, surly self, seated by the fire and sipping on her tea.

I approached her, reluctantly admiring how even sitting in a chair, she could look down her nose at me.

"I'm surprised you're out of bed, Eleanora." Her voice was tart but tired, and I worked hard to remember she came to check on me while I was sick, and my mind was foggy and feverish.

Perhaps because of my mother, or because of my own expectations of her as my grandmother, I was inclined to be upset with her at times. But she was the first one who had, as the leader of the Order, reaffirmed my dignity and gave me a new sense of purpose.

And as repulsive as some of her advice was to me, I now knew there was good reason for it.

After all, she'd told me to trust people only to the point where I knew they would betray me. I'd rejected the notion, seeing it as too cynical.

But she'd been right. The stinging soreness in my chest wasn't just from my attacker on the bridge.

"Eleanora? Are you well?" Lady Penelope glanced over at me quizzically.

"Oh, yes." My cheeks grew hot as I pushed my heart's humiliation away once more; Ferdy knew me well enough to believe I would break down, cry, and eventually beg for his forgiveness. And perhaps I would've, too, if I didn't feel so betrayed and insulted by the expectation.

"I figured you would require a day or two to recover, so you don't have training today. I've just sent Xiana out into the city to continue searching for Lumiere."

"Perhaps Didier could teach me about guns," I offered.

"Hmph." Lady Penelope wrinkled her nose. "Didier is taking on Lumiere's sins as his own, and he is refusing to leave his own locked room. He no doubt believes I will assume he is on our side if he behaves in such a manner."

Everything I had seen of him demonstrated his quiet thoughtfulness, but I knew Lady Penelope would never trust Didier after Lumiere's disappearance.

"What about Harshad?" I asked.

She took another sip of tea. "Harshad went out during the night, while Amir fussed over you. He is resting now."

Resting, I noticed. *Not sleeping.*

From the large, drooping bags under her own eyes, I had a feeling Harshad wasn't the only one who'd failed to sleep last night.

"That's probably for the best." I clasped my hands together behind my back. "May I join you, Madame?"

"There's no need for formalities." Lady Penelope gestured for me to sit down in the chair next to hers as she poured a cup of tea and handed it to me. "May I assume you've come to apologize for your recent recklessness?"

"No." I held my cup of tea with a delicate but determined sense of daring. "You've said yourself I'm getting better at standing up to you," I reminded her with a small smile.

She did not smile back. "Let me hear your excuses about what happened, and we'll be done with it, then."

I sat down and explained what happened, without telling her quite everything; I still wasn't sure what I would do about Ferdy, but for now I decided to leave him out of the Order's business. "Lumiere was missing, and I went out to see if I could find him. I didn't set out to get attacked."

"I gave you strict rules about remaining here, and you know why."

"Yes, I know." I kept my tone as light as possible. "That's actually what I came to discuss with you."

"Oh?" She arched her brow at me.

I swallowed the nervous lump in my throat. "I say we venture out into Society this weekend. If Karl still needs my cooperation to maintain support for his council, his plans would be disrupted if I openly rejected him ... wouldn't they?"

Hearing myself say it aloud suddenly made me feel extra senseless, especially given my numerous and recent failures.

"You must still be feverish. That is foolish." Lady Penelope's gaze narrowed, and my palms began to sweat.

"Well, yes," I admitted. "But if I am bound to secrecy and silence because of reputation and propriety, surely Karl is, too."

"He is bound by different standards; men must keep their finances pure and pristine, while women guard their virtue. You will be ruined if people find out the truth."

"But my virtue has not been lost," I murmured as my cheeks warmed over. "If anything, it has been secured."

"In the eyes of God, perhaps, but not in the eyes of Society, and Society is a much crueler god." Lady Penelope sniffed indignantly and shook her head. "After all the scandal with your supposed elopement, we must tread more carefully than ever. The elites will not excuse many trespasses, even with money and connections."

"I still think my idea has merit. That was part of my original role, wasn't it? To distract our audience. And with Lumiere gone, we need to find Karl more than ever."

"Hopefully Lumiere will be back shortly." Her voice was curt, devoid of hope. "And all Karl would have to do is show up to discredit or discard you, and you will never be allowed to go out in Society ever again."

"But we will be able to capture him." I clasped my hands more tightly around my teacup. "One does what one must, propriety be damned, remember?"

"Propriety still has its place, as damned as it may be."

"I understand the risks." I held my ground.

Lady Penelope gave me a calculating gaze. "Are you that tired of being stuck indoors, Eleanora, that you would put yourself in such danger?"

"If I am tired of being stuck waiting, I imagine Karl is, too."

She looked back toward the fire. For long moments, we sank into a contemplative silence. I watched every miniscule movement on her face, studying each pinched lip and twisted wrinkle, waiting for her final judgment.

"I don't suppose you think this course of action will make up for your mistakes yesterday, do you?" she finally asked, arching her brow at me.

"My mistakes are in the past, and there's nothing I can do about the past." My tone was too matter of fact for her taste, but she couldn't deny my logic—after all, it was the same as her own.

"It is good to see you're learning something from all your failures at least." She set down her teacup lightly. "I will call Marguerite and tell her to prepare a new dress for you, and Amelia and Jaqueline can get one for me, too. We should go out shopping while they work."

"So, you agree with me?" I asked, leaning forward in excitement.

"Yes. Perhaps you are right. It is feasible we can draw Karl out." She nodded once, quickly and decisively, and then stood up. "We have worked too long in the shadows if we are afraid of the light."

Hope stirred within me. My struggle had led to triumph. Lady POW had resisted my idea, but in the end, I'd made my case for it—and I'd won.

"But if we are going to do this, you can't reject Karl," she said, and immediately my heart sank and my stomach turned. "While we are out, you'll have to act the part of his completely devoted wife."

THE ORDER OF THE CRYSTAL DAGGERS

"Ugh, please no." I moaned. "Why can't I reject him and tell everyone what he's doing with the League and Louis Valoris and everything else?"

"Don't be this naïve. They will not believe you," Lady Penelope said dismissively. "These are people completely obsessed with gossip—money, sex, and power. They live in an imaginary world where real life never has a say, and I'm afraid Karl's plan is all too real for them to handle. It's best we keep them in the comfort of their illusions and the safety of their ignorance."

"But they should know," I argued.

"Even if they did know, would they care? And if they do, what can they do about it? They would be trapped by helplessness until mass hysteria or mob rule ensued. And we cannot allow that, especially when innocent people are the ones who would suffer."

I swallowed hard, thinking of how I'd been appalled at Lady Penelope's previous advice. True, it had been too harsh for me to take, and it would have been better if I'd listened more carefully.

Slowly, I nodded. "All right. If you think it's best."

"I do." She ignored my gagging. "Lumiere might be with Karl, and he will not be expecting us to ignore his disappearance."

"But we're not, though."

"The others will keep looking for him, but Lumiere and his father will be more worried about what we're doing." Lady Penelope said. "So, are we agreed, then?"

My fingers curled into my palms. The thought of playing Karl's smitten wife before the world still made me feel absolutely sick inside. "Yes."

Lady Penelope placed herself between me and the fireplace, blocking me in my seat. "You didn't come up with this plan after learning Karl is at *Vyšehrad*, did you?"

At her question, the disgust I'd felt at the idea of pretending to be Karl's blushing bride instantly transformed into blunt shame. It festered inside my stomach, twisting into knots.

I quickly took a sip of tea to disguise my discomfort.

"It's a good enough plan, if a risky one, so long as we know he's trapped where he's at," Lady Penelope continued. "But certainly you knew that already, didn't you?"

I had to swallow my tea carefully to stop myself from choking. It was too tempting to squirm in my seat like a child as Lady POW looked down at me.

"How did you find out?" I asked, my voice soft and weak.

"I imagine you can guess." Lady Penelope crossed her arms over her chest. "This morning Ferdinand and I had a very lively discussion before he left."

"Left?" My palms clasped around my cup as they began to shake, as I thought of how I'd stood outside his room earlier. It hadn't even crossed my mind that he wouldn't have been in there at all.

Lady Penelope nodded. "Yes. It seems he is rather annoyed with all our spy business, and he eagerly stormed out of here after we were finished talking. I'm not sure he'll be back."

"He'll come back."

She arched her brow at me. "Are you sure?"

"Yes." My heart was racing as my mouth went dry.

A moment passed, and then she shrugged. "Perhaps you are right."

"He will," I insisted, as my temper flared in anger.

"Well then, I envy your certainty." She crossed her arms over her chest. "Men are such odd creatures, aren't they? But we should be grateful for that; it makes them easy to manipulate. They are easy to lie to, and they are too quick to fall in love with an illusion. Especially an ideal one."

She turned to me with a small smirk. "It seems our family has a history of taking advantage of this male deficiency in particular."

I was already angry, so I was ready to argue with her; so many of my own illusions about my mother had been smashed of late, it did not make sense only men overindulged in idealism. But then, I realized she was likely talking about Ferdy, or possibly even my father, especially given what Amir had told me about *Máma* and her secrets.

I stirred my tea around in my cup, furious and frustrated as I struggled to control myself.

"I know you didn't approve of my mother's marriage, or mine, but you don't need to insult my family," I finally said.

She blinked in mild surprise. "It was not my intent to cause offense; I was merely stating a fact. It does no good to deny the reality around us, no matter how grim and bleak it may be."

I bit down on my lip. She was right, but she was also rude, and the remark seemed to be too insulting for me to easily dismiss.

"I imagine Jakub was fairly relieved when we parted ways. I know Arthur was glad to be done with me. That's how I managed to get a good amount of his money, even if the title has gone on to his sons." Her smirk softened into a genuinely amused look. "I have my own legacy to contend with, Eleanor."

"Eleanora," I corrected.

"Yes, yes, of course," she murmured. "Forgive me. You remind me of her so much—reckless, willful, dutiful … deceitful, secretive, strangely optimistic. She was better about obeying me, however."

"Not all the time," I said. "I wouldn't be here if she had listened to you, after all. She got her way when she wanted to."

"That is sadly the truth." Lady Penelope sat down next to me again, and before I could argue, I saw her eyes shift into a more melancholic mood, reminding me of *Máma* from my dream. "I knew she didn't want to be part of the Order, you know. She was very happy about the baby."

"Well, I know you weren't."

"You're certainly right about that."

"My goodness, how can you be so callous?" It was my turn to stand up, ready to leave at her remark. "Were you happy when Nassara died, and Amir and my mother split up, too?"

"Eleanora!" Lady Penelope shot up out of her seat and followed after me as I made my way to the exit. For an older lady, she was quick when she wanted to be, and she managed to cut me off. "Stop. You don't understand."

"Yes, I do," I said, tears filling my eyes. "You were the one who poisoned her, weren't you?"

"What? No. Never. That's not part of the Order's code." She reached forward and put her hand on my arm, almost like she wanted to comfort me—or capture me. "I told you that we protect the innocent the night I gave you your mother's dagger."

"It's the Order that's always more important with you." I pulled away. "Family should come first."

"Really? And should freedom take precedence over truth?"

I scowled at her in silence.

"Or what of love? Should that be first?" she pressed.

"What about love, indeed? It's clear that you've forgotten all about love. You're just as bad as Louis, aren't you? You're incapable of seeing anyone's value outside of their use." Despite the uncertainty I felt in accusing her, I remained still as Lady Penelope's nostrils flared dangerously. "That is what's wrong with you, isn't it? You only care about yourself."

"That's enough," Lady Penelope hissed as she stepped back from me, and for a moment, I thought she would order me to be beaten, just as Cecilia had done before. But she only backed away from me. I could see her hands, wrinkled as they were, grasping tightly at her skirts, and I knew then that I had pushed her beyond her usual limits.

"Eleanora, you don't understand," she finally said. "You do not know what it is like to live in the world as I have. You've been very fortunate to have grown up here."

"You mean away from you?"

"No." Her lips tightened into a pinched line. "The losses you have suffered are nothing compared to my own."

"I lost *Máma*, too."

"Eleanor is my greatest loss, but far from my only one," Lady Penelope said firmly. "I grew up in a harsher world, and perhaps you can tell. But I believe in love, and truth, and freedom; I believe in a higher calling and a duty that is honorable—precisely because I come from a world without any of that."

Harshad had told me before about some of my grandmother's past and how she'd grown up in a brothel.

"Repeatedly, my belief in each of those things has been tested by the world, and often at the expense of each other. I lost Jakub when he became blind to the truth of Louis' betrayal. I lost my marriage to Arthur when I realized safety and security was not a suitable replacement for love and affection. And I lost my family, to time and chance, and others' interference."

She glanced down at my midsection, and I was surprised to see the regret and shame in her gaze. It was shocking to see that *Máma* losing Nassara had been hard for Lady Penelope, too, even if she had not wanted her in the beginning.

I exhaled a soft sigh of relief; she hadn't been the one who'd poisoned my mother.

"I have spent years working for the Order in hopes of bringing the world into a better place for my family, only to lose them in the end," Lady Penelope said quietly. "And the largest reason I have failed in this is mostly because of Louis Valoris."

I said nothing, but my anger diminished at her admission of failure, too.

"You might as well know." Lady Penelope pursed her lips. "Years ago, several works of art went missing in London, and Queen Victoria asked me to step in to find them. Art is at the heart of a culture, and it's easy to demoralize a nation if their art is compromised or destroyed. Eleanor was supposed to distract Society—"

"Much like we'd planned here in Prague," I said.

She nodded. "But then she was pregnant, and Amir objected to her going out at all. And then, of course, after she miscarried … well, she was too distraught, and there was a lot of fighting."

"Do you really believe my mother miscarried?" I asked quietly.

The silence hung in the air between us like a shroud. There was only the small flicker of flames, and I felt the heat in the room exponentially increase as I waited on her answer.

"Belief in these instances is a matter of choice." She wrinkled her nose. "She wrote to me a few times after she married your father, you know. She said she had reason to believe that I'd poisoned her. I suspect she'd imagined these things, out of guilt or regret."

"She didn't do it herself," I insisted, unable to stop myself.

"As I said earlier, it's no good to ignore reality around us, no matter how grim and bleak it may be." Lady Penelope looked at me somberly. "Harshad told me much later that he saw her teacup that day, full of silver thallis residue. It turns blue in the blood, but it has a silver sheen on its herb. Eleanor would've known how much to mix in so she wouldn't die, just the baby. I can't say what the truth is for certain."

I frowned. I still didn't believe her, but I couldn't deny her logic. "It had to be someone else. Like how my father died."

Lady Penelope's eyebrows shot up in surprise, but she frowned a moment later. "Perhaps. Maybe I will ask Tulia about it."

"Tulia?"

"She was here around the time of your father's death, and she might remember something," Lady Penelope explained. "But never mind that for now. Regarding your mother, Harshad and I don't talk about what happened. There are many reasons it upsets us. After Harshad told me, I accused Amir of it instead, for obvious reasons, though of course he wouldn't do such a thing. But Harshad thought of your mother as his own daughter in many ways, and after his discovery, he couldn't look at her quite the same, devastated by what we believed she'd done. He feels awful at her death, especially because they did not reconcile before she passed."

I recalled Harshad's outburst the other day, when Lady Penelope had almost told me the truth, and I nodded slowly. His eyes had been raw with hurt and anger, and I recognized it now for what it was—a heartbreak that had never quite healed.

"What happened to the art thieves?" I asked, changing the subject. I couldn't think about everything all at once; it was too overwhelming, and Lady POW was right: it was in the past, and I wasn't able to change the past.

She seemed grateful for the change in conversation, too.

"Because our attention was divided, most of them ended up dying." Lady Penelope's eyes went dark. "Louis sent assassins to kill those who had evidence against him. It's hard to kill someone with my connections, but for those poor souls, they relied on the income from working with him. He took advantage of their poverty and talent. He was always good about finding others' weaknesses and exploiting them in his favor."

"I'm sorry." She was being open and vulnerable with me, but I saw how much of her strength came from dehumanizing herself. She seemed weak and lonely as she spoke, enough to where I was tempted to reach over and pat her hand.

"It wasn't the first time he'd gotten away from me, of course." Lady POW shook her head. "Eleanor knew what she'd cost me at the end. That was why she agreed to go to Prague, to investigate the growing revolutionary movement."

"She had other reasons for leaving." I thought of Amir divorcing her, of Harshad believing the worst of her, and of Lady Penelope furious at failing in her mission.

Máma would've wanted to escape such a prison.

"Of course. But Louis managed to slip away from justice, again, and I ruthlessly blamed her. So you must forgive me, Eleanora, if I am not entirely pleasant with you at times. This mission is deeply personal to me now that he's involved. I lost that which I have loved most because of him. Nothing would give me more pleasure than to shoot the man dead. But thinking about the past won't help me bring him to justice now."

"It might help me to trust you more," I offered, and she snorted back a laugh.

"I doubt it. Harshad was right; you are Dezda's avenging angel, not her redeemer."

"Of course I wouldn't be her redeemer," I said. "She might have quit the Order, but that doesn't mean she failed. She had her own losses, but she still got what she wanted. And even if I am here in her place, I am still myself."

Lady Penelope eyed me carefully. "Tell me then, Eleanora. Do you regret joining the Order?"

"No."

And that was the truth. I didn't regret it. I had a new family, new friends, and new skills. I was stronger and freer, more of myself, and more of who I wanted to be. I had an intimate connection to my mother's life, and I had a new foundation for my future.

If I did regret anything, it was my own failures.

Failing to see Ferdy for who he was, in more ways than one.

Failing to save Ben from more pain.

Failing to stop Karl, then failing to save him.

Failing to navigate my questions and fears and feelings, only to flounder in doubt.

THE ORDER OF THE CRYSTAL DAGGERS

But even with all that, if my failures meant progress, I would relive them a thousand times over.

"Good." Her tired, sad eyes shimmered. "Now tell me, Eleanora, can you believe in something even if it brings you loss? Even if it fails you? Even if you are not able to articulate its importance properly? Even if you only understand why it is so important once it's gone?"

I hesitated and then gave the only answer I could muster. "I guess it would depend on what it is I believe in."

Lady Penelope pursed her lips together. "You say Louis and I are similar, and you're not wrong. We are powerful people with connections, and we've had our share of losses, both incidental and intentional. We are both determined, smart, and ambitious people. But … "

She turned away from me again.

"But you're not a monster," I said quietly, feeling foolish for so much in that moment.

"Oh, I wouldn't say that," Lady Penelope said. "I do not happen to enjoy being a monster, but I am one."

"I don't think you are."

"Sure you do," Lady Penelope replied easily enough. "You've said so in different ways before, how I do not allow myself to be vulnerable or give my heart away or completely trust my friends."

"Well—"

"But I would rather be a monster a hundred times over than let the true monsters in this world win."

I swallowed. "I do not think it's wise to become like the people you hate."

"Wise? No. Necessary? That's a different question," Lady Penelope put her hands on my shoulders and patted my curls affectionately. "We do not live in a world of easy choices. We live in a world where we get to choose which side we will fight for, and which side we will fight against. But how we fight is a different matter, Eleanora. I chose to become a monster to stop other monsters, and I did so willingly, so you may also choose your own way to fight."

I stood there, speechless, as her eyes shined with unshed tears.

Not for the first time, I was tempted to hate Louis for all he'd done. I didn't want to disappoint Lady Penelope, or fail my mother; I wanted to protect others from his villainy, so that no one else would face the losses my family had borne.

In that moment, I silently vowed I would kill him myself, if necessary.

Lady Penelope cleared her throat, and sniffed indignantly. A second later, the tears were gone, and her eyes were hard again. "Either way, I should have earned your trust by now."

I hesitated, and then I held my hand out to her. "Trust is something built between people, Madame. Both sides must work together, and I'm willing to do that—if you are."

Lady Penelope looked at my hand. After a moment, she took it and held on firmly.

"I will hold you to that." She nodded soberly. "Now, let's get going. If we are going back into Society, we should see about adorning the proper armor."

Almost reluctantly, I smiled, glad I would get the chance to get out of the house.

I would draw Karl out, and I would use my charade as a way to find Ferdy and Lumiere.

I paused, briefly wondering if Ferdy had really deserted me.

What if he doesn't love me anymore?

All too clearly, I remembered how Ferdy had told Ben about finding me again, thanks to our arguments outside Wickward's, and I worried for a moment that Lady Penelope had a point about falling in love with illusions and ideals. Ferdy had been so surprised and dismayed to see me when we'd found each other the night of the Advent Ball when I'd come to rescue him.

Was it possible he had been in love with who he thought I was, instead of who I actually was?

A moment later, I dismissed the thought. Ferdy and I had fought each other in a small fight, a disagreement, and the perfect trust and faith I'd had in him was broken. But it was still there, and we could rebuild it.

And we will, I thought with renewed determination. If I could find a way to make peace with Lady POW, surely, I could do so with Ferdy, too.

All I have to do is find him.

13

◊

If the best part of going back out into Society was knowing Ferdy and Karl were both going to be upset with me, the worst part was knowing I was making a spectacle of myself, and it was no longer one of goodwill.

All day and nearly all night, Lady Penelope and I went from shop to shop, and then ball to ball, party to party, and so on and so forth, whether we were invited or not.

I was polite but memorable, dignified even when I was disparaging.

But a foreboding sense of the inescapable followed me as we moved through the crowds of the people we did and did not know. It did not matter if I was laughing or dancing, or pretending to drink champagne; the more I tried to hide my despair, the more hopeless everything seemed—even if my plan was working. By the time the clocks chimed midnight in Prague, it was universally accepted Karl and I were more than happily married.

Even if Karl himself had not made an appearance.

It was nearly dawn as we made our way out of Lady Taaffe's house party. As we waited for the carriage to be brought around, I caught sight of myself in a large mirror in the hall.

I watched my reflection with a growing sense of regret and shame.

The light reflected off the princess combs in my hair, as taunting as it was elegant. They perfectly matched my sapphire gown with its ruffles, cuffs, and simple stitching, and the soft dancing slippers that covered my chilly feet. A new cloak lined with fur was draped across my shoulders, and muted rouge was spread across my lips and cheeks. Yet still my eyes were hollow and full of worry, and any attempt I made to smile only seemed to mock all that was sacred and holy.

Quickly, I looked away; I was all dressed for a night of ballrooms and dancing and lively discussions, but my heart was still crushed by the weight of forced enthusiasm.

"You did very well tonight," Lady Penelope told me. "Hopefully it won't take long for our prey to hear of our return, thanks to your acting skills."

"Thanks." I tightened my grip on my cloak, wistfully thinking of the one I'd lost in the Vltava. "If this doesn't work out, I suppose I can still have a career on the stage."

"So far our charade is working just fine."

"If you say so." I watched a footman lead Lady Penelope's carriage closer to the exit, still feeling like a fool.

There had been no sign of Karl, no sign of Ferdy, and even Lumiere failed to make a surprise entrance; I honestly couldn't say who disappointed me the most.

"Are you well, Eleanora? You aren't still upset at what those women were saying at the milliner shop earlier, are you?" Lady Penelope asked.

"No, I'm not upset about that," I muttered.

Before, when we were shopping—and sending the large bills to Karl's former residence at Roman Szapira's house— we had run into several ladies of Society, including some of Lady Hohenwart's friends, each one more gossip-hungry than the last.

Their greeting was full of cynical excitement, and I could see their disappointment as I began rhapsodizing over my marriage. I lauded over how happy I was, and how Karl and I would soon leave Prague for another tour of the continent.

183

After I convinced them my virtue and good name were intact, they were visibly eager to spread the news, even if it was not as scandalous as they'd hoped.

I wrinkled my nose distastefully. "I'm just tired."

Lady Penelope nodded. "It's been more than a fortnight since we've been out in public. We are out of practice."

"Thank goodness we're finished for tonight." I glanced outside again, staring at the cityscape before me. When I'd gone out looking for Lumiere the night before, I was free, and the city was full of beauty and truth. Now I was back to donning another mask, and Prague became a world of lies and uncertainty.

Lady Penelope chuckled lightly. "Navigating Society's treacherous waters can be difficult, but you have a natural instinct for it."

"Navigating the waters is preferable to drowning," I replied before I remembered my mother, and guilt plagued me.

"True." Lady POW thankfully ignored my tasteless jesting. "Still, you could have been a very successful Original."

"I think I've just read too many books." I gave her a tired smile. "Though perhaps not *The Ladies Guide to Excellence and Etiquette.*"

She chuckled. "You would've had your pick of husbands and prospects if you hadn't joined the Order."

"I'm not worried about my choice of husband," I said, this time through gritted teeth. Until that point, I would've said Lady POW and I were getting along, but Ferdy was still a point of contention between us.

"Eleanora, hush." Lady Penelope hurriedly stepped in front of me and squared her shoulders, turning her full, blistering attention onto the man suddenly standing before us. Disappointment struck me hard as I saw it was Lord

Maximillian, instead of Karl. "I wish I could say what a pleasure it is to see you again, Your Grace. Alas, there are no words to do it justice."

His large, fluffy mustache twitched with an amused grimace. "I feel the same way about your manners, Lady Wellington."

Watching his practiced gallantry, I decided disappointment suited him.

"Mrs. Marcelin." The way he said it made what little warmth there was in the air disappear entirely. "What a lovely surprise to find you here."

I scowled back. "We are more surprised to see you, as opposed to rotting in prison after all your treachery against the Bohemian Crown."

"You might have captured Lumiere, but any evidence he's given you can easily be discounted as fraud," Lord Maximillian argued.

"Yet you still have not been out in Society either of late," Lady POW reminded him. "And neither has Karl, we've noticed."

"I regret to say he is indisposed tonight." Lord Maximillian exhaled sharply. "Rumor says he is fatigued from fawning over his beloved bride, but I personally know he has other reasons for taking to his bed."

"What have you done with him?" I hissed.

"I'm merely here to tell you he will be at the Potocki ball tomorrow, to honor our great friend the Count."

"Oh, really? You wouldn't be lying, would you?" Lady Penelope looked doubtful. "But then I suppose you wouldn't want Eleanora to inform the public Karl has decided to retire from public service now that he's a happily married man."

"Such a truth could have easily been a reality, had Karl bothered to marry my daughter instead of chasing after you." Lord Maximillian gave us a quick, mocking bow as our carriage pulled up to the house. "He will be there tomorrow. Now, excuse me."

Lady Penelope curtly nodded. "You should go, before the former Empress learns of your presence here."

"She can't do anything to me," Lord Maximillian snapped, but I saw him grip the folds of his coat nervously.

I didn't know why he was worried; Karl wasn't concerned about her at all, from what Ferdy had told me.

"Eleanora." Lady Penelope tugged me along into the carriage, even though I wanted nothing more than to push Lord Maximillian into the coat room and force him to tell us all his plans.

"Why did you let him go?" My voice nearly cracked in anger.

"We did enough," Lady Penelope explained. "We know where Karl will be tomorrow night, and even better, we know where he is tonight. We can easily make the arrangements to intercept him."

I frowned. "I still don't see why we couldn't capture Lord Maximillian, too. He could be a good source to incriminate Louis."

"I know," Lady Penelope said grimly. "But if he doesn't return to *Vyšehrad* tonight, Karl will undoubtedly fail to show tomorrow. Let him believe we are letting him go as a measure of thanks. He'll be more likely to make mistakes in our favor if he thinks he's in control."

Once more, I felt trapped. I wanted all of this to be over and settled, and my heart ached knowing I would be stuck waiting again.

But I nodded glumly. "Yes, Madame."

As we drove through the city, I looked out the windows, searching for any sign of Ferdy. I was still mad at him, just as he still likely believed I was a fool.

At least if I am following Lady Penelope's orders, he can't say I'm a fool.

Unless he thought her to be one, too.

"I'll get Ben to come along with us tomorrow," Lady Penelope said, interrupting my thoughts.

"I don't know if he should be out of the house just yet," I murmured, knowing Ben wouldn't appreciate my objection.

"He can ride on the top box with Harshad," Lady POW said, pointing to the top of the carriage. "We'll benefit from another pair of eyes at Count Potocki's tomorrow night. Xiana already has her assignments, searching the city in the daytime and making some antidote for us."

"Antidote?"

"Yes, to counteract the Order's poison," she explained. "Harshad and Amir are out looking for Lumiere as well as your attacker."

"My attacker?" My tongue felt thick as I dully repeated her words. All my weariness caught up with me, and I didn't seem to be able to do much of anything other than repeat the words I heard.

"Yes. Given Lumiere's involvement, I believe your attacker is a sign that Louis is either here or nearly here in Prague."

"I didn't think of that," I admitted.

"Who else would attack you?" She shook her head. "It's the same with the attack at Prague Castle, and the man who burned Tulia's house. There's a pattern to these things that cannot be overlooked or deemed merely a coincidence."

"How would anyone know it was me, though?" I wondered, trying to picture my attacker again. I couldn't see anything but a small, black blur inside my head and feel the echoes of small, powerful punches on my chest. I laid my hand softly over my heart. "Ferdy saw everything that happened. He might be able to tell us something else."

"I doubt it." Lady POW frowned. "I do not think he will be back when we get home, Eleanora."

I felt my nostrils flare in anger.

"We will see, Madame." I looked away from her and kept my tone as light as possible. I did not want her to be right, and I was appalled how she instinctively assumed the worst.

But when we arrived at the manor, Ferdy was still nowhere to be found.

Between his absence and all the lies and stress from my performance, I was grateful I was too tired to cry myself to sleep.

I couldn't help but feel like my faith had been misplaced, and I'd failed all over again.

14

◊

"Ella."

Ben's voice would've been more welcome if he'd only called me Nora as he used to, and then it would've been easier to pretend I only had a day of chores and errands to complete—although, that was about the truth, except Lady Penelope was in charge instead of Cecilia.

I grumbled out a barely intelligible response before burying my face under my pillow even further. I reached over beside me, feeling the empty bed where Ferdy should have been. I already knew he was still missing, but I still felt disappointed.

It was all too easy to imagine him back down at the Port of Prague, entertaining himself with fist fights or gambling, or back at the Cabal, where Clavan and Jarl and Eliezer would argue over what to do with him. Or he could have gone back to Prague Castle, too, where the former Empress would self-righteously chide him for marrying me.

I shuddered. Such thoughts were worse than nightmares.

"Come on, you need to get up." Ben put his hand on my shoulder and shook me, harder than he had to, but still more gently than he could have; it was his form of brotherly kindness, and it was because of that I finally rolled over and sat up.

"What time is it?" I asked, rubbing the bleariness out of my eyes.

"Nearly four in the afternoon."

"That late?"

Though I had not drunk any champagne the previous night, I felt groggy and sick and sluggish. Still, I was surprised Lady Penelope had allowed me to sleep without interruption.

"It's time to get ready to go to your party." Ben flopped down on the bed beside me, clearly much more excited about the mission than I was.

"Watch your leg, *brácha*. I don't want you to get hurt," I mumbled out my concern, and predictably, Ben frowned.

"My leg is doing fine." He stood up again to show me how he could move around without his crutches. "Amir and I finished the new brace, and he says my leg's even a little straighter now. I might be able to get by with just a walking stick when it's stronger."

"He told me that might happen." I curled my hands around my sheets, feeling guilty. Ben's leg had broken close to the knee, right about where it had broken before. Nothing that would stop him from living a normal life otherwise, but Ben would never walk without a limp.

"I'm just going to ride up on the top box tonight," Ben said. "So you see, Ella? It'll be fine."

"Does this mean you'll forgive me?"

The question was meant to be more of a jest than a serious inquiry, but when Ben sat down and put his arm around my shoulders, I almost caved into the temptation to cry.

Ben knew me better than anyone, and he knew what I needed.

"I'll forgive you for my leg before I forgive you for Ferdy," he said.

I peeked over toward the empty space beside me on the bed. "That's fair."

Ben snorted back a laugh, and I felt much better.

"Well, forgiving you is easier than forgiving him," Ben said. "He knows what will happen to him if anything happens to you, Ella."

"If you do forgive me, why don't you call me Nora?" I felt my nostrils flare slightly in helpless frustration.

"Ella is who you are now," Ben replied, much more easily than I'd expected. "As much as I might disagree with his tactics, Ferdy is right; it's a name that suits you."

"I am still your sister."

"Yes, but you have a duty to others, now, too, and I've never wanted to hold you back from being who you wanted to be." He looked out into the distance thoughtfully. "And you should be the one to choose that."

"Ferdy chose the name, truth be told."

"And you chose him." Ben rolled his eyes, before his mood turned darker and more serious. "But you know, Lady POW calls *Máma* Eleanor, and Harshad says Dezda, and Amir calls her Naděžda. I remember her when she would have sad days. Sometimes now I wonder if she just didn't know who she was."

"She still loved us," I insisted, putting my hand on his.

Ben nodded. "I know. But that's not enough. Human love has its limits."

He stood up again. "Anyway, you're stuck with me, just as I know there's no escaping you, and Amir is right; you are family, and I might as well forgive you and move on. It's better if we can work together for the Order."

"I guess that's what he does with Lady POW."

"For all the good it does him some days." Ben shrugged. "I should have better luck with you than he has with her."

A knock sounded at the door, and I heard Marguerite calling to me from the other side.

"Nora? Madame sent me to dress your hair for the evening."

I saw Ben's mouth twist into a grimace. "What is it?" I asked. "Tell me."

He seemed unwilling to say anything, but perhaps in light of our awkward truce, he answered me.

"She calls you Nora. I wish she wouldn't, that's all."

"I like it when you call me Nora. And I wish you would, too. It'll remind me of who I was, and where I came from." I curled my hands around my blankets. "So much of *Máma's* past seems like a dream now that we know the truth. If she'd have had a brother who was as good as you are to me, I'll bet she wouldn't have suffered as much."

"It's no wonder you and Ferdy get along so well," Ben grumbled. "You're both good at manipulating people when you want to."

I smirked to hide my sadness. "It's a family trait, remember?"

Ben rolled his eyes, but he patted me on the head playfully. "I guess we'll see after tonight, *ségra.*"

I'd hoped he would agree with me, but I was satisfied. He was still calling me *ségra*, even if he didn't want to call me Nora.

"Hello, Nora? Are you awake yet?" Marguerite's voice sounded out patiently from the other side of the door.

"I'd better let her in," Ben said gruffly. "We need to hurry if we're going to capture Karl."

"Ben?"

He shot me an irritated look over his shoulder. "What is it?"

I bit my lip and then decided to confess. "I was awake when you and Ferdy were arguing before. After he brought me home the other night."

"So?"

"So … that doesn't mean it'll always be just us. You can still find someone, too."

I glanced back at the door meaningfully, and then back to Ben.

But he only shook his head. "I doubt I'll ever be in a favorable position where a woman will want to consider marriage."

"If she loves you, I'm sure an unfavorable position would be fine with her." I blushed, thinking of the night of the Advent Ball. "I was in love with Ferdy before I knew he was a prince."

"Nora?" Marguerite called louder and knocked louder from outside the room. "Can you let me in, please?"

"We don't have time to talk about this now. Just worry about the mission for now."

Ben opened the door and excused himself brusquely as he walked by Marguerite. I saw her eyes dart down briefly, before her cheeks turned pink and she smiled to herself.

As she hurried to my side to help me out of bed, Ben paused at the door. I was just about to ask him if there was something else, when I saw he wasn't looking at me; he was watching Marguerite, in a sad, lovely sort of way.

I was stunned; I would've thought their relationship was all one-sided if I hadn't seen that look of soft longing on his face.

THE ORDER OF THE CRYSTAL DAGGERS

Ben saw me, and in a blink of the eye, he slammed the door carelessly. I could hear his uneven footsteps echo down the hallway as he hurried away.

My cheeks flustered, both in anger and sisterly protectiveness, as I saw there was indeed some spark of feeling there between them. What the exact nature of it was, I couldn't be sure.

And I didn't like that.

Ferdy had known about that, too, I remembered angrily, thinking of his earlier remark to Ben.

All the more reason to find him. All the more reason to punish him.

But first, I had to save Karl.

15

◊

From the top of the carriage, the gentle *pat-pat-pat* sound pounded like a quickening heartbeat as we rode toward Count Potocki's mansion. It agitated me, but I also smiled at its music.

Ben was tapping his foot as he rode on the top box. Weeks had passed since the accident on the *Salacia*, and this was the first time he was allowed out into the city since then. From the sound of things, he was excited for our mission tonight, and I envied his enjoyment.

As the Potocki mansion appeared in the distance, I could only pray nothing would happen that would make his leg worse.

And that was only one reason I was anxious tonight; I had plenty of others, too.

"Are you listening to me, Eleanora?"

"Huh? Oh, um … yes, Madame." I blushed.

From the look on her face, I knew Lady Penelope didn't believe me. She was sitting on the opposite bench, and as I met her gaze, I could tell she knew I was lying.

Thankfully we'd already gone over tonight's plan several times.

We were to infiltrate Count Potocki's party; she would take the lead, claiming she would "forget" she'd been uninvited, while I would look for Karl, continually announcing to any and every person alive that we were beyond happy in our marriage.

It was a simple plan, and I didn't think we would have a problem carrying it out once we got there, even if I was uneasy about seeing Karl again.

"Are you afraid?" Lady Penelope asked me.

"No. I mean, I have plenty of questions," I replied, more honestly this time. "But I'm too nervous to think of them."

"There's nothing to be nervous about."

"I'm afraid that's not how nerves work, Madame."

She gave me an amused smile. "If everything goes well, Amir or Xiana should have Karl in custody before he gets here. They'll send us a message if they get him first. And if he manages to slip by them, we will get him here."

"Yes." My tone and thoughts were glum as we pulled up to the front of the Potocki mansion.

Lady Penelope patted my arm reassuringly. "Think of it this way, Eleanora; if he shows up, we will be able to leave early."

I laughed, feeling a little better at her attempt to comfort me, and also pleased she'd called me by my proper name, and not my mother's. "That does sound good to me."

Ben helped me down out of the carriage. He was donned in bright-colored livery for the night, as was Harshad, who was still sitting up on the top box, watching the others who were arriving. I wanted to say something to Ben, something that would make me feel better, but I could barely speak.

"You'll be fine," Ben said instead. His voice was steady and calming. "We'll be here if you need us."

While I felt better at his kindness, I still could only give him a nod before Lady Penelope called for me to follow her.

"I'm glad you and Benedict seem to be getting along again," Lady Penelope remarked on our way into the house.

"Even if we weren't, we would still work for the good of the mission," I insisted sullenly, thinking of how Amir had forgiven Lady POW for their past struggles. She might have never forgotten his supposed sins against her, but they could still work together for the good of others.

They were still like family in that way.

Even if their bond was overshadowed by the past.

Lady Penelope and I were ushered into Count Potocki's party, and once we were inside, I was momentarily swept up in another world.

It was too easy to think of my first ball, where I'd felt a similar sensation. Everyone was sparkling with jewels and dressed in rich fabrics, and the music was a stream of magic and moonlight. But a moment later, the luster faded, and I was able to see the defects as well as the delights. The walls were covered in a ghastly dark green silk; there were places where I could see it had been hastily adhered to the wall. The newer curtains on the windows and several mirrors looked grand, but they were randomly placed around the room. There were candelabras covered with flowers, but the winter bluster already left them wilting.

I could almost hear Lumiere's voice inside my head, mocking the choice of décor. When I let out a nervous chuckle, Lady Penelope arched her brow at me.

"What is it?" she asked.

I could tell from her sharp, impatient tone she was just as tense and anxious as I was, though she was better at hiding it; after all her years of experience, it was nice to see her façade of perfectionism slip, even if it was just a little.

"Lumiere was right," I said. "Count Potocki should pay Roman Szapira to remodel his house anyway."

"Oh. I hate to give Lumiere any credit, but he's certainly not wrong in this instance." She nodded, ever so slightly, and then went back to scanning the crowds. A moment later, she nudged me with her reticule. "Stand up straight. Here comes Lady Hohenwart."

The cheery, plump woman I'd met seemingly ages ago sauntered over to us. She was wearing another one of her large turbans, and it jiggled on her head ever so slightly as she made her way through the crowd.

"Penelope! So good to see you again." She gave Lady POW a cordial hello before turning to me. There was a smug look in her eye as she assessed me. "Oh, my dear, I'm sure you know what a great deal of trouble you've given your grandmother. It is good to see you and your husband have returned or I'd fear the worst."

"Oh, yes," I murmured delicately, dismayed at the possibility of another passive-aggressive conversation. "Well, the course of true love never runs smooth, as Shakespeare said."

Lady Hohenwart chuckled. "No wonder you and Mr. Marcelin get along so well. You're both so good with your words. Wouldn't want to be overtly scandalous, would we?"

"No, of course not, Madame." I cleared my throat to stop myself from rolling my eyes.

I knew I was supposed to be lying to everyone, and well enough they believed what we needed them to believe, but it was irritating to hear people agree Karl and I were perfect for each other.

It was also irritating because Lady Hohenwart's comment was so close to Ben's earlier observation about me and Ferdy.

"How is your own husband doing of late? Will he be joining us here? I do not imagine he and Alfred get along since he took over his position as Minister-President." Lady

Penelope stepped in to give me some cover with Lady Hohenwart.

"Oh, nonsense. The Count is always a gracious host," Lady Hohenwart said, waving away her concern. "He's standing over there with my husband and some other gentlemen."

She pointed to the far corner of the room, where there were several men gathered together, each of them more finely dressed than the last. I only just recognized our host as he was drinking champagne from a glass as others talked; I thought he seemed bored.

It was then I noticed Lord Maximillian was standing beside Count Potocki. I tugged on Lady Penelope's skirt lightly, and we exchanged a quick look; we both knew if he was here, Karl had to be on his way.

"Excuse me, ladies," a voice spoke up from behind us.

Speak of the devil.

My stomach sank as my spine tingled and my body went cold.

Karl's voice had very little of the enchanting charm it used to, but it was still able to command attention.

I forced myself to keep smiling as I turned around, but it was harder to do so when I finally saw him again.

I'd thought Count Potocki's house lacked the proper care it needed, but Karl was in a much worse condition. His hair was loosely brushed back in the current style, and while his clothes were as fine as ever with their silk lining and velvet trim, they seemed a size too large, as though he'd lost weight since we'd last met.

All in all, Karl was clearly miserable, and it was evident enough that I even felt a little sorry for him.

But I still couldn't let his pitiful state interrupt our plans, I reminded myself. He'd already gotten past Amir and Xiana somehow, so Lady Penelope and I had to ensure we captured him. If we didn't, all our plans would have been for nothing, and I would miss my best chance to fulfill my promise to the former Empress.

"Oh, there you are, Karl," I said brightly. Before he could say anything, I grabbed his arm and dragged him toward the dancing floor, moving so fast I nearly tripped on my skirts.

"Your manners have devolved since we last met, Madame." Karl snorted disdainfully. "Is that Ferdinand's doing?"

I whirled around at once. "Excuse us, please," I called back to Lady Hohenwart, who was clearly both pleased and insulted by my lack of proper etiquette. I saw Lady POW's smirk of approval, and I pushed forward.

"You might already know this, but I'd rather not dance with you," Karl muttered as he trailed behind me.

"Would you prefer to leave with Lord Maximillian?" I asked through gritted teeth as I took his hand and forced him to join the promenade of dancers. "I'm sure he wouldn't mind retiring for the night, given your mother is calling for his return as well as yours."

Karl flushed, but he reluctantly took my hand and began to dance. Briefly, I saw him scowl over in Lord Maximillian's direction.

"Mother will have to wait," Karl said as he twirled me around in such a painstakingly graceful way, I could only think of Ferdy. "I know it distresses her that I am putting myself at risk, but things will get better in the long run. She is not used to seeing a strong sense of leadership."

I did my best to remain smiling, even if I only wanted to shake him. "You're a fool if you believe that."

"You're the fool for not joining me," Karl snapped bitterly. He cleared his throat, looking shocked he'd said such harsh words to me. "I still believe my brother has blinded you, Ella."

I frowned, tempted to point out he'd just insulted me. "Do you really think I'd be happier with you?"

"Of course. I know Ferdinand quite well, even if we fundamentally disagree on certain topics. Ferdinand is far too idealistic; he sees you as who he wants you to be," Karl said as he pulled me around into another turn. "But I see you for who you are. I know you've lived in poverty and service, and you've faced unjust hardship. Yet you still are your father's daughter."

I didn't know whether or not I should be insulted, but I wasn't happy to hear him talk of *Táta*.

"Your father was loyal to mine," Karl reminded me. "If Bohemia regained its sovereignty, and I was crowned king, we could honor your father's legacy and make life better for everyone in the kingdom. Can't you see it? No more Nationalists fighting to keep hold of their heritage. No more politicians buying votes and trading favors. No more trade issues that the Diets have to argue over, or send to the *Reichsrat* for a vote. We can do a lot of good, and the kingdom will benefit from our loyalty, to it and each other. No one who hates this nation can take care of it properly."

I drew back, uncomfortable at how true his words were, not just about Ferdy and myself, but my father, too.

For a moment—just a moment—I thought about what Karl was offering.

Lady Penelope and Harshad had come to Bohemia to make the region stable for trade and travel; Karl had gotten a lot of support in recent months, and he was partially right; there were things about the country that could be adjusted and

THE ORDER OF THE CRYSTAL DAGGERS

fixed, and it was possible to make things better for more people. And I wouldn't be opposed to that, if they were indeed fair and just changes.

But I had seen Karl, and I had seen his mask slip; he was content to say these things and not really mean them. He was also condoning violence when deemed necessary, as a means to his end, and I couldn't stand by that—especially since Ferdy had nearly been killed twice by his plans. And while I did think Karl was happy to proclaim his love and adoration for me, I didn't really think he was in love with me.

For all his talk of Ferdy's idealism, Karl too failed to see me for who I truly was; he only saw me as the person I could be if I was with him.

"No." I shook my head. "You've been working with people who do not think twice before poisoning and killing their opponents."

"You don't think the Order of the Crystal Daggers has done that, too?" Karl asked. At my surprise, he sneered at me. "Oh, yes, Lord Maximillian and I have talked at length about your secret organization and how they tried to kill my father during the Spring Revolution."

"That's not true," I objected fiercely, thinking of my mother. She had come to save the former rulers, and even protected Karl himself before he was born.

"It's dangerous to be so naive," Karl warned. "You're a part of the group, and you should know what it's capable of."

"I know what we're capable of, just as I know the Order protected you and your family," I argued.

"Your father protected mine," Karl said. "Not the Order. They have their own history full of lies and secrets, and they've only survived as long as they have by pandering to the powerful and lying to the gullible."

I scowled. "We are loyal to the truth, if you must know."

"Ha." Karl sniffed disdainfully as we headed into a final lap around the room. The music was drawing to a close, and I was grateful. "What is truth?"

"The truth is that everyone is capable of good and evil, and we all need to decide to stand up for what is good, and stand against what is evil," I said. "I see the Order as a way to help people."

"Yes, they help the people who pay their bills and keep them in power."

I bit down on my lip to keep myself from arguing with him. I already knew that if I let him, he would spend the rest of our time pointing out my side's flaws and imperfections while ignoring his own hypocrisies.

My hand brushed against my side, where my mother's dagger was securely hidden, and I felt braver knowing it was there.

I took a deep breath. It was time to regain control of the current situation.

"If you're that concerned about the Order, I'm surprised you haven't tried to kill me," I said.

"I'd still rather not," Karl said, ominously enough that I suddenly felt afraid. I stumbled as we turned, nearly falling over before Karl caught my hand at the last possible second. He pulled me tight against him as he whispered into my ear. "And between you and me, I am hoping to win you over yet."

I pushed him away and quickly turned it into a flirtatious movement, laughing as we moved together with the dying musical current. "Oh, Karl, you're so funny," I said, loudly enough others could hear me. Softening my voice, I added, "That will never happen."

"Honestly, I do not understand the appeal Ferdinand has," Karl muttered. "Why would you want a harder life, with little safety and comfort?"

"I am better served having one with freedom and truth." I pulled away from him as the music faded into its dénouement. "And your brother's not the only one who struggles with illusions. Your plans to take Bohemia back will only cause more chaos, and you're doing it for yourself."

"They are not mutually exclusive." Karl blushed as the dance ended. "But I do wish for you to come with me tonight."

"Where?" I asked, glancing around. "I doubt Count Potocki has his gardens open this time of the year."

"No, come with me back to my quarters." Karl gave me a bold look, assessing me from the hem of my gown to the top of the jeweled princess combs twisted up in my hair. "Give me one last chance to convince you that my side is the winning one. I've convinced Lord Maximillian we still need you."

"No, thank you." I smiled my most bitter smile as the music ended with a small round of applause.

Karl inhaled deeply. "May I ask what your objections are?"

"I've already given them," I said. "But more to the point, Ferdy and I are married now."

"What?" Karl blanched before his face mixed over with crimson and scarlet. He looked sick, and I almost enjoyed his sudden discomfort.

"Your father approved it," I added. "And your mother couldn't stop it."

Karl took a long moment to compose himself, long enough I could hear the whispers starting to stir around us. He then straightened his waist coat, before he finally shook his head. "Then you are truly lost to me."

I shook my head and lost my smile. "You never had me."

Karl's scowl deepened. "Well then, it is time I departed. I suppose I can, in good conscience, leave you here to die and rot with the rest of them."

In the middle of the ballroom, he gave me a curt bow before he turned on his heel and walked away. I heard a few gasps as gossip flooded over the crowd's waggling tongues.

"Wait," I said, leaping after him and grabbing onto his sleeve. "What do you mean?"

"What I mean is farewell," Karl snarled, slapping my hand sharply before he smoothed out his jacket. "And hopefully for good. You can take comfort knowing I will celebrate your death with a toast, dear *sister*."

His words were laced with hurt and anger, and they stung more than I expected. For a moment, I could only stare at him as he headed toward the exit.

But I swiftly regained my senses. Karl never worried about the people he might hurt, and while he had never done the work of killing his opposition himself, he did not deserve my remorse.

I glanced around for Lady POW. When I didn't see her— and when I saw the various other people giving me side-glances and speaking in soft, speculative tones—I hurried after Karl.

"Karl!" The instant I was free of the eyes from the crowd, I hiked up my skirts and chased him down a darkened hallway until I caught up to him.

"Leave me be," he snapped, trying to push me aside.

"No." I grabbed his arm and twisted it behind him, making him gasp in surprise at the aggressive move. He fell to his knees in pain. He tried to shift away from me, but his whimpering only increased. I held on firmly. "Your mother wanted me to bring you home. And I intend to keep that promise."

"Let me go," Karl demanded. I pulled harder on his wrist, making him cry in pain. "You'll kill us both."

I was just about to ask him how that could happen when a new pair of hands grabbed me from behind.

Before I could protest, a handkerchief was plastered over my mouth, and I could smell a sweet-smelling foulness.

Chloroform.

Panic set in fast. My arms and legs began to fight back, but pressure came down hard around my neck, and I could feel weakness pouring through me.

"I'm really getting tired of rescuing you, Prince Karl," Lord Maximillian scoffed.

Thinking quickly, I fell forward, forcing him to carry my full weight. I heard his grunts and groans, and I did my best to hold my breath.

When he finally dropped me to the floor, I gasped for breath and crawled away from him as fast as I could.

I'd been shaken by the surprise attack. Lord Maximillian was considerably bigger than me, and my evening gown added an unwieldly quality to my weight, even if it provided enough padding to keep him from fully choking me.

Nausea rippled through me as they began to argue.

"I told you it was a waste of time to court her," Lord Maximillian said to Karl.

THE ORDER OF THE CRYSTAL DAGGERS

Karl stood up hastily and brushed himself off. "Did you light the fuse?"

My eyes went wide, and I coughed in disbelief at what I was hearing.

"Of course I did," Lord Maximillian replied. "Unlike you, I'm reliable."

"And I am the one properly in line to the throne," Karl snapped back. "If you want me to marry your daughter, you'll do as I say."

"If you want to get the throne at all, you'll do as *I* say." Lord Maximillian scowled with displeasure. "Now, help me with her."

He stepped toward me again, slamming his booted foot on my skirts as I fumbled for my dagger. I was still a little light-headed from the chloroform, and I desperately wondered where Lady Penelope had gone.

"No." Karl stopped Lord Maximillian. "We can leave her here."

"What?" he asked.

"Leave her here," Karl repeated, clearly irritated. "I'll get public sympathy sooner."

"Killing her at the Tripartite Council would leave a greater impact." Lord Maximillian's mustache fluttered as he exhaled sharply. "Besides, if we take her now, you can finally have her the way you always wanted."

Even in my compromised condition, I heard the threat behind Lord Maximillian's words, and I struggled harder to back away as he stood over me.

"She's a lovely young lady, as you've always said. Surely you still want such a prize?" The dark tone in Lord Maximillian's voice mirrored his morbid amusement as he looked at me.

THE ORDER OF THE CRYSTAL DAGGERS

"You'd already deemed her more important than my financial support. Besides, perhaps forcing yourself on her might convince her to give up on the Order."

"No," Karl said. "I am not going to do that."

I was grateful Karl seemed to have some sense of honor, even if it was only enough to stop himself from defiling his brother's wife. I was about to commend him, but then he continued talking.

"It's better to have her die tonight, anyway."

"Die?" I feigned more shock than I felt as I moved slowly, struggling with the damask layers of my dress, grabbing for my dagger. I had to keep them talking if I was going to free myself.

Karl cleared his throat. "Lord Maximillian and I have been at odds before, but we are in complete agreement regarding the future of Bohemia. And there cannot be any great victory without great loss."

"Yes." Lord Maximillian gave me a menacing stare. "As it happens, I've been developing a weapon to make the progress we desire a reality. You've already seen its work for yourself."

Fire filled my memory; I pictured the dark wine cellar in Prague Castle, of Tulia's house, and even the carriage moving Ferdy's friends back to Silesia. And then I thought back to Ben's observations in the barn.

"Nitroglycerin." I barely whispered the word as I felt the blood drain out of my face.

"Not quite, but close," Lord Maximillian corrected. "Nobel holds the patent for dynamite, but I've determined my recipe is close enough to his that it'll work the same, if not better."

"Yes, and thanks to me, Count Potocki imported several barrels of it into his pantry tonight, just like Mother did for the Advent Ball," Karl boasted. "It won't be long before it explodes. All we had to do was light the fuse."

"Why?" I looked from Karl to Lord Maximillian, unable to comprehend how little they cared for the lives they were about to destroy. "Why are you doing this?"

"What do you mean, 'why?'" Lord Maximillian scorned me. "A better question is 'why not,' don't you think?"

"After people die here, Bohemians will see they need new leadership," Karl said. "The Emperor doesn't care for us, and the Nationalists will rise up and propel me back to the throne."

"And then you will marry my daughter," Lord Maximillian finished.

As Karl nodded glumly, I saw my moment—and I took it.

I whipped out my mother's dagger, leaned forward, and plunged the blade into Lord Maximillian's leg.

The larger man jumped back and hollered in surprise and pain; he struggled to stay balanced, and in all the confusion, I pulled my skirts out from underneath his foot.

"Why did you do that?" At the sight of blood and violence, Karl scampered back several steps, looking ill. He put his hand over his mouth, as if he was about vomit.

While the two of them yelled, I escaped down the hall. The chloroform had not worn off entirely; I ran for several large steps, and then stumbled and crashed into a crevice near a door. My one hand steadied me against the wall as my body shook. I breathed deeply, carrying my dagger in my other hand as Lord Maximillian cursed at me.

"I can only hope you'll die quickly!" he yelled back at me while Karl supported him.

THE ORDER OF THE CRYSTAL DAGGERS

"Who's worried about poor manners now?" I murmured, flinching as I saw Lord Maximillian's leg was bleeding out in small spurts.

Together with Karl, he limped away in the other direction.

Where is Lady POW when I need her?

She had said we would leave early if Karl showed up, but she wasn't supposed to leave me behind. Without her, I couldn't do anything to gain the upper hand against them both.

I could only hope Harshad and Ben would catch them as they left.

"Not again," I muttered, as another wave of dizziness took over me. Feeling hopeless, I slid onto the floor as they disappeared from my sight.

I was stuck there, my body shaking with stunned rage and weakness.

I wanted to cry at the unfairness of it all. They were so close, and yet still out of my reach, and my own body was incapable of capturing them. The only thing I could do was follow them, but that would mean the people in Count Potocki's mansion would die from their trap.

A hand reached out and took hold of my shoulder. I jerked around, ready to stab anyone who would dare try to stop me. The shadow behind me avoided my attack and then knocked my dagger from my still-trembling hands a second later. I was reaching for it again, terrified my attacker from the bridge had come back, when the figure spoke out from the darkness.

"I'd rather hoped you'd forgiven me enough not to try to kill me, *chérie*."

It was Ferdy.

16

◊

Ferdy.

Shock and anger flooded through me, mixing into relief and even hope, before transforming into its final, aggravated form.

He smelled of the streets, of pipe tobacco, river water, and kitchen smoke. In the dim lighting, I could see he was wearing a set of livery easily two sizes too small. I could only wonder what he'd been doing, and I honestly didn't really even want to know.

Ferdy had returned to me at last—just in time to be put back in danger. After several days of silence, here he was right in front of me, just as explosives were set to go off.

Will this man ever stop frustrating me so?

"What are you doing here?" My voice was cold as he pulled me up off the floor and returned my dagger to me. Forcefully, I shoved my blade back into its sheath. "Lady Penelope said she wasn't sure you would come back."

"Well, that was always a possibility," Ferdy replied cheerfully, making me even angrier.

"Oh, so I should be grateful that you've come back at all?" I put my hands on my hips. "That you've only left me for a few days instead of years or perhaps the rest of your life?"

"What?" Ferdy looked surprised.

"If you've changed your mind about our marriage or realized I'm not the woman you thought I was, you should just tell me and be done with it."

211

"Ella, are you listening to yourself?" Ferdy frowned at me. "I went looking for Lumiere. I was going to come back once I found him."

I felt flustered and foolish, but I wasn't going to let that stop me. "Well, did you actually find him?"

"No ... not exactly." Ferdy shrugged. "But I got a lead. It shouldn't take me much longer to track him down."

"I must say, it's so very nice you're letting me know you're leaving beforehand this time," I snapped.

"I told your grandmother I was leaving," he said. "She should've told you."

"No, *you* should've told me." I did not like defending Lady POW, especially when she had chosen not to tell me why Ferdy had gone. But he couldn't put all the blame on her.

"Now you know how I felt the other night when you went into the city without me, and how I had to come track you down here tonight," he argued.

"Excuse me? I was doing what I had to do!"

"And I thought if I could find Lumiere, that would keep you safe and make you happy."

"I don't need you to do things to make me happy!" I threw up my hands angrily, secretly groaning at the memory of Lady POW fighting with Xiana. "I need to be able to trust you."

Ferdy took me by the shoulders. "I can't do anything about that, but I've trusted you for a long time. Remember the night you saved me at the castle? You protected me, even to the point you risked your life, and I knew then I really was in love with you, without a doubt—the real you, not one I'd imagined. Even if you were a spy and assassin."

"Oh, please, we're not arguing about that now." I glared at him. "You knew I didn't want you to leave the house after what happened to me on the bridge."

"Of course I knew that," Ferdy agreed. "But you were sick, and that was part of the deal: I told Lady Penelope where Karl was and then I left to get Lumiere back. She was supposed to make sure you were safe while I was gone."

He gestured down the hall where Karl had made his exit. "I guess I shouldn't be surprised to find you in danger again. She didn't keep her word."

"It probably depends on your perspective," I murmured. Lady POW hadn't been eager for my plan, but she had given in to my reasoning. I could only assume she'd meant to keep me safe, even if she didn't keep me at the manor. "Besides, you're in danger now, too. Lord Maximillian and Karl are eager to repeat the events of the Advent Ball. They've already got explosives planted and the fuse is lit."

"Leave it to Karl to ruin things." Ferdy groaned and looked for an exit. "We need to get out of here."

"Wait," I said. "We have to save the others first."

Ferdy's hands tightened around me. I knew he was wrestling over what to do, and I felt my heart soften at his torment. He wanted to protect me, but he couldn't ignore my reasoning, either.

"Ferdy, please," I whispered. "We can't just leave them to die."

"I know, I know." Ferdy's angry expression crumbled into despair. "But my goodness, Ella, do you just hate me? I almost lost you twice already. I can't lose you now. Why are you making me suffer like this?"

"You know I don't hate you." I put my hands on his chest, bracing myself against him. As we stood there, I thought of all the times I'd been worried for him, fearing the worst—even before I really knew I was in love with him. I recalled hoping he was safe after learning of Dr. Artha's murder, how I'd looked for him in town after joining the Order, and how I'd surprised even myself by admitting I was in love with him at the Advent Ball. "And I've almost lost you before, too, remember?"

Ferdy shook his head. "It seems we are destined to make each other suffer."

"*Absolument.*" I pressed my forehead against his to encourage him. "But we'll have to do that later. We have work to do right now. If we won't save these people, who will?"

"Do you really believe we can?" Ferdy asked softly, and I could hear the slight tremor in his voice.

"We can, if we trust each other," I said. "I know you think I am a fool—"

"Oh, Ella. You might be a fool, but I am a fool for you." Ferdy crushed me against him. My arms slid up and wrapped around his neck instinctively, and I inwardly reveled as the full force of his warmth washed over me.

It felt so good to be back in his arms. I almost couldn't believe it had been two whole days since I'd seen him.

"Maybe you should leave," I whispered, suddenly more afraid of losing him, too. "It might be too much if both of us are acting foolish."

"No. We'll stay together and work together." He looked at me and tried to smile. "Just as we promised. For better, for worse, for richer, for poorer—and in magic and madness, in spy work and in civilian life, right?"

"Until death do we part." I curled into him briefly, listening to the beat of his heart as it pounded. I wanted him to trust me, and I had to trust him, too. I wasn't sure why, but hearing him joke irreverently about our wedding vows gave me a strange sense of peace.

"All right." Ferdy let me go, looking unhappy but resolved. "What's your plan?"

I bit my lip. It was the worst time to hesitate, but I couldn't risk failing again—not with so many lives at stake.

"Go find Ben," I said. "He came with us tonight. He'll know more about the explosives than me."

"All right," Ferdy agreed. "And then you will get out of here?"

He was hopeful, but I knew he was not expecting me to be so sensible.

"No, I'll find Lady POW, and we'll get the people out of the house," I said. "I don't know where she went, but this was definitely the worst time for her to leave."

"She's outside by now. Amir sent for her," Ferdy told me. "He ran into me as I arrived to come and rescue you."

"Amir is here? Why?"

"Lumiere sent a runner to let Amir know Karl was out for the night," Ferdy explained. "I offered to pose as the messenger boy, and then I stayed in the kitchens as a charity case—"

"—and when they weren't looking, you stole a footman's uniform and came to find me," I finished, looking down at his tightly fitting tunic with a newfound amusement.

It was almost like the time at the Hohenwart Ball. He'd been rescuing me from Karl back then, too.

"Ah, you know me so well, *chérie*." Ferdy grinned, the first genuinely happy smile I'd seen from him all night.

"And yet I love you anyway." I picked up my skirts in one hand and blew him a kiss with the other. "Go. I'm going to get these people out of here, and then I'll meet you in a bit."

"Do I know we will meet again?" Ferdy's words harkened back to that night outside the *Stavovské divadlo*, and if I had more time, I might have boxed his ears.

"Of course we will," I said through gritted teeth. "How else will I be able to punish you for distracting me right now?"

"Well, that's fair." Ferdy let out a quick laugh, and I could still hear him as he headed out to retrieve Ben.

Watching him leave felt painful and frightening, as though my skin was being ripped off my chest.

I shook my head to clear my mind. Lady POW was likely with Ben and Amir, and Ferdy was on his way to them; now, it was my job to save everyone else.

It was hard to feel brave as I looked out at the ballroom again; I saw all the beautifully clad people so happy and so ignorant and felt overwhelmed.

But how? How do I get all these people out of the house?

It didn't seem prudent to reveal myself as a member of the Order of the Crystal Daggers, especially to a large crowd; as Lady Penelope told me before, it was possible they wouldn't believe me, either about my mission or the danger.

And it would be too scandalous if they learned the truth about Karl. I'd spent the last two days establishing our overly romantic narrative, I realized with dismay. I'd spent all my goodwill on them, and they would rightfully reject me now.

Some of the guests waved to me, but I couldn't move, not even to wave back; I was stuck in an indecisive trance.

Until I caught sight of the wallpaper again.

THE ORDER OF THE CRYSTAL DAGGERS

Just off to the side, there was a small strip of it hanging loose in one corner of the room. To help hide it, a candelabra and a pedestal with a vase of flowers had been strategically placed in front of it.

An idea took hold inside of me—one I did not like.

But I liked everyone dying inside the house even less, and I could even hear Lumiere cheering me on inside my head as I moved forward.

"Come now, he was going to get Roman to redo the house anyway … go ahead and give him some flaming incentive … might do us a world of good, too, before other people start ordering such a grisly color …"

At the memory of Lumiere's rampant laughter, I didn't hesitate.

I approached the curling wallpaper, grabbing a glass of champagne as a server passed by. As I pretended to examine the flowers and gaze at the candelabra, I glanced to the side, watching the crowd as nonchalantly as possible.

No one was paying attention to me.

I took a deep breath, praying my plan would work.

And then I threw the champagne onto the wilting flowers and the wall, and shoved myself into the candelabra hard enough it fell over.

The sparks flew all around and caught, and as the crowd took notice, I screamed and pointed at the spurting flames.

"Fire!" I pretended to slap at the flames, but I was only intent on spreading them.

Several in the crowd seemed confused, and I clenched my fists.

Don't they know they need to get out of here? What are they waiting for?

To hinder my apparent incompetence, several footmen were running with water and wet towels. They began beating the flames out, and I suddenly wished I'd lit the whole hallway on fire.

"It's too much!" I cried. "We need to leave!"

"Madame, we can stop it," a footman said, but I began shrieking hysterically.

"Everyone, get out," I yelled, wildly gesturing for people to leave. Some of them scowled and dutifully moved out of the room. Others stood there, drunkenly staring at me, as I hurried around in circles and pushed them toward the exit.

I never felt so embarrassed in all my life, acting like a foolish madwoman. As I continued to usher people out the door, I had to remind myself over and over that it was for their own good, that I would worry about the fallout later— or, preferably, I would never think of this moment ever again.

"I sure hope the house doesn't fall," I hollered, and more whispers erupted into shouts.

"The house is going to fall!" Lady Hohenwart screamed as she rushed by me, holding down her purple turban with one hand and barely holding onto her skirts in the other. She stumbled toward the exit, and I was grateful to see others follow her.

We might save them yet.

It helped that the fire was still spreading, and the wallpaper was falling down in sweeping lines, as though offering itself up as kindling.

I was just helping a gentleman stand up after he'd been knocked down when I saw Ben waving at me from the other side of the room.

"Ben!"

He looked at the fire behind me. "What did you do?"

Despite the footmen working hard to slow the spread, it had crawled toward the ceiling and extended across the wall. Some of the wallpaper was falling on the floor, too, lighting up smaller piles of fires.

"Reality needed to get too real for the crowd," I hastily explained. "Where's Ferdy?"

"He and the others are helping the guests outside into their carriages," Ben told me. "He offered to carry me inside, and I told him no. I figured you would be happy about that."

"Thank you." I could barely whisper out the words, but Ben nodded in understanding, and then I hurried to describe what had happened with Lord Maximillian and Karl. I told Ben how they'd planned to set off dynamite to gain sympathy for their political cause, and his eyes lit up in recognition.

"Dynamite?" Ben scowled. "I had a feeling about the time in Prague Castle. It couldn't have been just fire and wine that made the ballroom collapse."

"They said it was in the wine cellar," I said.

"We have to find it then." Ben grimaced. "And we'll need to hurry."

Together, Ben and I made our way down into the servants' hallways. I told the workers I saw about the fire. I ordered them to get out while they could, while Ben asked for directions to the wine cellar. It didn't take long for us to arrive at our destination.

And as we walked into the wine cellar, I already knew something was wrong.

"It's too warm in here," I murmured, and Ben nodded in agreement.

"Look!" he pointed toward the back of the room, and a small rise of smoke rose up from one of the wine barrels.

We made our way over, and Ben carefully pulled the cork out of the barrel. More smoke and the smell of oil immediately poured out.

"There's something burning inside," I said, trying not to cough. I glanced around at the other barrels nearby.

Ben eyed the smoking barrel and then the others alongside it. "This barrel was meant to be kindling."

"This must be the fuse Lord Maximillian was talking about," I said, as Ben knocked on the barrel next to him, listening intently. I didn't know what he was doing until he rapped his knuckles against the wood again.

"Whatever's in this barrel, it's not wine. It's more solid," Ben said.

"It can't be frozen."

"Yes," Ben agreed. "From what I've read, Nobel mixed the nitroglycerin with some earth and minerals to make his dynamite. It's similar to gunpowder, only stronger."

"So, it will explode."

"Yes, just like it happened at the Advent Ball." Ben tapped the barrel again. "This likely has powder inside."

"Are you sure?"

"Best guess." Ben gave me a teasing smirk. "But Ferdy might not want to bet on it."

"I'm not sure. He seems to think he's pretty lucky when it comes to gambling." I eyed the barrel nervously. "Can you stop it from going off?"

"Yes. And if we stop the fire in here, we can stop everything." He pointed to the barrel that was leaking out smoke and fumes.

"I hope you're right. Please hurry."

Ben took hold of the top of the smoking barrel. "It's better to be right than fast."

"It's best to be right *and* fast," I argued.

"That's why I'm doing it, not you."

I groaned, but he laughed, and I felt a little better. My nerves were already shattered for the night, and things couldn't be all bad if Ben was trying to get me to relax a little, even if this was absolutely not the right time for it.

It was not the right time to panic, either, I reminded myself as Ben started trying to smash open the cover. I winced at the loud noises and kept looking over at the door, almost expecting someone to come and try to stop us.

After a few more blows, the wood appeared only slightly cracked.

That's when I pulled out our mother's dagger.

"Here," I said, offering it to Ben. "Pry it open."

"Thanks." His voice was gruff, and I could tell he was hiding his own nervousness. "If you want to help some more, you can stop tapping your foot, too."

"Huh?" I'd barely noticed I was fidgeting.

"Actually, go see if there are any other barrels we need to check," Ben ordered. "That'll help us, and I won't have to worry about you distracting me, either."

As he began digging the dagger's blade around the edge of the barrel top, I looked through each line of barrels carefully.

I leaned down close to smell for fire, and I knocked on the barrels, just as Ben had, to hear what was inside.

At the last one, I let out a sigh of relief. "There's no more fire," I called.

"Good." Ben pried the wooden top of his barrel off, and several oily, burning swaths emptied out onto the floor. Ben smothered the flames with his boots as I ran back to him.

"Ouch."

I saw him crouch over and back away; a spark had caught onto his brace and burned him. I hurried over, trying to ground the fire into the stone floor. My dress burned in some areas, but my skirts were thick enough I didn't feel it.

The fumes made us cough as the smell of burning oil filled the room. I tore off a section of my petticoats to tie over my mouth. I offered one to Ben, but he declined.

My skin was cold, even as we stood there next to the flames. I couldn't escape the feeling that trouble was coming, and I wouldn't be able to stop it or save anyone.

But after the fire dwindled down, I let out a shaky laugh and collapsed onto the ground in relief.

"Oh, thank you, Lord," I whispered.

"Are there anymore?" Ben asked, looking around again.

I shook my head. "No."

"All right." He nodded, clearly pleased by my report. Using my dagger again, he opened the barrel next to us. He was right; the barrel was full of a strange, brownish powder. He sniffed at it, and then shook his head. "It's different from gunpowder, but it's close."

I scanned the room. "Either way, it definitely doesn't belong here. If it went off, the wine would add to the flames, too."

THE ORDER OF THE CRYSTAL DAGGERS

"You mean like it did upstairs with your fire?" Ben was more relaxed as he teased me.

I ignored him, even if I was grateful. "What do we do now?"

"We'll have to remove the powder barrels out of the manor." Ben eyed the cellar's entrance with a calculating look. "I think that's a problem for Lady POW. She'll need Potocki's cooperation."

"I agree." My nerves were more than strained, and I welcomed the chance to hand responsibility over to someone else.

"Here." Ben held out my dagger. "Thanks. I'll have to get one for myself, one day."

I stepped back, realizing I'd forgotten how much Ben missed our mother, too. "Maybe we can share it."

"No." He shook his head and pushed the dagger back toward me. "It belongs to you. You should be the one to uphold *Máma*'s legacy; I'm the one responsible for redeeming *Otec*'s."

"We are both their children," I said, suddenly feeling apologetic. "I know you miss her, too. So we should share it."

"And we will, when we can. Like we did now." Ben placed my dagger back in my hand, and I finally put it away, only a little reluctantly; I was still grateful it was mine, and I was glad Ben was content to leave it in my care.

We headed out to find Lady POW, and that was when I remembered Ferdy was back, too.

"Did you see that Ferdy's here?" I asked. "He went out looking for Lumiere. That's why he was missing these last couple of days."

"Really?" Ben gave me a skeptical look. "Did he find him?"

"No. But he said he was close."

"Maybe it takes a rogue to find a rogue." Ben shrugged. "I'll admit I'm not eager to deal with Lumiere again so soon, but it'll be better if we get him back, especially if we weren't able to get Karl tonight."

"Oh, no, you're right." I wrinkled my nose. "I forgot about that."

"How could you forget something like that?"

"You know, I'm not entirely sure." I waved my arm back toward the cellar, stocked full of explosive powder. "There must be something else on my mind."

Despite the danger we'd faced, Ben and I shared a laugh, and for once I felt as though I had succeeded in an important mission—not just in saving lives, but rebuilding the trust between me and my brother.

I looked down at my mother's dagger, tucked away just at the side of my soot-covered dress. I felt much better as we walked outside. This time, even though it was chilly, I felt only warmth.

Máma would be proud of us.

17

◊

The fire was still smoldering inside Count Potocki's ballroom as Ben and I walked out toward the stables. A small spout of smoke fluttered out of the mansion's roof, its pale, wispy tail wafting upward into the wintery night.

I grimaced at the scene before us. "I was hoping that the fire wouldn't make things worse."

"I just hope no one saw you start it." Ben's voice was light, even though it was concerned. "And that they can stop it before it reaches the wine cellar."

"At least most of the people seem to be outside," I said, glancing around at the fairly large crowd. Many eyed the house with grim expressions on their faces. Several men offered their greatcoats to the ladies standing around in the cold, while others called out for their friends and companions.

I was still a little afraid about the fire, but a sense of satisfaction swelled up within me as I surveyed the scene.

Karl failed—again.

"There you are, Eleanora." Lady Penelope made her way over to us; there was enough worry in her irritated gaze that I could tell she was glad to see us. "I must apologize for my disappearance earlier."

"You should also apologize for failing to tell me why Ferdy really left," I retorted. She could've eased my doubt if only she'd explained everything to me, but she'd chosen not to.

"I was legitimately concerned he wouldn't come back." Lady Penelope did not look sorry at all, and I didn't know why I was surprised. "You must realize that I had to make

225

sure you would still be able to work on the mission, even if he did leave for good."

"Ferdy wouldn't do that," I insisted.

"Maybe not this time," she snapped back. "But what of next time, or others, Eleanora? Will you be able to keep your resolve to finish the mission if I disappear? Or Benedict? Or any of the others in your life? This is the price you pay for your love."

She narrowed her eyes behind me, and I turned to see Ferdy. He was still in his stolen livery, leading horses toward the waiting carriages. No one seemed to realize he wasn't really part of the Potocki household.

"Well, I guess you'll never have to worry about facing such conditions," I scoffed, turning back to Lady POW.

Ben stepped between us, and I was both grateful and angry for his interruption. "Were you able to capture Karl on his way out?"

"No." She crossed her arms. "But we know where he is. We will go to *Vyšehrad* tomorrow night. Right now, we still have work to do here."

"We need Count Potocki's help to empty out his wine cellar," Ben said. "Especially if Ella's fire isn't put out."

"Hey, it's not my fire," I tried to argue.

"Don't worry about that. It's already been largely taken care of," Lady Penelope said. "The smoke will take some time to disappear."

As angry with her as I was, I was relieved by her assessment. "So the house will stand?"

"Yes."

"Assuming we get the dynamite out," Ben murmured beside me.

Lady Penelope nodded brusquely. "I will speak with the Count about that. He was eager for renovations; now he has the perfect excuse to pour even more money into his house. But you should be especially proud of yourselves tonight."

I looked back to the smoke-filled night doubtfully. "Why?"

"Karl's plan was to destroy the mansion and harm those inside. With your fire, you took something meant for evil and used it as a way to save others," Lady POW explained. "True justice always results in mercy for the innocent."

"Thank you." I clenched my jaw, hating how much I enjoyed her approval. "But don't think you can get away with insulting me by giving me compliments."

Lady Penelope rolled her eyes. "You should go home, Eleanora. Clearly your nerves are overwrought. You've done your job, and you've done it well. There's no use pretending you'll be needed now."

"We still have our own business to settle, Madame. I want to know why you didn't tell me about Ferdy—"

"You have your orders." Lady Penelope glared down at me and then turned to my brother. "Benedict, come follow me; we will see to the explosives. Eleanora, you can see to yourself."

Ben gave me an apologetic look, but I waved him on. He was still excited to be here, in the middle of the action, and Lady Penelope was right. I was tired and my nerves were strained, and I did want to go home.

Especially before I ended up fighting with Lady POW all over again.

"I know that look," Amir said, as he appeared at my side. "It is best to forgive her, Eleanora."

I crossed my arms. "I hate how she keeps undermining my trust in Ferdy."

Ferdy himself was also good at undermining my trust, but that was for the two of us to discuss, not for Lady POW to further damage.

"It is still best to forgive her."

I scowled. "I'd think of all people, you would know how it hurts to deal with her vitriol."

"Yes, and of all people, I know it is best to forgive her for it." Amir's soft rebuke stung even more than Lady Penelope's scorn. "You have to be able to stand up for yourself, Eleanora, no matter your choices. And to be fair, at least you know she doesn't want you to get hurt."

"I don't think she cares if I'm upset, so long as I'll keep working through it."

"Even if it's more because of the mission, she is still trying to protect you."

"I don't want her to." Angrily, I stomped my foot. "It's *not* fair."

"Life isn't fair," Amir agreed. "But Lady Penelope knows what it's like to be hurt, too, remember?"

I looked back at the mansion, where the smoke was dying down. "But no one's died here—so far, anyway."

"I know." Amir put one hand on my shoulder and the other on the hilt of his own dagger. "And thankfully, from the way she's talking with Ben and the others, I doubt we'll have to worry about it tonight. But there are other ways to lose people."

I nodded silently, unable to do anything else. Amir was right, of course.

"You should go home and rest," Amir continued. "If Lady Penelope let you have a break, you should take it."

I glanced back at Ben, watching him hobble after Lady POW. He was talking with Ferdy as I watched them, and they seemed to be getting along.

Amir cleared his throat. "I'll stay and watch over Ben for you. After we're done here, I'll take him on a round through the city."

"He seems tired."

"He still needs to build up his strength. Lady POW wants you to work despite your emotional burdens; Ben needs to work even in light of his physical ones."

As we approached Lady Penelope's carriage, I remembered what Ferdy had told me inside the house. "Ferdy said you received a letter from Lumiere."

Amir nodded. "He wanted me to know Karl was heading toward the Potocki mansion using the secret tunnels that run throughout the city."

"Secret tunnels?" I repeated the words, but didn't fully understand them. "What did he mean by that?"

"Everyone has secrets, even the city, it seems." Amir gave me an amused smile. "After Karl I, the first king of Bohemia, was crowned, he began to construct a secret underground. He wanted them in case of a coup. Over the years, some of them have caved in due to erosion and the city's weakened foundation in different places, but they are still there."

"I never knew about them." I wrinkled my nose. "If they were built to stop a coup, it's ironic this Karl is using them."

"Yes, and it's disquieting that Lumiere knows of them," Amir agreed. "But it does explain why Xiana and I did not intercept him on his way over."

"Where is Xiana?" I glanced around, but didn't see her. I hadn't seen her since I talked with Lady Penelope the morning after the bridge attack. Part of me wanted to confide

229

THE ORDER OF THE CRYSTAL DAGGERS

in Amir how I felt she was upset with me, but I didn't want him to think I was imagining it, either.

"I am not sure," he admitted. "I tried to find her before I came here, but she'd already moved from her post. I imagine she saw something and took off to investigate. Have you heard anything from Xiana, Harshad?"

I looked up to the top box, where Harshad was waiting and watching over the scene patiently. He seemed more alive in the night, as if he was infinitely more comfortable.

"No, I've received nothing from her," he said. "But it could be as you say. We'll surely see her back at the manor within a few hours."

"Ben and I will look around for Xiana on our rounds," Amir told Harshad. "Lady Penelope wants Eleanora to go home."

"I'll drop her off and return for Pepé." Harshad gave Amir a concerned look. "Don't be out too late. And don't draw any attention to yourself. There are rumors about murder again."

I recalled that a Turk was to blame for the murder of Ferdy's friends. Even without a deadly ending, tonight could cause a lot more trouble yet.

Amir assured Harshad he would be fine, and then he nudged me up into the carriage. "Go home and rest."

I didn't fight back. I climbed up into the carriage, and once the door was shut and we began to move, I collapsed against the cushions.

Only to fly out of my seat as the other door of the carriage whooshed open again, and Ferdy appeared, half-hanging out the door.

"You weren't going to leave without me, were you?" he asked, trying to stay calm as he reached for me.

I saw he'd scrambled to climb inside as we moved, but he'd lost his footing.

"Oh my goodness, Ferdy." Quickly, I hurried to help, grabbing him and pulling on his arms. Less than gracefully, we fell back together, and he landed on top of me. The carriage door slammed shut, and the sounds of the streets became more muffled.

Ferdy smiled. "It's nice to see you'll still fall for me, Ella."

"Falling for you is one thing." Immediately, I pushed him off and swiftly moved away to shut the carriage curtains. "But I'd rather not fall for your lies."

Ferdy sighed dejectedly as he scooted back onto the other bench. "Why are you upset again? I was doing what I was supposed to do, just as you were. And we did work together back there."

"I'm glad you were able to help back there," I said. "But after everything that nearly happened, I want to make sure you know not to lie to me—even if it's to keep me safe."

"I'm supposed to keep you safe."

"No, you're supposed to keep me," I retorted. "That's what you said before. I didn't know what you meant when you said it, exactly, before we got married, but I certainly didn't think you were going to try to imprison me. Otherwise, I would've said no. I've lived enough of my life being trapped by others."

"I didn't tell you about Karl because I was trying to keep him imprisoned, not you," Ferdy argued. "I did apologize, and I did my best to make it up to you."

I crossed my arms and slumped over, looking away from him. Every unrealized fear I'd had in the last hour started raging inside of me, even if my anger seemed easier to handle.

"You look beautiful tonight," Ferdy said after a while. "I always thought you would look perfect in the princess combs. I was right."

I gave him a quick nod and then turned back to the window.

"You're welcome, by the way."

"For what?"

"For not telling you the truth," Ferdy said, giving me one of his charming smiles.

The last of my self-control suddenly snapped; I could almost hear it breaking as I glared back at him. "Don't do that. Lumiere says things like that, you know. He gives me nothing but trouble, and then he assumes I'm thankful for it, and I'd rather you not resemble him right now." I wrinkled my nose. "Or ever, really."

"He has his moments."

"Why aren't you going after him now?" I asked, thinking back to the small moments we'd been able to talk inside the Potocki mansion. "You said you were close to finding him."

"I'll follow up on my lead later. I'd rather spend the time with you."

I snorted disdainfully. "Well, everyone has regrets."

"I don't. Not where you're concerned." Ferdy suddenly leaned forward, snatched me right off my seat, and pulled me into his lap.

"Ferdy!" I objected. "What are you—"

My words fell away as he pressed his lips against mine.

For only a moment, I mindlessly kissed him back. Whatever anger I felt at him, I'd missed him, and no matter how tired I was, I still ached for him.

But soon, I came back to my senses and pulled away. "No. Not if you don't trust me."

"I do," Ferdy insisted.

"Fine. Then not if I can't trust you."

"You can."

"Then why didn't you tell me about Karl?" My fingers dug into his chest as we once more came to the impasse between us. "You said it was to keep me safe. That's not good enough, Ferdy. What kind of woman do you take me for? You know we are going to face trouble at some point. The fact that it's from your brother means very little to me right now."

"It was for your benefit—"

"No, it wasn't. What are we going to do when we have to spend the holidays with your family? What about if we go abroad?" I suddenly clung to him even more tightly. "What about when I find myself pregnant?"

"Are you?" he asked, glancing down at my midsection briefly.

"No." I narrowed my eyes. "But I need you to tell me the truth, no matter what it is. And I need you to be there for me."

"Ella, please … I didn't keep the truth about Karl from you because I didn't trust you," Ferdy said quietly.

"Oh, really?" I arched my brow at him. "It sure seems like it."

"No, I promise, that's not it." He sighed. "I didn't say anything because I didn't want to force you to choose between me and the Order. If I'd told you about Karl, and gave all the reasons for leaving him alone, you would've fretted over whether or not to say something to your grandmother. Even if I asked you not to."

I tried to imagine how things would've happened if he'd told me. He wasn't wrong; even Amir had said Ferdy's reasons for keeping Karl locked away under Lord Maximillian's watch were sensible enough, and I hadn't been willing to tell Lady POW the truth even after learning it, even knowing about the danger Louis posed.

"Were you worried I would choose her over you?" I asked slowly.

He'd told me before he knew of the Order, and while he didn't think I would kill him, he was adamant the Order had its history of assassinations; yet he still insisted he loved me and wanted to be with me.

"No," Ferdy said, surprising me. "But if my plan failed, you would have blamed yourself. And, knowing you as I do, I also knew you wouldn't forgive yourself if you failed."

Tenderness suddenly filled my heart where all the anger had been simmering. I softened against him, and he quickly drew me closer to himself.

"I thought it might be easier for you to forgive me," he said. "A foolish thought, perhaps."

No, it wasn't.

I couldn't bring myself to say it, but he knew. How could he not? He knew me so well.

I buried my head into his shoulder. "Where was this calm, rational Ferdinand the other night?"

"You'll have to forgive me for that, too. You said we would have trouble, and some of it is bound to come from either one of us." Ferdy cupped my cheek and smiled at me. "I was especially upset when I found you were gone from the manor the other night; I was blindsided by your absence. So I was not at my most reasonable."

"I wasn't, either."

"No, you weren't," Ferdy agreed with a small chuckle. I started to object, but he ran his fingers reverently down my face, and I leaned into his touch. "But that's fine. I can love you within reason as much as without."

The last of any resistance I'd intended to keep gave way, and I leaned up and kissed him with renewed, fervent desperation.

He met me in the middle with equal passion. I felt the rest of the world disappear as his mouth moved over mine possessively. Soon the chill of winter was forgotten as we held onto each other.

"Loving you is magic," Ferdy whispered, pulling back from me only to catch his breath.

"I thought it was madness," I murmured back, too lost in him to be playful as I wrapped my arms around his neck.

"No," Ferdy said. "It's the thought of losing you that's madness. I'm certain of that now."

I met his gaze with mine. "I don't think there can be one without the other."

"I know." He kissed me again. "But if the cost of loving you is losing my sanity, it's a price I'll pay."

"I don't think that's the right way of putting it," I started to say before his hands moved down my body and I lost all but the most basic semblance of thought. "Ferdy, Harshad is outside and I don't think—"

"I don't think we'll make that much noise," he assured me with a mischievous grin. "I'll even bet on it."

Before I could argue any further, his lips found mine again, and I ceased thinking entirely.

THE ORDER OF THE CRYSTAL DAGGERS

Hours drifted by before I stirred awake in my bed. As I stretched, my hand bumped against the small table beside my bed, carelessly knocking my mother's dagger onto the floor.

"Ugh." I cringed at the scuffling sound. It seemed louder than it was against the dark, early morning stillness.

"What is it?" Ferdy's slurred and sleepy voice was muffled from underneath his pillow.

"Nothing, my love," I said, pulling the sheet over top of him.

He mumbled out some unclear words before burying himself even further under the covers.

Ferdy had promised me that he would resume his quest to find Lumiere after he tucked me into bed, but two days of running around the city, searching through nearby ports, napping in alleyways, and questioning different runners had all taken their toll on him.

He meant to tuck me in, but it seemed better for me to put him to bed.

"Ella." Ferdy was still half-asleep as he reached for me.

At first, I resisted; I wanted to retrieve my mother's dagger and see if Lady POW and Ben and the others had made it home yet.

But Ferdy persisted, and I gave in.

Time deepened, pulling us into a small pocket of memory all our own as I lay beside him. My fingers trailed down his arms, feeling the strength and tenderness there. How strange and splendid it was that this person I loved so much loved me back so potently, yet still so imperfectly.

Paradoxes are not the same as contradictions.

THE ORDER OF THE CRYSTAL DAGGERS

For a small moment, I thought of his deception and felt the dull heartache of disappointment.

I'd trusted him so completely, and it seemed wrong how loving someone meant they could cause pain that would otherwise be impossible. I grimaced as my heart clenched up like a fist, jealously grasping at my inner bitterness.

The rush of righteous pain, self-righteous or not, was intoxicating at first, but the longer I clung to it, the more hollow I felt. If I let it fester like an open wound, it would only grow bigger and more painful as time went by.

I let out a long, slow exhale, forcing my heart to open again. It was like chiseling away a layer of rock and stone, desperately digging and hammering away inside of me, all in hopes of finding underneath it all, I would still be able to go on and live.

"I forgive you." My voice was barely audible, and I was sure Ferdy was asleep, but I needed to say the words, almost as if I needed to hear them to believe them.

And I needed to let him know our impasse was over, so we could move forward—together.

His heart was beating steadily and his breathing was even, but a moment later, he shifted over and kissed my shoulder. "Thank you, Ella."

I drifted back to sleep, still smiling as Ferdy held me.

18

◊

It wasn't much longer before I woke up again, but this time I jolted awake, already searching for Ferdy. My hands reached over into the sheets, where only a small shadow of his warmth remained.

Ferdy was gone.

I sat up and put my head in my hands; it was almost like a premonition of the worst sort. Despite the rest we'd had, I felt a dark cloud hanging over me, as though something bad was just on the verge of happening.

"Sorry if I woke you."

My head jerked up and there he was, dressing in the far corner of the room.

I exhaled deeply and almost laughed at my fretfulness. "I thought you'd left."

"I thought it would be best to tell you myself when I'm leaving," he replied, his voice lighthearted and teasing, before coming over and pressing a kiss to my forehead. I grabbed his hands and clung to him, reaching up for a true kiss.

I desperately wanted more time with him. "Let me get dressed and eat breakfast with you," I said, already moving out of bed.

"If you hurry," Ferdy said with a hint of challenge in his eyes as he grabbed his boots. "After all the excitement of last night, I'm starving."

I blushed, thinking of how Ferdy and I had excused ourselves to our room when we'd arrived back to the manor. I didn't have time to see Harshad's face as we ran away, but my appetite dried up at the memory.

I put on my housedress and reached down for my fallen dagger on the floor. As I grabbed it, I saw a flicker of white.

There, on the floor, hiding just underneath my bed, along with my still-soggy tunic, was the water-damaged sketch I'd received from the older man on the bridge.

I picked up the paper and unfolded it carefully. I could still see it as clearly as I had in the moonlight, even where the older man had pointed out its imperfections.

The city of Prague was majestic and sad, yet still full of hope and promises.

I glanced over at Ferdy, who was still putting on his boots.

Even if our relationship had its imperfections, I thought, it would be wrong of me to abandon him. It was too easy to leave, to tear down in temporal rage what I'd pledged myself to in hope; it was an act of love and trust to remain and rebuild the broken parts.

Did I really love him if I wasn't willing to sacrifice something of myself, especially in hopes of bettering both of us?

"Are you ready?" Ferdy asked me.

"Almost." Delicately, I put the sketch down on my night table again and reached for a band to tie back my hair.

"Aw, you're not wearing the princess combs today?" Ferdy teased.

I smiled. "No. They're very lovely, but they're heavy. And they really should only be for you."

"I like the idea of you wearing only them for me." Ferdy tussled my hair and kissed me before I could say anything about that.

Hand in hand, we walked down the quiet, empty halls of my home, heading for the kitchen as we talked in soft tones.

We were passing the library when Cecilia's voice cut through the air like a knife.

"Is that you, Tulia? What could possibly be taking you so long this morning? All we wanted was tea!"

Ferdy let go of my hand to cover his ears. "I didn't know your stepmother was part banshee."

I gave him a sympathetic look. "Give me a moment. I'll take care of her."

"If you're going to kill her, you shouldn't tell me about it first. I might feel compelled to stop you," he said.

I held back a laugh as I walked into the library. "What is wrong, Cecilia?"

My stepmother jumped up from her chair at my entrance. She was visibly irritated, much like the last time I saw her.

"Your Highness," she hissed in greeting. "You'll have to excuse my trespasses. Priscilla and I have been waiting for some time for our morning tea. But your crippled prison keeper seems to think it's funny to make us wait."

"You should be grateful you're here, and not under Lord Maximillian's watch. He is not a kind host; I have seen the evidence myself." I scowled, thinking of Karl's ragged appearance the night before. He seemed angry and more than humiliated by his forced performance at Potocki's ball. After our encounter last night, I had to wonder if Karl was relieved to be back in his own fortified prison this morning.

"Cruelty is in the eye of the beholder." Cecilia crossed her arms against her chest. "I was not so cruel to you and your brother when I was in charge."

"No, you were much worse, Madame," I assured her, wondering if she'd truly forgotten how she'd treated us.

"I could've turned you out at any time once your father died," she snapped. "Yet I gave you a room and a job."

"Would you like a job, too, Madame? Is that what you're telling me?" I was amused at the thought of her scrubbing the floors or attempting to do the laundry.

"Why, you spiteful child. You should have understood where I was coming from, in my position. I still did my Christian duty."

"Christian duty is nothing without Christian love," I retorted. "And by your logic, you should understand where I am coming from in my position now."

I bit back a sigh. There was no point in reasoning with the unreasonable. Cecilia had been a tyrant in our home, and now, as its displaced ruler, she was upset she was no longer in her seat of privilege and power. To make it worse, she was still unapologetic regarding her past actions, and she had nowhere else to go.

"When this mission is over, I will make sure you are taken care of," I promised. "And Prissy, too."

"You mean to have us murdered?" Cecilia looked shocked.

"What? No." I shook my head. As cruel as she'd been to me, I did not want to be like Cecilia; I didn't want to keep her here and make her suffer, even if I was amused by it. Truth be told, I didn't even want to really see her at all. "No, I meant I'll figure something out for you. I'll see if I can find a place for you to go and live."

I wondered if I could get a small cottage for her, and have Lady POW send her a quarterly allowance through the bank. That way we could both be rid of each other, even if she wouldn't live in the grandeur she'd always wanted.

Or maybe she'll get married again and I won't have to worry about her at all …

THE ORDER OF THE CRYSTAL DAGGERS

I could only hope for that.

"I'll check on Tulia for you." I excused myself.

Ferdy was still waiting for me outside. "I'm glad I didn't have to stop you from killing her," he joked.

"I don't want to kill her," I murmured. I couldn't bring myself to hate her enough to kill her. "I don't know what to do with her, either."

"If you'd like, I can see about getting her a room in my mother's service. She could use another lady-in-waiting."

"I don't know if being kind to Cecilia means I should be unkind to your mother," I said, but the more I thought about it, the more tempting the offer became. "Still, thank you. I appreciate it. Especially since she doesn't deserve it."

"Well, I don't deserve you." Ferdy kissed the back of my hand gallantly. "You are too kind, Ella."

"I'm not always kind." I shook my head. "*Máma* once said it takes more courage to be kind. Cecilia doesn't make me feel very brave, that's for sure."

"Still, you owe her nothing, not even kindness," Ferdy reminded me. "And if you ask me, it means less if kindness is the default and one is incapable of cruelty."

I nodded, grateful for his support. "I'm sure Lady POW can find a way to deal with her. She's still useful to us in that regard."

I was just about to share my cottage idea with him when we rounded the corner, and I ran into Betsy.

"Betsy!" I was happy to see my friend, but I quickly lost my smile when I saw her tear-filled eyes and her quivering lip. "What's wrong?"

"Oh, Nora, it's terrible," Betsy murmured, barely able to speak.

A shiver went down my spine as I suddenly smelled blood in the air. "What happened?"

"It's Tulia. She's hurt, and it's bad," Betsy whispered, and then she ducked her head and cried. Her blonde curls bounced with shame and horror, and as much as I wanted to comfort her, I needed to remain calm myself.

Gently, I put my hands on Betsy's shoulders, trying to project an aura of strength even though I was suddenly terrified.

"Go and rouse Graves," I told her. "He'll know what to do. And if not, he can find Lady Penelope and Mr. Harshad and they'll know what to do."

"Yes, Your Highness," Betsy mumbled, bowing and scrambling down the hall before I could tell her this was not the time to worry about etiquette.

"You should go with her." Ferdy's voice was full of worry as he glanced toward the kitchen.

"No." I pulled out my mother's dagger and shook my head at him. "We work together, remember?"

He said nothing, but I knew he wasn't happy as we walked into the kitchen.

My stomach turned at the sight.

There was a mess of overturned pots scattered on the floor. Bread was thrown all over, while baskets of vegetables and fruits were on their sides, spilling onto the counter.

The only thing in order was a tray of tea, still warm, that was set out and ready to be served—and just below it, on the floor, was Tulia.

Her face was splattered with blood, her gray hair was wild and frazzled—and a large knife was lodged inside her chest, all the way down to the hilt.

"Tulia!" I hurried and kneeled down next to her. Carefully, I cradled her against my legs as I watched, horrified, as her topaz eyes glazed over with tears and approaching death. "What happened?"

I wanted to ask if there had been an accident, but I also knew it was foolish to be so naïve.

I glanced down at Tulia's fingers, which were moving as they spelled out a response.

I killed him.

"You killed him?" I watched as she nodded. "Who? Who are you talking about?"

Your father.

"What?" My mouth dropped open in shock, and I nearly lost my grip on her.

"What did she say?" Ferdy asked, but I ignored him.

She looked up at me, and I couldn't be sure if she was telling me the truth or if she was lost in some hallucination brought on by her injuries.

But she weakly reached up and took hold of my hand.

Forgive me.

I sat there, still and unmoving, watching as blood trickled down her front, and she struggled to breathe.

Nothing was going to stop her from dying now.

Forgive me. Her hand curled in mine; her silent words were sure, and her dying wish was unmistakable.

"Nora."

I looked up as Marguerite came down to kneel by Tulia's other side.

"Marguerite?" My voice was scratchy as my throat constricted with fear—and something beyond fear. She held out a towel and pressed it down gently on Tulia's wound. The cloth was quickly drenched in blood.

"I can't do anything for her," Marguerite whispered sadly. "I don't even think Mr. Qureshi could save her now."

Her words were muffled inside my mind; I could barely process what was happening. My lovely morning with Ferdy had transformed into something beyond surreal, and as I sat there, thinking through all the times Tulia and I had shared as friends, it was impossible to imagine her killing my father.

Tulia weakly poked at me. *Forgive me.*

"Why?" I murmured. "Why did you kill my father?"

"What was that?" Ferdy asked.

But I ignored him, focusing all my attention on Tulia. She was fading fast—but I had to know.

Jakub. I promised Jakub.

"My grandfather?" I frowned in confusion.

The last of the light in her eyes went dim, and Tulia's head slumped over. Her fingers twitched again.

I'm sorry.

I shook my head, crumbling as I began to weep. I took her into my arms and held her, wishing I had more time with her. I wanted to ask her questions, to speak with her, to let her know how I felt, assuming I could even understand how I even felt.

It was all so complicated.

Tulia was my friend, my companion, one of the last links to my mother—but she was a kidnapper, a conspirator, and now a murderer?

How could I mourn for her loss? And yet, how could I not cry at losing her?

"I forgive you." I whispered the words as I held her; I felt her lips smile one last time against my cheek, and then her breathing stopped along with her heartbeat.

And then all I could see were my tears, and all I could feel was my heart screaming in agony.

She was gone.

Ferdy put his arm around me, keeping me warm as Tulia's body went cold.

I didn't know if I truly forgave her, but there was nothing to be done now that she was dead.

"I'm sorry, Ella." Ferdy leaned against me in comfort. "Did you see what happened, Marguerite?"

"There was a commotion, and when I came in here, she was on the floor like this." Marguerite looked down at the floor. "I went to see if Mr. Qureshi had returned. When I couldn't find him, I came back here with a towel. But it was too late."

"Did you see anyone else?" Ferdy asked.

"Some of the maids and cooks," Marguerite said. "They came rushing in here after me, and I told them to leave."

"Thank you," I whispered. My voice was as scraggly as ever, but I was grateful for Marguerite's kindness. Betsy and my other friends had already seen too much horror at the world's hands, and I was glad they'd been spared.

"There was something else," Marguerite said. "As I was heading here, I saw someone dressed all in black turning down the other hallway."

"In black?" Ferdy's voice was full of hidden fear as he squeezed my shoulders.

I barely understood that Tulia's killer might have been my attacker from the bridge.

"Yes. At first, I wasn't sure if what I was seeing was really there, since it's still dark out. But I'm certain I saw someone." Marguerite looked down at Tulia. "Do you think it was really her killer?"

In response to her question, Lady Penelope spoke up from behind us. "We will find out."

All of us turned to see her standing in the doorway. She looked distressed as she came forward. Harshad and Ben were both behind her. I noticed Ben was watching Marguerite with a worried expression on his face; when he saw me looking at him, he frowned.

"What happened?" he asked.

"Tulia killed *Táta*," I blurted out. I knew that wasn't what he'd wanted to know, but I needed to tell him.

Ben looked shocked. "What?"

I couldn't look at him as I spoke. "She told me before … before … "

The last time we had been together, I remembered Tulia insisting that it would be better for me to hate her, and how horror-stricken her face had been when Cecilia accused her of wanting to poison them.

She'd wanted to tell me. But why now?

I still clung to her, unable to discern anything from her chilly flesh. Maybe she supposed I'd find out soon enough and thought I truly would've hated her for her deception. Or maybe after our arguments on the *Salacia*, she might have felt some measure of guilt.

My tears slowed, but my heart ached with fresh pain and betrayal, mixed with the weight of loss and grief. Beside me,

Ben was still and silent, and I was just grateful he and Ferdy were both there for me. Carefully, I moved Tulia off my lap and wiped my eyes with the back of my hand.

Harshad stepped forward. "Was this tea sitting here like this when you arrived, Miss Marguerite?"

"Yes, sir," she answered. "I didn't touch anything when I saw her. I just got the towel, and that's all, I promise."

"The tea is for Cecilia," I said, as Ferdy and Ben both helped me up from my position on the floor. "She's waiting for it in the library with Priscilla."

"There's a note here," Lady Penelope said, picking up a small, folded sheet of paper from under the teapot. "It says the tea was for you, Eleanora. You ordered it."

"No, I didn't." I reached for it, and she gave it to me. I was shocked to see there was indeed a small scribble that resembled my own writing, calling for tea to be sent up to my room. "I didn't write this."

Harshad poured the tea into a cup and sniffed it. After careful examination, he put it down with a somber look. "This tea is poisoned."

"Poisoned?" I looked over at the pots and pans which were overturned. "Tulia was fighting with someone. Maybe she saw the person who did it."

"The man in black," Marguerite whispered. "That has to be who it was."

Which means Tulia was protecting me.

Just then, I was glad I'd forgiven her. Tulia hadn't wanted me and Ben to know of my mother's history with the Order, and she'd objected to Lady Penelope's tutelage—and to be fair, she likely had her reasons against trusting Lady POW to see to our wellbeing.

I still couldn't understand why Tulia had killed my father, forcing me and Ben under Cecilia's care, or lack thereof, but I believed she did her best to look out for us after he died.

As for my grandfather, I couldn't imagine why he would want Tulia to kill my father. Jakub was a Bohemian Loyalist and a member of the League, and he had died a year after *Máma*.

My thoughts circled back to Lumiere. He knew of the Bohemian Loyalists, and if he was the true owner of his pocket watch, he would know why my grandfather would tell Tulia to do such a thing.

We have to find him.

Lumiere could have left to meet up with Louis, to stay with Karl, or even to just run away. But once more, I wanted to find him, and it was mostly for personal reasons.

"This is the Order's poison."

I glanced up in surprise, both at Harshad's hard tone and his words. The rest of us turned to face him, but he only looked to Lady Penelope.

Together, the two of them had another one of their silent conversations, and then Lady Penelope's expression soured.

"Where is Amir?" she asked.

Harshad shook his head, and I immediately objected.

"Amir wouldn't do this," I exclaimed.

Ben nodded. "She's right. Amir and I just came home a little while ago. He wouldn't have had time to do this."

"Go and get him. If he is innocent, I will need him to mix up some more antidote. I don't think we have any more now." She gestured to the pots on the ground, where a small puddle of silvery liquid shimmered against the floor.

"Amir is innocent," I insisted.

Lady Penelope and Harshad exchanged another glance, but neither of them seemed willing to explain anything to me.

"We will talk about this again later, Eleanora," Lady Penelope said. "We have other things to do now. We need to see to Tulia's burial."

She began issuing orders. Ben headed out to get Amir, and Marguerite quickly followed him. As they left, I saw her reach for his hand, and I even saw him let her take it.

I was about to tell him to wait for me, but Ferdy put his hand on my arm.

"It's fine, Ella," Ferdy whispered softly to me, as if he could see what I was thinking. "She really does care for your brother, even if he doesn't believe it, and you don't need to fear being replaced, just as I didn't replace Ben in your eyes."

I still didn't really know what to think about Marguerite and Ben; she was a sweet young lady, and Ben had wanted a unique wife, I remembered, thinking of our conversation months ago.

So why didn't he seem excited that he'd possibly found one? He seemed a little uncertain of his ability to provide for her—but I thought he was even more unwilling to believe he was worthy of her.

When I looked over at Ferdy, I understood how Ben felt.

"We will need more herbs for an antidote," Lady Penelope spoke up a moment later.

"Ferdy and I will get them from Eliezer's wife again," I volunteered, eager to get away from the house. The thought of going back to the Cabal cheered me some, if only a little. "We were going to go out and look for Lumiere anyway."

Lady Penelope looked irritated, but she only nodded. "Let me give you a list before you leave."

As she began scribbling on the back of the fake note, Amir came in, followed closely by Ben.

"You sent for me, Madame?" he inquired, and I saw the grim resolution on his face.

"Yes." Lady Penelope gestured down to Tulia. "Did you do this?"

"Of course he didn't!" I insisted, angry all over again. "Why are you so cruel?"

Amir shook his head. "It's all right."

"No, it's not," I objected. "She can't just accuse you of something like this—"

"Eleanora." Amir's tone was hard but sure. "Lady Penelope and I have worked together for years, long before you entered our lives. Please calm yourself."

"Why?" I pouted. "I'm on your side."

"Should there be a fight, I will only lay down my arms," Amir told me quietly. "But there is no need for fighting, is there, Madame?"

Lady Penelope shook her head. "No. Of course not."

"Then I trust you will forgive Eleanora for her interruption," he said, making me frown further.

"I have never trusted you with my affections, Amir, but I have always trusted you with my life." Lady Penelope gave me a slanted look, and then gestured down to Tulia's corpse. "Did you do this?"

"No." Amir's voice was thick with emotional upheaval, but there was nothing uncertain in his response. I watched as he clasped his hands together, his left hand covering the mark of the *noon* on his right.

The sight of it brought tears to my eyes. Amir really had given up so much for my mother. After breaking away from his family, I had no doubt he was prepared to stand up to Lady Penelope and the Order, too.

"Then you know what this means," Lady Penelope said, looking over at Harshad, and then back to Amir.

Once more, I was excluded from their conversation.

"We will need to take care of the matter at once," Lady Penelope said, her voice uncharacteristically soft.

"You will have to excuse me." Harshad's head fell to his chest. "I do not believe I can assist you in this matter. I would only hinder your work."

"Harshad." Lady Penelope put her hand on his arm. "We all have our weaknesses. You must forgive yourself."

"If only I could." He shook his head again and left.

There was a moment of silence, and then Amir reached for his dagger. "Thank you for saying that, Madame."

"It doesn't matter." She wrinkled her nose. "There's nothing we can do."

"It matters more than you know," Amir said. "I have never forgiven myself for leaving Naděžda; I only wanted her happiness, and I thought leaving was best. But I was wrong. And I can forgive you, Madame, for all your crimes against me, however horrible or slight they might have been, because they are nothing compared to mine against her. There is nothing we can do about the past, but for the present, it is good we acknowledge the truth. And that includes our weaknesses."

Lady POW gave him the slightest nod, before clearing her throat. "Go with Eleanora and Ferdinand and retrieve Lumiere. I will feel much better if he can give us some corresponding proof regarding this development."

"What development?" I asked, but no one answered me.

Instead, Lady POW merely handed me the list of herbs we needed from Zipporah. "After we have Lumiere, we will march on *Vyšehrad* and retrieve Karl, and then use him as bait to find Louis."

She excused herself and I said nothing as she headed out in the same direction as Harshad.

I wanted answers, but no one seemed to care.

Ferdy took my hand. "Are you sure you want to go with me?" he asked.

"Yes." I nodded. "You heard Lady POW. We'll get Lumiere, and then we'll get Karl later tonight."

"Lumi sent me a message last night," Amir said. "I know he is not with Karl or Lord Maximillian."

"I have my lead," Ferdy said. "We'll find him."

"Good," I said. "He's the only one who can tell me why Tulia would kill my father. We can stop at the Cabal on the way back and get the herbs from Eliezer's wife."

"Assuming she has them." Ferdy looked grim. "And assuming we won't run into more trouble along the way."

"There will be more, I'm afraid." Amir looked back over at me apologetically. "There are other, unexpected matters we must attend to now."

"Like what?" I asked.

Amir looked back at the tea set on the counter. "Like finding Nassara's true killer."

19

◊

"Are you sure this is the right place?" Ferdy looked at the Church of Our Lady of the Snows with doubt. "Lumiere seems more suited to gaming hells or clubs or taverns … or brothels."

"The Church of Our Lady of the Snows is where Dr. Artha was killed," Amir reminded us. "And Father Novak, too. Lumiere would know this place."

"That's what the runner meant by 'the church of the light.' There aren't any other places known by that name," I said. "Light" was the code name Lumiere used for himself.

Standing there, I remembered Tulia had her own code name, too—*Míra*, meaning "peace."

At my sudden sadness, I could only hope Tulia truly was at peace. Maybe she was with Dr. Artha now, I mused, before I stopped myself. It was still too hard for me to think about her in the afterlife. Not when I'd seen her body go limp with death only this morning.

"Let's go. There's no reason to stand here." I pulled my bonnet further down over my face and quickly traced a small cross over my heart in prayer—not just for Tulia, but for answers, too.

Despite his insistence that Nassara's killer was on the loose, Amir would not explain himself without proof. He said we would get it when we found Lumiere.

And that wasn't all we would get. My hands tingled with the memory of Tulia's last, silent words to me.

I would get more information about my father's murder, too.

"Well, the runner didn't seem like he was lying," Ferdy said as he took hold of my hand. "If you're both certain."

Walking into the church, I saw it was no less grand to me than it had been the night of Father Novak's murder. The foyer opened into the presbytery, where I turned up my face to see the high vault; its patterned supports zigzagged all across the ceiling, like a puzzling labyrinth.

It stirred hope in my soul that, as complicated and chaotic as life could be, I was secure in my hope that every question had an answer, and all the questions I had would lead me to where I was supposed to be and help me do what I was supposed to do.

The organ music played in the sanctuary as we began to walk through the pews. I saw Amir's smile, and then I recognized the music's tune of "Amazing Grace," John Newton's work. Amir had told me once how he loved music, even though he had grown up believing it to be *haram*, a sinful indulgence.

Suddenly, I was very aware of so much I took for granted.

"Would you like to go pray?" I asked Amir quietly. "Ferdy and I can look around on our own."

I could see the tired gratitude in his eyes as he nodded. "I would like that. Thank you."

As Amir excused himself, I scanned the alcoves, looking for signs of Lumiere's bright, golden locks.

There were scattered sets of people, here and there and all around; some were lighting candles at the front, others were kneeling in the pews; others were simply sitting down, looking up at the majestic altar with varied expressions ranging from listlessness to feigned interest to holy wonder.

It was only when I caught sight of the closed confessionals that I paused. "Huh."

THE ORDER OF THE CRYSTAL DAGGERS

"What is it?" Ferdy asked.

"Lumiere was joking the other day about how he'd wanted Lady POW to capture him," I explained. "I guess he wasn't really joking. But he said he'd stay until he was unable to bear his guilt. Then he would head straight for the nearest monastery to confess his sins. I didn't think he meant it."

Ferdy followed my gaze. "I could try stealing a set of priestly robes."

"I don't think you'll have to. Look." I nudged his hand toward a small area behind the confessionals, where several altar boys and a priest were hauling a swaggering body away from the sanctuary. Even from where we stood, there was a fineness of the cloak and a cleanliness to the boots I knew all too well.

Ferdy and I moved as quickly and quietly as possible. We caught up with them just as they reached the side door.

"Come now, Father," Lumiere's voice was muffled. "I didn't intend to get drunk on the communion wine."

"Where is your self-control, sir? This is the second church you've disgraced yourself in this week," one of the boys said. "I heard Father Bercik at St. Cyril tried to perform an exorcism on you, but I admit I didn't believe it at first."

"Hey, your priests aren't supposed to be sharing my list of sins," Lumiere reprimanded. "I don't care how entertaining I am, nor do I care how boring your life is. I sin for my own pleasure, not yours."

Another altar boy sniggered into his sleeve. "Sorry," he said as the others glared at him. "But I heard he went to *Týnem*, asking for asylum and vowing to dedicate his life to the service of God, and then he got thrown out two days later for poor behavior."

I glanced over at Ferdy. "Should we stop them from tossing him out, or just get him outside?" I whispered.

There was no hesitation in his answer. "Outside."

We enjoyed a quiet laugh before we headed out to retrieve Lumiere's disgraced form. He was on the ground in the alleyway, facedown and defeated, as I came up beside him.

"Lumiere." I shook his shoulder hard as Ferdy kept watch and guarded us.

"*Oui, c'est moi, chérie,*" Lumiere greeted me with a happy, drunken slur. "Are you here for me at last?"

"Yes, unfortunately," I said. "You've been misbehaving again, by the sound of it."

"Did you really do all those things they were talking about in there?" Ferdy asked.

"What? Never!" Lumiere let out a loud hiccup, his expression shocked and horrified, and then he grinned up at me, still playful. "I was at *Tynem* for three days, not two. I counted very carefully, you know. I might enjoy pretending to be mad, but I do so very much want to emulate my Lord and Savior."

I hauled him up into a sitting position. The streets were extra cold, and it spoke to the high degree of Lumiere's torment that he allowed himself to sit neatly on a pile of slush and garbage. "From what I've seen, your messiah is Bacchus, not Jesus."

"Even Bacchus would have approved of Jesus after he turned the water into wine." Lumiere gave me a half-hearted smile, before he sighed dejectedly. "But Christ had no beauty or majesty to attract us to him; there was nothing in his appearance that we should desire him. Seeing as how I am shamefully pure charisma, it's a doomed hope that I should be like him, right from the very beginning."

"Oh, my goodness, Lumiere … " I sighed and rubbed my temples in exasperation.

How could I have missed such a monster?

"Anyway, it's not my fault I got thrown out of the churches," Lumiere muttered. "I couldn't achieve the first requirement of my stay. They set me up for failure."

"What was it? Donning the plain robes of a monk?"

Lumiere shuddered. "Don't even jest about such things, Ella. That's the least funny thing I've ever heard."

"What was it then?"

"As my primary penitence, I had to receive your forgiveness for my great transgression against you."

"What?" I was tempted to laugh, but then I saw the stark, deadly serious look on his face. There were too many ills and inconveniences Lumiere had given me in our short time of acquaintance, and while they were all annoying, there was nothing I could imagine that would cause him such misery. "You're serious?"

"I am." His green eyes were blurred over, but the thought behind them was as sharp and clear as ever. "Do you know how it feels to wish so badly to be someone the opposite of yourself?"

I watched him carefully, unsure if I should say anything at all. And when I didn't reply, he waved me away.

"Of course you don't," he said, taking my hand before I could scoot away from him. "You're just like Naděžda, really. She was funny and smart and effortlessly lovely."

"She had her flaws, too."

"She certainly did." He drew up his knees to his chin and curled his arms around himself protectively. He looked like a small, princely child, sitting on his throne of garbage. "I told her not to go, you know."

"Go where?"

"To London. To see Lady Penelope and Amir again." He watched me as I felt my breathing grow shallow. "It's my fault she died."

At first, I could only hope he was joking. But I saw Lumiere's face—his proud, haughty, luminous face. In place of his usual effervescence and vitality, I only saw repentant despair.

Shock rushed through me first, followed quickly by anger. "What are you talking about?"

"The poison," he finally said. "I was the one who told her she'd been poisoned. I found out my father had made the arrangements. When I came to visit her and your grandfather, she confessed about Nassara—and I wasn't expecting it at all, and then, of course, it's no easy thing, to get a woman to open up about her sadness. Why women like to believe their suffering will go away if they just ignore it, I'll never—"

"Lumiere!" I snapped, practically strangling him. "Are you telling me that you killed my mother?"

"Ella? Are you all right?" Ferdy asked, inching closer to us.

Lumiere and I both ignored him, even though I was grateful for his presence. He would stop me from doing anything too drastic.

And as good as it might have felt, I did not want to kill Lumiere.

Not yet, anyway.

"What? No, never." Lumiere shook his head fiercely, his hair flinging out in a thrashing wave of blonde. "*Non, chérie.* I loved her dearly. She was my sister in all but blood. I used to imagine she really was, you know, even if it meant Pepé was my mother. But I so loved her and Jakub that I could pretend even that … my father was just as awful as you might've guessed, and … "

"How did you find out she was poisoned?" I asked slowly.

"My father and your grandmother were fighting over Europe's favorite art collection when your mother was pregnant with Nassara."

"I heard about that," I said. That was the mission Lady POW had told me my mother caused her to lose to Louis.

"Yes, well, you probably didn't know your grandmother was very close to winning," Lumiere said. "And that it would have been the end of him. So he did something very naughty—and very shocking, even for him."

He looked up at me, and then at my stomach. He shook his head, and a knot of pain twisted inside me.

Louis knew about Nassara—and he killed her.

"He didn't do it himself, of course; he found an accomplice to give her the poison. I wasn't around to stop him; I didn't even learn of it until much later, after Naděžda told me what had happened and I asked *mon père* about it." Lumiere scowled. "He was quite proud of it by then."

"Where were you when … ?" I didn't finish the question. I could barely speak. Even Lumiere was having trouble telling me what happened.

"I was … rather indisposed, if you must know."

"In prison?" My brow furrowed in impatience.

"That's one way to describe Ireland." Lumiere snorted disdainfully. "I suppose that's the other reason you irritate me at times—all that Catholicism. Protestants won't pay money to assuage their consciences, so they channel their guilt into evangelizing. But Catholics pay their indulgences and gain interest in guilting others. It's one thing to convince a man of his need for the Lord Jesus and his sacrifice, and then it's another to constantly remind him of his sin."

"Please, Lumiere, we don't have time to go through any catechisms." All over again, I was realizing how much he just wanted attention, and I hated him for it. We had just been reunited and already I wanted to scream in frustration, and for more than one reason, too. "Tell me why I should forgive you."

"You shouldn't." Lumiere laughed all of a sudden. "There is never a right time for conversations such as this, Ella, no matter where life finds us."

Ferdy sat down beside me, and without saying a word, he took hold of my other hand. At his touch, I remembered Tulia.

"Tulia's dead," I said.

"Oh." Lumiere didn't seem surprised to hear of her death.

"You didn't do it, did you? Someone spotted a man dressed all in black at the manor," Ferdy said.

"No, it wasn't me," Lumiere replied glumly. "I adore black, but it's far too colorless for me to enjoy wearing it. Especially if it's the only color." He glanced down at his ermine-lined crimson cloak, his bright leather shoes, and his gold-embroidered jacket, before he grimaced. "But I've instructed several of my henchmen to wear it, as has my father. Of course, that just means I shouldn't wear it all the more. I'm not the help, after all; I'm the second-in-command."

I ignored his narcissistic rambling. "I can't see you using a knife, either. You killed Alex without a qualm back on the *Salacia*, but you used a gun then."

"Yes, well, the bastard deserved it from all the rumors I'd heard," Lumiere said. "And Tulia deserved to die, too. I told you so myself, though I can see you're not happy about it."

"No. Of course not." I swallowed hard. "She told me she killed my father."

"She told you?" Lumiere huffed. "Well, I lost that bet. At least she's dead and I don't have to pay her now."

"You knew? Why did she do it?" I held my breath, unsure of how I would feel about his answer. "Tell me."

"He deserved it, really, that's why."

"Lumiere!"

"Calm down, Ella. Adolf was not fond of me, and I didn't like him—God, I hated him, if truth be told; he was a poor substitute for Amir, who is still a prince among men."

My jaw clenched with impatience. I should've known he would enjoy taking as long as possible with his story. "Tulia said she killed him because of my grandfather."

"Yes." Lumiere sighed. "You see, Jakub was a good and honorable man. His only defect in the League was that he was a very loyal Bohemian. When Naděžda returned to Prague in 1847, and met her Dolf again—"

"Again?"

"They met before in Constantinople," Lumiere explained quickly. "Naděžda flirted with him for information, and he was easily besotted. When they met again, he proposed, and since he was one of King Ferdinand V's closest advisors, she accepted for the sake of the mission."

I frowned. It was hard to think of my mother as a practiced flirt; I also didn't like how pragmatically she'd agreed to marriage to my father. The thought left a bad taste in my mouth.

"Then my mother got pregnant with Karl," Ferdy said.

"And soon enough, Naděžda got pregnant, too," Lumiere agreed. "At Jakub's prodding, she resigned from the Order, but Adolf didn't know about her past."

"I see," I said. My mother had grown to love my father after they married, and then he'd grown to resent her after she died.

Lumiere's drunkenness began to wane. "When she told me about Nassara, Naděžda wondered aloud if she'd been poisoned. She'd sought answers and sent out letters to Pepé, in hopes she would come here to Prague. Your grandmother predictably refused, even though she sent money and anything else asked of her. Naděžda planned to tell her about you and Benedict when everything was settled."

"But *Máma* went to see her after you told her the truth about Nassara's death." I slumped over. "And then her ship was lost at sea."

"Afterward, your grandfather asked Tulia and me to make sure that Adolf never learned about the Order."

"But my father did find out." I thought about my dream, the one where I'd remembered how my father was learning Arabic.

Lumiere nodded. "Yes, so it appears. And then because of his carelessness, Max found out about Karl, and so here we are. Tulia was right to kill him before he made it worse."

"Lumiere." I shook my head. "That's not fair of you to say."

"What kind of person would I be if I didn't say it anyway? Don't be like that, Ella. You know life is not fair, and there's no use pretending niceties and euphemisms somehow make it easier." Lumiere's head sank even further against his chest. "Jakub died less than a year after your mother. He was

263

devastated at her loss, you know. And so was I. Just like you, I lost my family—or at least, the one of my own choosing.”

We sat there, surrounded by snow and garbage, with the echo of church hymns and liturgies. Ferdy held onto me, and I even held Lumiere's hand tightly in reluctant solidarity and sympathy.

A few moments passed before Lumiere brightened a little and nudged Ferdy's shoulder companionably. “The former empress liked the promise that Adolf—and Naděžda herself—would protect her family, but she hid her second pregnancy even more than the first.”

“How did you find out, then?” Ferdy asked. “You knew about it before we were even introduced.”

“If you haven't noticed, I have a way with getting information from various sources, including priests and other clergymen,” Lumiere said, nodding back towards the closed church doors behind us. “They remember my antics more than my questions, and since I am an egregious sinner beyond repair, they frequently forget about me if I am quiet enough.”

He laughed, but it was hollow and dry, reminding me of how cold I felt.

I didn't know what I could really do for him, any more than I really knew what to do with him. Lumiere was a strange man, shameless but full of guilt, a victim as much as a victimizer, and as fake as he was genuine, trapped in a world in which he imagined himself free.

Perhaps that was the reason he'd found such a refuge in my mother's friendship; they were the same.

Wordlessly, I could only pray.

Many times in my life, I had prayed for a sign or a specific outcome; I had been certain of what I'd wanted, and I'd asked for it with the childlike faith that confounds the adult.

THE ORDER OF THE CRYSTAL DAGGERS

I'd had moments when the heavenly bowers went silent, and my faith seemed to waver. But I also knew that there were times when no such sign was warranted at all; I did not need a sign or a specific answer to know what to do.

And right now, I had to be brave, I had to be kind, and I had to be steady. My mother wasn't here, but I knew she did not want Lumiere to carry the burden of a sin he was only guilty of covering up, not of committing.

"I forgive you," I said. The words still felt harsh and foreign as I said them for the second time that day, to a person I didn't truly know if I could just simply forgive. Lumiere was another soul I would have to forgive again and again, perhaps on a daily basis, until the habit was woven into the very fabric of my soul.

Lumiere crumpled. "I need a drink."

At that moment, I knew it was time to leave. Together, Ferdy and I hauled Lumiere to his feet; he seemed more stable as we walked.

"We've got to head to the Cabal first," Ferdy reminded me. "Lady Penelope wants more herbs for the antidote."

I nodded in agreement. "Perhaps Clavan can get Lumiere settled, too."

My heart, nestled inside its crater of fear and grief, cheered a little as Lumiere began to fume over his dirty clothes. I envied his self-concern; it was as admirable in its breadth as much as it was lamentable in its depth. But he didn't seem to let the past bother him.

Well, but then it wouldn't, I thought. He'd just settled it with me. He'd gotten what he wanted—perhaps even what he needed.

Lumiere brightened as Amir came outside to meet us, and even raced to hug him. I smiled as Amir made no objection at

Lumiere's show of friendship, even if another wave of weariness took hold of me.

"Ella?" Ferdy took hold of my hand again. "Are you able to keep going?"

"We have no choice. But I can do it."

He pressed a kiss on my cheek. "There is no need for you to do so alone."

More than gratefully, I clung to him.

Lumiere and Amir talked companionably as we made our way through the city toward the *Josefkà*. Ferdy and I followed them, keeping a close watch. Now that we'd found Lumiere again, I was determined that we weren't going to let him get away.

We were almost to the Cabal when they stopped short, and Ferdy and I came to a quick halt behind them.

"What is it?" I asked.

"What else would it be, *chérie?*" Lumiere pointed ahead. "Trouble."

That was when I heard glass breaking and tasted a whisper of smoke on the wind.

The Cabal was under attack.

THE ORDER OF THE CRYSTAL DAGGERS

20

◊

"Ella." Ferdy clutched my hand even more firmly, and I couldn't say whether it was to steady me or hold me back.

A sadistic, musical barrage of destruction emitted from the small publican house as flames appeared and smoke poured out of the roof.

"Ugh," Lumiere groaned. "Look. Here comes even more trouble."

I followed his gaze up the street, surprised to see Lady Penelope climbing down from her carriage. Ben quickly jumped down from the top box, and even Marguerite followed after him.

"Why did they come?" Amir asked Lumiere, who only grimaced.

Another crackle of broken glass made me look back to the Cabal. My fear grew, but I could no longer stand around and do nothing.

Amir and Lumiere could worry about the others, I decided. I headed into the building as Ferdy followed close behind me.

A small group of annoyed patrons filed past us as we entered, with several of them still carrying their mugs.

Behind me, I could hear Lady Penelope calling for me, but I ignored her.

"Faye!" I yelled into the emptying pub, desperate to locate my friends. I pushed my bonnet back, letting it fall to the floor as I called out again. "Jarl? Mr. Clavan?"

"Let's check in the back," Ferdy suggested, as he pulled me into the kitchen.

"Faye?" I called again, much more hesitantly this time. "Mr. Clavan?"

"Back here. This way." Ferdy said as he headed toward the back room and the street exit. I followed after him closely, my eyes already stinging at the clouds of smoke as a new dread settled inside me.

Are Karl and Lord Maximillian behind this?

They didn't know about Ferdy's trips here, or our friends, or how I enjoyed my visits. Lumiere was the only one outside the Order's circle who knew about the Cabal, and he'd been terrorizing churches for the past several days.

I frowned. There was nothing I could think of that would point them to this place, and that only made me more confused and angry.

Then I saw Clavan kneeling on the floor, a line of blood dripping down his forehead. He was holding onto Helen, who was unconscious.

"Mr. Clavan." I saw he had another array of cuts on one of his arms, and his shirt was torn at the elbow. "What happened?"

"Never mind that," Clavan said, looking down at his wife. "We need to get her out of here."

Ferdy knelt down on the other side of Helen's unconscious form and carefully looped her arm around his neck.

"She's bleeding," I said, noticing the blood pooling from the back of her head.

"We can take care of it outside," Ferdy said, but I was already pulling out my dagger and cutting strips from the bottom of my dress.

"Here." I handed them to Clavan.

At first, he didn't take them; he was staring at my dagger with an intrigued wariness on his face.

"It seems you have quite the adventurous life, Ella," he said, as he finally took the cloth from my hand. "Especially if you are truly a member of the Order of the Crystal Daggers."

For some reason, I felt flustered. His observation was without admiration, nor condemnation; it was a fact, and from the way he spoke, it was a foreboding one.

I looked to Ferdy, who turned away from me, and I decided we would have to worry about it later.

"Where's Faye?" I asked.

"Faye went upstairs," Clavan said. "To get her dress."

It took me a second to remember Faye's wedding, and then I bit down on my cheek. She'd been so happy, looking forward to it, and I didn't want to think how the Cabal could burn down.

But for the safety of everyone involved, I had to face the reality that it was possible.

While Ferdy helped Clavan carefully arrange Helen's body across his back, I watched the smoke build up. I relaxed only in the slightest to see it was burning white; I knew from Ben that the dynamite concoction at the Potocki mansion would burn black.

Faye suddenly appeared at the bottom of the stairs, carrying her copy of *Jane Eyre* and a large ball of fabric that could only be her wedding dress.

"I'm here," she said, and despite the danger, she gave me a smile. There was a grim, resigned quality to it, but Faye was still hopeful and determined; she had the best of her father as well as the loveliness and grace of her mother.

Helen was finally secure in Clavan's arms. Thanks to Ferdy's help, his wound wasn't being further exasperated, and we were ready to leave.

We headed for the back door—only to see it was blocked.

Not by the fire, but by a figure, all dressed in black.

A hood covered his face, but I still felt the shock of recognition.

I felt the blood drain from my face. "You're the one who pushed me off the bridge."

There was no reply from under the hood. Instead, his hands only moved to a fighting position.

I gripped my dagger and swallowed hard. "You killed Tulia, too, didn't you?"

No response.

"Ella." Ferdy's whisper was one of fear and warning.

But I shook my head. "Get them out of the building. Use the side door up front. I'll take care of this."

My voice sounded unusually calm, even though I was terrified.

Ferdy shook his head. "No."

"Yes," I insisted. "I'm trained for this. And I have to protect you."

I thought back to that night at the port, where I'd told him before that I wouldn't die for a prince, but I would die for him.

The time had come for me to prove myself.

In the end, Ferdy gave in. There was no way for him to stop me without letting go of Helen, and neither of us wanted our friends to be harmed.

"Fine," he said. "But I'll come back for you."

"Be careful," Faye whispered as they left.

I was about to promise her I would be quick as well as careful, but the figure in black was already lunging forward. His first attack lashed out with lightning speed, right at my chest.

I only just managed to dodge it, and rebound into a defensive stance.

And then the battle truly began.

Our movements were swift, but familiar. I was grateful for this; it allowed me to be more prepared than I'd expected.

Dodging another blow, I slipped under his arm and shoved into his chest this time, crying out as I slammed the full weight of my body into his. He fell back into the door, and I landed a left hook on his face. Despite the circumstance, I was thankful I'd cut off a portion of my skirts for Helen's injuries; I was able to move much more freely without their full length, and even though I was still at a disadvantage, I'd been practicing enough to know I could win.

We battled with each other's punches in a synchronized harmony as the smoke worsened, and my eyes grew wet with grief, fear, and determination.

It was too easy to block out the rest of the world in those moments; perhaps it was the real sense of danger, or maybe it was how I wanted to protect Ferdy and my friends, or it could have even been my grief over Tulia's loss.

But no matter what it was, I kept my eyes on my enemy, and I set my heart on victory.

Finally, I grappled with his arm, yanked it close to me, and pulled him down to the floor as I slashed out with my dagger. I shouted in horrified triumph as the blade struck true and drew blood as it sliced through his shoulder.

The smallest gasp of surprise sounded out from underneath the hood. I pulled back briefly, struggling with an unbelievable thought as I stood there, struck by the sudden familiarity.

Is it possible … ?

The figure suddenly pushed me back hard, grabbing my dagger and forcing it out my hand. Another kick landed on my chest, sending me flying into the wall by the stairs. The last of my breath flew out of my lungs.

I couldn't stop staring at my attacker—even as my own dagger was turned against me and thrust toward my face with headlong speed.

Finally, I shut my eyes, unable to do anything else.

Only to hear a familiar *clash*—the sound of metal scraping against metal.

My heart was pounding as I looked up at my rescuer.

"Amir." I gasped, feeling winded and beyond relieved that he'd saved me again.

Amir didn't appear to hear me. His *Wahabite Jambiya* glimmered as it held back my own dagger's deadly blade.

"That's enough," Amir said quietly. "You can stop now, Xiana."

"Xiana?" I looked back at the figure in black, and the earlier dread I'd felt flashed through me again.

It couldn't really be Xiana … could it?

A long moment passed as the hooded figure stepped from us, staying back out of reach, outlined by rising flames and flowing smoke.

And then, in a graceful, sweeping move, the hood came down, and Xiana stood before us in silence. Through the smoke, her eyes spoke of hatred and anger and shame.

What had been unthinkable was suddenly inevitably true.

"Why?" I wailed, unable to understand it and unwilling to believe it. "Why did you do this?"

"She was manipulated into doing it," Amir said. "She tried to poison you earlier, and then she was forced to kill Tulia."

"You are wrong." Xiana scowled at him. Her voice sounded hoarse as she spoke, and she turned her blazing eyes on me. "I sought to kill Eleanora on my own. Louis said her death would not affect Madame quite as much as he'd hoped, so he would allow it."

"Louis?" I blinked. "You're working with Louis?"

And then I shook my head.

Of course she is.

Lumiere had told me earlier that Louis had poisoned my mother with the help of an accomplice. And Xiana had seen *Máma* take it firsthand—though my mother hadn't known herself.

"Xiana." Amir shook his head. "No matter what has happened, Nassara did not deserve death by your hand, and neither does Eleanora."

He knows.

Amir had finally found out the truth of Nassara's death, and I could only envy his calm composure at the news.

"And did I deserve such anguish by your own hand?" Xiana's uncharacteristic cry was as jarring as her sudden bloodlust. She lunged at him again, still armed with my dagger.

Amir expertly parried his weapon against my mother's blade. "Suffering in this world is unavoidable, Xiana. We may experience it differently, but we are all able to decide to inflict it on others or not."

"Then what is your choice now, Amir?" Xiana glared up at him. "Will you inflict even more suffering on me?"

"I will not allow you to hurt Eleanora," he said firmly. "But you've already hurt yourself more than I ever could. You've killed my daughter, broke my wife's trust, and worked against your friends by siding with the enemy. As much as I've lost, you've lost even more. You might have felt alone before, but now you are more alone than you've ever been."

His voice was breaking as he finished, and my tears began to fall at the sadness he carried.

"In truth, I pity you—for you truly do not know what you've done, or even what you are doing now." Amir shook his head. "I will pity you even more if you really believe there's no hope for forgiveness and reconciliation."

Amir was struggling to speak now, and she pulled back from him.

"I do not want you to forgive me," Xiana growled as she resumed her fighting stance. "I only want you to suffer now. It is too late for us to reconcile."

Amir stood his ground, and I could only watch.

But I barely blinked, and then Amir grabbed her arm, hit her hand with his knee, and freed my mother's dagger from her grasp. After he shoved her backward, he nudged the dagger back in my direction.

"Go see Lady Penelope," he ordered, his *Wahabite Jambiya* ready as Xiana pulled out her *jian* from the hidden sheath on her back.

"Are you certain?" I whispered, suddenly feeling sick as I inched back toward the front room.

"Yes." He gave me the briefest smile. "Thank you, Eleanora."

My heart had been pounding nearly the entire time I'd been at the Cabal, but as I grabbed my dagger and slid past Amir, I felt it stop, and then fall into despair.

21

◊

Guilt hounded me as I hurried back to the front of the Cabal.

I did not want to leave Amir. He'd told me before Xiana was hard to defeat. She'd seemed angrier and more emotional than ever, and I could only hope Amir would find a way to overcome her.

I tucked my mother's dagger back into its sheath, and wiped my eyes.

The menacing fire slowly filled the publican house. The place was empty like a tomb as I stood there.

Suddenly, I realized Ferdy hadn't come back to find me, and my dread increased exponentially.

Where was he?

"Ferdy?" I called. "Faye? Mr. Clavan?"

A soft, familiar voice spoke up from behind me.

"Everyone is preoccupied at the moment, and it is no coincidence they are busy. But I'd be happy to help you if I can, Madame."

I whirled around to see an old man sitting at a table near the door. He was calmly sipping at a teacup, as though he was used to surrounding himself with chaos.

At once, I recognized him. With his pristine white hair, his cloak, with the University patch on the side, it was the old man from the bridge.

I wasn't sure why I felt nervous. I swallowed hard. "What are you doing here?"

"Enjoying a nice cup of tea." His voice was easy and light, and he seemed amused by my concern. "My dormitory is well furnished, but the tea here has always been unmatched in my esteem."

Lady Penelope suddenly burst through the door.

"Eleanora." Lady Penelope was more than capable of ignoring the condition of the Cabal as she glared at me. "I've been waiting for you outside."

"Lady Penelope." My mouth felt dry as I forced myself to speak. I was about to warn her about Amir and Xiana when she handed me a paper.

I looked down to see it was the sketch from the old man— the same old man who sat before us now, surrounded by oncoming death and destruction, as calmly as though he was on holiday by the sea.

"Where did you get this? Tell me," Lady Penelope demanded.

"Where else would she have gotten it, Pepé?" The old man shifted in his seat behind us, clearly pleased. "She got it from me."

Lady Penelope turned toward him with a bitter look on her face. "So, you have arrived."

I examined the paper again. At the corner on the front, just under the drawing, there was a small name scribbled—small enough I'd missed it, and large enough I shouldn't have ignored it.

L. Valoris.

It was then I understood.

"I've been here for some time now, Pepé." Louis Valoris chuckled as he stirred his tea with a spoon. "I do believe it is time we were formally introduced, Lady Eleanora."

THE ORDER OF THE CRYSTAL DAGGERS

"It's you," I whispered, shaking my head in shame.

"I must say, you look so much like your mother. Even in the moonlight, I could've sworn you were her ghost, the first time I saw you for myself."

"Eleanora." Lady Penelope gave me a deadly scowl.

I gave her an apologetic look, but I knew it wouldn't do any good. She'd warned me before Louis was crafty and full of cunning, and I'd been completely caught off guard.

"I must commend you on her progress, Pepé," Louis continued. "But she's still very naïve, and that's dangerous, especially for one who carries the weapon of the Order. How do you know she won't betray you when she learns all your secrets?"

"Eleanora is a loyal member of the Order," Lady Penelope said, her voice full of resignation instead of pride. "She will not betray me."

"Oh, that's a shame. It would be nice to see her live up to her mother's legacy."

At his disparaging tone, a heady, hateful fury rocked me to my core. Lumiere had told me less than an hour ago how Louis had a hand in poisoning my mother and killing Nassara—and now I knew he'd used Xiana to carry out his plans.

"The dead deserve some respect, Louis." Lady Penelope put a hand on my shoulder, as though she knew I'd wanted to attack him. "I'd rather talk of the present, now that we've come to our final rendezvous."

She let me go to pull out her own violet-colored dagger in one hand and a pistol in the other.

"I regret to inform you that this is not our last reunion," Louis said calmly. "I merely stopped by because I was invited."

He looked to me again and winked. Shame sliced through me.

"There is nothing to stop me from killing you, even if it's not in your plans." Lady Penelope cocked her gun at him, and I pulled out my dagger, too.

"Oh, I wouldn't say that. I do have my contingencies." His green eyes glimmered spitefully in the growing firelight. "After all, Maximillian Chotek is eager for his bloodline to reclaim the Bohemian throne. There's no telling how long Prince Karl will last if I am not there to stop the Duke from disposing of him."

"You wouldn't kill Karl," I said, suddenly feeling as naïve as he'd asserted earlier.

Louis laughed. "As it happens, I prefer he remains alive. For now."

"Do you actually believe he will be king of Bohemia one day?" I asked. "The people will not accept him."

"We'll worry about that if we need to," Louis assured me. "Either way, it's best for him if you leave me alive this time, Pepé. Put the gun down."

I didn't know how much he was bluffing, but I looked back to Lady POW with pleading eyes. As upset as I was at Louis, I still needed to return Karl to his mother.

"Please," I whispered softly.

Lady Penelope scowled at me with a ferocity I'd never seen as her finger slipped back from the trigger ever so slightly.

It was the smallest act of surrender she would give.

"You never had any respect for national sovereignty," Lady Penelope said, turning her attention back to Louis. "I can't imagine why you would start now."

"Change is part of life, my dear Penelope," he replied, giving her name a caressing French accent. "And conflict is as inevitable as change. Look around—conflict is already here, *n'est-ce pas?*"

"Only because of you."

"I have helped it along a little, yes." He beamed with pride. "But it is a *good* thing. The world is getting smaller, and as it shrinks, it grows weaker. Look at the Hapsburgs; scattered throughout European royalty, yet all of them are weak. They've been made soft by traditions they no longer understand, strangled by the bureaucracy they'd imagined would make life easier. How can they fight for their own slow, inevitable suicide? It's better for the world to tear down the weakened institutions of the past."

He gestured around us, as the fire and smoke muted the air, proud of his handiwork, and happier still to show it off.

"I didn't want to believe you're this intent on sending the continent into war," Lady Penelope said. "You're even more foolish than I'd thought. Perhaps you are getting senile in your old age."

"I'm not senile; you're just shortsighted," Louis replied. "My plan will send the world around us into the fire of war, perhaps—but a new, stronger, better empire can be reborn in its ashes."

I glanced nervously at Lady Penelope; Louis wasn't exactly wrong or delusional, even if he was dangerous—and just like before on the bridge, I couldn't articulate my disagreement with him.

"You might be right, but you are also wrong," Lady Penelope said. "It's true our leaders are weak. But tearing down corruption only works when corruption is complete; we need to repair and build up the good."

"How can it be good when the foundations are imperfect?" Louis shook his head. "You waste time on repairs and rebuilding. A new beginning is much more efficient."

"Patience has its place, and its reward. Anything worth having requires time," Lady Penelope countered. "Recklessness like yours will lead to war, and despite what you believe, war throughout Europe will not reinvigorate the nations. It would only destroy the people and their spirit."

"Have you seen these people in question, Pepé? How many of them are content to be loathsome quislings, proud of their narcissism and ignorance, or boasting of their worldly incompetence and meaningless arrogance? Even Queen Victoria herself vaunts her pitiful failures and her deference to her advisors—men who are beholden to their egos and purse strings more than national pride." Louis sniffed, disgusted at the thought. "Such specimens are better off in the grave. It is no wonder that empires and their foundations are rotting. The Order would not disagree with me, given its own darker histories."

Lady Penelope shook her head. "The Order is called to protect and preserve our rulers—yes, sometimes at the cost of human life. But we seek a better future. We don't burn everything to the ground."

She glanced around at the Cabal as it continued to fill with smoke and flames, giving him a pointed look.

But Louis only shrugged.

"You're still standing here," he replied easily enough as he stood up from his chair. "And you've allowed your family and allies to remain inside here, too. You can't be too worried."

I couldn't speak for Lady POW, but I was certainly nervous. I was just about to suggest we move out of the burning building and let Louis leave when I heard Ferdy call for me.

"Ella!"

His voice made me feel both more alive and more sick than ever. I felt even worse as Louis sneered at me with sinister pleasure.

"Are you going to ignore a cry from your prince, Lady Eleanora?" he asked me. "He's always been good to you, from what I've heard. When he lies to you, it's only because he loves you, and he wants to protect you from the pain of the truth."

"Leave him alone," I snapped, determined not to allow him to intimidate me over Ferdy. My throat was getting sore from the smoke, but I held firm. "He's fine outside with the others."

"Are you certain?"

The confident amusement in his voice sent another wave of nausea through me.

"Eleanora, get away from him." Lady Penelope took a step forward and raised her gun again. I could hear the soft *click* of a new bullet entering its chamber.

"There's no need for that. I don't intend to stay for much longer," Louis said, gesturing toward the smoke rising out of the kitchen. "I have what I came for."

"Oh? And what is that, exactly?" Lady Penelope asked.

Louis was against the far wall, and there was no room for him to make his escape; the pistol in Lady Penelope's hand remained unwavering, and her own dagger still gleamed with malicious intent.

"*Moi,* of course," Lumiere said as he walked inside, with Ferdy just behind him. We all turned to look at them, and I was shocked to see Ferdy shaking with anger.

I didn't understand. "Ferdy, what—"

And then Louis caught me from behind.

His arm suddenly clutched around my neck, choking me with more strength than I'd thought possible for a man his age. I dropped my dagger in surprise, and I heard Lady Penelope and Ferdy both yell in anger before Lumiere fired his gun.

The bullet shot into the ceiling—a warning shot. He did not look happy as I watched him.

Louis scoffed. "I never appreciate your late entrances, Lumiere, but at least they are predictable these days."

"Ella!" Ferdy reached for me, but Lumiere caught him by the neck.

"Now, now, that's not what we agreed, *mon ami*," Lumiere admonished him, as he put his still-smoking gun to Ferdy's forehead.

"Lumiere, stop," Ferdy snapped, wrestling against him.

"Come now." Lumiere held onto him firmly. "Be a good little prince as I deliver you to my father. Just as I promised I would."

And then I realized Louis had me, while Lumiere had Ferdy. Lady Penelope was caught in the middle, unable to do anything.

Louis knew our weaknesses.

"I'm disappointed, *chérie*." Lumiere looked back at me with an arrogant sneer. "It was too pitifully easy to let you think I was your captive."

Panic threatened me like never before, and I thrashed with anger and fear. I struggled to breathe as Louis tightened his grip on my neck. Pain laced through my head and spots began to appear before my eyes.

THE ORDER OF THE CRYSTAL DAGGERS

"Ferdy." I gasped out his name, feeling more helpless than ever.

"Is this necessary, Lumiere?" Lady Penelope asked, scowling at him as she put down her pistol.

"What do you think?" Lumiere squealed with delight. "After all these weeks of torment, you are finally getting your comeuppance, Pepé! *Mon père* wanted both princes, and now he'll get them, thanks to my undying loyalty and selflessness."

No.

My heart was weak, and my mind was muddled, but I continued to fight against Louis' hold with renewed anger and desperation. I looked down at my dagger powerlessly, as it lay on the floor in front of me.

"It's been a pleasure, my dear Penelope," Louis purred. "But don't fear. We will meet again. I always enjoy watching you fail."

"Why not just kill me now and be done with it, then?" Lady Penelope arched her brow, practically daring him to do it.

"I might be a monster, but I'm a very organized one," he said. "And your part in my play is not over yet. But don't worry. It's worth the delay. Patience has its own reward."

He pressed harder around my throat, unleashing pain down my spine. I yelped with pain as Ferdy struggled against Lumiere again.

"Please, stop," Ferdy pleaded. "You can have me. Just let Ella go."

"You're already my prisoner," Louis told him. "I knew I would be able to get you if I had her. By all accounts, you've been quite smitten with your princess for years now."

"Hard to blame him," Lumiere said. "Eleanora is very much her mother's daughter."

"It would be a shame for you to see her die, young prince." Louis tightened his grip on me again; the bones in my neck crackled in warning. "What do you say, Penelope? Let us go, and you'll have your Eleanora back, and before I break her neck. I might be old, but I've still got a few tricks left."

Before I could hear Lady Penelope's response, my body went limp; I fell forward as the world spun, before dissolving into an ocean of gray spots and swirling colors.

Louis' grip on me lessened as I rested inside the whirlwind, as everything spun out of control and into chaos.

But I heard the click of a trigger, and blood rushed back into my head. As everything began to return to normal, I saw Lady Penelope was pulling me up from the floor.

"What happened?" I coughed as my throat stung with smoke and pain.

"Oh, Eleanora," Lady Penelope murmured. "I told you marrying him wasn't a good idea."

I didn't know if she was insulting me intentionally or not, but I pushed back against her. I rubbed my neck, massaging it, as I slowly looked toward the door.

"Ferdy." My voice croaked as I said his name.

"We have to let him go for now." Lady Penelope grabbed my arm as my balance faltered. "I promise you, Eleanora, I hate to see Louis win as much as you do."

Through the smoky windows, I watched Louis step in front of two carriages. Lumiere and Ferdy climbed into the one in front, while Louis headed for the other one.

"Wait!" Tears stung my eyes as I ran outside.

I was still weak and disoriented from nearly being strangled, and I couldn't let him win.

I could not let him hurt my family.

THE ORDER OF THE CRYSTAL DAGGERS

Not again.

"Ferdy!" I raced to reach him, nearly slipping, still too dizzy and out of breath to run properly. I ended up clinging to Ben, who was suddenly at my side, helping me stay on my feet.

"What's wrong, Ella?" Ben asked, but I ignored him as Louis nodded his head to me.

"It was lovely meeting you, but I've got to get back to Karl now, before he's killed," Louis said as he climbed up into the carriage. "You remind me so much of your mother, Lady Eleanora."

"Why, you bastard!" I balled my fists as Lady Penelope held me back. "I'll kill you!"

"Still, you have my thanks." Louis only laughed. "And in more ways than one. You know, Naděžda was sent to kill King Ferdinand V during the Revolution. It's fitting that you would be the one who delivered his last heir to me."

"Excuse me?" I stopped fighting against Lady Penelope as shock overwhelmed even my hate and grief. "What?"

"Your mother was sent by the Order to kill the king," Louis repeated. "Isn't fate just so amusing—and just so cruel? Call me a perfectionist, but I do love to see a job finished, even if it has been grossly delayed and mismanaged."

My mind scrambled to make sense of his words.

But all I could think of was Ferdy telling me the Order was full of assassins; Karl asserting the Order wanted his father dead; and I even recalled the look Clavan had given me after seeing my weapon, just moments ago.

And as I looked up at Lady Penelope for her denial, another memory stirred again—Lady Penelope telling me about my mother's last mission in Prague.

"Your father was part of her last assignment," Lady Penelope said. "She was supposed to come down here with some others and take care of King Ferdinand V during the Revolution of 1848."

"Take care of … " I said the words aloud—the same group of words I'd heard *Táta* use as he joked with my mother about Jakub murdering Lumiere.

"Oh, Eleanora." Lady Penelope sighed.

That was the moment I knew that Louis was right.

There was no denial coming.

I closed my eyes, stunned and betrayed—stupefied and unable to live with the truth.

"Ella." Ferdy called out to me as the carriages rolled away, but I only shook my head. I couldn't face him.

Not when he'd been right about the Order—and not when my own mother had been called to assassinate his father.

"Ella, I'll be fine," Ferdy shouted back. "I still love you."

"Our time together was very enjoyable, *chérie*." Lumiere waved back at me as their carriage sped off, closely followed by the one Louis was riding in. "We will see you again, when the time is right."

"Stop them," I begged Lady Penelope, but it was too late.

The carriages took off, and sped away.

I watched them move bluntly through the crowded streets. Their drivers had no concern for human life, and all I could think about was how Lumiere betrayed us.

Lumiere betrayed me.

I clenched my fists. He'd insisted he wanted to be like Christ, but he was more like Judas.

THE ORDER OF THE CRYSTAL DAGGERS

Lumiere's carriage turned down one street, and Louis' carriage went onto another street. I kept looking for Ferdy, hoping against hope he would escape.

Please, God. Let him break free. Let him come back to me …

Once more I felt my prayers went unanswered.

"Ella?"

I looked to the side, looking at my brother with blinking, disbelieving eyes. There was blood all down Ben's front.

"Ben! What happened? Are you all right?" I gasped, suddenly afraid again.

He nodded and quickly explained how he'd helped Clavan and some of the others. Marguerite was still tending to some minor injuries.

I was glad he was all right, but I barely heard him. I wiped my tears off and reached down my side for my mother's dagger—only to remember I'd dropped it inside after Louis had grabbed me.

"Good. You've stopped your blubbering," Lady Penelope said. "It's quite embarrassing."

"You!" I scrambled to face her, angry and vengeful, and more upset than ever. I couldn't believe I'd listened to her, after she'd lied so many times. "You are no monster, Madame—you are the very devil incarnate. How could you do this to me? How could you lie to me about *Máma* and let Louis take Ferdy hostage?"

Lady Penelope held firm. "Your mother's mission is in the past. Clearly, she didn't go through with it, so I don't see why you're upset about it—"

I leapt at her, eager to inflict her with all the damage and pain I felt. I screamed, but Ben grabbed me before I could do anything too damaging.

"Eleanora, calm yourself," Lady Penelope ordered as she sidestepped my clumsy rage. "This is just what Louis wants— he wants you to hate me. You're just going to let him win again if you can't control yourself."

My head pounded with renewed pain. Ben put his hand on my shoulder, trying to reassure me, but all I could do was just stand there and stare at Lady Penelope.

How could she really think I was upset that Louis had won this round? How could she truly believe I cared about his supposed victory more than Ferdy's life?

"Well, Louis got what he wanted," I finally shouted. "Now it's time for me to get what I want. I want Ferdy back!"

"You heard Louis." Lady Penelope grimaced. "He'll meet with us again."

"When?" I hollered. "Where? There were two carriages and they went in different directions. Where did Lumiere and Ferdy go?"

"Louis is likely heading back to *Vyšehrad*, where Karl is being held. I'm not sure where Lumiere took Ferdinand, but we'll find them soon enough," Lady Penelope insisted. "Louis said I still have a role to fulfill in his little play, remember?"

"But why did he want Ferdy?" Ben asked, distracting me momentarily. "He's already got Karl."

"I'm not certain." For once, Lady POW seemed willing to admit the truth. "But we should get to work. If he thinks I'll just wait around by the fire at home for him to come knocking on my door, he's dead wrong."

"If only he were dead," I muttered darkly, before pulling free of Ben and heading back into the Cabal.

"Where are you going, Eleanora?" Lady Penelope asked me brusquely. "The building's going to come down."

"I need my mother's dagger," I snapped back.

"Oh, yes. Go and get it." She nodded approvingly, and I scowled back at her.

I didn't need her patronizing looks right now. I turned back toward the door and took one last breath of fresh air before stepping inside.

"We need to go back to the manor and prepare to go to *Vyšehrad*," I heard Lady Penelope say. "If we're going to win against Louis, we can't leave it to chance. Where is Amir?"

I froze.

And then, as if to answer her question, a loud cry came out from behind the bar.

My breath left me in a sharp exhale. "Oh, no!"

22

◊

Stinging heat cloaked me as I raced inside the Cabal. In the few moments since I'd been outside, the smoke had grown into dark, deadly clouds, and fire framed the building.

But that didn't matter to me. Not now.

Ashes danced in the air, and fire simmered all around, but I swiped my dagger off the floor, thankful Louis and Lumiere had ignored it earlier, and hurried to the back room where I'd left Amir.

Only to stop when I saw he was still alive.

"Thank you, Lord," I whispered.

Amir was standing in the middle of the room, while Xiana was supporting herself against the burnt, blackened wall. Neither of them appeared to have noticed me, or the fire that was creeping up from all around them.

"Attack me properly," she yelled at Amir, clearly upset. "You cannot avoid me forever."

"I do not wish to fight with you," Amir insisted.

"You will fight me!" Xiana launched into another attack.

Amir parried with her thrusts expertly, managing to throw off her footwork in the process.

Her eyes were wild with their sun-colored fire, with hate and sorrow burning up from inside her very soul as she stumbled back.

"Xiana, please stop." Amir took hold of her hand and stopped her.

"No," she yelled back.

"You have always been driven to succeed," Amir told her quietly. "But this is not a victory you truly want."

"Eleanora." Lady Penelope appeared behind me. "What are you … "

Her voice faded as she saw the scene before me; she uncharacteristically faltered at the sight of Xiana dressed in her full form as an agent of the enemy.

Even in the fire, I saw her eyes glisten, and then she set her jaw and moved between them.

I didn't see that her gun was back in her hand until the very last second. Lady Penelope took aim and fired.

My eyes squeezed shut in horror, but I opened them a second later, curious and terrified of what had happened.

Xiana and Amir were both still; neither of them had been shot, and even with all the ash in the air, I breathed a deep sigh of relief.

"That's enough," Lady Penelope said. "Amir. We have work to do. And Xiana, you're dismissed from my presence—for good, this time."

"Madame." Xiana looked at her, stricken. "You would dismiss me after all the training I took on? After all the work, after all I have learned?"

Lady Penelope only paused for a small second, before she nodded. "Harshad and I have given you what we could, but after what we know you've done, you should be grateful I'm not here to kill you."

"All I have ever wanted was your love and to be part of your family!"

"You were part of my family, until you decided your own happiness was more important." Lady Penelope shook her head scornfully. "I would kill you myself, and quite cheerfully, too, if it weren't for Harshad. For the sake of his love for you, I'll spare you, just this once."

At once, Xiana's shoulders dropped, and she lowered the sword in her hand.

"Now, depart from me; I see now that you never really knew me." Lady Penelope waved her away.

Amir bowed his head to Xiana, and then he spoke to her.

"I forgive you." There was pain and agony laced in every word.

I looked down at the floor, hoping Amir truly had peace at last.

Together, Lady Penelope and Amir walked toward the exit where I was waiting. Amir gave me a small, tired smile, but I knew he was miserable.

A board from the ceiling broke and crashed down around us. Xiana remained standing in the fire, unaffected by the destruction and fire around her.

She wanted to stay and burn, and I was content to let her.

But I reached for Amir, wanting to comfort him. He'd saved me, again, and after Ferdy's capture, I was so glad Amir was still with me.

But then I blinked, and Xiana moved with deadly precision—aiming her sword not at me, not at Amir, but at Lady Penelope.

I cried out in warning, but it was already too late.

Time slowed and stretched, filling me with even more horror and agony, as Amir pushed Lady Penelope into me and stepped in front of her to shield her from Xiana's attack.

I couldn't hear anything else as I screamed. I saw Xiana's eyes widen with anger and shock and horror, and Lady

THE ORDER OF THE CRYSTAL DAGGERS

Penelope gasped; I could even hear her berate Amir for saving her as he fell to his knees, Xiana's *jian* still lodged deep into his stomach.

"Amir!" I screamed. "No!"

Xiana jerked her sword free from Amir, and he writhed and groaned with renewed pain.

"He's going to die," she told me bitterly. "I put the Order's poison on my sword. There is no antidote left. I made sure of that."

Her eyes looked up from his fallen form to Lady Penelope. Xiana glanced at the gun still in Lady Penelope's hand, and I realized what Xiana wanted.

She wanted Lady Penelope to shoot her.

She wanted to die.

But instead, Lady Penelope only knelt down on the other side of Amir's body and took him in her arms, letting him fall against her knees, much like I'd held Tulia in her last moments.

She ignored Xiana entirely.

I wanted to yell at Lady Penelope, to tell her to shoot Xiana. I grabbed my dagger, ready to give Xiana the death she so desperately wanted.

But at my approach, Xiana finally turned and left. She leapt through the labyrinth of fire and broken boards, and then disappeared. I saw one last glint of light on her sword's poisoned blade as she disappeared into the darkness.

I had no words to say; I was beyond rage, shaking my fists at heaven for Amir's fate, cursing Lady Penelope's foolish weakness, and crumbling under the weight of another failure.

I fell to my knees, sobbing with rage as I took Amir's hand.

Amir squeezed my hand in return. Already I could feel his weakness. Warm blood splashed between our palms, and I couldn't find my voice; my throat seemed clogged, and my tongue felt too thick and dry to say anything.

"Ella, what happened?" Ben's voice seemed to call to me from miles away, and I barely looked as he appeared beside me.

"Oh, Ben." My lips quivered, and I couldn't say anything.

Lady Penelope pulled Amir's head up onto her lap. "My son."

Her voice broke, and she finally began to cry.

Amir used his other hand—the one marked with the *noon*—to embrace her. He whispered something I couldn't hear in her ears, and she only shook her head and buried her face into his shoulder.

"Ben." Amir's voice was stalling, but it was still sure. He groaned as he reached for his *Wahabite Jambiya*. He was breathing heavily, with sweat streaming down his brow, as he handed it to my brother. "Here. I need you to be strong and brave now, for my sake, and for theirs, too."

Ben took the dagger with shaking hands, and the two men exchanged a look—one I hadn't seen on my brother's face since *Máma* was alive, and *Táta* was still pure in Ben's eyes.

Amir was giving Ben more than a weapon; he was giving him a legacy, one a father would give to a son out of reverence and love.

"I will." Ben's voice was shaking, but it was still strong.

Amir's breathing went ragged as he looked up at me.

"I'm sorry," I finally blubbered out. "I'm so sorry."

Why was saying "I'm sorry" so insufficient, and yet it was the only thing I could hope to say?

I loved Amir, and I hated how my life had served to only make his more miserable, whether it was the constant reminder of my mother, or my own insolence at learning the waltz, or cutting into his soul with my carelessness a thousand times over.

"Oh, Eleanora," Amir gasped through strangling breaths. "Naděžda imagined herself too cowardly to live, but I am not afraid to die."

"I'm afraid of losing you," I whispered back.

"You won't," he promised. "We will all be together again one day. And you'll get to meet Nassara."

I tried to smile, but I couldn't. Even dying, Amir was the one comforting me. A fresh set of tears streamed down my cheeks.

The fire was still growing around us, and I could barely breathe, but I refused to leave Amir's side.

He turned to look up at me and smiled brightly, one last time. He no longer looked so tired, even if his body seemed much weaker. And then his head dropped back, and his hand fell out of mine.

"Naděžda."

He spoke my mother's name like a song, and then, as the sound died on the air between us, so did he.

For a long moment, with the fire eagerly blazing around us and the building slowly collapsing around us, we said nothing.

It seemed like a long time later when Lady Penelope eased Amir back down to the floor and wiped her eyes. "We have to leave," she said.

I barely felt anything at all as Ben hauled me to my feet and Lady Penelope led us out of the kitchen.

I looked back at Amir, just in time to see his body catch fire.

As we made it outside again, the taste of ash and soot clung to my dried lips. It served as a bitter reminder that I was alive and alone—and that I'd failed all over again, and more spectacularly than ever.

THE ORDER OF THE CRYSTAL DAGGERS

23

◊

Time passed in a slow, grueling fashion, dragging and pushing me against every bit of anguish inside of me as the Cabal finished burning down.

I couldn't do anything but stand and watch as it burned. It felt as though my own world was burning down, too—and not only had I failed to save it, but I'd hastened its demise.

I forced myself to watch the flames as they rose higher, and I did not look away until the fire gradually recoiled into itself, like a snake curling up to die.

The flame-tipped ashes wafted away in the wind, taking Amir with them.

After fearing dynamite and nitroglycerin, it was hard to admit I'd forgotten how a simple fire could cause such damage all on its own—and how swiftly, too.

It was only hours ago my life had been so very different. Lumiere was almost a friend, Amir was alive, and Ferdy had been at my side.

But now, Louis had earned another victory.

Ferdy was captured, Amir was gone, and Lumiere had betrayed us; and in addition to that, I was left without trust in Lady Penelope's leadership, Karl was still kidnapped, and I had no more admiration for my mother's role in the Order.

There was no certainty of truth, and I was numb from pain too great for me to bear.

I was angry beyond rage and tired beyond belief. I could only cry.

Lady Penelope was much more productive than me. She had sent a runner to retrieve Harshad, while Marguerite helped take care of our collective injuries. Ben stood beside me, until I made him help Marguerite instead.

I wanted to be alone.

I *was* alone.

I was so alone that I didn't see Faye as she came up beside me. It was only when she took hold of my hand I noticed her. Together, we stood there; she was mourning her losses, with the death of her dreams and the destruction of her home, while I was just lost.

"I'm sorry." I whispered the words after what seemed to be a lifetime. I couldn't find the courage to admit I'd been the one to lead Louis to the Cabal. "I'm sorry about your wedding."

"Ella." Faye put her arm around my shoulders. "Look."

She nodded toward the alleyway, where Jarl was currently helping some of the others squelch out some of the smaller piles of flames. He'd come after hearing the news and quickly started running around, issuing orders to volunteers and even assisting Lady POW.

"We might be down for a bit. But life will go on, and we will rebuild," she explained. "So this is not the end. Even if it feels like it."

She gave me a brave smile, even if her eyes were still full of tears. "Not everything is always as it appears."

I nodded in easy, tepid agreement. My throat was scratchy and sore from inhaling all that smoke, and I didn't want to say anything else.

I was glad when Jarl called over to her and Faye left me by myself. She gave me one last hug before she headed off, promising me that she would let me know what would happen with her wedding.

Faye couldn't comfort me, and Ben couldn't comfort me, either. From time to time, he stopped working with Marguerite to check on me. But I just shook my head at him, and he went back to work.

After a while, he seemed to understand that I didn't want to be consoled.

I wanted blood.

I wanted to give into my anger and hate and rage.

I wanted to kill Xiana, I wanted to kill Louis, and I wanted to kill Lumiere, and maybe even Karl, too.

It was so antithetical to who I believed myself to be, it was all I could do to just stand there and suffer, to try to hold onto the good and not to let evil consume me.

I had already lost Amir; I did not want to lose myself, too.

It was only when Clavan came up to me that my inner warfare called a momentary cease-fire.

"Ella." He gave me a respectful nod, wincing briefly at his wounds. "Thank you for your help today."

"How is your wife doing?"

I was happy to play along and be polite, even if I couldn't feel the depth and breadth of my emotions. It was too draining, and too tempting to give in against my baser instincts for blood.

"She's well enough," Clavan told me. "We were in the kitchen when that intruder came in and lit the fire. As bad as things look, it's fortunate that it wasn't worse."

I swallowed the lump in my throat and only nodded. Clavan likely knew someone had died, but I doubted he truly knew how much of a loss Amir was to the world, and to me.

"Here. I wanted to give this back to you." Clavan reached into his back pocket and pulled out Lumiere's watch.

Gently, I took hold of it. Some part of me wanted to smash it into the ground and spit on it, but the delicate outline of the *fleur-de-lis* reminded me too much of my father's watch.

I couldn't punish Lumiere without blemishing my father's memory.

"My friend wasn't able to fix it," Clavan said as I opened the watch and saw it was still set to midnight. "Apparently, it broke some number of years ago, and there's quite a bit of rust. He offered to replace the parts, but I said I would talk with you first. It's a rare item, and one that seems to be more sentimental than functional in its use."

"Thank you." Mindlessly, I ran my ashen palms over the golden design, before I saw Clavan looking at the dagger at my side. I put the watch away and held my weapon out to him. "Did you want to look at this, too?"

Wariness briefly lit up into his eyes again, but he took it a moment later. He lifted his small eyeglasses up and studied it carefully; he tested its weight and its balance and swung it through the air with a few moves.

"It's been well-preserved," he said. "The alloy is unique to the Middle East, but its rarity only contributes to half its value. Hardly anything made today would be able to compare with its craftsmanship."

"Thank you." I gazed at the Cabal, my eyes already tearing up again. "For all the good it did me today."

"You helped save Helen," he reminded me softly.

"I know. But it wasn't enough to save everyone," I whispered, putting my hands over my eyes.

Nothing I had done was enough to save Amir, and nothing I'd done was enough to stop Louis.

"You can't save everyone, you know," Clavan replied. "And not everyone wants to be saved, either. But the important thing is that you do what you can, and hope some are saved in the end."

I shook my head. I wanted to explain that everything I did only seemed to make things worse. Xiana escaped, Louis walked out, while Lumiere had Ferdy at his mercy.

Why was it that only the worst sort of people were the ones who survived?

"Here." Clavan gently pried one hand away from my face and gently pressed my dagger's hilt into my palm. I looked down at it through tear-soaked eyes.

"Fighting, and then losing, is not the same thing as surrender, Ella," he told me. "You've fought the good fight, and you've seen failure. But you've never seen a self-defeat, and I pray you will not start now."

My mother's dagger was usually a source of comfort as well as courage, but I felt nothing as I stood there and held it— nothing but disgust and disbelief, and even betrayal.

"I don't know," I mumbled, feeling as weak as Louis believed the nations to be.

It was possible he was right; if I was this pathetic, how could an entire nation of people be strong enough to stop him and others like him?

"Yes, you do," Clavan said. "And since you are a member of the Order, you know what's at stake, especially with the Emperor on his way here."

My mind was muddled with grief and anger, and it took me a moment to respond. "What?"

"The Emperor is coming to Prague. His ship is due to arrive later today at the fort at *Vyšehrad.* He's called for the Tripartite Council to commence this week at Prague Castle."

"But it's not supposed to happen until March, or even until later this year," I said, recalling what Lady Penelope had said, only days ago.

"Something's happened that made him move it up." Clavan glanced around. "At first, I thought it was the war between France and Germany. But now I suspect it's something more personal—perhaps an issue with succession?"

He looked at me intently, and at first, I couldn't imagine what it was that he was trying to tell me. But when I realized he meant Ferdy, or Karl, or maybe even both now that Louis had them, I coughed in surprise.

"Um, I don't know." I stuttered out the words, unwilling to ask him directly if he knew the truth about Ferdy; I preferred to leave that as a mystery, and I had a feeling he did, too.

"It might be best to find out," Clavan replied gently. "The Order is known for its courage and determination—*In Hoc Signo Vinces.*"

"With this sign, you shall win." I repeated the words that formed the motto of the Order, feeling further away from anything even resembling victory than ever.

"You should know it's not the sword, or even the wielder, that leads to victory, but the faith behind it." Clavan gave me another smile. "It takes courage to believe in truth, and even more to live a life dedicated to it."

I tightened my grip on my mother's dagger. As much as I felt conflicted over her past and her choices, there was

THE ORDER OF THE CRYSTAL DAGGERS

nothing conflicted about how much I wanted Ferdy back, and how I wanted him safe from the likes of Louis Valoris.

"Ella."

Ben called out to me, and when I looked over at him, he pointed down the street.

As I watched, Harshad and Didier climbed out of Lady Penelope's carriage.

I didn't see what difference it would make at this point if they were here or not, but when Ben waved for me to come over, I nodded and excused myself to Clavan.

"Thank you, for everything—again," I whispered. "I must go now."

Clavan graciously bowed his head to me, and as we parted ways, I couldn't help but envy him; he was going off to his family, and they would survive this difficult time together. He seemed to be the kind of person who had things figured out, and even if he didn't, he had enough peace about the possibilities that would allow him to recover from life's brutalities.

My steps slowed as I saw Lady Penelope speak with Harshad. While I couldn't hear the words they spoke, I knew she was telling him about Amir's death and Xiana's treachery.

As I watched, Harshad drew her into a slight embrace. For a long moment, he held her there, and she seemed to weaken only slightly against him. In contrast, he stood there, still and strong, unmoved by the worst of circumstances.

I wondered how he could be so blasé about everything, but then I remembered how he'd excused himself after seeing the poison.

He probably knew what Xiana had done.

I approached them and I heard him speak to Lady Penelope.

"I am sorry I was not here," he said to her. "But thank you. You did all you could."

My mouth dropped open in shock. "Excuse me?"

Both of them looked at me, and at that moment, all the fury I'd been trying to control raged inside of me with renewed vigor; all the words I couldn't speak earlier came rushing out all at once.

"What do you mean, she did all she could?" I pointed at Lady Penelope, adamant I would not say her name or give any indication I considered her even the slightest bit human. "She didn't kill Louis when she had the chance, and she let Lumiere take Ferdy away. She did *nothing*."

"Need I remind you that I saved your life and Ferdinand's by allowing Louis to leave?" Lady Penelope's jaw clenched. "I understand your grief, Eleanora. But don't be ridiculous."

"I'm ridiculous?" I could barely believe her. "You could've killed Xiana, before *and* after she stabbed Amir. I saw her; she *wanted* you to kill her. She was daring you to do it, and you ignored her, just like a coward."

"Eleanora." Lady Penelope sighed. "There are times when life is much more of a punishment than death—and there are times when some things are more important than justice. Don't forget your mother did the same."

"What are you talking about?"

Lady Penelope crossed her arms over her chest. "She didn't kill Ferdinand's father, after all."

I was disoriented at her mention of King Ferdinand, but I would not let her win this argument. Lady POW was wrong, and not even my mother's past would stop my tirade.

"How dare you mention her at all," I hissed. "Especially after you lied to me about her mission."

"I didn't lie—"

"You misled me, and Ben, too." My voice was getting louder and stronger as my anger boiled over.

"Stop yelling," Lady Penelope hissed. "Look, Eleanor wasn't under direct orders to kill him. But it was the first option on a very short list; honestly, if you know history at all, you know it was a miracle the issue was resolved without his permanent disposal. It would have been easier to poison him, allow others to believe it was a natural death, and then discuss the line of succession with more optimism."

"That doesn't matter," I yelled. "You still didn't tell me the truth."

"The truth is complicated, Eleanora," Lady Penelope retorted.

"Yes, and now Amir is dead, and Ferdy's gone," I shouted back. I whipped out my dagger and took a menacing step forward. "All of this is your fault, Madame, and I will never, ever forgive you for this! Not that you would ever ask for it yourself."

"Eleanora." Harshad stepped between me and Lady Penelope. "Please … I am sorry I was not here for you."

Harshad was old, and tired, and just barely taller than I was, but he still remained an imposing figure; I didn't know if he was protecting me from Lady POW, or the other way around—but I lost all my bluster as he stood there before me.

He took my shoulders and hugged me close, but I couldn't embrace him back.

His affection was nothing like Amir's had been. Standing there, I felt empty and absent of true warmth. But Harshad was still trying, and because Lady Penelope was still watching me, I stopped myself from crying again.

He let go, and I stepped back, sheathed my dagger, and turned away from both of them.

"I'm sorry," he said again.

I crossed my arms as a new lump formed in my throat. "It's not your fault. You didn't know what … what Xiana would do."

"Nevertheless, I taught you about weaknesses, and it's my own that has brought us to this point." Harshad sighed. "It is always much easier to teach the lesson than it is to learn it, and I have failed to live up to my own standards in this regard."

"No." I narrowed my eyes, murderously glaring at Lady Penelope. "It wasn't your weakness that led to this. It was *hers*. She let Xiana leave."

"Xiana will face her fate at the appointed time," Harshad said solemnly. "But she was as much a daughter to me as your mother was, and I am as grateful as I am conflicted that she did not die."

Especially by Lady Penelope's hand.

The words were unspoken, but I knew what he meant.

I shook my head. "I don't care. I can't forgive her. And I *won't.*"

"It may be easier to forgive Xiana after she receives justice for her sins," Harshad replied neutrally. "In the meantime, we cannot do anything for Amir any longer. We can rescue your beloved Ferdinand, and his brother, too. Once we have them back, we will see to Louis and his plans for Prague."

"Fine." My eyes fell to the ground.

Harshad was right, even if I was still in pain.

THE ORDER OF THE CRYSTAL DAGGERS

Xiana wasn't the only one who had to face justice, I thought, thinking of the old man who'd seemed so harmless before.

I should tell them about the Emperor.

I whirled around, ready to tell them what Clavan told me. But Harshad was already talking to Ben, hesitating just the slightest as the sight of Amir's dagger in my brother's hand.

A slight shadow came up from behind me.

If I wasn't so despondent, I might've jumped at the sudden sight of Didier.

"What are you doing here?" I asked, unable to hide the bitterness in my voice. "Why aren't you still locked up in Lumiere's bedroom, worried about earning Lady POW's trust?"

"I've never been fond of an exercise in futility," he replied, almost making me smile. "When she called for Harshad to come here, I had a feeling it was time."

"Time for what?"

"Lumiere told me that if trouble should come, I was to give these to Ben and Ferdy." He pulled out a pair of dueling pistols, just like the ones they'd been working with the day I'd stumbled outside, worried the manor was being attacked.

"Lumiere's a traitor." I practically spat out the words as I thought of how pathetic I'd thought him to be only this morning. "He took Ferdy as his prisoner."

"Lumiere is indeed a traitor," Didier agreed. "But not to you. He's on your side."

"Ha." I sniffed, my nose drippling with snot from all my earlier tears. "He's on his own side."

"Well … that is a better way of saying it," Didier agreed. "But right now, your goals are aligned. He might have Ferdy, but I know he will keep him safe from Louis."

Hope briefly stirred inside of me. I didn't know if I could trust it to be true, but if I was going to save Ferdy, I had to believe it was possible—until it wasn't.

"Where are they going?" I asked. "There were two carriages. Lady POW says Louis went to *Vyšehrad*, where Karl is being kept. But where did Lumiere go? Surely you have some idea?"

"I've known Lumi for many years, but the man is still an enigma." Didier smiled. "However, he did tell me that he trusts you to find the right place and time for the knowledge you seek."

"He also said it was too easy to fool me." I crossed my arms over my chest glumly, thinking of how miserable Lumiere had been earlier, when he told me there was no proper place and time for some conversations.

But then I stopped.

I pulled out the pocket watch Clavan had given back to me, and I thought back to its connections with the Bohemian Loyalists.

Lumiere's watch … and Louis' patch on his sleeve.

"The University." I heard myself say the words more than I said them, but it was the only sensible answer.

Louis was staying at a dormitory, posing as an art student. In the University's *Karolinum*, there was a display for the Bohemian Loyalists—and there was more than that, I thought, recalling what Amir had said about the secrets of the city.

The tunnels.

There were secret tunnels under the city from *Vyšehrad*. There was no telling where they all went, but there had to be one that led to the University.

"Harshad?" I stepped up beside him. "I have to talk with you."

"What is it now?" Lady Penelope asked, her blatant bitterness clear despite her curiosity.

I frowned at her. "I want to talk to Harshad, not you. I have a plan."

Quickly, I explained what I'd found out, and all the clues I'd put together.

As I finished, Lady Penelope sighed.

"Oh, Eleanora," she groaned. "Louis is right about you. You're naïve and too idealistic by far."

"I know," I snapped, my voice harder this time. With renewed determination, I gripped my mother's dagger in my hand. "But don't worry, Madame. After this mission is over, you will never have to deal with my naivety and idealism ever again."

"We'll see," she muttered.

"No." I straightened my shoulders. "*You'll* see."

24

◊

Much like I'd felt earlier, standing before the Church of Our Lady of the Snows, I felt very small and uncertain as I looked up at the large, rounded entrance of the University's *Karolinum*.

I could only hope I would have better luck finding Ferdy than I'd had trying to find Karl—and Lumiere, and Louis, too.

"Are you sure he's here?" Ben asked, as if he knew I was suddenly doubting myself.

"Shhh … " I put my finger to my lips.

Ben's question was reasonable enough, but I didn't particularly want to answer him.

Lumiere was not a creature I considered beholden to reason. His little quips and barbs over the past weeks could've been clues—or merely the half-drunken ramblings of a madman still lucid enough to believe himself sane.

I was gambling on the former, but the odds were the same for the latter.

I bit back a smile, and then forced myself not to tear up again. Ferdy would approve, and not just because he was the one we were trying to save.

"It's been about two hours since we left the Cabal," Ben said. "Harshad and Lady POW should be near *Vyšehrad* by now."

"If you wanted to go with them, you should've said something," I whispered back.

"I'm only letting you know. Clavan said Emperor Franz Joseph is expected to arrive before the end of the day, if he's not there already. If you want your plan to work, we need to hurry."

"I know."

"And anyway, I'm not leaving you. We're family."

"Then it'll either be easier or harder to forgive me if I'm wrong about this."

"I've forgiven you for much worse," Ben said, provoking me as well as comforting me.

A little reluctantly, I smiled. Ben's loyalty was touching, even in light of his impatience. "Well, thank you, *brácha*."

"Ben." Marguerite appeared at his side and tugged on his sleeve. "Be nice to your sister."

"I wasn't trying to be mean," Ben objected.

"We're fine." I didn't mind that Marguerite had joined our group to come to the University, but I didn't need her to defend me; Ben and I had grown up knowing hurting each other and helping each other were not mutually exclusive.

Still, it was difficult to soften my sarcasm. "Perhaps I'm more worried about forgiving myself."

"You told Lady Penelope that you knew what you were about." Didier shuffled next to me, his large form cloaking me in an extra shadow; his dark eyes twinkled down at me. "I'd hate to think you would doubt yourself now."

"That's part of my naïve charm." I glanced up at the sky, realizing there was more than one reason to hurry. It was getting darker, and it looked like it might rain. The clouds were gray and feathery, as uncertain of themselves as I was of myself and Lumiere. "Come on."

The old door to the University was off to the side of one of the city's markets, and the busy streets were enough to give us sufficient cover as we crossed into the building's threshold.

Stepping inside, I tripped on my skirts. I grimaced as I stopped myself from falling. I regretted not wearing my stealth habit. The bright morning I'd had with Ferdy seemed like a lifetime ago as my day increasingly devolved into madness, fear, and death.

As one of the university's oldest sections, the *Karolinum* often housed both the German and Bohemian Diets, along with the *Reichsrat*, and it was still a place of reception for foreign leaders, ambassadors, and diplomats. It had been born of a coming together of nations, with Czechs, the Bavarians, the Polish, the Slavs, the Saxons, and more. As we made our way through the outer rooms, I saw the long history of Bohemia and its people was housed there. Some of the architecture was rough and pagan, while others were Christianized, but all of it showed Bohemia's complicated history, both in its conquests, and even its current struggles to maintain the unity in the diversity of its ethnic roots.

The University was a place of both chaos and order, ideas and histories, and histories revisited in light of new ideas; it was a place of judgment and record, a place of destiny, death, and rebirth.

Yes, I thought, Louis would appreciate such a place—and Karl would, too.

We entered into the vestibule of the Great Hall, where the walls were lined with paintings enshrined in elaborate and elegant frames; their painted eyes all looked down at me and offered up their varied, silent judgments.

"We don't have time to linger," Ben reminded me.

"The dormitories are upstairs." Marguerite gestured toward a staircase down the hall. "Maybe we should look there."

"That's likely where Louis has been staying," I said. "But I don't think Lumiere will be there."

"Where do you think he is, then?" Ben asked.

"The Great Hall." I nodded toward the doors in front of us and then looked back at Didier. "I can't imagine Lumiere would settle for anything less than greatness. Would you?"

Didier gave me a smile. "It depends on what you mean by greatness."

"So much depends on so much," I murmured, pushing the doors open.

Inside, flags adorned the walls along with paintings and elegant architectural décor, and the room was capped with a dome ceiling. There were two lines of chairs circled around a podium, and in the middle was a chair, where the leader of the room would sit.

I was surprised to see it was empty; I'd been expecting Lumiere to have claimed it for his own.

My shoulders slumped. I'd been wrong.

"Ella!"

My heart leapt as Ferdy called for me. I whirled around to see him sitting down on a chair, just tucked into a far alcove, near the entrance to the small chapel of St. Margaret.

"Oh, thank you, Lord," I whispered, hurrying over.

Only to stop abruptly in my tracks, as Xiana stepped directly in front of me.

"Be careful," Ferdy warned, his voice full of glum fear.

Xiana was still in her ash-covered cloak, the white and gray specks clinging to the cloth, covered in little splashes of Amir's blood. Her eyes were still full of fire and vengeance, but I could see the regret in her gaze.

She was not nearly as calm as she appeared. And—to my great relief—I saw she was not armed. I still had my mother's dagger, and as long as I kept it this time, I could win against her.

"Ella." Ben came up beside me and held up his fists, too. "We can do this together."

I nodded. Ben and I had both lost so much with Amir's death; it was in his right to be there alongside me.

I couldn't say who took the first step, but soon, Ben and I were locked in combat with Xiana.

The sounds of our battle muffled out the rest of the world; Xiana's breathing increased as my own heart thundered, complemented by the *click-clack* of Ben's brace as we fought.

I watched her moves, the feints, the ducks, and rolls, and I saw her weaken briefly as I went to the defensive, and Ben whipped out Amir's dagger.

The *Wahabite Jambiya* surprised both me and Xiana, and Ben used that against her.

A long streak of blood appeared on her chest, and her eyes narrowed even further as she retreated.

"I see Amir managed to slip one more surprise by me." Xiana finally spoke as she glared at Ben with malice. "But it will be his last."

She lunged off to the side, away from us, and I was momentarily puzzled—until I saw she meant to attack Marguerite.

"Marguerite, watch out," I called, but Ben was already moving.

He dipped down low and fell forward, deliberately intercepting Xiana's attack. His movement awkwardly propelled himself into her. The two of them tumbled over. I

THE ORDER OF THE CRYSTAL DAGGERS

heard Ben's brace *clank* against the floor. His leg came free, but he still managed to trap her.

I was about to hurry over when suddenly Lumiere's laughter rang out from behind us.

"Ah, Ella, there you are. I was just beginning to wonder if you would show at all, *chérie.*"

I froze and whirled around to face him.

Lumiere was sitting at the front of the altar by St. Margaret's chapel, calm and smiling.

I could've sworn the chapel was empty besides Ferdy just a moment ago, but I was breathing too hard to say anything.

"Not now, Lumiere." Xiana kicked herself free from Ben's hold, and he grabbed at his leg where she'd struck him. "This is not a good time."

"*Oui, oui, j'accord,*" Lumiere muttered as he came over to stand in front of Xiana. "But we will make it better, *non?* Where are our good manners?"

"I can't imagine what you mean," I muttered, struggling not to curse Lumiere as he gave Marguerite a curtsy and bowed to Ben on the floor.

Xiana and I both scowled at him.

"Ah, *mon ami*, it is good to see you again." Lumiere put his hand on Didier's shoulder. "I trust you will forgive me for my sudden departure?"

"Of course." Didier clasped his arm in return. "You can count on me to forgive you, just as I can count on you to be unpredictable."

Lumiere shrugged. "I'm not as unpredictable as you'd think."

"Lumiere," Xiana's voice growled. "This is—"

"*Pardonnez-moi*, Xiana, but surely you must know how I've always hated your poor manners." Lumiere's bubbly, dulcet tones went low and deadly as he jerked away from Didier and whirled around to face her.

I gasped at the sudden sight of the gun in his hand. Lumiere had pilfered it from Didier's front coat.

It's just like before, on the Salacia. *He's going to—*

I didn't have time to finish my thought as Lumiere squeezed the trigger and shot Xiana straight through the chest.

Blood rained out from her wound, and she was too taken aback to do anything but drop to her knees in shock.

"That was for Amir," Lumiere told her, his tone full of condemnation. "It turns out he had an additional last surprise for you, *Saghira*. But that should have been expected. For what fellowship can light have with darkness?"

Xiana began to choke; she fought death, even as any movement only hastened her inevitable fate.

"Just so you know, my father would shoot you, too, just like a horse with a broken leg."

"I am ... not ... " Xiana seethed, barely able to move her lips.

"Please. You're just a tool to get work done. My father offered you apples and sugar cubes for your tasks, but now you're really no longer useful to him—or, more importantly, to me." Lumiere gave her a cruel smirk. "Am I not such a good actor? Blackmailing you into helping me was fun, but I must admit, it feels good to shoot you now."

Xiana's lips quivered, and, before she could try to say anything else, Lumiere shot her twice more—once in the stomach, and then straight through the head.

THE ORDER OF THE CRYSTAL DAGGERS

"That's for Nassara and Naděžda." Lumiere's eyes lit up with wicked pleasure as Xiana fell forward. Her body began twitching as he laughed. "Yes, it's *very* good to shoot you—a most impure delight. Now I'm only sorry I didn't do it earlier after our little *tête-à-tête* in the west parlor back at Pepé's house."

"Lumiere!" I was taken aback by his violent delight. "That's enough."

"*Pourquoi?* Should I not have my own surprises?"

"You always do," Didier said. "I'm surprised you used the gun this time."

Lumiere grinned. "Oh, I know. It'll be a dreadful mess to clean all the gunpowder off my sleeves. But I didn't have any poison, and swords are too hard to conceal. And I do rather like how quick and painful it was for her. It really adds to the surprise."

Xiana's body lay on the floor, her blood gathering in scarlet pools.

"Lumiere," I muttered.

There was no cheery smile on his face, no hint of remorse; his green eyes were filled with expectancy and satisfaction.

"You're welcome," Lumiere told me, gesturing toward Xiana's body, and then to Ferdy. "A punished murderer, and a saved prince. And you needn't worry about his condition; I strapped him down myself so she wouldn't suspect I had other plans."

He turned back to Didier. "Thank you for bringing the guns. I'll be sure to get you more in the near future, and some nice bullets to go along with them, too."

"I would like my stock replenished," Didier agreed.

"You still have extra rounds on you, *oui?*"

The two of them were talking so normally, and it was all the more jarring. They chatted amicably as I struggled to find the words I wanted to say—if I could even think of what to say. It was good to see Xiana dead, but I still didn't appreciate Lumiere's style.

"Ella." Ferdy said my name, and the spell was broken; he was still stuck in his chair.

"Oh, yes." Lumiere gestured toward Ferdy. "Please, finish rescuing him now, Ella. I'm done."

"Done?" I gritted my teeth.

"You didn't have to be so loud about it, Lumiere," Ben said from behind us. I noticed he was leaning against Marguerite as he stood. "What if someone else comes in here?"

"I reserved this room for a special chapel time, in memory of the Bohemian Loyalists," Lumiere said. "But we should hope others will arrive soon. We'll need someone to clean up this mess. Even God himself didn't want to do it. Why else do you think she fell forward away from St. Margaret's alcove?"

Ben and I exchanged an irritated look, and then he shrugged. I bit down on my cheek as Didier and Lumiere went back to chatting with each other.

I went to see to Ferdy's care. After I unceremoniously stepped over Xiana's corpse, I saw he was tied down to his chair with thick ropes.

"I'm glad you're here." Ferdy gave me an irreverent grin as he held up his wrists. I saw he was wearing a familiar pair of manacles. "I may need to make a stop at the men's withdrawing room before we leave."

He was trying to make me laugh, and I almost hated how kind he was being to me.

"I'm just glad you're all right," I whispered. "I was so worried when … "

My voice trailed off as I thought of Louis revealing my mother's past, and how afraid I'd been at Ferdy's loss.

My fingers seemed numb and weak as I stood there, realizing I didn't deserve Ferdy's forgiveness. My vision was once more blurred with tears, and my hands were now shaking as I was unable to look at him.

Ferdy put his hand on mine. "Ella—I'm sorry about Amir."

He knew I was upset.

"Xiana came here a little while ago, and Lumiere more or less guessed what happened," Ferdy continued. "I wasn't surprised Lumiere killed her, really. I was more surprised he let her live as long as he did."

I nodded, still unable to say anything. I knelt down and tried to untangle the knots at his feet. I thought about using my mother's dagger, but I didn't even want to think of her in that moment.

"Ella." Ferdy reached for me. Even wearing Lumiere's iron shackles, he pulled me close and held onto me tightly. "What's wrong?"

Once more, someone who I should have been taking care of was the one taking care of me.

"I'm sorry," I whispered, my voice breaking.

I thought of my own mother being sent to kill his father, how I'd doubted Ferdy when he'd told me the Order was full of assassins—and how I'd been so content to believe that since I was a member of the Order, they were all like me, instead of acknowledging I was on my way to becoming like them.

I'd been content to be ignorant, and now I was truly so undeserving of Ferdy and his love.

Shamefully, I bowed my head down onto my chest. "I'm so sorry."

"This is hardly your fault." Ferdy lay my head onto his lap, running his hands through my curls with loving care.

"I meant … I mean, I'm sorry about my mother … and your father." I barely whispered the words. I didn't want to look up at him as I asked the question that burned through my soul. "Can you still love me?"

"Oh, Ella." Ferdy cradled my face in his hands and smiled down at me, tenderly amused. "You are your mother's daughter, but don't forget, you are your father's daughter, too."

He nodded toward the far wall of the chapel, and I glanced behind me. On a small plaque, my father's name was carved in gilded lettering, with an embossed *fleur-de-lis* underneath.

That's right, I thought, turning back to Ferdy with widened eyes.

My father saved King Ferdinand.

"I didn't doubt for a minute that you would come for me this time. But no matter your family's history, you are your own self. And you've never backed down from trying to save me." Ferdy chuckled lightly and then, leaning down, he pressed his forehead against mine. "How could I not love you?"

"You are too wonderful for me." After a long day of tragedy and loss, I felt truly hopeful again. I felt warmth and love, and I knew I didn't deserve anything as good and perfect as what I had.

"We can revisit that topic later," Ferdy said. "Can you get me out of these ropes first?"

THE ORDER OF THE CRYSTAL DAGGERS

I wiped my eyes with the back of my hand and gave him a tremulous smile. *"Absolument."*

Soon, Ferdy was free of his ropes.

The instant he stood up, he kissed me. His mouth was firm, yet patient, against my own and I succumbed to the pleasure of holding him again.

I'd been so afraid I'd lost him, and I kissed him back, letting the downpour of love in my heart wash away all my fear.

It was only when both Lumiere and Ben groaned that I pulled back.

"Ferdy." I was a little embarrassed, even if I was still pleased. "This isn't the right time."

"That is a matter of opinion." Ferdy grinned at me.

He looked so adorable and handsome, I had to busy myself with his shackles to stop myself from kissing him again.

I was about to call Ben over to see about picking the locks on the manacles, but I saw Marguerite was helping him tighten up his brace. She was being so careful, and Ben was being so patient. He'd risked injury for her wellbeing, and I couldn't bring myself to interrupt them.

Thankfully, Lumiere held out the key.

"I'd offer to let you keep my manacles if I didn't think we'd need them later." Lumiere gave me a playful wink. "They're quite a pleasure for nighttime activities, even if they are a little painful to wear."

"I'd rather you offer to wear them," I shot back, still irritated with him for kidnapping Ferdy earlier.

"Now, now, I'm sure your husband wouldn't be happy about that," Lumiere replied. "He means to keep you all to

THE ORDER OF THE CRYSTAL DAGGERS

himself, and I'm not particularly interested in such an invitation. No offense, Madame."

"What?" I suddenly blushed as I realized what he'd meant.

"You're right, Lumi." Ferdy took the key and unlocked the manacles. Once he removed them, he rubbed his wrists. "I do mean to keep her all to myself. But we should keep a hold of the handcuffs for Karl, after we get to *Vyšehrad*."

"Yes," I agreed quickly. "Once we get Karl free and stop Louis, we can deal with your transgressions, Lumiere."

I'd rescued Ferdy, even if he wasn't in as much danger as I'd thought, and Lumiere had, as he'd said, paid for his earlier betrayal.

Now all I had left to do was rescue Karl, and then stop Louis.

Preferably killing him after all the losses he'd caused me.

"There's no need for you to deal with my sins." Lumiere pointed to Xiana's motionless figure on the floor behind us. "I've paid you for them—and now, I even will gladly help you force my father to pay for his."

"Oh, really?" I crossed my arms, skeptical. "Are you sure you're not going to betray me again?"

"No, I'm done with that. Now, I'm going to tell you what to do." He gave me a wicked grin. "I'm second-in-command, remember?"

"Dare we even ask what you have planned, Lumiere?" Ben grumbled.

"Since you're here, I can guess Pepé's gone ahead to *Vyšehrad* with her Indian manservant running at her heels, hasn't she?"

I nodded. "Yes. I sent her there to take care of the Emperor while we saved Ferdy."

Lumiere cocked his brow at me. "What? *You* sent her? No wonder that's a foolish plan, then."

"Hey!"

"Oh, Ella, my father is there, waiting for her. That's all he needs to frame the Order for the death of the Emperor, and blame her for the resulting war." Lumiere sighed. "All of you will be hunted down while he puts Karl or Max on the throne. He'll probably favor Max, since he can take the dynamite as payment and then sell it to both sides."

All of the pieces of Louis' plan suddenly came together in a devastating moment.

Lord Maximillian wanted the throne, as did Karl. They were working with Louis to cause enough chaos for the Emperor to come to Prague. Using the Tripartite Council as a front, and Ferdy and Karl as hostages, Louis would murder him, blame the Order, and start another war across Europe—one that would destroy the old, weak foundations of the past and allow him to rebuild a new world using his wartime profits.

"But your father wouldn't really kill Karl, would he?" I asked.

"Karl would deserve it." Lumiere sniffed indignantly. "All of his recent bluster about freeing Bohemia from the Empire seems to have paid off, but when you appeal to a tyrant for your own purposes, you're only digging your own grave."

"Lumiere," I growled in warning.

"Ella, you know *mon père* and your grandmother are monsters of the worst sort. They only understand honor when it concerns their own, and they forget it easily enough when they want to destroy each other."

"We still need to work with Lady Penelope if we're going to stop Louis," I said.

"Oh, *chérie*, please. Naděžda discovered long ago what you should know now: You are far, far too good for their world, and they do not deserve you. And both of them know it. But both of them will still feast on your soul. It gives them new purpose, like vampires sucking the life from their victims. Sure, some of their intentions sound noble, and perhaps their cause is justified; but so what? Can anything be worth the loss of your own soul? The loss of your own freedom?"

I bit my lip. "And what if something is worth it?"

"If it is, then only you should truly make that decision," Lumiere told me. "It is your choice, and the consequences that follow will belong to you—even if they befall others besides you."

Both of us looked over at Ferdy, who shook his head.

"I'm not leaving Ella's side," he said firmly.

"Oh, you foolish children." Lumiere took me by the hand, and then Ferdy, too. "Several times, I have learned—and relearned—that the whole world wants to tell you what to do. Each person wants to tell you what to feel, how to act, what to believe. They will try to persuade you, berate you, threaten you. But you will be free if you stand up for yourself, if you take your proper place in standing against them—even if you end up agreeing with them in the end. You must listen to the voice of truth, and you must be willing to count the cost of your choices, your failures as well as victories.

"So now, I will tell you what you need to do, Ella—and that is to betray Pepé, as I will betray my father. They have led us into ruin, in the soul if not the body."

"Maybe." I squeezed Lumiere's hand, still conflicted. At the sight of Xiana's bloodied body on the floor, I remembered Amir's voice, telling me Lumi was a friend, how he'd been my mother's brotherly companion, and a victim of his father's neglect and abuse—as well as an abuser himself. He was a captive soul tormented further by his own debilitating choices. "But if I did betray her, I'd be doing what Louis wanted. He said my mother betrayed her, too."

"And Naděžda was right to." Lumiere shook his head. "The legacy we inherit doesn't have to be the one we leave behind. Of all people, your mother and I would be the ones who know this best."

In the distance, I could hear the soft chimes of the *Pražský orloj* ringing, as if to remind me time was not forgiving in either its pleasures or its pains.

"We have to hurry." Ben was full of impatience as I looked over at him. Marguerite had stepped back and he was walking again on his own.

"I know." Finally, I sighed. "I promised Empress Maria Anna I'd return him to her. This is a matter of my mother's honor, too."

"That's right," Ferdy spoke up. "Ella's mother didn't kill my father; and even more, she sent Ella's father to save mine. There's still plenty of good in the past. You can help us save it, Lumiere."

I gave Ferdy a grateful look.

Lumiere's expression softened, and then he sighed reluctantly. "You're right about that. I will do what I can to honor Naděžda. Even if it means following your orders when I agree with them."

I gave him a reluctant half-smile. "Thank you. Now, we've got to move if we're going to stop Louis. You know of the tunnels under the city. Use them and take us to *Vyšehrad*."

Lumiere scoffed. "I'll take you. That was part of my plan anyway. However, I have one condition."

"What is it?" I asked, exasperated.

THE ORDER OF THE CRYSTAL DAGGERS

"I will do this, but only if you make me, Ella." Lumiere nodded to Didier, who held out Ferdy's dueling pistol to me. "Who knows if I will truly have the courage to follow through or not? It's best to keep me at gunpoint."

"I won't argue with you." I took the gun carefully. It felt heavier in my hands than I'd expected, and I was suddenly afraid of its power. "It's a deal."

"*C'est parfait.* A deal between the prince of secrets and shadows, and the princess of Prague—ooh, how I love it!" Lumiere squealed with glee and then held out his wrists to me. "Handcuffs, please."

"Good idea." Ferdy quickly obliged, locking Lumiere in his own manacles. "Even I know some gambles are safer than others."

"So far, I like your plan, Lumiere," I admitted. "What happens after we get to *Vyšehrad?*"

"You'll see." Lumiere smirked as he looked back at Xiana's lifeless form. "But I can promise it'll be even more fun."

THE ORDER OF THE CRYSTAL DAGGERS

25

◊

"Why am I the one who has to do this, again?" I held the barrel of Ferdy's dueling pistol steady behind Lumiere's back as we walked through the *Karolinum* toward the tunnel entrance. "I don't even know how to use a gun."

I wished I could use my dagger to keep Lumiere in line. I had a long way to go in learning to use it effectively, but I had more experience with its use.

I felt better since Didier checked the gun to make sure it was properly loaded and ready to fire; if Lumiere had been the one to fiddle with it, I would've suspected him of setting me up for failure, even if he'd insisted he wasn't going to betray me again.

That's exactly what someone going to betray me would say.

"No time like the present to learn." Lumiere practically sang out the words before breaking out into obnoxious laughter. "Makes you wish you'd taken Didier up on his offer before, *ne c'est pas?* Anyway, this will convince *mon père* that you are serious. It's my brilliance at work with your own, which is what you wanted."

"You don't need to sound so pleased with yourself," I said through gritted teeth, watching as he secured his pocket watch back onto his vest. He seemed glad to have it back. "I'm the one who's supposed to make you suffer."

"*Chérie,* we are allies now, and that means we compromise on how much we make each other suffer. Almost like marriage."

"You might not want to tempt me any further then." I poked the barrel of the gun against his back, and he scowled at me.

THE ORDER OF THE CRYSTAL DAGGERS

"Watch how eagerly you ruin my cloak," he warned. "I'll make you pay for it. I made Xiana pay for nicking me the other day."

He rubbed his neck where she'd held him up against the parlor wall, but I only rolled my eyes. I was about to assure him I was already paying for my restraint when Ben interrupted us.

"Let's just focus on getting to the tunnels." Ben was clearly annoyed with Lumiere's behavior, but he didn't say anything in my defense, either. "I don't want someone to see us and wonder why we have a hostage."

"At this point, I'd say Lumiere enjoys it," I muttered.

"I'm sure he does," Ferdy agreed. "But that's all the more reason to make sure we don't let anyone else find out we have him. He likes the attention, remember? And there's hardly a surplus for it here."

Ferdy was right. We'd walked through several other rooms of the *Karolinum*, but they were largely empty.

There was an echo of organ music whispering around us as we turned down another hall and entered into the library of the National Hall. The room was two stories high and lined with books. There was a small set of stairs that enabled eager readers to easily navigate the collection. I smiled to be surrounded by music and books.

"Mr. Clavan would like this place." A new wave of guilt washed through me as I thought of the books back at the Cabal; while Faye had been able to escape with her copy of *Jane Eyre*, I doubted Clavan had saved any of his own.

Ferdy nodded. "He might be able to come here one day."

"No," Lumiere said. "This room was special to the king, and it's held in reserve for the Emperor now. Of course, since it's *moi*, you know I'm good at getting into places where I shouldn't be—right, Didier?"

Didier nodded. "We've certainly had some adventures."

Lumiere's manacles clinked together as he turned and faced a shelf of no particular distinction. He reached out and grabbed onto something in front of him, something I couldn't see, and twisted it. From the sound I heard, I would've said he was winding up a watch.

Then he stepped back down with a proud look on his face, and we waited expectantly.

For several long seconds, nothing happened. I was about to tell him he must've been wrong when there was a loud creak, and the bookshelf pressed inward, opening to a secret stairway that headed downward.

I could feel the dank chill in its air, and I could taste the musky scent of its fog.

"Don't be afraid," Lumiere said teasingly. "The music is what is making it worse right now. The organ pipes reach up to heaven, but they also remind the listener that death is but one breath away for all of us in the end."

"It's dark in there." I hurriedly gathered up my skirts and cut them up again, before grabbing a flag nearby and stripping off its colored fabric.

"What are you doing?" Ben asked as I broke the pole in two.

"Making a *flambeau*," I said. "It's not like we have a lot of candlesticks available right now, and it doesn't look like it's lit."

"I approve of torches," Lumiere agreed.

"I don't think one will be enough for all of us. Marguerite? Can you give me some of your skirt fabric?"

"No." Ben stepped in front of her. "No, she's not going with us."

Marguerite was just as surprised as I was by his statement.

"Why not?" she asked, looking indignant and hurt. "I have been with Lady Penelope for several years now. I can handle walking around in the dark."

"No." Ben's voice was hard. "You already almost got hurt back there, and you should go home now."

"You saved me."

"Yes, but now I'd rather you wait at the manor."

Ben had always been a perfect gentleman with Betsy and Mavis, and our other friends who'd worked under Cecilia. He was naturally protective, but I was still surprised at how brusquely he spoke to Marguerite.

I knew there was something between them, but I still couldn't say what, other than I could tell she was smitten with him.

Didn't he like her in the same way?

I'd caught him staring at her before. Had I been mistaken about his affections?

"Ella, let me help you with that," Ferdy offered, rolling up the fabric around the broken flagpole more tightly. "Why don't you go find a fireplace, and we can borrow some fire from it?"

He was practically pushing me out of the room, but he was also right.

"Watch Lumiere for me," I muttered reluctantly as Lumiere began betting Didier on who would win between Ben and Marguerite. I didn't have to look at Ferdy to know he was aching to put in his own wager.

Hurriedly, I located a fireplace and lit the torch. When I returned to the library, I slowed my steps to listen.

Ben and Marguerite were still whispering furiously with each other.

"I want to help you," I heard her argue.

I stopped moving, pressed my body against the wall, and cocked an ear toward their conversation. The flagpole in my hand continued to burn as I eavesdropped.

"I don't need your help. I need your cooperation," Ben insisted. "Please, go back to the manor. You shouldn't have come with us."

"I volunteered," Marguerite reminded him. "You can't order me around. Nora will let me come, just as Lady POW said I could come with you earlier."

Ben stifled a groan. "Marguerite … I don't want you to be in danger."

"Why not?"

"Because that's a very sensible position."

"But I don't want you to be in danger, either."

I smiled; Marguerite was good at holding her own against him. I didn't know if Ben would like that or not.

"I know we're not going to agree on this." From Ben's voice, I knew he was annoyed. "What can I give you, if you promise to go home and stay there and wait for me?"

"I can have anything?"

I held my breath as Ben paused.

"If you're sure you want it," he finally replied. "And if I can give it—then yes."

There was another scuffle of movement, and I finally glanced into the room as Marguerite wrapped her arms around Ben's neck, leaned up, and kissed him.

My eyes went wide as I stood there, watching as Ben softened against her, ever so slightly before he quickly—but gently—untangled himself from her.

"Thank you," Marguerite said. "We have a deal. But fair warning—this is the last time I'm stepping back, Ben."

"Thank you." Ben's cheeks were a light red as he saw me watching them.

I was stupefied at what I'd witnessed, but Ben glanced over at Didier.

"Can you take her home?" he asked.

"I will be glad to protect Miss Marguerite," Didier said. "Assuming Lumiere won't need me."

"We always need those who are loyal to us, and we'll miss you, but it's for the best you go," Lumiere replied. "You've seen only a sample of what my father is capable of doing. It's best if you're safe from him, too, this one, last time. This is no time for weakness, *mon ami*, my own included."

As Lumiere gave Didier another set of cryptic instructions for his contingencies, I walked up and stood beside Ben. "Well, I guess my prayers didn't work."

When he arched his brow at me, I smiled. "Marguerite's quite pretty, and you said you'd wanted an odd wife."

"Oh, Ella … I'm not talking about this with you. Besides," he muttered, "I said 'unique,' not 'odd.'"

"God knows what I meant." I watched as Marguerite headed out the door behind Didier. She turned back one last time to smile at Ben.

THE ORDER OF THE CRYSTAL DAGGERS

As I let out a small chuckle, Ben shook his head. "I'm still not talking about this with you."

"And that's for the best," Ferdy agreed. "We must go now. We've already been delayed long enough. Right, *mon frère?*"

Ben gave Ferdy a gruff nod, and I smiled; my brother knew Ferdy was rescuing him at that moment, and Ben was eager to embrace the offer.

"Lead the way, Lumiere." I handed the torch off to Ferdy as I picked up the gun again. "You should go first since you enjoy being such a *light* to others."

"Your jesting pains me more than bullets," Lumiere scoffed.

"You aren't going to be arguing all the way to the fort, are you?" Ben asked. "Maybe I should go with Marguerite."

"No, it's better you're here with us. Now we can tease you about her in person," Lumiere said.

Despite the tension surrounding us, I was grateful for the distracting banter as we headed down below the University and walked toward *Vyšehrad*.

The chill came up and settled around my exposed ankles, and the tunnels were narrow and cramped. The path was lined with stones and cement from ages before, and I had to breathe deep breaths to stay calm in the small, dark space.

This will all be over soon.

We would save Karl. Lord Maximillian would go to prison. Louis would be stopped. The kingdom would know peace, and I would defend my mother's honor.

Or at least, I hoped so.

26

◊

It seemed like a long time passed as we walked under the city. I heard the gentle *splish-splash* of the Vltava's waves through the walls until we came to a stairway.

We climbed upward, and Ferdy stepped forward to open up a hidden gate.

And then we were free.

"Thank you, Lord." I was grateful to be back outside, even if it was dark now. The air was still cold, but it was much more pungent and fresh, and I could breathe much more easily. I tossed my makeshift torch into the water eagerly.

I looked around to see we came out on a stone path on the riverbanks, far down below the actual fort of *Vyšehrad*.

"Hold up." Ben held up his arm, and the rest of us went still.

Two pairs of guards appeared, walking across the battlements above us.

"We should head for the fort's cemetery," Ferdy whispered as they walked by. "There's an entrance there that no one guards."

"How do you know?" I asked.

"My parents often brought me and Karl to *Vyšehrad* when we were younger. I didn't ever imagine I'd try sneaking into it. But I remember enough to know this is the southeast side."

It was too easy to forget sometimes that Ferdy had grown up as a hidden prince of Bohemia. I glanced down at the common street clothes he wore. His copper hair was more red than ever against the wintery background, and his eyes twinkled with silver mischief as he smiled at me.

Ferdy craned his neck toward the gatehouse. "If I had to guess, Karl's going to be in his assigned chambers here, or Lord Maximillian might have even put him in the king's rooms. I'm not sure where Louis would be."

"We'll get Karl first," I said. "That's the most important part of all of this."

It was what I'd been working toward for the last several weeks, and if it hadn't been for all the anguish I'd suffered so far today, I would've almost been excited to be there.

Ferdy took the lead, and the rest of us followed without issue—even Lumiere who seemed oddly quiet as we climbed up stairs, hid in alcoves, and ducked down on the ground as we made our way toward the keep.

As we came to the top of the bailey, we passed by a cellar. Inside the large stone chambers were a number of barrels and boxes. Behind them, several doors were on the other side, and Ferdy nodded when I asked him if they led out to the landing port.

"In times of war, this area would be filled with weapons and supplies," Ferdy said. "These barrels are likely full of food and water and other supplies for the castle's occupants."

"I doubt it. Look at the ground. Several barrels have been brought in and out of here recently," Ben said, pointing at tracks on the ground. There were several footsteps and scratches where large items had been moved.

Using Amir's dagger, he pried open one that was nearby. Inside, there was a large quantity of the sand-colored powder I'd seen at Count Potocki's house.

"Looks like Lord Maximillian has already paid Louis for his services," Ben said in a disgusted voice.

"Louis wants the dynamite to sell to both sides of the war." I glanced over at Lumiere. "Isn't that what you said?"

"Yes, but I don't know if they've officially concluded their arrangements or not." Lumiere shrugged, before he nodded to Ferdy. "You can probably make the guards tell us. They are Bohemian, and they should listen to you."

I brightened. "We could try that."

"No." Ferdy's face blanched over before he shook his head. "I'm not really a prince, Ella."

"But what if you could stop this now?" I asked.

"I doubt I could. Karl hasn't been able to leave this place. He only came out for Count Potocki's ball," Ferdy reminded me. "If Karl's not in charge, I can't see why I would be able to order anyone around here, either."

"We could still try."

"When we were younger, Karl would always play the crown prince in here, terrorizing the guards," Ferdy said, looking up at the twin bell towers of the basilica before us, and then to the yard full of graves off to its side. "But not me. I've never wanted a prince's power or authority."

"But—"

"No," he insisted, more sharply this time. "Some men need a king to follow, but no man deserves to be a king. It's too much for me, Ella, and it's too tempting—"

"You can do so much good with it, though. And it would help us now," I argued. "Don't be such a coward."

"I'd rather be a coward than a tyrant," Ferdy shot back, surprising me with the sudden flare of his temper. He glanced over at Lumiere, and his eyes went dark with vengeful lightning. "My brother tried to kill me, and he succeeded in killing my friends. It's already too tempting to use any means for my own satisfaction."

"Oh, Ferdy." My heart ached at his sadness and anger. I'd known that feeling myself earlier.

Lumiere let out a loud, disgruntled sigh as I passed Ben the gun, and I slipped into Ferdy's arms.

"Do you know why I love you?" I asked him.

Ferdy attempted to smile. "My charm, my wit, my good looks?" His joking fell flat, but I still smiled.

"No. I love you because you give me such hope." I rested my head on his shoulder, willing him to be comforted. "Even now, when you're afraid and you suffer, you don't stop me from doing what ought to be done. And even more, you come with me and stand beside me, trying to protect me."

"I'm not that scared," Ferdy muttered, irritated more than angry now. "Just cautious, and rightly so, given my brother's tendency toward despotism."

"You are not your brother," I reminded him, keeping my voice kind. "You are your own self—just as I am, remember?"

Ferdy paused for a moment, and then he gave me a small, rueful smile. "Well, I can see why we're perfect for each other."

"Because you remind me who I am, and I tell you who you're not?"

"No," Ferdy said with a soft chuckle. "Because you make me afraid like nothing else."

"You want to know what I'm afraid of?" Lumiere asked from behind us. "That you'll mess this up, and all because you always stare into each other's eyes and moan about how much you're in love. That's not going to stop *mon père*."

I wrinkled my nose at Lumiere. "You're just jealous."

Ferdy laughed, and he seemed to be back to more of his usual self. But then he tightened his grip on me. "I've already lost so much. I can't lose you, Ella. If I lose you, I'll lose myself, too."

"You won't lose me," I promised.

"Are you done now?" Lumiere huffed. "I'm getting tired of sappy speeches."

"You've had your own share of them," I reminded him.

"I still wouldn't count on any of my supposed princely authority." Ferdy interrupted our fighting by returning us back to our earlier concern. "We don't know who's really in charge, and I don't exactly look like a Bohemian prince right now."

"Would that really be an issue?" Ben asked skeptically.

"Probably." Ferdy gave him a sheepish look. "More than once, Philip took my place here while I snuck out to the city."

"If you don't want the authority, you should've started with that argument. No one wants to take orders from a beggar or a farmer, unless they're American." Lumiere eyed Ferdy's attire disdainfully before turning back to me. "If you're done playing the role of the good wife, take the gun back from Ben. I don't want him holding me hostage."

"Why not?" I asked with a renewed sense of suspicion.

"He's the better shot, and he's much better than your husband, too." Lumiere scowled. "But also, you'll need to be in control when we run into *mon père*, Ella. He needs to see you're in charge, and the person in charge is usually the one who's got the most threatening weapon."

"Usually?"

"You have to consider that I'm the one telling you to keep it," Lumiere said, sneering with snide pleasure. "I just hope I don't have to tell you when to use it, too."

It was tempting to ask him if that meant I should use it on him, but I resisted it and focused on what needed to be done. "Where are Karl's rooms located, Ferdy?"

"In the keep."

"What do we do about the dynamite powder?" Ben asked, gesturing toward the small collection of barrels. "We can't just leave it here."

"We're not going to be able to do anything about it now," I said. "We need to get Karl first."

"We can come back for it later," Ferdy said. "For now, follow me."

Ben was reluctant to leave the barrels, but Karl needed to be rescued first.

Ferdy led us through the last hidden trails of the graveyard, walked through a small vineyard, slipped through the basilica, and headed inside the fortified keep.

Immediately, we all scrambled to hide in a courtyard bower as another pair of guards passed by.

They'd just missed seeing us, but they were busy talking about the "little prince" who was fortunately imprisoned in his room.

Finally.

Ferdy smiled as we slid out from our dark hiding spot. "For once, I'm glad Karl likes to talk so much."

"Me, too." I thought about how it was too easy to coax information from Karl when I'd danced with him.

After that, all of us were able to get to Karl's door without trouble. There were guards that patrolled through the hallway, but none that were standing in front of his room.

There was no obstacle to freeing Karl—other than his locked door.

"Ben?" I was about to ask him to pick the lock when Karl started pounding on the door.

"Hello? Hello, guards? I can hear you, and I demand you let me free at once," Karl called out. His voice was a little hoarse, as though he'd been yelling for some time. "I know you're there."

Lumiere groaned. "Do we have to free him?"

Before I could answer, Karl began ranting and raving about why he shouldn't be locked up when the Emperor was coming to visit, and how he and Lord Maximilian were equal partners in their political arrangements.

Karl was in full tantrum mode, but at least we'd found him, and he was alive.

"Doesn't sound like an equal partnership to me," Ben grumbled. "Keep watch for us, Ferdy."

"I'm good at that." Ferdy grinned.

"Yes," Ben said tersely. "I know."

"Of course, *mon frère*," Ferdy said, as I held back a giggle. It was too easy to recall Ben's objection to Ferdy spying on us after seeing us outside Wickward's shop.

A moment later, thanks to Ben's handywork, the knob clicked open, and Karl yanked open the door.

"Finally, it's about time you … "

His voice trailed off as he stared at all of us.

I imagined the sight surprised him as much as it angered him. All of us were tired and ragged, covered in dirt and sweat, and my arm ached as I still held the gun to Lumiere's back.

Karl was a little surprising himself. While he wore the formal jacket of a king, with its gold braid and shining buttons paired down the front, I could see stray threads peeking out from the frayed cuffs and collar. His gray eyes were darkened from stress, while his cheeks were hollow and thin. His jaw was tight, his hair needed a trim, and there were even a few strands of light grey in his ebony locks.

He had been miserable at the Potocki ball, but I could now see it wasn't just because he'd dreaded seeing me again.

Karl remained speechless as Ferdy motioned to Ben that the guards were coming, and Ben quickly ushered all of us into the room and shut the door again.

It was very nice, with large windows and elegant furniture. The floor was graced with Oriental rugs, and the room was covered in a much nicer green-colored silk wallpaper. A desk was off to the side, littered with papers and ink and books, and further off to the side, there was an alcove in the back for sleeping.

Karl might have been held against his will, but he was still surrounded by comfort and security.

"Why are you here?" Karl finally found his voice again as he glared at us in disbelief. "If you've come to take the throne away from me, you're not going to succeed."

"The idea that we're 'taking the throne' from you implies you have it in the first place," Ferdy argued.

"You're happy to be a pauper. You can't imagine the loss I feel. If you weren't my brother, I would challenge you to a duel!"

"You've already tried to have me killed. That would be a step up for you and your so-called notions of honor."

"You don't deserve honor," Karl hissed. "You stole Ella from me and you've twisted her mind, and now you want Bohemia to suffer."

"Bohemia would suffer if you were its king."

"Stop," I ordered, stepping between them. "Karl, Bohemia is part of the Empire now. Nothing you do can—"

"I refuse to believe that," Karl snapped.

Lumiere chuckled. "This is exactly why I told *mon père* that it would be much better to keep you two separate."

"Be quiet, Lumiere," I snapped.

"You know I'm right, Ella. They'll always have their little squabbles, over you as well as the throne. Can you believe my father didn't agree with me at first? It took me some time to convince him otherwise, too. He's getting old."

Ferdy and Karl began arguing again as I thought about Louis' appearance in the Cabal. He was calm and even very polite, but when Lumiere appeared with Ferdy in hand, he'd seemed largely unimpressed and even expressed derision toward his son. "He likely has good reasons to disagree with you at times."

"Good reasons, no. His own reasons? Yes."

"You're just as bad as he is when you say it that way."

"Wisdom is seen in how you use knowledge, just as virtue is how you choose to contend with opportunities," Lumiere drawled. "I'm working toward my goals while he has his own end in mind."

"And what are your goals, exactly?" I asked, suddenly curious.

"His end, of course." His eyes glimmered. "I should thank him, really. Thanks to my father's investments—the more legitimate ones—all I have to do is secure his arrest and trials, and I'll have enough money to live out the rest of my days as I see fit. And while he's all excited at the thought of profiting off worldwide warfare, I prefer to be left alone."

"You wish for freedom." I suddenly wondered how I'd never realized it before.

"Of course I do. Men like my father want power—the ability to determine truth and its meaning, and how it should be used. What a waste of a life, if you ask me." Lumiere eyed Karl with clear disgust. "And look at this one here. The promise of power seduces the worst sort of men, and somehow manages to make them even more repulsive."

"Excuse me?" Karl took a break from arguing with Ferdy to scowl at Lumiere.

"Cloaking your degeneracy in decency never works, young princeling." Lumiere smirked. "That's why I've always worn my sins so well. I don't have to lie about them in addition to covering them up."

"You are clearly a deviant, sir, and I will not be lectured by the likes of you." Karl was incensed. "I don't have to guess to know this is all your doing, Eleanora. Is the Order here to kill me if I don't cooperate?"

"No," I said. "I promised your mother I would bring you back to her. Given your current circumstances, it might be the best option for you right now."

"That is preposterous."

"All of us heard you yelling just now," I told him. "You're stuck as a prisoner here, and you're not going to tell me that you agreed to it?"

THE ORDER OF THE CRYSTAL DAGGERS

"I did at first." Karl flustered. "It seemed sensible. Max was compromised, and I couldn't afford the scandal of a broken engagement—"

"Especially when you'd lost your bride to your own brother, no less," Ferdy interrupted with a smug grin, and I shook my head at him in warning.

Karl's mouth twisted in displeasure. "And certainty not when the public was so enthralled with Eleanora."

"They'll soon forget about me," I said. "I was a sensation, but I wasn't that popular. And Society will forget me soon enough."

"They'll remember you longer than you think. If I was to free Bohemia from the Empire, I needed money, and I needed Society's blessing. It was the perfect time to act, and you would've helped me," Karl said. "You provided the social influence—intrigue, connections, money, and historical prestige. It was perfect. Until I found out you lied to me."

"Lord Maximillian killed people with his dynamite at the Advent Ball, and you're complicit in his crimes. And you tried to kill me, and everyone else, at Count Potocki's. I ruined your plans to kill people, and that was a good thing," I said, much more calmly than I felt. "You're lucky I'm not here to kill you after all of that."

"Your death would have been a point of sympathy," Karl explained, as if I'd be honored by his self-concerned intentions. "It was Max's idea to build on the outrage of the Advent Ball incident. But Louis said we should wait until you were here along with the Emperor. He said if we killed you here, it would anger the Bohemians even more."

I glanced over at Lumiere, who nodded. "*C'est vrai, chérie.* You make a good prize, dead or alive."

"Ella's not going to die," Ben said. "And we're not leaving here without you, Karl."

345

THE ORDER OF THE CRYSTAL DAGGERS

Karl eyed Ben carefully. He'd only seen him a handful of times, if that, and when I saw Karl look at Ben's brace and wrinkle his brow in disdain, I almost hit him.

"So are you going to come with us to go see your mother, or are we going to drag you out of here?" Ben's tone was a bit harsher as he spoke this time, and I knew he'd seen Karl's judgmental assessment.

"Do I have a choice?" Karl scowled.

"Do you?" I asked. "Louis and Lord Maximillian don't seem eager to let you do as you'd like."

Karl's wan face blushed over crimson again. "I suppose you have a point."

"I think you should stay here," Ferdy said, before I could tell him to stop aggravating his brother. "Your handlers wouldn't like it if you disobeyed them."

"I'll go where I want, *brother.* You can't tell me to stay," Karl snarled. "If you've unlocked the doors, we can leave now."

He marched toward the door as Ferdy gave me a quick wink and one of his charming grins. I could almost hear him bragging about manipulating Karl. I bit back a smile, before turning to Lumiere.

"All right, Lumiere, let's—"

I was suddenly interrupted by the sound of a trumpet and marching soldiers, followed by a lone gunshot that crackled like lightning.

Terror ran down my spine, and I could feel the tension around us thicken with the threat of danger.

All of us headed for the windows.

"Look, Ella," Ben whispered, pointing down toward the riverbank. I followed the direction he indicated to see a small line of palace soldiers heading toward *Vyšehrad*. "It looks like Harshad and Lady POW were able to do what you wanted."

A rush of happiness overwhelmed me.

Lady Penelope and I had agreed we would get more done if we split up our party; I went after Ferdy and Lumiere, and she'd gone to catch Louis. But before heading out for *Vyšehrad*, I'd wanted her to go see Empress Maria Anna and inform her about Louis' plans.

Even if we hadn't yet rescued Karl, I'd suspected the former Empress would be willing to aid us if she could. Ferdy offered to write a letter to his mother himself.

And now, thanks to the approaching regiment of soldiers, even if Louis had sought to trap us, he was the one who was now trapped.

"This is good." Ferdy exhaled with relief. "It'll be better having my parents' guard here."

"Yes, they know you and your real face better," Lumiere remarked from behind us.

"We should still get Karl out of here," I said. "It'll be safer for him if he's further away from both Louis and Lord Maximillian. Come on, Lumiere."

"Try to make it more convincing, would you?"

"Fine." I held the gun up to his chest. "Let's go get Karl, Lumiere, or I'll shoot you."

"That's an improvement, but I think you can still do better. It's not like I want to go on a nice jaunt around the fort here."

I gritted my teeth. "You've been sitting or lying around the manor for weeks now, drinking an excess of alcohol and spirits. You should thank me for making you move your bloated form along. You need the exercise."

"Are you calling me fat?"

"I didn't say that. Specifically." It was hard not to laugh at the horrified look on his face, but he'd wanted me to be more convincing, and his vanity was an easy target.

It helped that he did seem to be a little more robust since I first saw him in the Cabal, or even when he'd donned Hawaiian coconuts and colorful flowers at the Estates Theatre. It could've been his clothes, but as I examined his midsection, I wondered if I'd been right.

And then I felt bad, because I remembered how Lady Penelope would stare at my stomach for any signs of pregnancy or laziness.

Thinking of her, I gripped the gun in one hand and pulled out my mother's dagger with the other.

I hated how alike we were at times, but in this one instance, it was to my advantage.

Lumiere crossed his arms. "That was better. I'll humor you for your efforts."

"Thank you for your cooperation," I murmured, prodding him with the gun again; in spite of his egregious graciousness, I figured he could use the extra incentive to move.

"Ella." Ben took my arm briefly. "I'm going to go to the front and see if I can find Lady Penelope and Harshad. I'll let them know you've got Karl so she can concentrate on finding Louis, and maybe Harshad and I can do something about the dynamite powder."

I didn't like the thought of separating from Ben this time; if we had run into this situation back when we first started training, I wouldn't have let him go.

"I'll be all right," Ben promised. "My leg's doing well enough. I also have the other gun and Amir's dagger."

It was touching and insulting that he knew me so well, especially my weaknesses.

Reluctantly, I nodded. "That's probably a good idea," I conceded. "Be careful."

"I will."

Ben walked away, wincing as his limp was a little exaggerated because of the fort's stony floors. I almost called him back, but Ferdy brushed up beside me.

"Your brother will be fine," he said. "My brother, on the other hand … "

Karl sniffed loudly from behind us. "I'd rather you stop talking about me as though I'm not present. I can hear you just fine."

"I'm sorry." I apologized without thinking, making Lumiere laugh at me.

Ferdy frowned at Karl. "Stop talking to my wife."

Karl eyed him maliciously. "*Your wife* can handle me speaking to her."

"I don't care. You stop talking to her, or I'll—"

"You'll what?" Karl sneered, his voice suddenly more vicious than I'd ever heard it before. "Kill me?"

"You'd be so lucky," Ferdy snapped back.

"Please stop." I didn't want to beg them to behave, but I could see Karl had less incentive than ever to help us out. He'd been gallant enough to refrain from forcing himself on me, but he was starting to realize his plans had all failed. "You're family, for goodness' sake."

I took Ferdy's arm. "You told me that Karl always looked out for you when you were younger," I reminded him. "He saw to your well-being."

349

THE ORDER OF THE CRYSTAL DAGGERS

"If only to keep him from embarrassing me and the rest of our royal heritage," Karl snapped.

"And you," I said, trying not to let my anger overtake my voice. "You should realize that Ferdy is not the one at fault because your father favored him over you."

Karl's face turned purple. "Is that what he told you?" Karl sputtered; he was so angry, I knew I'd spoken the raw truth. "What utter rubbish. My father was a king, and he was an awful one. I shouldn't have lost the crown because of his incompetency. I don't care if he liked Ferdinand better."

"You shouldn't get a crown just because of your bloodline, either," Ferdy said, and I shot him another warning look.

"You're still brothers, and you're still family," I repeated, more angrily this time. "You might not trust each other, but you should still have some affection for one another."

There was nothing repentant on either Ferdy or Karl's face, and I sighed, eager to give up.

Reconciliation was a dream, and just then, I could only hope we would be able to contain Karl's anger long enough to get out of *Vyšehrad* safely.

I only had one gun, and I needed it to move Lumiere along.

At the thought of him, I turned to see he was staring out the window now with a look of interest on his face. "What is it, Lumiere?"

"We'd better hurry if we're going to leave," Lumiere said. "It's getting dark, but I can still see it."

"See what?" Ferdy asked, moving over beside him.

"The Emperor's flagship."

Just as he spoke, a round of gunfire sounded out from near the entrance of the fort.

THE ORDER OF THE CRYSTAL DAGGERS

A sinking feeling tore through my knotted stomach. I didn't know how, but I knew we needed to get out of there. And fast.

Quickly, I gathered up Ferdy, Karl, and Lumiere, and we ran out into the open air of the courtyard.

The fort's guardsmen were running and gathering in small groups, heading for the battlements as the sounds of battle began increasing from the front.

"What are Lady POW and Harshad doing?" I wondered aloud. "They should be able to get in with the former Empress' soldiers coming, shouldn't they?"

A new voice answered my question.

"The guards here are under my orders." Lord Maximillian's voice was precise and formal as I whirled around to face him. "And I've told them not to let anyone else in, especially now that you are here, Lady Eleanora."

27

◊

"Karl." Lord Maximillian stared down at Karl angrily. "Why are you out of your room?"

"I didn't have much of a choice." Karl clutched at his fraying sleeves as he gestured to me and the weapons I held. "Besides, if you hadn't locked me up, we wouldn't have such an issue."

"That's no way for a man to talk to his future father-in-law—or his future king."

"I'm the one who will be the king," Karl insisted. "Not you."

"You're not in charge here," Lord Maximillian reminded him. "You've already caused me too much trouble in Bohemia. Now that Louis and I have finalized our deal, you will serve me and follow my orders—or you will die."

Lord Maximillian had said before he would gain power when Lady Teresa Marie married Karl. Now it was clear that he intended to rule himself.

Beside me, Karl stiffened with fear. I held my breath, while Ferdy looked worried and Lumiere yawned.

"But you're not the king, or even an immediate heir," I said to Lord Maximillian. "Why would Bohemia accept you as their king?"

I was stalling for time, desperate to think of something.

Lady POW and Harshad were still outside *Vyšehrad*. Ben had gone off to find them. I didn't think I'd be able to shoot him, and I didn't actually want to kill him. Lord Maximillian was a witness to Louis' crimes in Prague and Silesia, and he

352

had also implicated himself with the development of a dynamite-like weapon that could be used for war.

At least he wasn't armed, I noticed.

"They know a respectable leader when they see one." Lord Maximillian sneered at me and stepped forward carefully. I noticed he was limping a little, thanks to how I'd managed to injure him the other night.

"Do they?" I asked quietly.

"Lady Eleanora has an excellent point, Maximillian."

All of us turned toward the sound of Louis Valoris' voice.

The evening starlight reflected off the pristine white of his hair and the little golden threads in his embroidered tunic. Louis was stylish and stately, calm and in charge, ever the master of both chaos and order.

Behind me, I heard Lumiere shuffle, and I quickly held my gun at the level of his heart.

Louis didn't seem to mind. "*Bon nuit* to you, my honored guests. I know we had such a lovely time earlier, but I'll admit I didn't prepare for your arrival quite this soon. I pray you'll forgive me."

I was about to tell him he should pray for something else when he turned back to Lord Maximillian.

"I'd like to hear your answer to Lady Eleanora's question. Do Bohemians truly know a respectable leader when they see him?"

"Excuse me?" Lord Maximillian was caught off guard by Louis' question.

Ferdy tugged my arm, trying to pull me back toward a stairway, where there was an alcove, one that we could use for cover.

353

"I wouldn't move if I were you, Lady Eleanora." Louis spoke firmly, leaving our small group frozen where we stood. "You want to know the answer to your question, don't you? You asked for it, after all."

"Well, Maximillian?" Louis looked at him expectantly.

"I am a duke," Lord Maximillian finally answered. "I am rich, and I've worked with weaponry and warfare for years. I own my own land, and I have grown my vineyards, made my own wine, and sold it for profits to fund my research for years."

"That describes you; it says nothing of Bohemia, or its people." Louis smirked. "I think you'll find much more resistance than you'd like to believe.

"Take the guardsmen here for example. You may believe they'll listen to you, but they've worked for me for years already." Louis gestured toward the battlements. "They're enjoying their playtime with you here, but they all know who they answer to in the end."

Before Lord Maximillian could reply, Louis pulled out a gun of his own and shot him.

I swallowed the scream in my throat as Lord Maximillian fell to the ground, writhing in pain as he clutched at his torso.

Louis laughed. "I'll admit, I must thank you, Maximillian. Your explosives will greatly profit me now that France and Germany are at war, and soon the rest of Europe will be too, including Bohemia, and all the countries in the Austria-Hungarian Empire."

So that's what he wanted.

Louis didn't care about Bohemia's kingdom, or its ruler. He just wanted war across the continent.

"I'll kill you for this," Lord Maximillian hissed angrily, still grappling with the pain in his side.

"We've had a very good partnership. But now that your weapon is being mixed up in more factories, and all your research is in my hands, I don't need you anymore. You're just a broken man."

"No more good to me than a horse with a broken leg," Lumiere whispered behind me.

"No more good to me than a horse with a broken leg," Louis continued, walking closer to Lord Maximillian's fallen form.

He shot his gun again, and this time, Lord Maximillian grabbed his leg. His shrieks of pain echoed throughout the courtyard as blood poured out, and Louis shot him in the other leg.

"Stop it," I cried, unable to bear Lord Maximillian's screams any longer.

"It's not me doing this." Louis was still as calm as ever as he smiled at me. "Why would you and the Order of the Crystal Daggers take care of a duke like Lord Maximillian like this?"

"But the Order's not—" I stopped, shutting my mouth as I realized Louis didn't need Lady Penelope to frame the Order for any crimes.

I was present—and armed with a gun.

Louis was amused as he turned his gun on Ferdy, and then he moved it to Karl. "What do you think? Who should die for the Order next?"

"No." My nerves shattered with dread. I stood there, unable to move, barely able to breathe.

From the look on Karl's face, he was in just as much turmoil as I was. Ferdy looked on Louis' steady figure with a grim expression, but all elements of his irreverence and lightheartedness were gone.

Gunshots and fighting was still going on from the entrance, and Lord Maximillian was whimpering as he crawled away from the courtyard.

"Come now," Louis persisted. "I'll even let you choose, Eleanora. Which prince would you save? The man you love, who's been hidden even more carefully from the public eye, or the prince willing to destroy the world to restore Bohemia's national pride? I only need one of them alive to get the Emperor to realize cooperation with me is not optional."

I swallowed hard. "You can't kill either of them."

"That's not very fun," Louis said.

"I can't choose between the two of them." I shook my head. Ferdy was my heart's future, and Karl was my mother's past. "But I have a better idea."

Louis laughed. "The Emperor isn't here yet. Who would I kill instead?"

I lowered the gun I held. "Take me instead."

"Oh?" Louis arched his brow at me. "I'd rather not kill you. I like having a scapegoat alive. It's rather fun to watch them squirm."

Lumiere cleared his throat behind me.

"Ella," Lumiere whispered, deliberately interrupting me as I was trying to save Ferdy and Karl.

"Lumiere." I hissed through gritted teeth. "What is it?"

"The gun he's using is a Smith & Wesson Model 3. It has five shots before he needs to reload."

"So?" I barely registered his words; I had no idea what he meant.

And then Lumiere suddenly burst into tears.

"Oh, *Papa!*" Lumiere cried out in sniveling relief. "I am so glad you're here. Ella has captured me, and she's going to kill me next if you don't save me!"

I saw the slightest twitch along Louis' jaw. "Not now, Lumiere."

He was enough of a distraction that even if I lost my composure, I was able to regain my resolve.

"Lumiere is not wrong." I held up my gun again, pointing it carefully at Lumiere's heart. "But not for the reason you might think."

Louis arched his brow. "You're quite bold, Eleanora, but you're also naïve and innocent. I'm not interested in a trade for him, and I know you'd never kill him."

"I would if I had to," I said, doing my best to keep the nervousness out of my voice. "And that's why you should take me instead of killing Karl or Ferdy. Take me as your apprentice."

I saw the flicker of surprise on his face.

"You're right about me, Mr. Valoris," I told him, my eyes filling with tears. "I am idealistic and inexperienced, and I don't have the confidence like you. But I would do anything to save Ferdy. And Karl, too."

"Ella. What are you doing?" Ferdy asked.

"The only thing I can do," I said, keeping my gaze on Louis. "I've thought about it, and you've been right about me, and so much more, in the short time I've known you, Mr. Valoris."

He was watching me with interest now. "Such as?"

"Such as weakness, and how imperfections can ruin everything." I swallowed hard, but I straightened my shoulders.

I had to do this, I told myself.

I had to.

It was the only way.

"I've seen that Lady Penelope is unfit to instruct me as her pupil, and my mother was right to leave her."

"That's enough out of you, Eleanora." Lady Penelope's voice called out from off to the side, but it never sounded more grating. "Stop this foolishness."

She appeared in the east side entrance to the courtyard. Harshad was close behind her. Both of them were armed with guns, and Lady Penelope was carrying the dagger of the Order in her left hand. There were still gunshots ringing around us, and I figured she'd left the palace guards to fight off Louis' men as she made her way here. Quickly, I looked for Ben, but I didn't see him.

"No, that's enough of you, Madame," I snapped. "You say I'm a disappointment to you, but what of yourself? You failed to kill Louis when we met in the Cabal earlier—

"You asked me not to," Lady Penelope interrupted, but I kept talking over her.

"—and you didn't shoot Xiana after she killed Amir—"

"I can kill Louis now," she offered harshly, but I intentionally moved and stepped in front of Louis.

Lady Penelope and Harshad both looked shocked, and I could almost feel Louis' amused approval from behind me.

"No," I said. "You are a coward. You've always blamed me for our troubles. But now I know you're the one who is weak. You can't even keep your own family safe!"

Lady Penelope's eyes suddenly shimmered with angry tears.

"Eleanora," Harshad said. "Please stop."

"But I'm right!" I insisted.

"That's true," Louis agreed cheerfully. "I may have lost money and investments throughout our history together, but I have taken what you love most, Penelope."

I turned toward Louis. "You've said I've made good progress in my learning. Well, if I'm going to be better, I need a good teacher, Mr. Valoris. One who is accomplished and successful. Lady Penelope is unfit for the job, and a failure."

"That is also true." Louis nodded.

"So if you will keep Ferdy and Karl safe, I will pledge myself to your tutelage and work to become worthy as your partner, your right-hand man."

Louis looked at me, maliciously pleased and impressed. "Your offer is enticing."

"That's enough of this, Eleanora." Lady Penelope's voice trembled as she scolded me.

I would not let her deter me. I would not give into guilt, I vowed, as I scowled back at her.

"I'm tired of your failure. You ruined Amir's life, and my mother's, too. And because you couldn't see Xiana's treachery, I lost a sister."

"Louis is the one who's responsible for her death," Lady Penelope reminded me.

"Only because you failed to stop him," I pressed. "You've always hated Louis Valoris because he was the successful victor, and now, I will serve him. Even at the cost of my honor. It's clear to me that your honor only serves you, Madame. That will not be my fate. I'm not like you—and that's the greatest failure you could ever have."

"Death or defeat, Eleanora!" Lady Penelope insisted. She pulled her gun level up to me, and I couldn't say if she would

THE ORDER OF THE CRYSTAL DAGGERS

shoot me or not. "That is the only way a member of the Order leaves."

My knees buckled, but I couldn't back down now.

"No, Ella," Ferdy insisted. "What are you doing?"

"I love you," I told him. "And I can't lose you."

Lady Penelope looked stricken, and Louis only laughed.

I turned to face Louis. "I will do anything it takes to keep my family safe. Even if it means betraying you. Even if I have to kill for it."

"I must admit, I wasn't expecting this when I arrived here," he said.

Lumiere groaned loudly. "I'll agree it's been fun, but if you are going to accept her offer, will you have Ella release me or not, *Papa?*"

Louis gave me a thoughtful look. "Your offer is a good one, but I already have Lumiere for my second-in-command."

"I must inform you, sir, that Lumiere is not a good partner for you." Slowly, I secured my finger around the gun's trigger. "My offer will be more enticing to you after I tell you Lumiere is a traitor. He's been giving Lady Penelope information, and he only pretended to kidnap Ferdy earlier. He also killed Xiana."

Louis gave Lumiere a questioning look. "Well, Lumiere?" His voice was still cheerful and amused. He didn't seem bothered at all by my news, until Lumiere smirked back at him.

Slowly, Lumiere moved backward and stood in front of the wall of the courtyard. He held up his hands in surrender.

"Ella is right," Lumiere said, the easy pride in his voice full of amusement. "I guess it's for the best I tell you the truth at last, Old Man. I'm done following your orders, and I've decided to defect to Lady Penelope's side—officially, of course. I have been undermining you for years already. And I know I'm perfectly safe, since you will always protect me, *ne c'est pas?*"

There was absolute silence as Louis' expression completely lost its good humor.

"You see?" I said. "I've seen it myself, and I know how you feel about imperfections like this, Mr. Valoris. I used him to find you, but I will turn him over to you now as proof of my desire to serve you."

Louis's lips thinned into a barely perceivable line.

"I know I'm not your flesh and blood," I continued, my resolve strengthening. "But that's even better, isn't it? I'm Lady Penelope's granddaughter, and Jakub's, too. I would serve under you, and my blood would give you both her disdain and his approval. My family has suffered from opposing you for years, and it's time I make that right— especially if I want to save my own family now."

I glanced at Ferdy, meeting his eyes with mine. He shook his head, and I had to look away.

"What do you say?" I asked. "Do you accept my deal? Will you let Karl and Ferdy go?"

The whole world seemed to hang on my question; I could almost see Louis thinking over my offer. Lady Penelope seethed behind me, and Karl was back to whimpering, while Ferdy's eyes were full of disappointment.

"This isn't right," Ferdy objected. "Don't do this, Ella. You'll only hurt me if you forfeit your honor."

"I would do anything to keep you safe. How could I live if I lost you? And don't you want to have a family one day?"

"Well, yes, but—

THE ORDER OF THE CRYSTAL DAGGERS

"Then this is my only choice," I told him. My voice was full of resignation. "And I'm not sorry in the least."

"That's a good start," Louis said. "I will agree to your offer, Lady Eleanora."

I let out a sigh of relief, while Ferdy's face crumpled in despair.

"For your first assignment, you must kill Lumiere for me."

My skin began to tingle with disgust and uncertainty, but I swallowed hard and turned toward Lumiere.

"Come now, *Papa*, this is ridiculous," Lumiere scoffed. "She's wanted to kill me ever since she found out I admitted I was the masked assailant who nearly killed King Ferdinand."

"What? You were the one who attacked my father?" Ferdy stepped toward Lumiere threateningly, but Louis stopped him with a look of warning.

"Now, now. Eleanora is the one who has the decision to make. You're still my captive till then, little prince." Louis looked over at me. "Well?"

"Shoot him, Eleanora," Ferdy snarled.

I thought back to Ferdy's vehemence at the Order's history with his family, and his anger at Lumiere, even though he insisted Lumiere was a friend.

Lumiere must've caused the attack to fail.

"Yes." Louis grimaced. "Shoot him."

Despite the sickness I felt, I nodded and tightened my grip around the gun, and turned back to Lumiere.

"You've asked for this, Lumiere," I said bitterly.

"Please. If it's one thing I'm familiar with, it's giving into temptation. You're enjoying this moment." Lumiere sneered as he gracefully ran one of his shackled hands through his blond hair.

He wasn't wrong. Once I might've enjoyed this moment, I thought. But just then, I didn't know how to feel, other than awful and unsure.

Carefully, I aimed for Lumiere's heart and looked into his green eyes.

His gaze was steady and peaceful, and I almost wondered if he was giving me his blessing. My finger seemed stuck as I tried to squeeze the trigger.

But there came a point where there was the distinctive *click*, and the bullet surged forward out of the shaft.

The sound echoed all around us, filling the courtyard like a demon's cry.

My eyes flew shut as the bullet shot out of its chamber, and I only opened them in time to see Lumiere's eyes widen with shock and pain.

Time seemed to slow, as he grabbed his chest, fell to his knees, and then slumped forward.

His cloak fluttered peacefully around him, gently falling over his still form like the wings of a bird wrapping around its body before it sleeps. When he finally settled to the ground—the dirty, sullen ground—I lowered my head to my chest.

Tears shot to my eyes, and I felt my lip blubber out in regret and self-disgust.

What have I done?

As if to answer me, Louis clapped. "Well done, my new protégé. I wasn't sure you would do it. But you have proven you're willing to kill for those you love, and that's a fine start."

THE ORDER OF THE CRYSTAL DAGGERS

"Thank you, sir." I did my best to compose myself, and I turned to Lady Penelope. "At last, I am free of you, Madame."

Her mouth was hanging open in shock. "You've betrayed me," she gasped.

"You only have yourself to blame." I held up the gun again, this time aiming at her. "Perhaps I should kill you next? Or should I leave you alive to suffer?"

Louis came up beside me. "I must say, you are quite an impressive creature. But now, we will need her alive just a little longer. The Emperor will be here, and that's when we will frame Pepé for his murder."

At the mention of the Emperor, Karl finally spoke up again. "What of my kingdom?" he yelled. "If you kill Franz Joseph, the Empire will go to Prince Rupert."

Louis waved him away. "We can draw up a treaty first." He started to explain more of his intentions to Karl, but I could only stare at Lumiere's corpse.

Then the sound of marching soldiers rang from the courtyard entrance.

Ben burst through the courtyard archway. "Get away from the southwest wall, everyone. The cellar is going to explode!"

I looked over to where Lord Maximillian had been shot earlier.

His body was gone, but there was a steady trail of blood on the ground. It led to a doorway down near the riverbank, where the cellars were located.

They were still likely full of dynamite powder.

"Ella." Ferdy and I exchanged a quick look. "Do you think—"

The rest of his words were cut off as a large, loud explosion of fire and stone rippled through the fort.

28

◊

Instinctively, I reached out and took hold of Ferdy. We gripped onto each other, just as we had the night of the Advent Ball.

Together, we fell to the ground.

Smoke and flames appeared along the far wall, and the doorway through which Lord Maximillian had escaped through was now a firepit of flame and death.

"Ella?" Ferdy whispered.

"I'm here," I said, feeling dizzy as we sat up. My voice was a whisper, but I felt as though I was screaming.

Everyone else around us was on the ground.

The tremendous force had sent everyone reeling. Lumiere's body hadn't moved much, but Harshad knelt beside Lady Penelope as she smothered small flames on her skirts. Ben was using a courtyard pillar to pull himself back up to his feet, and his brace seemed a little bent from the sudden force.

Ferdy let go of me to haul Karl up from the ground, but Karl was already shoving him away.

I forced myself up off the ground. My sleeves were torn and my hands were bloodied from my fall, and I'd dropped my gun. I looked around before I saw it laying on the ground nearby.

I let it stay there, too preoccupied with the scene around me. There was fire and death and blood, and it was all chaos—but not by Louis' hand, this time.

Lord Maximillian had gotten his revenge against Louis.

Louis.

He was on the ground, too, and it was the first time I'd ever seen him so disheveled.

His perfectly combed hair was all blown out, and the white tips were covered with ash and dirt. Of all the people around us, he was the only one unable to get up. He grabbed at his side, biting his lip in pain.

"Eleanora." Louis stared up at me as I stood over him. I think he expected me to help him.

Is he injured? What happened to him?

And then, behind us, Lumiere's laughter rang out. "Oh, no, *mon père*! Tell me you didn't break your hip."

Ferdy, Karl, and all of us turned around to see Lumiere stand up, still laughing as he took off his manacles and walked toward us.

Relief washed over me, and I almost ran to hug him.

Louis looked savagely stricken as Lumiere approached us. "You're alive."

"Of course I am," Lumiere said. "Ella doesn't know how to use a gun properly."

"Lumiere," I growled at him, but he only laughed harder.

"It also helps that I wore some plate armor," he said, pulling up his tunic a little to show me the thick layer of metal that covered his skin around his torso. "Of course, you missed me anyway."

I frowned at him, but I didn't say anything, either.

That explains why he looks so much thicker.

"Eleanora." Lady Penelope called over to me as she limped over to us.

Lumiere smiled. "Don't tell me you're suffering from the same fate, too, Pepé? I suppose you've both had a good run of things after all these decades, and it's only fitting that you should be forced from the front line."

"I can still walk," Lady Penelope snapped at Lumiere. She held out her gun and pointed it down at Louis. "And I can still shoot you."

"Good," I said, enjoying the surprise I saw in Louis' expression. "Shoot him."

"Ah, but that's not part of my plan." Lumiere handed his handcuffs to Lady Penelope as he picked his father up off the ground. "It's time for *mon père* to face the ultimate suffering: Paying for his crimes against humanity in court—while I live off his hard-won labor."

"Lumiere!" Louis barked. There was a thick undertone of pain in his voice, and he was still holding his hip with both hands.

Lumiere laughed at him. "I've waited a long time for this day. Let me enjoy it, *Papa*—goodness knows you've robbed me of so much enjoyment in my life, you'd think you'd allow your one and only son to have some happiness. Even if it's at your own spectacular failure."

"Yes, and it is a complete failure," Harshad agreed. "Benedict warned us about the dynamite, and the palace guards have your men in custody by now. Also, because of the fire now, the Emperor will not dare arrive at *Vyšehrad*."

"And both Karl and Ferdy are safe," I added, beaming with pride.

Louis was beyond weary as he looked at me.

"You don't really think I was serious about joining you, do you?" I crossed my arms over my chest. "I might be naïve and inexperienced, but I'm good at manipulating others when I want to."

"And that's why we're so good together," Ferdy agreed.

All the heat around us was nothing compared to the burning fire I saw in his gaze as we looked at each other.

Lady Penelope cleared her throat. "You didn't have to be so convincing, Eleanora. I didn't know if you were telling the truth or not, given some of our recent conversations."

"It wasn't hard to hate you. You're just fortunate that I hate Louis more." I turned away from her abruptly, eager to see the end of Louis. "Now, Louis, you can die, knowing all your plans have failed."

"I already said no, *chérie*." Lumiere shook his head. "I need him for the courts."

"But she said she could shoot him." I looked at Lady Penelope expectantly.

Anger boiled up inside of me again as she only sighed.

"I'm not going to do it, Eleanora," she said, putting her gun away.

I gaped at her. "What?"

"I hate it, but Lumiere is right," she said through gritted teeth. She'd told me before how much she loathed to give Lumiere any credit, and I felt more offended than ever at her bitterness. "I can't do it."

"This is the man who killed my sister, used Xiana against my mother and Amir, and laughed at causing you pain," I shouted, angrier than ever. "He's Lumiere's father, and he's escaped justice for years. He has contingencies, remember? How can you let him live? Shoot him! It's a matter of justice as much as security."

"There is more at stake than justice," Lumiere said. "His crime syndicate workers are all over the world. We need his cooperation to get all the information out of him, so we can prevent even more damage from being done."

"What?" I shook my head. "I don't believe this."

"Ella, please." Ferdy's soft whisper made me even more upset.

Everyone seemed to think it was just fine to leave Louis alive after all the terrible things he'd done.

After all the disgusting things I'd said to trick him.

After I'd nearly sacrificed myself and Lumiere for the chance to stop him.

After all the sadness and sorrow I felt.

All I wanted was some peace. And I wouldn't have it.

"I was right about you!" I shoved Lady Penelope in anger. "I can't believe this. I can't believe how weak and cowardly and foolish you are."

"You don't see things the way I do," Lady Penelope argued back. "We can't sacrifice long-term good for short-term pleasure."

"Speak for yourself," Lumiere muttered, but no one paid him any attention as I battled with Lady Penelope.

"You've always done this," I shouted. "You've always regretted it, too. He's killed *our family*, and he's gotten away. Can't you see this is one time when you should do things differently?"

"As I said, Lumiere is right. Louis' cooperation can help prevent other people's further troubles," Lady Penelope said. "This is not just about you, or me, or even about your mother, Eleanora."

"Lumiere." Louis let out a gasp, and we all turned to look at him.

Louis had lost his balance, and he was falling forward out of Lumiere's grip—or so I thought.

Time seemed to slow down as I suddenly saw the gun hidden away in his left hand. He took aim for Ferdy as he pretended to fall.

"No!" I shouted, and I lunged forward into Louis.

There was one shot, and then I had my hand around his wrist. Louis grappled with me, twisting me against him and choking me again.

Behind me, Lady Penelope struggled as she and Lumiere were caught off balance.

"This is the end," Louis huffed beside me.

"For you," I growled back. I was stronger, younger, and less injured than he was, and now I was more experienced in fighting with him, too. I pulled out my mother's dagger, and sliced the blade into his other side.

He gasped in renewed pain, and I slipped free of his grip.

But then my shoe tripped over a stone, and I fell forward.

I glanced back just as Louis once more aimed his gun.

One shot left.

"Ella," Ferdy cried out.

Out of the corner of my eye, I saw Karl grab onto him. "Let her die," Karl said. "I can still use her death—"

The next second of my life blurred over as Ferdy pushed Karl away from him—right into Louis' path.

The bullet left his gun in a deadly echo and caught Karl directly in the chest.

Blood surged out where he was struck.

I screamed, while Ferdy grabbed hold of me and dragged me away from danger.

Lumiere took hold of his father again. The gun was empty, and Louis had no choice but to be shackled. Lady Penelope looked confused as to what had happened in the last few seconds, while I pushed away from Ferdy's hold.

"No, Ella," Ferdy told me.

"Why did you do that?" I yelled at him, pounding my fists against him. "I was supposed to protect Karl. I was supposed to take him back to your mother."

Ferdy braced himself, keeping his hold on me firm. "I didn't shoot him," he said. "But either way, I won't let you die for a prince, Ella. Even if it's supposed to be me."

I finally wriggled out of his grasp and went over to Karl's body. I shifted him onto my lap as my tears began rolling down my cheeks all over again.

Karl's listless eyes narrowed at me, and then at Ferdy.

"Karl?" I whispered. Hope fluttered up inside me. Maybe he would be all right.

"I … hate you," Karl moaned, before his eyes turned sightless and his body went limp.

All I could do was sit there, more helpless than ever. Ferdy sat beside me, but I didn't want him to touch me; I was devastated.

I cried as the rest of the world faded away, and I was left all alone with my failure.

Even my mother's memory was of no comfort to me as I sat there, completely shattered.

A few moments, or perhaps an eternity, passed before a shadow fell over me.

I looked up, surprised to see Lady Penelope standing over me. The fires were still burning high around us, and in that moment, she reminded me of a demon.

And that was how I saw her.

"Stay away." I shook my head, desperate to ignore her, wishing she was just a figment of my imagination. I bowed my head over Karl's dead body. "Stay away from me."

"I'm sorry, Eleanora," she said.

"No, you're not," I snapped, still crying. "You could have just killed Louis like I wanted, but no. You had to break *Máma*'s promise to the former Empress and dishonor her memory one last time."

"These things happen," Lady Penelope tried to explain carefully, but I shook my head.

"It doesn't matter now," I said. "Get away from me. I'll never forgive you for this. I don't want to see you or talk to you, ever again."

She grimaced. "Yes, I know, so you've told me."

"Just go then," I screamed. "Go!"

I don't know how long I was there, or how long the chaos raged around me. I just knew the night was still full of burning flames when an elegant pair of Hessians stood before me.

"Huh?" I looked up to see a familiar-looking man in front of me. I said nothing as I stared up at him; my mouth couldn't seem to make words.

"Cousin Franz," Ferdy whispered. He hurriedly stood up and bowed.

The Emperor looked back at me. "Are you Lady Eleanora of Bohemia?"

My eyes were still full of tears as I nodded glumly.

He didn't smile, nor did his expression change, but for some reason he seemed pleased all of a sudden. "I have been looking forward to meeting you."

THE ORDER OF THE CRYSTAL DAGGERS

29

◊

The Emperor was much more kind and gracious than I'd expected.

Shortly after we introduced ourselves, Lady Penelope and Harshad explained what had happened, while Lumiere lent his support to their claims where needed.

The Emperor nodded and asked questions, and when it was all over, he offered to send Karl's body to Prague Castle with a small escort of troops.

Several pairs of hands came forward, presenting a board transformed into a makeshift litter. Together, they pried Karl's body from my stiff, bloodied hands.

"No," I whispered, knowing my objection was futile.

There was nothing I could do now.

Karl was dead.

Louis was captured, Lord Maximillian was gone, and the Emperor was safe—and the Tripartite Council was likely canceled, or indefinitely postponed.

But Karl was dead, and I'd failed in my most important task.

I'd failed Karl, the former empress, and my mother, too.

I'd failed.

"Ella."

I shook my head, but Ferdy took my hand.

He pulled me up from the ground and held me.

I let him. I was still angry with him, even though I knew that was senseless, too.

It had been a very long day, full of hours of fighting and tears and walking and sadness.

"Come with me," Ferdy said, and soon we were walking back to Prague Castle with Karl's body.

It was just like my father's funeral, I thought.

There were pallbearers and a royal escort forming a procession, and though the night had settled in over Prague, along with its cloudy skies, we gathered at the gates of *Vyšehrad*.

"Lady Eleanora." Franz Joseph appeared before me again, just before we were about to leave. This time, without Karl's body on top of me, I was able to give him a proper curtsy, even if I still couldn't smile.

"Your Imperial Highness." I mumbled the words, wishing I had more energy to care as much as I perhaps should have about my poor manners.

Franz Joseph didn't seem to mind. He had been trained in war, and as I looked back up at him, he seemed to recognize how much the day had drained me.

"I must commend you on your efforts today," the Emperor said. "You and the Order have been of service to my empire, and our country."

"Thank you."

I glanced behind the Emperor to see another group of guards put Louis on a chair and use it to carry him. He seemed to be in considerable pain, but he didn't make a move to stop them or fight back. There was a thick bandage around his hips, and one side was red from where I'd stabbed him.

I wondered if Louis was silent with shock; I was half-hoping to see him realize he was defeated.

"I also understand that I should welcome you to my family," Franz Joseph continued, nodding toward Ferdy. "Though we have not known each other long, I am glad to meet you, and I am hoping you'll join us at court. I would be grateful for you to remain in service to the empire, as your father had done for my great uncle."

I swallowed the lump in my throat as I nodded. "Yes. *Táta* always was good to King Ferdinand. He would have been good to you, too, especially if you had been coronated here, Majesty."

"I have offered to get coronated here before," Franz Joseph said quietly. "But empty gestures and performances won't be enough to convince the people I am now their king, even with my great uncle still alive."

"I doubt it would be seen as an empty gesture." I glanced around. "Not like the Tripartite Council you've arranged."

"Fortunately, we don't have to worry about the Tripartite Council as much as it seems," he said, confirming my suspicions before giving me a tired smile. "But I will share a secret with you. I believe there are things more important than making people happy, all in hopes of securing their acceptance. I'd rather honor King Ferdinand during his life, and I hope I'll be assessed by what I do as an emperor than be judged for what I didn't do as king."

"History will judge both aspects of your reign," I said, still blushing as I spoke candidly with him.

"Perhaps it will judge me more kindly if I have your allegiance," Franz Joseph replied.

From his voice, I knew he didn't want to hear any more arguments, and I didn't really want to make them, anyway.

I merely nodded, and then I bowed again. "If you are certain, Your Imperial Highness."

"I am."

I didn't have the heart or energy to explain the Order's loyalties or exact history or our skill sets. But perhaps he already knew. Either way, I was glad when he spoke with Ferdy instead, confirming we would attend a commendation ceremony in the near future.

We parted ways shortly after Franz Joseph congratulated Ferdy on securing me as his bride.

Once he was done thanking Ferdy for his own service, Franz Joseph headed back down to his ship.

We made our way out of *Vyšehrad*, walking through the streets of Prague, still escorting Karl's body to Prague Castle. I heard from Ferdy that Franz Joseph was heading back to his ship, and then he would pull into the Port of Prague. After that, he would be taken to the castle by carriage once he landed on shore again.

The Emperor seemed sincere as a ruler, and thoughtful as a man. Karl died believing him to be an obstacle, someone to dethrone, but I mostly pitied Franz Joseph.

My sympathy grew as I saw the people watching us as we made our way to the castle.

Even if Louis had not succeeded in murdering the Emperor, there would likely be others who were just as discontent with his rule. Karl's death would be hard for those like him, and it could possibly raise another usurper—one who might even fulfill Louis' dream of a global war.

I shuddered at the thought.

We might have delayed such a fate, but it was awful to think it was still possible.

Ferdy and I walked in mostly silence for the rest of the trip, until we came up to Prague Castle's grand entrance.

THE ORDER OF THE CRYSTAL DAGGERS

"Ella." Ferdy squeezed my hand. "Don't let go of my hand this time."

I didn't even consider the possibility—until we met with Empress Maria Anna.

When Karl's fallen form was gently laid before her, the cry that left her lips was utterly inhuman in its agony.

She fell beside his corpse as she wept. Her large skirts billowed out around her, and her headdress shifted dangerously on her head until she finally tugged it free and let down her limp, thin, gray-black hair. She had none of the calm repose I'd always associated with Mary, the Mother of Jesus; instead she wept so hard that her cheeks swelled with her salty tears and her nose ran.

It was then that I tried to rush forward to comfort her, but Ferdy held me back. His own silver eyes were full of regret and shame, and he could only shake his head.

We both knew there was no comfort we could offer her that would heal her broken heart; it was the same for any mother who lost a child.

When Ferdy did speak several long moments later, all he said was, "I'm sorry, Mother."

Her eyes snapped up, and she pointed at me accusingly. "You were supposed to protect him. You promised me!"

"I ... I don't ... I'm sorry—"

I tried to say something, but there was nothing I could say. I wanted to believe it wasn't my fault Karl was dead, but I didn't even believe that.

I replayed the whole scene out in my head, wishing I'd stabbed Louis harder, or knocked him out, or held onto Lumiere's gun.

I wished I'd have done anything else, rather than face such dreadful failure.

"This is all your fault," Empress Maria Anna wailed at me.

"No, Mother." Ferdy stepped forward to defend me, still holding onto my hand. "It's my fault that he's dead. I'm the one who caused him to die."

"Ferdinand." Empress Maria Anna gasped out his name, and then she howled again.

"Ferdy," I whispered, but he shook his head at me.

His mother sobbed. "How could you do this to your only brother? How could you do this to me?"

Ferdy looked down at the ground. "I pray you will forgive me, Mother," he said. "I did not want him to die."

Her face scrunched up as she began weeping again, and she wasn't able to say anything I could understand clearly.

Finally, she waved us away. "Leave us. Leave me."

Ferdy bowed, and I followed in suit. He had to lead me out of the room; I still wanted to say something else—that I was sorry, that I'd tried, that I didn't mean for it to end this way.

But, of course, I couldn't.

Once we were out of the throne room, Ferdy tugged me down the long hallway.

I didn't know where we were going at first, but then I recognized a little bit of the castle. I could see the ballroom where the Advent Ball had taken place months before; it was still in disrepair, but it didn't look as bad as I remembered it.

Perhaps Faye had been right, I thought. Life would go on, and we could still rebuild.

"This is where I told you I loved you for the first time," I said as we turned down another hall.

THE ORDER OF THE CRYSTAL DAGGERS

Ferdy nodded. "I'd already fallen in love with you several times over before then. But there was nothing like catching you when you fell."

For the first time in what felt like a long time, a small smile managed to curl on my cheeks. My face was full of pain and my expression felt stiff, but the anguish in my heart felt a little lighter.

"Where are we going?" I asked.

"To see my father." Ferdy turned us down another corridor, and then he pushed open a door and led me into the indoor garden where Karl had once taken me.

I stopped as we entered inside. It was chilly, and the lack of sunlight had caused the flowers and plants to wilt since I'd last been there. Many of them were brown with death.

That was when I noticed the smell of rotting leaves in the air.

"This is my father's favorite place," Ferdy told me as he walked down a row of small succulents, which were somehow still alive. "I'd come here sometimes and help him plant new seeds. We would spend hours in here, sometimes just in silence. Karl never liked it much in here after he started school, even though we would play here sometimes if I begged him. He preferred his study; once he went away for schooling, he would stay in his room to write letters to his friends and instructors."

Ferdy's voice thickened as he spoke. He still didn't really feel like Karl was gone for good, I realized.

"Ah, Ferdinand."

Ferdy and I looked up to see his father, King Ferdinand V, appear at the far door ahead of us. The older man looked weak and small, with his large robes wrapped all around him, and he leaned heavily on his cane. But there was a broad smile on his large face as he made his way over to us.

"You're back," he said. "Come to help me with the weeding?"

Ferdy gave him a small smile. "There's not much left to do here, I'm afraid."

The king nodded. "You're right. There's a hole in the roof near here. All the heat is leaving the room."

"Will it be fixed?" I asked, looking around the desolate garden.

"Perhaps." The king shrugged. "When the rest of the castle is, likely."

He reached out a ring-covered hand to poke at some of the different plants and walked slowly but steadily around the garden.

"Father." Ferdy cleared his throat. "Karl died."

His father didn't look up from his plants. "When?"

"Earlier today," Ferdy told him. "He was shot by Louis Valoris."

I held my breath, waiting for the king to dissolve into tears like Empress Maria Anna had, or for him to possibly have a seizure.

But he didn't do either of those. He only shrugged. "His mother will be sad."

"Will you be all right?" I asked, coming up beside him.

He smiled down at me with a simple, gentle expression. "Eleanora. I didn't mean to ignore you. You are tired today."

"Yes. I'm sad about Karl," I said, trying to redirect him back to our conversation. "Aren't you?"

"I am." He shrugged again. "But I never knew him very well. And he didn't know me very well, either."

King Ferdinand looked back over to Ferdy. "Have you come to help me in the garden today?"

"No." Ferdy took my hand. "I wanted to show Ella your flowers."

"They're not in good condition right now." The king tapped one of the shelves with his cane. "But neither am I."

"You're still the father I remember," Ferdy replied, and the king grinned.

"Not the king, but a father." He nodded, and then he sighed. "Karl never saw me as a father. He only saw me as a deposed king."

I gave Ferdy a questioning look, and he said nothing. His father was nowhere near as upset at Karl's death as Empress Maria Anna.

Soon after that, Ferdy excused both of us.

"Ferdinand. Don't come back until your mother summons you," King Ferdinand told us. "She won't want to see visitors for a while."

"Yes, sire." Ferdy gave his father a quick hug. The king patted him in a mechanical sort of fashion, but I saw his eyes shimmer with tears as we left.

"Your father loves you," I said. "And he loves you as a father loves his son."

Ferdy nodded. "He says he didn't know Karl very well. I don't think he knows me very well, either."

"But he loves you." I took his hand and leaned against him. "I don't think it's easy for children to know their parents. I imagine it's hard to see them as real people. I would've never guessed some things about my mother, or my father, either."

"Yes, that's true." Ferdy gave me an irreverent smile. "I'm glad your mother decided not to murder my father."

"Ferdy."

"It's fine," he told me. "I'm sorry if it's too soon to joke about it. But as I said before, your father saved mine. So it all worked out in the end."

I pursed my lips together for a moment. "Was it really Lumiere that attacked the king when my father saved him?"

"Assuming he wasn't lying when he told me, then yes," Ferdy said, his voice full of irritation again. "He told me a few years ago when we met. He also told me some of the more nasty truths about the Order, and his own involvement on the continent with his father. Lumi seemed to want to impress me. But after everything that's happened this week, I think maybe he wanted out, and he saw me as a friend who would help him."

My hand tightened around his. "You would be a good person to trust with that."

"So you think." Ferdy smiled a little. "He worked with your mother to make sure my father survived."

"I'm surprised he told you." I wrinkled my nose. "He arranged for your friends to be murdered."

"He explained that by telling me how Louis had been unhappy with his recent performances, and especially in the last few years when Lumiere 'accidentally' freed Didier in America," Ferdy said. "He said it was good my friends died, so it looked like he was still competent."

"What?" I clenched my jaw. "That's awful. About your friends, I mean. But I'm glad about Didier. And Lumiere's still pretty callous."

"There are a lot of stories he should tell you," Ferdy said. "I guess he needs a few successes here and there to keep his

THE ORDER OF THE CRYSTAL DAGGERS

father from finding out the truth. Or at least, he did. Hopefully he will stop now that he's openly betrayed Louis."

I nodded and then blinked. "Where are we?" I asked, looking around. "We're supposed to leave the castle, aren't we?"

"We just have to stay out of my mother's way for a while," Ferdy said. "And it's cold, and it looks like rain, and it's past nightfall. So I thought, well … "

He looked toward a long flight of stairs, and suddenly I knew where we were going.

Ferdy reached his bedroom door and opened it, and I welcomed the familiar sight.

The candles on the candelabras were smaller, and there was a small layer of dust, but the books were still all over the floors and shelves, and there was a lingering scent of lavender and mint.

This was the room he'd brought me to after the Advent Ball had rendered me unconscious.

"Come on," he said, before leading me to the bed and pulling down the covers. "You deserve to rest now, my princess."

"I won't argue about that." My body's guard dropped, and I let myself fall into bed next to him. I was already asleep by the time my head hit the pillow.

30

◊

I didn't know if hours or days had passed when I finally shifted out of sleep completely. There was no way to tell for sure, since it was raining when I sat up in Ferdy's bed.

I didn't bother trying to find out, either; I was too enchanted at the sight of my husband sitting down on the window seat, looking through a pile of books.

He didn't notice I was awake. The way he thumbed through the pages, looking them over before stacking them up quietly, made me think of my mother's journal.

Maybe Ferdy can teach me and Ben Arabic so we can read it, I thought, suddenly dreading having to search through Amir's room and his possessions when we got back to the manor.

"What are you looking for?" My voice was harsh and low against the silence around us.

"Ella." Ferdy looked back and smiled at me.

He was still sad, but he was much more energetic, and I was glad to see he'd been able to rest. I'd had a few nightmares, but I was too tired and sad to do anything but wait until they passed.

I had a feeling some of my nightmares would return.

Ferdy briefly put the books aside. "Go back to sleep. We're not going to be able to leave until the rain's finished."

"Why not?" I asked. "It's just rain."

He gestured toward a stack of books and patted them affectionately. "I was going to take those to Clavan. To see if he wants any, to start a new collection, or sell some, so he'll have some money to rebuild the Cabal."

"That's very kind of you." I chuckled a little. "Although I doubt he would be able to sell any to Wickard. Not for profit, anyway."

"I don't want the books damaged by the rain," Ferdy continued, gazing at them and then looking all around the room. "And I don't imagine I'll be coming back here any time soon. If at all."

At his sudden despondency, I got out of the bed and went to sit down next to him. Distractedly, I rummaged through another small pile of books he had been sorting through. There were several with the same title, and I picked one up with loving hands.

"How many copies do you have of *Le Morte d'Arthur*, exactly?" I asked.

"What does that matter, if it's not the right book?" Ferdy replied. "I know the one Ben sold was red. That's all I know for sure, other than the title."

"There's an inscription in the cover." I opened the book, trying to remember it. "It was originally for Ben, you know. *Táta* gave it to him the birthday before he broke his leg, I think. I didn't want Ben to lose it. The book was a reminder of better times, when we had a better father, and I didn't want Ben to forget that."

"He didn't," Ferdy said.

"How do you know?"

"I can tell." Ferdy shrugged. "That's why he's sour toward him. It's easier to hate someone if they've always been awful to you. But if you know there's some good, and it's just been taken away, it hurts so much more."

I wondered if he was thinking of Karl when he spoke, and I decided I didn't want to contemplate that.

For reasons I hated, I was already thinking of Lady Penelope, too, and I wanted to think of her even less.

Ferdy sighed. "Anyway, go back to bed. Get some more sleep."

I put his book down on the window seat again, and then I cradled his face in my hands. "I'll go back to bed if you come with me."

I leaned over and kissed him, and soon Ferdy was kissing me back.

We were still kissing each other as I led him to the large bed and pulled him down on top of me.

THE ORDER OF THE CRYSTAL DAGGERS

31

◊

Ferdy and I waited until the rain stopped to return to the manor, but no one was waiting for me as they had been the last time I'd come home from the castle.

Days of colorless grief settled around us, and while I had my husband, my brother, and plenty of friends, I felt numb and bland as the long days slowly passed, an impasse between listlessness and restlessness.

Franz Joseph had ordered Louis to pay for his crimes in Bohemia; all of his assets within the country and the Empire's territories would be confiscated and turned over to the imperial authorities.

After that, Louis was to be sent off to London to be tried in Queen Victoria's courts. Didier told me that Lumiere would be going with Lady Penelope, and while they were away, Didier would stay here and help Harshad and some of the others keep an eye on Prague.

There was still the possibility of turmoil, with the fights breaking out between the Bohemian and German Diets more frequently after the news of Karl's death.

It wasn't the first time in recent weeks that the rumors made me furious. Rumors said it was possible he'd been killed by a German Confederacy supporter, or even a Jewish anarchist.

It angered me even more that the truth wouldn't come out, and more people had the chance to believe whatever they wanted, no matter how wrong or depraved or irrational it was.

And then I saw Lady Penelope, one last time, before she was to return to London with Louis and Lumiere.

Shortly after Ferdy and I returned to the manor, she arrived to pick up her luggage.

She called me and Ben to the west parlor to say goodbye, but I didn't go.

Instead, I crossed my arms and stood on the manor's battlements, the same one I'd beaten Alex on, the day she'd arrived on the manor's doorstop.

I watched her as she headed toward her carriage.

I didn't exactly know how I felt about her departure.

I was happy to see her gone.

I was angry she would leave me here now.

I was puzzled when she didn't insist that I come along with her.

And I hated how she didn't fight with me any longer.

As I watched her step into the carriage, she glanced up my way.

I froze.

From where I was, I could see her nostrils flaring, and as much as I hated her, I think that was the moment I realized I hated myself for what had happened, too.

But everyone lies, and everyone has secrets, and everyone has regrets—and sometimes the most egregious lies, the most treacherous secrets, and the hardest regrets we have are the ones about ourselves.

I buried that last little bit of hatred inside of me, and despite my better judgment, I was determined to nurture it, and yet still forget about Lady Penelope entirely.

I decided I didn't care, but I cared too much to let myself truly know how conflicted I was.

She entered the carriage, and then she was gone.

THE ORDER OF THE CRYSTAL DAGGERS

Good.

Then Lumiere appeared behind her, and he looked up at me, just as she had.

"Goodbye, Ella!" he called, waving up to me. He blew me several kisses. "Don't get too pudgy while we're away! And make sure you let Didier teach you how to use a gun. I'll be eager to see your improvement when I get back!"

I shook my head and walked inside, heading for the library.

Once I got there, I saw my mother's portrait looking at me again. She was my mother, and as much as I'd loved her, I needed to accept that some part of her would always be a mystery.

"I'm not going to miss Lumiere that much," I told her. "I don't care if you loved him like a brother. To me, he's just an infuriating clown."

"You'll miss him more than you'll admit, *ségra.*" Ben appeared behind me and put his hand on my shoulder. He had a new scabbard for Amir's dagger on his side, and along with that, and a bath and some food, Ben appeared much more healthy and cheerful. "He's a strange man, but there's bound to be some good in him."

"Ferdy and I have a bet about how long it will take before Lady POW throws him overboard," I said, and Ben and I shared a much-needed laugh.

By the time we stopped, the carriage was already far off down the road.

"Where's Marguerite?" I asked, looking behind him.

Ben lost his smile. "She's not going to follow me around all day, like you do to Ferdy. She's still here, working with Prissy, and Betsy and Mavis, too."

"Really?"

THE ORDER OF THE CRYSTAL DAGGERS

"Well, since Amelia and Jaqueline are with Lady Penelope, Marguerite is teaching the other girls how to sew like she can." Ben frowned. "So they can replace her in Lady POW's service when she gets back. That will free Marguerite up so she can stay with me."

"Since you're getting married, that'll be good," I said. "She doesn't need to work with our grandmother."

"I'm not thrilled that she's not interested in setting up a household of her own," Ben admitted. "She wants to go on missions with me."

"Well, we don't have any missions right now," I said. "And it'll take some time for Lady Penelope to return here. Longer, if court drags on for Louis. Perhaps by then she'll be more eager to settle down with you and start a family."

Ben sighed. "I don't know why I agreed to this."

"You promised. And you do love her, don't you?" I was certain he did love her, otherwise I knew he would've found a way to wiggle out of their previous agreement.

"Yes." Ben scowled at me. "You have it easy with Ferdy, you know. He doesn't have to be here with us. He's a prince. He can provide for you without trouble."

"He was born a prince, and he'll always be one to me." Momentarily, I slumped forward and put my head in my hands. "But you should've seen Empress Maria Anna's face, Ben. After what happened to Karl, I don't know if Ferdy will ever see her again. I think he's more content to be here than at the castle anyway."

"He still doesn't have a bad leg to stop him from a regular income."

I gave him an irritated look. "Your leg won't stop you from getting your inheritance from *Táta*, now that Lady POW and her man of affairs took care of it."

"It's not the money—"

"And you've more than proven you can handle your leg," I reminded him. "Even better, Harshad told me that Cecilia is going with Lady POW to London. She'll be working in the household of the new Duke of Wellington. Lady Penelope's stepson had an opening for a lady's companion for his spinster aunt, apparently. So she'll be gone, even if she deserves much more of a punishment."

"She might deserve less, but Marguerite deserves more."

"Well, I can't argue with that," I said with a smile. The way Ben asserted that fact made me so proud to be his sister.

"I don't want her helping with the Order," Ben said. "I've been hurt before, but I don't want to see her injured, either. And being a spy is not a respectable job."

"I know Society feels that way. But you can at least look on the bright side," I said.

"What's that?" Ben asked.

I grinned playfully. "You'll be able to commiserate with Ferdy much better now. He says the same thing about me."

Ben only groaned as I laughed, and I was still chuckling as he left me and went off to the kitchen for some food.

I thought about following him, but in the aftermath of everything that had happened, my appetite was practically non-existent.

Instead, I looked around for a book, and then sat down and curled up to read it. Hours might have passed before I heard Harshad say my name.

"Eleanora."

I looked up as he appeared in the room.

I was shocked to see the broken quality of his gaze.

THE ORDER OF THE CRYSTAL DAGGERS

He had always seemed so solid, so unmoved by the world, but as I watched him sit in Lady Penelope's usual seat in the library, as I saw him gaze at my mother's portrait and then out the window, I saw that his pain was ongoing, universal in both his movements and his moments.

"Harshad?" I put down my book and stood up, moving closer to him even though I was uncertain of what I should do—or if I should do anything at all. "Are you well?"

He surely couldn't be this lost without Lady POW, could he?

"Grief is a masterful devil in its own right; it does not want to take a final shape, only allowing us to see its presence is marked by the absence of our loved ones." Harshad sighed and shook his head.

My eyes filled with tears, and I tried to push back the memory of Amir's hand in mine. I tried to picture Amir at his best, when he was helping me waltz, teaching me to fight, when he would talk with me and share with me some part of my mother's secret lives.

I didn't know if remembering Amir like that helped or not, because I knew the ending.

I was surprised when Harshad's hand touched mine. I was even more surprised when I fell into his arms and cried.

This time, I didn't hesitate to embrace Harshad.

"This is not the end, Eleanora. Amir is at peace, just as Dezda is," he told me, as he held me. "We are the ones who mourn for our loss, and the world's. But we do not mourn for them."

"You have a bigger heart than me," I said, as my tears finally slipped free. "I'd rather the world suffer if it meant I didn't have to lose them."

"There are some philosophies in this world that say all life is suffering—that love is an act of violence upon the soul. To

394

love is to have something so good that everything else is able to be seen for the tragedy it truly is." Harshad squeezed his hand over mine. "I have seen this in my own life. And this is why I believe what I believe, and more importantly, I know whom I have believed. God is merciful in our most vulnerable moments; not that he takes away our pain, but that he took on that pain himself."

"I know death makes us turn toward God, but I can't help but feel he's deserted me." I buried my face into Harshad's shoulder.

I did not really want to talk about Amir and the others. It was too painful.

"On the contrary." Harshad paused. "If you think of how God experiences time, he sees it all at once, like a line of blood on a paper. And so, he is always able to see the cross. He is always on the cross.

"God is love, and he suffers for it—he suffers for me. And so I, in turn, must suffer, too."

Harshad stepped back from me, but he still held onto my hands with his. "In all the world, in all the places I have been and the people I have met, I have never seen such an answer to suffering as this. God remembers the cross and experiences it each day. Right now, we carry those we love, as he does; we experience that pain we feel, that sharp absence of love. You've carried your mother this far, as I have, and you've honored her in your memory. Now, you will go on and carry Amir, as will I. That loss is part of our cross to bear."

"I am too weak to carry such a loss."

Amir had spent so much of the last months of my life teaching me to be strong. It broke me even further to know I couldn't do what he'd sought to teach me.

I'd failed him all over again.

THE ORDER OF THE CRYSTAL DAGGERS

Harshad let go of me, and I expected his rebuke.

But Harshad was not Lady Penelope, and he gave me a small kiss on the top of my head, reminding me of *Táta*. "Then I will help you carry it, as much as I can. And so will the others who love you."

When Harshad finally stepped back from me, I felt a curious warmth; some people would mistake it for distance, but I knew it was an act of trust.

My hand went to my mother's dagger at my side. I took the weapon with a small sense of resolve. Amir had warned me once not to make my mother's mantle my mission in life. We were different people, and after all that had transpired, I knew this was true more than I would've liked at times.

But I had a better life, too, that she'd helped to give me—both in my own life, and in giving me Ben as a brother. My mother had never had a brother like him.

I thought of how Amir had passed his dagger onto him. I hoped Ben would be sure not to let himself get caught up in pleasing Amir the way one would please a false and truly faceless idol; but then, Ben had me, too, and now he also had Marguerite, half of Lumiere, and perhaps even Lady Penelope, and most certainly Harshad … there were more of us than ever in our lives.

Perhaps we would never establish Liberté, I thought. But I could rest easy knowing Ben and I were free in a way we never had been before.

Now, we only have to keep it that way …

I wiped my eyes with the back of my hand before I straightened my shoulders. "I'll be here if there's a new assignment," I told Harshad.

Harshad nodded. "Your new assignment right now is to recover from the previous one. Pepé and Lumiere and the others are with Louis, who is in chains and under tight guard, and they'll be sailing off in the morning. Everyone needs time, Eleanora."

"Including me."

"Including both of us." He nodded, and then his eyes cleared of their sadness; it was time for us to return to business. "I know you do not wish to work with your grandmother again. For now, until there is a change, I will manage your assignments, and I will be keeping you here in Prague as much as possible."

"I can go other places," I told him. "I'm sure Ferdy won't mind."

"But I do." Harshad clasped his hands together. "As much as you might disagree, you are a princess now, and you have a country as well as a family to oversee. I heard you speak with Franz Joseph the other night in *Vyšehrad*. You agreed to become part of his court."

"But that doesn't really mean anything—"

"Yes, Eleanora, it does," he said, surprising me by his interruption. "Even if the kingdom does not know about you, you should still be here for them. Your beloved Ferdinand belongs here, too."

My heart fluttered; I was grateful Harshad approved of Ferdy.

"One day you might be called away, but this is your home, and you should stay here when you can. You should protect and provide for it as much as you can, for as long as you can."

"At least Louis is on his way to court, and then jail," I said. "He can't do anything too upsetting from where he is now."

"He's always had his contingencies." Harshad frowned. "While Louis did not succeed in starting all the wars he'd

THE ORDER OF THE CRYSTAL DAGGERS

planned, he was successful in showing us how weak and divided the people are. He's left a path of destruction in his wake, and if we are not careful to rebuild the good, and create new life where there was only death, he will still win in the end."

I shivered at the thought. "I hope that day never comes."

Louis was not a madman, even if he was ambitious. He'd wanted to orchestrate wars across Europe, all for his own profit, prestige, and amusement. And he was right; Bohemia and other smaller countries were at the mercy of their neighbors' continued benevolence and honor. It wouldn't take much to bring us down, and using our own principles to do so.

"I pray that, too," Harshad agreed with another weary sigh. "But I pray more that if it does come, we will survive and learn to do better. The past is full of blood and tears, and the future is likely to be much of the same. Even if it's different, there will always be poverty and depravity."

"But there will still be good people, too," I said, thinking of Ferdy and Clavan and Amir—and my mother and father, and Harshad and Ben and even myself, and my other friends and associates who would stand up against evil and stand up for truth and justice.

Perhaps I could even include Lady Penelope in that list, but I didn't want to give her any credit; any good she was capable of seemed more like a divine accident than her direct intention.

"Yes." Harshad agreed.

I smiled, looking back at my mother's portrait. "There are reasons to hold on."

"Yes, there are reasons to have hope, despite the temptation to despair. Hope is like happiness in this regard;

THE ORDER OF THE CRYSTAL DAGGERS

we see it better when we give it away." He gave me another small smile. "You have learned well, Eleanora."

"I've been taught well."

"I will tell you a secret, Eleanora," Harshad said. "You can have the best teacher and still fail to learn, just as you can show up and make all the right choices and still lose. So it is something special when you do learn, and when what you've learned leads to victory."

"I will try to remember that," I promised. Learning things was hard, but relearning things seemed even more painful. "Thank you."

"You're welcome." He nodded toward the door. "Go and rest now. Louis is taken care of. You have your friend's wedding in a few days, and you should be ready to go."

I was surprised he'd known about Faye's wedding, but I nodded.

But before I left, I gave Harshad another quick hug, surprising him right back.

Hours later, Ferdy and Ben headed out to practice shooting with Didier, and I made my way back to the library again, eager to read a book and escape from reality for a little while.

But when I entered, I saw Harshad was still there, standing by the window, looking outside despondently. He had his hands tucked behind him as he stoically faced the world outside, and inside of one hand was a bright, white scroll with Lady Penelope's signature on it.

THE ORDER OF THE CRYSTAL DAGGERS

I bit my lip before I gave into my curiosity. "What is it?"

Harshad didn't flinch or move. "Louis is gone."

"Gone?" I felt the blood rush out of my head. "You mean, he escaped?"

"No. He is dead. He poisoned himself."

"Was it the silver thallis poison?" When Harshad nodded, I hesitated for only a moment. "Are you sure Lady Penelope or Lumiere aren't responsible?"

"Fairly. He had the poison hidden away in a small packet, sewn into the inside of his jacket."

"Oh. I guess he was the kind of man who would have everything in order."

"His last contingency, and it was a cowardly one." Harshad shook his head.

There wasn't much else I could say.

I couldn't say if Harshad believed Lady Penelope or Lumiere was responsible, but even if he did, I doubted he would tell me. Eventually, silence between us spoke of shared frustration, even if there was firmer foundation for trust.

We stood there, together, facing the known and the unknown before us.

"So at long last, Louis Valoris is gone." Harshad shook his head. "And he managed to escape justice. After all these years and all our losses, he will not endure punishment for his crimes or face the people he has hurt."

I came to stand next to him. "He will have divine condemnation, if not earthly judgment."

"Yes." Harshad nodded grimly. "But I fear the world will face more trouble by his hand now. There's no telling how many of his projects and investments remain active, or how many of his underlings will seek to take his place."

Briefly, I thought of Lady Penelope, telling me about Louis' attempts to steal art from all over Europe, and then I recalled Louis himself telling us about his various investments in war and medicine.

Eventually, I put my hand on Harshad's arm, attempting to comfort him as well as steady myself. "The Order will stand for justice, and it will stand against them, too."

He patted my hand gratefully, and then we both turned and stared out the window for a long time after that, eventually listening to Ferdy and Ben as they argued between taking turns shooting the targets outside.

After a while, I excused myself, forgetting about my books, and headed outside to join them.

The Order was ready to stand against evil, but if we were going to do it effectively and efficiently, I figured it was time I learned how to use a gun properly.

THE ORDER OF THE CRYSTAL DAGGERS

32

◊

An ominous, eerie calmness settled over the house as the next weeks passed. I aimlessly moved through the various routines of my life.

Even with Louis dead, Lady Penelope was off for London with Lumiere, Cecilia, and her traveling company; she seemed to take the bitter fire inside of me along with her, and I once more hated how I was indebted to her in that way.

Harshad had ordered me to recover from my mission, but such a recovery was largely a mystery, one I had to solve all on my own.

Not that I was alone in doing so.

Ferdy seemed quiet and contemplative by his standards, but he still teased me, talked with me, and tenderly held me, and I responded to him in love, patience, and passion.

To help pass the time during the day, Ben offered to work with me on our fighting skills. He was getting much stronger, and said he wouldn't hold back any longer, as long as I didn't either.

Even if I lost, I was just grateful we'd been able to grow back together.

Ben would always be one of my weaknesses, but it was a weakness that would grow smaller over the years, even if my love for my brother would grow deeper into my heart.

He didn't seem to mind losing to me as much, either; Marguerite was there to help take care of him, and it didn't take me long to see she'd been just as diligent in healing his physical injuries as she was in healing the wounds in his heart.

For her part, Marguerite kept her promise; I never saw her step back from Ben's side.

Despite all the things I had to be grateful for, there were still random moments when I only felt numb inside.

I'd never imagined before how nothing could feel so heavy.

Perhaps holding Karl as he died had made some of me die, too.

It was only when I got a new invitation for Faye's wedding that something dead inside me began to stir alive again.

Harshad quickly insisted Ferdy, Ben, Marguerite, and I attend.

He didn't have to work too hard to force us out of the house. Spring was well on its way, and we were eager to leave the house, even if I still had to be discreet about my appearances in the city. Karl's tragic death left me as his widow in Society's narrative, and that meant I was unable to rejoin them. I didn't know if it was a permanent retreat, but I had a feeling things would change once more when I was called to Franz Joseph's court in Vienna.

The worst part of the journey was walking across the Stone Bridge to get there. While I hated thinking of Louis practicing his sketching on the bridge, it was even more irritating since after Karl's passing, a new ordinance had passed, and the Stone Bridge had been renamed as the Charles Bridge.

While it was the anglicized pronunciation of his name, and not quite the honor Karl sought, it was the one he'd received—and unfittingly so. I was glad people ignorantly credited the name to Bohemia's first crowned king instead.

The second worst part of getting to the wedding was passing by the burnt remains of the Cabal.

It was still a long way from reconstruction, but Jarl's Uncle Rhys had purchased a modest townhouse near Market

Square, and Faye and Jarl made the official ceremony arrangements with a church nearby.

I felt much better as we walked into the *Kostel Matky Boží před Týnem*, the Church of Týn. Its tall towers reached upward in an effort to touch heaven—a goal that was beyond reach, but not beyond wonder.

"You're here," Faye called out to us.

She was radiant in her lovely cream-colored dress; it complemented the light in her eyes and contrasted with the curls of her hair. She gathered me into a hug, much as she had the last time we'd met, and I could feel her delight.

She was full of joy as she and Jarl finally spoke their vows, and their two souls were knit together, in hopes they would create a new, blessed legacy.

My eyes filled up with tears again, and I was full of wonder and humility. For the last few months, I'd been immersed in a world all about the people and the physical realm in which they existed, and where they died and fell into depravity and disillusionment.

But as I saw Faye and Jarl walk down the aisle as husband and wife, I felt the pull of heaven.

There was another way to see the world from outside of this one, and I only needed to look around me to see it.

Prague was my home, but it was not made of mere walls and lumber, paint and bricks and fabric and gold; it was a city I could see as just that, but I knew it to be so much more.

And just as Prague was more than the physical, so was I, and so was my marriage; it was a home that would be fruitful and multiply, and bring joy into my heart that my soul magnify; and even after all the physical things had passed away, I would be left as mirror for God's graciousness and

THE ORDER OF THE CRYSTAL DAGGERS

mercy, a memory that embodied hope and sought to stir it in others.

Ferdy took my hand as we stood and the music rang out from the organ pipes behind us. "I am sorry if you didn't get the wedding you wanted, Ella," he said. "This one was very beautiful."

"It's all right." I smiled up at him as I wiped the tears off my cheeks. "I got the groom I wanted."

"You don't regret anything, then?" he asked. "I was worried you were upset we didn't have a lovely wedding such as this one."

"No, I'm not upset."

"Those are happy tears, then?"

Clavan came up behind us. "Of course they are," he said to Ferdy, while dabbing at the moisture in his own eyes. "For we are free men, and in moments like these, while freedom is found in truth and the struggle for it, we celebrate the victory that is already here, as well as the one to come."

"Is that so?" Ferdy chuckled. "I thought it was just a very nice wedding, with a very happy bride and groom."

I nodded. "After fighting as much as I have, I am glad to celebrate something good."

"As it will be at the final wedding feast in the new heaven," Clavan said. "Much sorrow often lies in waiting for us, and our scars will still stand out brightly on our hearts long after we find rest. But only a free man can weep at the thought of an enslaved one, and only a free man can weep with joy in knowing freedom itself."

He was swept away by the crowd, and soon, I was swept up in the glory and the beauty of everything, too.

As the wedding finished and the celebration began, I watched as Helen cheerfully chatted with Eliezer and Zipporah; I danced with Ferdy, I joked with Ben, and I hugged Faye.

As the night went on, I thought of my mother and father, I thought of Amir with Nassara, I thought of all the good and beautiful and true things I had ever known. It was much easier to bear my losses in light of joy, and I found my appetite again.

And at the end of the celebration, I saw goodness, beauty, and truth were still there, even if they were hidden by the world's darkness. Seeing them, and realizing their staying power, I knew that despite my sadness and frustration over the last few weeks, I could go on and I could endure, too.

"Are you ready to go home, *chérie?*" Ferdy asked, taking my hand as it grew late. He was still full of energy and overly cheerful as he called for Ben and Marguerite.

"Yes." I tightened my fingers around his and gave him a kiss on the cheek. I looked at my friends and the beauty around us, and conviction settled deep inside of me.

I had hope.

I would continue on, and I would endure, and I would not do it alone.

In that moment, I was truly loved—and I was truly free.

THE ORDER OF THE CRYSTAL DAGGERS

Epilogue

◊

Vienna, 1875

"Ferdy."

His name was less than a whisper on my lips as I stood beside him, at the back of the grand resting place of Ferdy's family.

At the front altar, the reverend of the Capuchin Church recited the final funeral liturgy of the night.

Ferdy's eyes were fixed forward, his gaze empty and distant. The familiar silver sparkle in his eyes was dimmed by sorrow and tainted by loss.

For a moment, I wondered if he did not hear me, but I knew after the past four years of our lives, his heart was always so well attuned to mine—even if he did not hear me, he would know I was waiting for him.

When he turned to face me a moment later and gave me a half-hearted smile, I could only squeeze his hand in comfort.

"Are you trying to be brave?" I asked.

"I'm not sure." Briefly, his smile curled into a half-smirk, and he leaned over and kissed my forehead. "But if I succeed, it's likely because I have you to inspire me."

"I'm worried for you." I watched the priest as he flicked holy water over the coffin, cleansing it of this world's impurities, even though the stench of death would never leave the body inside.

"My father was a good, honorable man. And he had a good life. He had my mother, and Karl and me, too, even if it was just for a time." Ferdy watched the front of the sanctuary, where the coffin was on display for all to see. "He is with Karl now."

Assuming Karl made it to heaven.

The thought was sharp and clear inside of me, so persistent I barely managed to stop myself from saying it aloud. It spoke to the finest elements of Ferdy's character that he believed Karl to be in heaven, even as it demonstrated the worst of mine.

Ferdy sighed. "You might be worried for me, but I am more worried for my mother. She has already buried one child and lost another. I don't know how hard she is taking the loss of my father."

I looked forward and peeked through the various heads of the vast audience before us. In the very front, Empress Maria Anna stood, facing the altar.

"She has not lost you," I said, keeping my tone as kind and quiet as possible.

As if she had heard me, Empress Maria Anna turned her head ever so slightly. The large headdress, covered with a black veil and decorated with more pearls than seemed feasible, wobbled and clinked awkwardly with her movements. She had to be uncomfortable, this time in June, both because of her gown's dark colors and the heavy fabric.

Her outfit made me think of the one Cecilia wore on the day of my father's funeral. Just as before, I felt more than ragged in comparison.

I will need to get some new clothes soon.

I held back a smile, thinking of the horrifying things Lumiere would say at the sight of me. My gown was an older one, made of a deep purple damask and trimmed with black lace, while the stays were currently pulled tightly across my body. I always thought the violet went well with my dagger; I still wore it at my side, tucking it between the hidden slits of my skirts.

The pearls and heavy fabric jostled again, and I looked to see Empress Maria Anna glancing over her shoulder. Her eyes searched the sea of faces in the church as she held her rosary and crucifix.

I held my breath, waiting to see if she would spot us. Even tucked near the back of the crowded sanctuary, I could hear her movements, and I suddenly wondered if she could hear me, too. When she reverted her gaze back to the front of the church, I exhaled in relief.

As much as I was sure King Ferdinand would've been happy to have Ferdy at his funeral, there was no sure way of knowing how the former empress would feel about seeing Ferdy and me.

I could still perfectly remember Karl's dead body lying before her, and I'm sure she could, too.

"Mother." Ferdy's whisper was soft and warm, and I nearly teared up at his pained gentleness.

"Are you going to see her?" It was a question I'd held off on asking Ferdy as we traveled to Vienna from Prague, following behind the king's body on the way to its final resting place.

"I want to," he admitted. "But it might cause problems now. There are many details to attend to when a ruler dies, even a former one. When everything is more settled, I will go and see her."

If she will allow me to see her.

The words were left unspoken, but I heard them nonetheless.

Ferdy had called me kind after watching me at my own father's funeral, and I wish I could believe it after watching

THE ORDER OF THE CRYSTAL DAGGERS

him. He was hurting at the loss of his father, and it seemed so wrong that his mother might still turn him away. But he was still so understanding and patient, I wanted to curse the unfairness of the world all over again.

"I am sorry you have to wonder about that at all," I said. "It's all my fault."

"You know after Karl's death my parents rightfully disowned me."

"They still should not have done that," I said, keeping my tone light. I was appalled by his parents' decision, and even in that moment, I would've let Empress Maria Anna know of my displeasure if I had the proper chance.

Ferdy said nothing; he only glanced at me, allowing our eyes to meet for the smallest second before he turned back to face the front.

Karl should not have died, either.

Once more, words passed unspoken between us, and I was grateful I did not have to hear them.

We watched as the casket carrying the king was arranged on a pedestal at the front of the sanctuary.

I studied the altar of the church, awed over the eternal good of God and his providence, and I thought back to those dark hours and lonely moments when I used to look on the city of Prague in the distance from my home.

As I stood beside Ferdy in Vienna's finest church, baptized in the holy atmosphere, I knew I had been too focused on the city instead of the god behind it.

Even if my fairy tale kingdom would one day fall due to the deterioration of its roots and the crippled lines of its imperfect foundation, I knew there was good that would last; all of my life I had known that, even if I had just recently realized it.

Such constancy was built up with truth and everlasting love, and at its beauty, I knew we were not alone in our suffering and sorrow.

I did not like to think of the night Karl died, and I knew Ferdy did not, either. Over the past four years, the memories of Karl's untimely end had faded; Ferdy drowned out my guilt with his lovingkindness and his steadfastness. Every time I had nightmares, he held me and kept me close, keeping true to his promises that he would keep me, and he would keep me safe and only for himself.

I responded in kind, soothing his heartache as much as I could; I was his family, and while I was grateful when my own finally and fully embraced him, I knew Ben's gruff approval and Harshad's acceptance meant less to Ferdy than it did to me.

"Truth be told, I was worried for you, too, Ella," Ferdy murmured quietly. "I did not want this to bring up sad memories of Amir."

Hearing his name was both poignant and painful. I swallowed hard. My nose prickled, and my eyes were suddenly wet with tears at the mention of my friend and mentor.

But a moment later, I shook my head. Amir was home with my mother, and their daughter, too. Maybe he had even met my father and found a way to befriend the man who convinced my mother to give love another chance.

My lips trembled as I tried to give Ferdy my own brave smile. I found it much more difficult than I remembered it being when I was a child. "We have both lost so many."

"Death is an expected part of life." Ferdy wrapped his arm around me, letting his hand rest at my waist. "But I would rather stare down a thousand deaths than face this life without you."

"You should feel fortunate then," I said. "You get to do both, with all the Order does to keep us busy."

A gleam of amusement crept into his eye, and had we been anywhere else, I suspected he might've laughed.

"I have always been lucky when it comes to you," he agreed.

"Is that so? It seems that our rendezvous have only ever caused us more trouble." I glanced at his arm, where Alex had shot him so many years before. Though his formal jacket hid his scar, I could still picture the large, red divot running up his shoulder.

"Still, I have never lost a gamble when it comes to you." He smiled. "I am indeed extraordinarily blessed, far beyond even my luck's capabilities."

It was true that the Order kept us busy, but we were never too busy to love each other in a way that pushed back against the trials we faced.

We lived in a fallen world, but we had also fallen in love, and there was nothing more freeing than finding a home in each other's heart.

I was about to kiss him when I saw it.

A small, distinct glimmer of violet light flashed across the far corner of my eye, and even though it had been years, I stiffened.

"What is it?" Ferdy asked.

"Nothing."

"Ella." He raised his brow. I had spoken too softly and too swiftly, and he knew I was lying. "Tell me."

I gave in reluctantly. While we were risking a scene by coming to Vienna, I did not actually want to engage in one.

"*She's* here," I grumbled, nodding my head toward an alcove at the back of the church.

"Then why don't you go and see her?" His tone was serious, before he gave me a playful smirk. "Maybe on your way to the ladies' withdrawing room to take care of a personal matter?"

Ferdy was trying to lighten the mood with his levity, but I was not inclined to let him do so. "No. I don't want to leave you."

"I'll be fine for the next several moments, while the priest has another round of blessings and the choir has some Latin to recite," Ferdy assured me. "Go. You should talk to her regardless, just as I should talk with my mother."

He was not wrong about that.

"You should also go," he said quietly, "because it is something your mother would want. She would not want your heart to turn to stone all because of the Iron Dowager."

"All right," I agreed bitterly. "I won't be long."

"I'll be here for you when you're finished, *chérie.*"

Awkwardly, I shuffled out of the pew. Several others looked at me with half-disapproving stares as I left during the formal prayers for King Ferdinand, but I ignored them.

"Eleanora."

I nearly flinched as my estranged grandmother greeted me for the first time in four years.

While her authoritative tone had remained the same during our time apart, I was surprised to see how much the rest of her had changed.

The wrinkles lining her cheeks had increased, both in number and in depth. Her hair seemed to be a shade whiter than the last time, even though her cheeks and eyes were sharper. Her lips were thinner, giving her a more sour expression than I remembered. Her impeccable appearance seemed to be just slightly less so, with her hair bundled up with a wig to give an added layer.

"Lady Penelope." I gave her the smallest curtsy I could manage. "How do you do, Madame?"

"You can drop the act, same as before. I do not need your manners."

"Manners make matters such as this more—"

"More what?" Lady POW raised an eyebrow at me. "More comfortable? Hardly. I'll grant you they can make things more quiet and constrained, but you should be disciplined enough to manage that, even without the manners."

"Why are you here, then?" I asked, allowing my initial sympathy to wane. "I didn't think someone like you would be able to walk on hallowed ground."

At my jab, Lady Penelope smiled. "Good. Much better. Honesty is good between allies."

"I do not like to think of us as allies."

The truth was, I did not like to think of her at all. Even if I still did, and more frequently than I would've liked.

She seemed to sense my weakness in that regard, too, which only made me more disgruntled. "Ah, but we are. There is no denying the truth, no matter how grim and dark it may be."

"Just tell me why you're here."

That time, I saw her hesitate. "I must admit, I am surprised you came over to see me," she said.

"I'm surprised I managed to surprise you," I retorted.

"As you've no doubt already noticed, I'm getting older. It's actually somewhat refreshing, you should know, to find that life can still surprise me—even if it is not always enjoyable." She shrugged. "Old age makes one see things differently from time to time, with death nearing the horizon."

I bit my lip. I did not really want to antagonize her. She was still, after all, my grandmother.

I reached for the comfort and strength my mother's dagger had to offer.

"There is no need for violence," Lady Penelope said quietly. "I am merely here to pay my respects to the king."

"Even if you wanted him killed?"

She pursed her lips into an odd little smile. "Yes. Your husband is right. He was a good man, if a terrible ruler."

I softened, but only slightly. "I am sure Ferdy will agree his father had his faults."

"His favoritism was easily such an example," Lady Penelope agreed. "We might've avoided the whole Karl debacle itself if the king had only bonded with his eldest son. But then, I know from my own observations that terrible parents are not an absolute condemnation for life, even if the likelihood of suffering is more certain."

I noticed that she'd said observations, not experiences, and I might have slapped her for my mother's sake if we were not inside a church.

"I do not want to talk about this with you. I am not sure I want to talk with you at all."

"You don't. I saw Ferdinand push you to come see me." She crossed her arms. "I suppose he really does love you, to know how to manipulate you so."

"Sometimes it is good to be encouraged to do right, just as we need people to dissuade us from doing wrong."

I thought of my mother again.

Ben had told me, after learning more Arabic and deciphering more of her journal, she'd worked with Lumiere's plan to attempt to kill the emperor, and she was the one who convinced my father to go save him during the Spring Revolution.

So much of fate was a tangle. It was not unlike freedom, in that so much of it relied on so many other elements; between the timing, the indomitability of the human will, and the tendency of nature toward self-destruction, I was unable to believe fate was merely a sequence of coincidences.

It was indeed something greater, something so much greater, than I could fully contemplate—greater than my sadness, greater than my joy.

"I suppose you are correct," Lady Penelope said. "But no matter. To business, then."

"To business?"

"Whether or not you want to believe it, I have missed you, Eleanora."

My heart stung with hidden pain. I did not want to admit that I'd missed her, too, over the past several years.

Working with the Order, coordinating messages to Harshad and Lumiere and several others now, tracking down hostages and villains, recovering missing items, and gathering information—all of it was much less exciting than my first mission, even if it was safer than going after assassins and traitors.

Reporting on it to Franz Joseph was equally as cumbersome now, too.

Lady POW had once said she would never understand my generation's obsession with bureaucracy, and I was finally old enough and experienced enough I could agree.

"Her Majesty Queen Victoria has given me and Harshad another mission," Lady Penelope said. "You must know Her Majesty is greatly concerned with her new country."

"Yes, the Empress of India," I murmured, recalling the news with a nod. Just last month, Queen Victoria had been given the title, and it would be made official at the start of the coming year. "It seems while your mission to stabilize this region was a success, India still did not make it on its own."

"It will improve," Lady Penelope said. "Her Majesty has requested Harshad and I step in."

I did not believe for one moment that "stepping in" was all that was required to help a country.

But I did not question it.

I'd learned sometimes it was better not to ask questions, especially in matters involving my grandmother.

"I came here because I wanted to see if you and Ferdinand would come with us. We could use Ferdy's charm and your beauty as a cover," Lady Penelope said. "I know Lumiere has agreed to stay in Prague while you are here in Vienna. Why not just ask him to keep up the good work? I'm sure Didier wouldn't mind. He's become quite the beer enthusiast of late."

"He is enjoying his membership to the Cabal, now that it has been rebuilt," I agreed. "But … "

In that moment, I hated how hard it was to still hate her. Lady Penelope, while she had added significantly to my mother's misery and Amir's, not to mention my own, had never been my true enemy.

THE ORDER OF THE CRYSTAL DAGGERS

It was almost too painful to acknowledge that. I felt a gnawing pit in my stomach as I realized I still did not want to disappoint her.

But I also knew I was going to do just that.

She pursed her lips again, this time more tightly, in that surly way she had. "You're not going to say yes, are you?"

"No. Not today." I clasped my hands in front of me.

"No apology, either?" Lady Penelope nodded. "Good."

This time, I didn't stop my smile. I enjoyed earning her approval, even if I no longer needed it.

"It has been nice seeing you again, Eleanora. Perhaps we can do it again in the future."

Lady Penelope nodded curtly and then walked past me. I could feel the tension increase at our nearness.

She was the one who taught me that everyone had secrets and everyone lied.

But there were so many other things I'd learned, and as I stood there, watching her pass me, I thought of the many unspoken dreams and wishes of every human heart.

Ferdy showed me that everyone kept secrets, even from themselves; Ben had taught me everyone had pain, secret or not; Harshad taught me that learning often required failure; and Amir was the one who taught me that everyone carried regrets, sometimes throughout our lives.

And I was a better person, and more of myself, both because of and in spite of Lady Penelope, too.

I took a deep breath. "Wait."

Lady Penelope glanced over her shoulder. "What is it, Eleanora? Feeling sentimental? It's not a good feature for a spy."

"I am more than a spy. Just as you are more than a spymaster."

She blinked, and I knew I caught her off guard with the truth.

"You are also my grandmother," I continued. "So before you go, I have two things for you."

"Is that so?" Lady Penelope's lips curled in false amusement, and I wondered if she was thinking of the night of the Advent Ball as she glanced at my dagger.

"Yes," I said. "My gifts may not be as meaningful as my mother's dagger, or as practical as your ... special instructions. But I'd like to give them nevertheless."

"I appreciate your candor and bravery." Lady POW arched her brow, wryly amused.

Her mockery was a little infuriating. I could've used the time to satisfy all the rage and hurt inside of me I'd carried since our last meeting, and she was entertained to see me rise above my baser emotions.

I stood, reconsidering my intent, but I remembered how Lady Penelope had pulled out my mother's dagger.

She'd offered me freedom—freedom from servanthood— and gave me the tools I needed to find truth and fight against doubt. I had embraced her gifts, with all the blessings and burdens that came with them.

With the truth, I had a way to reach my mother—and embrace her, as a real person rather than a wraith of a memory.

But with her, I had embraced the past, and the past was gone. It had taken me a long time to forgive myself for Karl's death—and it was possible I would still need to forgive myself again in the future. But I would have to find a new way forward if I was going to honor my mother's legacy.

419

THE ORDER OF THE CRYSTAL DAGGERS

There was no freedom in being trapped in the past.

Louis had conspired against many nations, Xiana had been the one who had poisoned my mother, making her miscarry Nassara, and Tulia had been the one responsible for my father's death. I believed justice had been done where it could be, and I felt no need to hold their sins against them—at least, not to the degree I felt compelled to do so with my grandmother.

But I would not honor the hate I had inside of me. It was time to lay it down and let it go.

I blinked back the sudden rush of tears and clenched my fingers around the hilt of my dagger.

This was what Amir had told me all those years ago, as we stood together in the church where I'd married Ferdy. He'd told me that freedom had its limits, both from the outside and from within.

I had not known exactly what he'd meant, but I did now.

Amir had always been the better one between us; even now he was still teaching me. He had never let his own desires or delusions enslave him. He carried his disappointments in his heart and learned from them, never letting go of the beauty of my mother's memory as he clung to his faith, hoping above all else he would see her again.

"The first gift I have for you," I said to Lady POW through gritted teeth, "is my forgiveness."

She did not move as she continued staring at me; it was hard to determine if what I said had any effect on her at all.

I swallowed hard, trying to keep myself composed, even as there was nothing I wanted more than to fall to my knees and weep.

I was truly free in that moment, as the last of the poison in my heart against her was uprooted.

THE ORDER OF THE CRYSTAL DAGGERS

I'd needed to forgive her, just as I'd needed to forgive myself.

It wasn't enough to move on and keep carrying a burden I was trying to ignore.

"I hated you for so long for what happened before. But I know you are a woman of freedom. If liberty is the power to do what we ought to do, we can still fail to honor that power. When we met, you said there was a cost to knowing the truth. I didn't see it then, but I do now. And I know now that you and I will continue paying for that price for the rest of our lives."

The amusement in her eyes faded. "Yes," she agreed. "We will pay for it."

"I refuse to let unforgiveness rob me of even more of my life."

"A wise move," she intoned blandly.

I decided to hold back in reminding her about the church's teachings on the matter; she was not responding to me, and I did not think she would willingly reply to God either.

But after a moment passed between us, she cleared her throat, and I wondered if God had not spoken to her himself anyway.

"Amir taught you well, didn't he?" Lady Penelope whispered. Her voice was steady, but I saw she was struggling to remain composed. "You know, when he died, he asked me to forgive him."

I thought of that moment, before Amir had turned to Ben and me, when he'd whispered something to Lady POW.

She gave me another bitter smile. "But it was I who should have been asking for his forgiveness, wasn't it?"

"Yes." I almost smiled when she blinked; she had not expected me to reply aloud. "Yes, Amir did teach me well."

She rolled her eyes.

"The second gift I have for you is much like the first one," I said, changing the subject. "I wanted to tell you that you were wrong."

She laughed mirthlessly. "Oh, is that it? What was I wrong about?"

"You were wrong about how this will end. You said before that life as a spy would only end in death or defeat. You may be partially right. No one is getting out of this life alive. But my mother is proof that you were wrong, and I am now proof, too."

"You are quitting the Order?" She raised her brow in surprise. "I figured you wouldn't want to go to India, but I didn't think you'd let go of your mother's legacy."

"No, it's not that." I shook my head. "My mother quit, and she lived. She found my father, and found love, even if it was not the yearning she felt for another. She had Ben and me, and Tulia came back to her, too. She spent the last years of her life building a new one—even to the extent she wanted to see you again. And she was right to do that."

"Is that so? Not biased at all, are you?"

I ignored the sharp retort. "It does us no good to let the kingdoms around us burn down. We might start the fire and celebrate the sight of the ashes, but we will never truly live if we don't build up the good. So I choose freedom, which is only possible with truth and goodness, and I choose to build up a better future."

I paused for a long moment before I added, "Starting with my own children."

Silence fell between us as her eyes squinted at my midsection more carefully.

"Well, well … I suppose congratulations are in order," Lady Penelope said quietly. "And here I just thought you were getting fat."

The slight bulge was barely noticeable behind the dark colors of my gown, even if the fabric was drawn tight across my breasts and hips, but the proof of my growing baby was getting harder to hide every week.

I bit down on the inside of my cheek as I placed a hand on my stomach.

It was not easy to tell her the truth. Originally, I didn't want her to know about my offspring at all, but I remembered too clearly the night that she found out the truth about me.

I would not repeat my mother's choices, even if I truly understood them.

"I suppose I am getting old," Lady Penelope murmured, "if you are four months along and I did not realize it sooner. But then, I did see that your husband is still quite relentlessly cheerful, even at his father's funeral."

"Yes." I blushed, still unnerved by her bluntness after all these years. "Ferdy is quite excited about being a father."

I did not want to hide the truth, but I did not see a reason to tell her about his announcement to the Cabal, his staggering kisses as he told me he could not wait to meet his son or daughter, or how he promised to get started on a list of names and decorate a nursery.

"So, you say I am wrong." Lady Penelope shrugged. "In the end, maybe that is a good thing. I was sure you would give me your mother's dagger back."

"It is my dagger now, Madame."

THE ORDER OF THE CRYSTAL DAGGERS

And it was true. I felt a new bond with my weapon as I let the last piece of vengeance for my mother leave my heart.

Maybe that was the real reason I wanted nothing to do with Lady Penelope in the end. Forgiving her fulfilled my mother's last mission, and I did not want to say goodbye to *Máma* again.

But I knew *Máma* had never really left, either. She was with me, in me, and part of me. And what she'd left me, I would assess what was good, repair what had been damaged, and build on a new legacy for my own children one day.

After all, the legacy we inherit is not the one we have to leave behind.

"We can fight in other ways besides maintaining the status quo and protecting royals and statesmen," I said. "There is more to the Order's calling than to protect the present. We must prepare those who come after us, too."

"You are a wise young lady, Eleanora. You should know I am proud to call you my family, even if I have not earned that right." She cleared her throat. "Harshad and I will be leaving in a few hours for Delhi. Any message you would like to pass along to him? I'm sure he would be concerned to hear how pudgy you're getting, but at least you have a valid excuse."

"Give Harshad my best. He deserves it, that poor man, working with you."

"He will need it," Lady Penelope agreed. She paused for a moment; I could see her mind weighing her options, and I knew the instant she made her decision. "We have decided to marry."

My mouth dropped open in shock, before I quickly composed myself. "I assume because it is good for the mission?"

"Well, yes."

It was a little disappointing to see her swift agreement, but then I saw her smile—a real, genuine smile of happiness, one I had rarely, if ever, seen before.

I smiled back. "And because it is good for you, too?"

"Yes." She nodded and then actually laughed, letting the almost musical sound ring through the church alcove. "It seems you were right about things like love, Eleanora. Life is full of loss, but you can't lose what you never claim to have in the first place."

I nodded. "That is what *Máma* would want."

"She always called him 'Uncle,'" Lady Penelope said softly. She looked at me, and then past me; and then she nodded. "Eleanor loved him as much as her own *Táta*."

"Then please don't give Harshad a reason to regret his decision."

"I will have to do my best, and he'll have to accept that my best is not good enough some days," she said, waving the matter aside. "Perhaps we will see you on our way back to London, whenever the Queen calls us to return. Your son should be here by then."

"How do you know it's a boy?" My fingers tightened on my belly, protective and full of awe at the thought of Ferdy's son.

Would he have silver eyes like his father? That irreverent smirk, the pointed nose? Would he get my ebony curls, or Ferdy's wispy, copper-colored locks?

Lady Penelope smirked. "I told you a long time ago, Eleanora. You have good birthing hips. It'll be a boy."

I flushed over, half pleased and half embarrassed.

"Oh, come now. It's close enough to Christmas that he'll make a nice gift for Ferdinand. And Benedict will enjoy having a new pupil to teach when he gets back from Paris; after all, Harshad is getting older, too."

"Have you heard from Ben?" I asked.

"Yes." She smiled. "Marguerite still writes to me quite often."

"Their third anniversary is next month."

"I haven't forgotten." Lady POW lifted her skirts to show me the uneven hem of her underskirt. "How could I? I'm still looking for a seamstress with her level of talent. I know Betsy and Mavis are your friends, Eleanora, but as her replacements, they have been quite a disappointment."

I was tempted to argue with her, again, but outside the alcove, the music began to swell.

"They're almost finished with the service," Lady Penelope said. "You'd better get back to your husband. Assuming you don't actually need to use the ladies' withdrawing room?"

"Goodbye, Lady Penelope." I ignored her taunt and gave her another small curtsy. "I wish you all the best for your work in India."

She pursed her lips and then nodded. "All right. Farewell, Eleanora. For now."

She reached out her hand toward me; after only a moment, I reached out and took it.

We clasped each other tightly, knowing we were family, and we would continue working on building up the trust between us. No matter how slowly, progress was progress. With one hand, I held onto her, and with the other, I put my hand over my growing child.

And then we let go.

I watched as she walked away from me.

I kept my eye on her as she slipped into the main sanctuary. In the second I blinked, she managed to slide out of the church through one of the side doors.

And then she was gone.

For now.

I gripped my dagger at my side with one hand, pressing my other hand protectively against my stomach, unable to stop myself from smiling.

Even Lady Penelope was capable of change. There was truly hope to be had in this world after all.

My steps were quiet as I made my way back to Ferdy's side.

"Ella?" he whispered as he took my hand. "I'm here. Everything will be all right."

"Are you sure?" My voice was quiet and shaky, but I already felt a little better.

There would be trouble ahead. There would be sad days and lost battles and fearful nights. Such were the risks and realities of life and freedom. Yet I had survived everything life had brought me so far—and I wouldn't face the rest of it alone.

"Of course it will." Ferdy gave me a small grin. "We're going to live happily ever after."

"Oh?" I gave him a playful smirk. "How do you know?"

"Clavan once said that if you want proof that something is true, you only have to see how your joy is multiplied over time. There is no need to keep lying if there is joy." He reached down between us, letting his hand rest on my stomach. "And there is no greater joy I have than the joy I've found here with you."

Our baby—perhaps our son?—wriggled underneath Ferdy's touch, as if to prove his words true.

427

THE ORDER OF THE CRYSTAL DAGGERS

A new kind of wonder lit up in Ferdy's eyes as the church around us glowed with peace. My soul was never more firmly anchored at the foot of the cross as I stood there, caught between heaven and hell, life and death, between the past, present, and future.

"Clavan always seems to have the right answers," I said, smiling brightly, and happy tears swelled up in my eyes. I put my hand on top of his. "Lady Penelope says he'll be a boy."

"I'm glad," Ferdy said. "We won't have to wonder about naming him after her, then."

We shared a soft laugh. I looked back up at the altar, and then back at Ferdy. "I think I'd like to name him Nicholas."

My baby moved inside of me again, a small little flutter that echoed with the same hope and fear inside my heart.

"He seems to like it," Ferdy agreed. "As he should. He is our gift of wonder."

"Yes." I smiled at the thought of my son. Did he already know how much he was mine? How much I loved him, and what I would do to keep him safe?

My stomach lurched at the thought; all of my choices in the last several weeks—from traveling out to Vienna, to wearing restrictive clothing, to sleeping on my side—all of them came rushing at me, and I gripped my stomach, suddenly more afraid than I had ever been in my life.

"I love you." I opened my arms and fully embraced Ferdy, drawing his lips down onto mine.

It was the wrong time, the wrong place, and I knew we were going to get evil looks from any pearl-clutching spectators.

But I loved him. I wanted him, I needed him, I loved him.

And I loved him so much.

THE ORDER OF THE CRYSTAL DAGGERS

"Ella." Ferdy gripped me close. He knew as I did that we both wanted comfort, standing there in the ornate church, surrounded by the pain and the memories and the path we carried and the ones we wound not escape. "I love you. And you can bet on that."

"Is that so?" I asked, already knowing what his answer would be as I wiped the tears out of my eyes.

He grinned. "*Absolument.*"

THE ORDER OF THE CRYSTAL DAGGERS

C. S. Johnson is the award-winning, genre-hopping author of several young adult sci-fi and fantasy novels, including *The Starlight Chronicles* series, the *Once Upon a Princess* saga, and the *Divine Space Pirates* trilogy. With a gift for sarcasm and an apologetic heart, she currently lives in Atlanta with her family.

AUTHOR'S NOTE

Dear Reader,

If you're like me, there is always something a little bittersweet about coming to the end of a book series. I have traveled many roads and dreamed so many possibilities for my characters, so when we have come to the end of our time together, to the point where the dreaming must continue on without me, I always feel a little bereft. I am greatly comforted in knowing that you are the ones who continue on with them, and I know if you've read this far, they are in good hands. Thankfully, too, in this case, I am sure Ella and Ferdy, and all the others, have more than enough determination to survive if they so choose.

But in this case, I feel there is more of a sense of "finality for now" with this series. When I started these books, I was partially inspired to write this series, as some of you know, because I had heard Nabeel Qureshi, a favorite, beloved author of mine, had been diagnosed with stomach cancer. I was absolutely devastated by his death, believing as I had that he would be healed and allowed to continue his life here on earth as a testimony to God's healing and mercy. Before I could publish the first book, he had passed on.

I mourned for quite some time. It is only as I write this that I can smile at the thought of him in heaven. His voice, along with many others, have lent their insights into this series, and now I can really only continue on in my grief and joy. Both life and death have marked me, and now I rejoice as much as I grieve; and I must smile even more, because paradoxes are not the same as contradictions, after all.

I will be alright, but I will never be the same.

But for now, I must go on. I take great comfort in knowing I must go on, and that I am not alone.

In keeping with this, in this last book of the series, I wanted to tackle the question of freedom, and I always enjoy getting to see what I learn along the way as much as I enjoy the story. There is so much that goes into this book, and I am not apologetic in the slightest how it has a lot to offer for the one who is seeking for it. Life is full of surprises and questions, and there are complicated questions that can only require complicated answers.

For this book, I wanted to take a look at maintaining freedom. With its dependency on so much—both personal and universal aspects of morality, goodness, and perhaps especially identity—I wanted to see what it would take to not only secure it, but to keep it, and to keep ourselves from letting it slip away. The only way to do this is with power, love, and goodness; power without love is corrosive to the human heart, and goodness without love is feeling without meaning, and love cannot exist in its purest form without goodness.

I feel this is the same way about friends sometimes; it is easy to want friends, but harder to become friends, and sometimes, harder still to keep them.

While I heavily favor literary aspects, I am not a complete plot-hater, either, and I also wanted to bring up elements of forgiveness, hope, and fear. The trick is in the title, as always, because hope is both a gift and something to be born, and fear is grounded in respect for power, but only the fear of the Lord can be seen as the beginning of wisdom. This is reflected in the hero's journey, as the character's life includes innocence, trust—sometimes false trust—and wisdom.

That is where the paradox of freedom is. It gives power, but requires power, too, including the power (and goodness) to constrain itself.

We must be like Ella when it comes to such things as freedom, faith, and friendship: Determined, resolved, and intentional—and humble or hapless enough to lay down our arms when the battle we are fighting turns out to be one that is destroying us. We may not be armed with a crystal dagger at our side, but we can carry so much power in our hearts

THE ORDER OF THE CRYSTAL DAGGERS

through love and truth; it is really only truth that can link hope and fear and allow for true love to shine through.

Before you go, I have promised my most ardent fans to let you know that Amir is perfectly content with his fate, and that, to me at least, he is in story heaven with Naděžda, Nassara, and even Dolf is laughing with him as they celebrate the strange overlappings of their lives.

If you've enjoyed this book, I hope you will take a look at my other work, to come and find me again, and let me entertain you; I tend to genre-hop but I can promise you, my Shakespearean-Machiavellian-Khardashian influences all run through my stories, juxtaposing character with complicated fun, mixing the wisdom with the winsome and wonderous.

My books are not just words on a page or stories from inside; they are a piece of my heart, full of blood and sweat and tears, restless nights and ceaseless prayers, and so many words beyond all possible words. And with that, I can only thank you for the gift of your time. It truly is appreciated.

Until We Meet Again,

C. S. Johnson

P. S. If you do not know Jesus as your Lord and Savior, I pray that you will seek him and that you will find him. Death is a stark reality, a perpetual shadow on our souls. Many people object to religion, and several times, I have found their reasonings to be understandable, especially when we talk of religious people. But I do think Jesus himself should be taken more than seriously and I know he welcomes such scrutiny, especially if a relationship with you is the final prize. Risking your heart and pride is a great price, but the prize is more than worth the while. So in this regard, I hope you have yourself a bit of a gamble, as Ferdy might say.

Also: If you've enjoyed this series, look for the second companion novella to The Order of the Crystal Daggers, *City of Light and Sun*. It's a short novella featuring Ben and Marguerite on a new mission together in Paris.

THE ORDER OF THE CRYSTAL DAGGERS

AUTHOR'S ACKNOWLEDGEMENTS

EDITOR

Jennifer C. Sell

Jennifer Clark Sell is a professional book editor and proofreader. She works from her home in Southern California. With her years of professional and personal experience, she offers several quality packages for authors. Find her at https://www.facebook.com/JenniferSellEditingService.

Photo Credit: Savannah Sell

AUTHOR'S ACKNOWLEDGEMENTS

COVER ILLUSTRATOR

Amalia Chitulescu

Amalia Iuliana Chitulescu is a digital artist from Campina, Romania. Raised in a small town, this self-taught artist has a technique which is delineated by the contrast between obscurity and enlightenment, using dark elements in a dreamy world. Her areas of expertise include the use of theatrical concepts to create a macabre and surrealistic world that still maintains a highly recognizable attachment to reality. Bridging a diaphanous environment with light elements, an eerie view, she creates a dream world of dark beauty, done with a blend of photography and digital painting. Find her at
https://www.facebook.com/Amalia.Chitulescu.Digital.Art

Photo Credit: Amalia Chitulescu

Thank you for reading! Please leave a review for this book
and check out my other books for more adventures!